Praise for the ...t **series**

...nique

..., *The Fated Sky* dramatically
demonstrates the technical problems with going
to Mars—but the technical problems are the
not the only ones. Never backing down from
vital issues of race and gender, *The Fated Sky*
confronts the human issues of space travel in
a United States made increasingly desperate by
a massive meteor strike. Plausible, convincing,
and ultimately moving."

**Nancy Kress, author of the Hugo
Award-winning *Yesterday's Kin***

"*The Calculating Stars* is a wonderful,
scientifically accurate view of
what might have been. Kowal masters
both science and historical accuracy in this
alternate history adventure."

Andy Weir

"In *The Calculating Stars*,
Mary Robinette Kowal imagines an alternate
history of spaceflight that captures
everything I loved abou...

Cady Coleman,

THE RELENTLESS MOON

MARY ROBINETTE KOWAL

SOLARIS

Published in the United Kingdom in 2020 by Solaris
an imprint of Rebellion Publishing Ltd,
Riverside House, Osney Mead,
Oxford, OX2 0ES, UK

Published in the United States in 2020 by Tor Books

www.solarisbooks.com

ISBN: 978 1 78108 881 4

10 9 8 7 6 5 4 3 2 1

A CIP catalogue record for this book is available
from the British Library.

Designed & typeset by Rebellion Publishing

Printed in Denmark

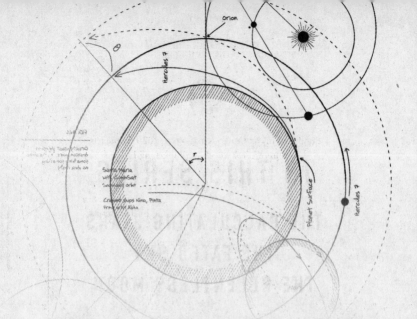

THE RELENTLESS MOON

A LADY ASTRONAUT NOVEL

IN THIS SERIES

For Alyshondra and Amara

I see the horizon. A light blue, a beautiful band.
This is the Earth. How beautiful it is! All goes well.

—Valentina Tereshkova, the first lady astronaut

PART I

ONE

HALFWAY TO MARS

John Schwartz, Special to The National Times

KANSAS CITY, March 28, 1963—If all goes as it should—and in space, that is no sure thing—then sometime today, thirteen brave voyagers will cross a Rubicon that no man ever has: the halfway point between our home planet and Mars.

It has been a mission of triumph and terror, of disasters averted and disasters tragically experienced, as thirteen astronauts and astronettes speed across the cosmic void.

The mission has been a test not just of technology, but also of ingenuity, resourcefulness, and the human spirit.

"Like Julius Caesar, we must prepare for the worst," said Norman Clemons, director of the International Aerospace Coalition, "that is our training. But we also strive for the best, and this wonderful team has trained for almost every eventuality."

The astronauts and astronettes, a group composed of so many nationalities that "Lady Astronaut" Elma York called it a "World's Fair in Space," have prepared years for this moment, and every moment of the months to come.

After tomorrow's milestone, the spacemen will have just
27 million kilometers to go before reaching the Red Planet.

HOW MANY PLACES do you call home? For me, it could mean my parents' home in Detroit. Or the Governor's Mansion that I share with my husband, Kenneth. Or my bunk on the lunar colony. But I've learned to not ask people where home is because after the Meteor, so many people no longer have their true home.

I have switched to the more innocuous "Where are you based?" which I was busily applying at the fundraiser tonight. While Ella Fitzgerald sang, I smiled at all the powerful men my husband wanted to charm so they would support his policies as governor.

My diamonds sparkled around my neck and made a striking contrast to the astronaut's wings pinned to the peacock-green taffeta of my evening gown. Being the glittering trophy wife was easier before I'd passed fifty, but I was in better shape than I'd been in my thirties.

I say that, but the arthritis in my feet protested each high-heeled step I took. I kept that masked along with my sigh of relief when Kenneth stopped us on the parquet floor for the umpteenth time. "You remember Mr. Vann, don't you, Nicole?"

I did not. Mr. Vann was yet another flaccid middle-aged white man with his glittering wife in tow. "How lovely of you to come!" My voice still had all the charm I'd learned in Swiss finishing school.

Thank God they taught us how to hide boredom behind glitter.

"A pleasure, Mrs. Wargin." His accent was from the Midwest. I'd need another sentence to pin it down, but his vowels leaned that way. "I don't believe you've met my wife, Bethany, yet."

Oklahoma. It was the only place you got Midwest and Southern twang mixed in quite that way, which meant they probably hadn't lost a lot of family to the Meteor and also meant that the last eleven years had been enough to remove the urgency from their minds. I smiled at them both. "Such a pleasure. Please do come visit me on the Moon."

"Now, now . . . I want Bethany here on Earth, where it's safe." Mr. Vann patted his wife's arm in a way that would have had Kenneth sleeping on the couch for a week. "I'm surprised that you're letting the little lady go up there, Governor."

Kenneth laughed, but his hand pressed on my lower back, letting me know that he could field this one. I leaned into him to accept his offer in a silent language that we've worked out over years of public service.

He smiled at the man. "I think you're mistaken, if you believe my wife is a woman that people 'let' do anything."

"Besides, living on the Moon isn't that different, really. In many ways, the lunar colony is just like being in a small town. Why, we even have an art gallery." Which I had set up, but the fact remained that it existed and that we had art.

"And you work with Elma York, don't you?" His wife's gaze focused on me, and what I had seen as vapidity was actually a boredom as thick as my own.

"Oh yes. Long before she was the famous 'Lady Astronaut'!" I was in the same class of astronauts as Elma, the first women chosen for the space program, but she would always be The Lady Astronaut.

Mrs. Vann's face brightened. "How did you two meet?"

"We met as WASPs during the Second World War." This is true. But the fuller truth is that I don't remember our first meeting. Oh, I know we were both Women Airforce Service Pilots, but it wasn't as though she was famous when we met. There were a lot of us. My first concrete memory of her is at a dance on the air base in Palm Springs where she was holding the hair of some hapless young pilot who had had too much to drink and was vomiting out her guts.

But no one wants to hear about that as a first memory of the famous Lady Astronaut.

Mrs. Vann sighed. "I'd join up in a heartbeat, if I were qualified."

If she were like me, her area of expertise was in planning menus, throwing fundraisers, and walking with a book balanced on her head. If not for being a WASP and having a husband who was, at the time, a senator, I never would have made the cut.

Ella Fitzgerald's song came to an end. I wanted to yell at the people who did not understand what a gift her voice was to at least pretend and clap politely.

In the pause before she started singing again, distant shouts sounded beyond the ballroom. They pulled my attention to the windows that stretched along one wall of the hotel. Beyond the filmy white curtains, there was a vivid orange glow like the base of a rocket at liftoff.

My spine straightened and I turned to Kenneth, leaning into him as if I were just being affectionate. "Is something on fire outside?"

"Hmm?" He followed my gaze. At the small of my back, his fingers tightened. "Nicole . . ."

"What—"

The window exploded in a shower of glass and flame. I grabbed Kenneth and spun him away, dragging us both down to a low crouch as my astronaut training kicked in. Something is exploding? Get low, seek cover, protect vulnerable body parts like your head and chest.

And here I was in an off-the-shoulder gown.

Screams sounded behind us. The haze of ennui that had coated me all evening evaporated. The room with its pudgy middle-aged white men and their glamorous wives and the waiters with their dark skin and white gloves snapped into focus as if I were in the seat of a T-38 jet. The best path to get Kenneth to safety was past the banquet tables and through the service door into the kitchen.

"Kenneth." I grabbed the sleeve of his tuxedo. "We need to—"

A swarm of black-suited security men, all square jaws and buzz cuts, surrounded us. "This way." One of them took my arm. Another had Kenneth's. Frustration at being managed filled me for a moment and it had no place here. These men were doing their jobs, protecting the governor and, by extension, his wife.

Me? I was hauled along the path to safety as if I were no more than a decorative bauble. And when I was on Earth, that was, in fact, my job.

*   *   *

IN THE BACK seat of our government car, Kenneth's hair gleamed silver gold in the sodium vapor streetlights. I sat sideways on the broad back seat, twisted to rest my stocking feet in Kenneth's lap. He massaged the ache in the ball of my right foot and stared out the window looking for more rioters as if he could do anything about them. But then, that's Kenneth to a T. He never sees a problem that he doesn't want to fix.

"Sweetheart." I drew my feet away and put my hand on the thigh of his tuxedo trousers. Don't fault me for finding my husband at his most attractive when he was concentrating. "I'm sure the UN has this well in hand."

"It's my state."

"Technically . . ." Both sides of Kansas City had been carved out of their respective states and redistricted to replace Washington, D.C. Not that you could replace Washington.

"Don't even." But he smiled a little and lifted my hand to kiss the fingertips.

I leaned against him even though it was too warm for snuggling. "The food shortages are not your fault."

"I'm the one who authorized accepting refugees from other sta—"

The driver slammed on the brakes. I slid forward in a hiss of taffeta, tightening my legs as if I could brace. We swerved onto a side street and I thought Kenneth was going to break my hand squeezing it so hard.

Out the side window, I saw why the driver had swerved.

Protestors with flaming trash barrels stood outside the high-rise where we had our pied-à-terre in the nation's capital. He looked in the rearview mirror. "Sorry, sir."

"Quite all right, son." Kenneth looked over his shoulder as the conflagration faded behind us. "Maybe we should try to head back to Topeka . . . I trust you to find the best route."

Biting my lower lip, I stared out the window as the driver wound through tree-lined older neighborhoods. "We could go to Cedar Air Park." I kept my Cessna in the 99s hangar there. Turning, I planted a kiss on Kenneth's cheek, careful not to get lipstick on his collar. "I can fly you home."

"Or we can just check into a hotel."

"And have reporters hound you? Nonsense. Besides, I have to be back out at the IAC in the morning to do some POGO instruction anyway. This will save me from taking the commuter train."

"Which you wouldn't have to if we—"

"Reporters. Rioters." I leaned forward to address our driver. "Do you think the governor should take the train tonight?"

"Um. No, ma'am."

Kenneth had the nerve to shake his head at me. "Now ask him if he thinks you should fly us to Topeka."

"Don't pressure him." Kenneth wasn't wrong. It would save me some travel if we just checked into a hotel, but the idea of having those people hounding my husband was intolerable. Besides, I would take almost any opportunity to fly. "It'll take no time at all to nip back to Topeka, so hush and stop arguing with your betters."

"See, this is why I do so well in debates. No one else has you to prepare them. I have another idea." Kenneth leaned forward and gave the driver the address of our friends the Lindholms.

The driver looked up sharply. "Sir, that's in the Black part of town."

"Son, I'm going to do you the kindness of pretending you didn't say that as if you were cautioning me against Black people." Kenneth's smile had all the disappointed weight of the grandfather he'll never be. "Dr. Martin Luther King is a personal friend of mine."

I shot him a glance, because that was true, but also not the address that he'd given the driver. I murmured, "Now this child is going to think he's taking us to Dr. King's house."

"Eugene Lindholm looks nothing like him. But he and Myrtle are staying far enough from downtown that I'm not worried about the riots getting out there." He kissed me on the cheek. "And you're right that checking into a hotel will call reporters down on us."

"Kenneth—"

"People were hurt tonight. I need to be here." He squeezed my hand with a sad smile. "Besides, tomorrow is poker night with the Astronauts' Husbands Club. I'd be back regardless."

"Tomorrow *night*."

"And tomorrow *morning*, you have to be back at the IAC anyway. I can continue on with my list of reasons to stay. Coordinating a response between the state and the city's police force. Visiting victims of the riots. Soothing our guests. Damage control at the UN. And upon reflection, I'm almost certainly going to have to do a press conference. If I'm here in the nation's capital, then I can share the stage with the president, which will be useful when I make my bid."

"Fine. You may stay." I compressed my lips and settled back in the seat. He hadn't announced it publicly, but becoming President Wargin was Kenneth's next goal, which meant he was already laying the groundwork for 1964. Even post-Meteor, election season was a never-ending battle for politicians, and he was right about needing to do a press conference. And right about the power of linking himself to the presidential stage. "As soon as you set the press conference time, let me know and I'll see if I can shift my training so I can be there with you."

Kenneth settled into his seat, lulling me into a false sense of security. You would think, as long as we've been married, that I would know better. The driver had nearly reached the Lindholms' before Kenneth spoke again.

He started by clearing his throat, which is never a good sign. "Nicole . . ."

"You already won this argument."

"This is a different argument." Kenneth never looks uncertain, even when he's completely stymied; the line of his jaw and the steadiness of his dark brown eyes always seem confident. The way you can tell he's uncertain is in the pauses between his words. They carry a weight then, which other people mistake for gravitas. I know that he's feeling his way across uncertain ground. Each word was a slow inch forward. "I think . . . it would be . . . for the best. If. You sat out this press conference."

"It will be fine. Clemons knows how important your support is to the program."

"That's . . . that's just it." He swallowed and the pause stretched between us. "I'm—Lord knows, I'm proud of your work at the IAC . . ."

"I'd be able to hear that 'but' from the Moon."

He laughed, kissing me on the cheek, and then sighed. "I'm sorry. I'm getting some pushback. A few people tonight raised the question . . . They wanted to know if my support of the space program was nepotism."

"Oh, for crying out loud. The goal is to get everyone off the planet. Do they call that nepotism?"

"But we won't, in fact, be able to save everyone. So . . . you see." He gave me that goddamned kindly smile of his. "I might need to be more circumspect in my support. We're trying to get the tax reform bill through . . . and. Well."

I know my job. I fly planes and rockets and smile for the cameras. "Well. I certainly don't want to be a problem."

"Nicole . . ."

"It's fine." The car rolled to a stop next to the tidy home that Myrtle and Eugene shared with their eldest son when they were home from the Moon. I let the driver open my door.

Just audible, sirens wailed in the distance. I forced my shoes back on and they made my feet hurt worse than before. That's the problem with taking off something that doesn't quite fit. Putting it back on is harder.

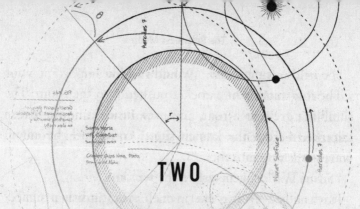

TWO

KANSAS CITY RIOTS SWEEP
CAPITAL CITY
2 REPORTED DEAD

Night of Terror in Kansas City Claimed by
the Organization Earth First After Civilians
Attack UN Guards

KANSAS CITY, March 29, 1963—Heavy fighting
has broken out between UN troops and civilians in
the United States capital of Kansas City. Unconfirmed
reports said two persons had been killed and about 80
wounded in the fighting, which began Thursday night.

THE MORNING LIGHT gleamed on the white linoleum counters
of the Lindholms' kitchen. Myrtle lifted a bright blue plate
with the last piece of toast on it. Her curls formed a close
cap framing her light tan face. When we'd met, she'd had a
cute bouffant, which she'd abandoned on the Moon. Turns
out that Black women have to use lye and heat to straighten
their hair and that's not friendly at one-sixth gravity. For
that matter, I'd switched to a pixie cut too. Not all of the
women in the astronaut corps did, but it had made things
easier before the engineers designed the "lunar shower."

She held out the toast. "Would you like—?"

The low rumble of a rocket pushed into the room. The rumbling grew to a roar, and even inside a house fifteen kilometers from the launch site, I could feel the sound waves crashing into me.

"Sirius IV?" Eugene asked the window.

It was a heavy lift rocket, which meant it was probably carrying people and supplies, although I couldn't tell you whether the crew was stopping at the space station or continuing on to the Moon. There was a time when I attended every launch, before the IAC added Brazilian and European spaceports. But now they were so frequent that I lost track of what was launching, to say nothing of whom. There had been a score of us at the beginning and now there were hundreds of people living and working in space.

Next to me at the breakfast table, Kenneth scanned the Lindholms' newspaper while remaining oblivious to the rocket. It was easy to tell which of us was not an astronaut. Kenneth wasn't being rude—well, I mean, by strict etiquette rules he was—but we all understood that he had to be ready to hit the ground running.

Across from me, Myrtle offered the toast again, raising her voice over the sound of the rocket. "Don't let this go to waste."

Eugene reached for the toast. "Happy to help."

She smacked his hand away. "Was I talking to you?"

"See, don't complain next time that I don't help around the house enough." Eugene lowered his plate with a comically loud mournful sigh.

Myrtle rolled her eyes at him and held the plate toward me. "Nicole?"

"Oh, I'm fine." I picked up a slice of bacon and waved it like a magic wand. "And I still have eggs."

Kenneth looked up from the paper and I could feel him study my plate to see if I was eating. I took a bite of bacon and let it fill my mouth with salt and fat. Beside me, he thumped the paper with the back of one knuckle. "Two people died last night."

Eugene winced. "I'm sorry to hear that."

I didn't want anyone to be dead, but I was terrified that it would be some of our guests. "Earth Firsters or . . . ?"

"A bystander who got trampled and a store owner who was trying to keep looters out."

"That's horrible." Sighing, I set my bacon down. "They say that they're protesting your policies, and then go after an innocent shopkeeper. It's just an excuse for looting."

"Earth First will deny involvement with the looting." Kenneth picked up his fork. "Now, Eugene . . . when you make your bid for lunar mayor, you'll have to be ready to talk about this. How would you respond to last night?"

Eugene lowered his toast and wiped his hands on his napkin. When he concentrated, you could still see the fighter pilot that he used to be, especially with his hair cropped so short you could see the gleam of his dark skin through the tight curls. His brows came together in a way that made him look concerned, rather than worried, which was a fine line and a good feature for a politician.

"I'd probably say something about how we grieve for

the loss of life and are listening to the cries of help from our homeworld."

I tilted my head. "That sounds like you're sympathetic to the rioters."

"That's because I'm sympathetic. Not to their methods, but to their fears." He pointed to a fork rattling on his plate from the ongoing sound of the Sirius IV. "Most people see this as a disruption. A reminder that they aren't going into space."

"Good point." Kenneth speared his last bite of eggs. "Sure I can't pry you out of the space program to be on my staff?"

Myrtle shook her head, pushing her chair back from the table. "Not a chance. I'm still not sure I should welcome you in my house after you talked him into running for mayor."

"Dr. King talked him into it. I just offered coaching." Kenneth passed his plate to her and looked pointedly at the eggs I still had left. "Your cooking sure is wonderful, Myrtle. No danger of anyone wasting food at your house."

I loved him and hated him all at the same time, but I picked up my fork so I could be a good guest and present her with a clean and empty plate. I said, "I still think you have to be careful about sounding sympathetic to rioters. It might be a good line for using on Earth, but when the Moon starts being self-governing, the people who vote for you will be the ones who have the least patience with Earth First."

Eugene nodded. "I know. But I also know that all my speeches will get transmitted downplanet. And, to be honest, I think it would be a mistake to ignore the Earth Firster fears. The number of applicants to the IAC has dropped."

Myrtle snorted and picked up Eugene's plate. "We've got more applicants than we have spots."

"Eugene's right. It's about the trend." Kenneth leaned back in his chair and settled his hands over his paunch. "Declining application numbers give us an indicator that the larger population is losing interest in the space . . ."

I lost the rest, because the sound of the rocket stopped. It shouldn't do that.

An explosion cracked the air.

I was out of my chair and halfway to the kitchen door before the rumble ended. Eugene was behind me, moving slower after months spent in lunar gravity. Myrtle reached for the radio, leaving Kenneth frozen at the table.

"How long?" I ran across the living room to the front door, while Eugene dove for the phone.

How long had we been talking while the rocket rose from the Earth? Two minutes? Three?

"Not sure." This mattered because it told us which mode of abort the crew would be in. Mode one bravo got deployed between 3,000 meters and 30.5 kilometers into flight. The Launch Escape System would haul the crew module away from the main rocket. Eugene continued, "We could hear it, so they were still in atmosphere."

Which meant that they hadn't gotten to a mode two abort. So the LES would have deployed. I threw the front door open and ran into the yard. You can't see the launch site from the Lindholms' neighborhood, but you can see the rocket trajectory. Up and down the street, people tilted their heads back to look at the smoke trail rising to disappear into the ever-present clouds. They were looking at the column as if the part of the trajectory we could see was significant.

I was looking for parachutes.

My fingernails dug into my palms. Clouds. Unbroken clouds.

Kenneth came out onto the Lindholms' front porch. "Who—?"

"I don't know." My voice hurt. "I should know. I don't know!"

He went behind me to wrap his arms around my waist to wait.

And wait.

And wait.

The clouds were constant now and had hit a point where you think of a high silver overcast as a beautiful day. But that damn cloud ceiling meant everything was hidden behind a layer of cotton.

We waited.

Eugene walked onto the front porch. "Circuits are busy. Anything?"

"Clouds." I realized that my hands were digging into Kenneth's wrists. I tried to unclench them. "What's on the radio?"

Kenneth said, "Just that there was an explosion."

Eugene grimaced and jerked a thumb back to the house. "I'll try again."

I don't know why I stayed in that yard, waiting. There

wasn't a damn thing I could do. I just remember when the Meteor happened, how I had been at my parents' Detroit home and we sat by the radio and the room had seemed to get smaller and smaller as the reports rolled in. I couldn't bear to be inside right now.

Someone shouted. A Black man down the street was pointing at the sky—at brilliant orange-and-white envelopes breaking through the clouds like the sun bearing a chariot. I tightened my hands on Kenneth and shouted toward the house. "Eugene! I see chutes!"

Behind me, Kenneth bent his head. "Dear heavenly Father. Thank you for delivering these brave men and women—"

I bit the inside of my cheek and let my husband pray. If there were a God, he would not have blown the rocket. He would not have slammed a Meteor into the Earth. But it gave Kenneth comfort and I would not deny him that, even if what had saved those people was science. Redundancies and methods and practice had saved them.

Eugene burst out of the house, with Myrtle close behind him. "Chutes?"

I nodded, stepping away from Kenneth, and wiped my eyes. "About twenty-five kilometers downrange."

"Oh, praise God." Myrtle raised her hands and closed her eyes for a moment. "Thank you, God, for this miracle."

"And thank the IAC for their training." I try not to get in the way of other people's faith, honest, I do. "Did you get through?"

Eugene shook his head. "Lines are busy, but we can go in."

So help me, I wanted to go with them. "You go on. We'll lock up."

Just because there were parachutes, that didn't mean the crew was going to make it to the ground safely. But there would have been nothing that needed me specifically. Kenneth, though, I could help prepare for the press conference. I couldn't tell him what to say about the riots, but I could coach him on the rocket failure.

I took Kenneth's arm. "Come on, love. We need to get you cleaned up and downtown."

THREE

MISFIRED ROCKET SHAKES
CAPITAL AREA

KANSAS CITY, March 29, 1963—An International
Aerospace Coalition rocket exploded during a routine
flight to the *Lunetta* orbital station early this morning.
After a flawless liftoff, one of the giant engines of the
Sirius IV rocket appears to have misfired, sending the
spaceship tumbling off course. The emergency Launch
Escape System separated the crew module from the rest
of the rocket before the tanks detonated over Kansas in a
stark reminder of the explosive power in the rockets that
pass on a regular basis over our nation's capital.

IN THE BRIEFING room at the U.S. Capitol downtown, I
nursed a cup of coffee as Kenneth got an update from
presidential staffers. Across the room, the door opened
and Director Clemons from the International Aerospace
Coalition strode in, trailing cigar smoke like a rocket. A
little bit of the tension in my gut relaxed. They wouldn't
have been able to pry him out of the IAC if there had been
any fatalities.

He shook hands with the president, who was a trim,

handsome white man in the Clark Gable mold, with dark hair just going silver at the temples. "Director. Thank you so much for coming out."

"I appreciate your offer to join the press conference." Clemons's plummy British accent made it sound as though everything were under control, but his eyes were pinched with worry. "Although I fear I may have made a tactical error in sending my two best spokespeople off on a three-year mission to Mars."

Stetson Parker and Elma York. The First Man in Space and The Lady Astronaut. I was always amazed at how well Elma hid the toll that being in the spotlight took on her. It's not a problem I ever had—other problems, yes, but anxiety was not one of them.

Setting my coffee cup down, I slid out of my chair. The joint of my big toe twinged as weight settled on it. I'd wager no one could tell that it hurt to walk, any more than you could tell how much pain my pointe shoes used to cause. I walked toward Clemons, wishing that I'd brought my blue IAC flight suit with me so I could represent the astronaut corps, if needed, instead of the sober navy blue pencil skirt and jacket that I'd opted for as Governor Wargin's wife. Still, I had my astronaut wings and could pin them on if the director needed me.

I paused just outside the social arc created by the two men and waited to be noticed, which gave them the illusion of being in control of the situation. The president was still talking to Clemons and glanced briefly at me, acknowledging that I'd approached. "What does the Mars Expedition crew think about this?"

"We aren't telling them." Clemons turned the cigar over in his hands. "There's nothing they can do and I do not want to cause them undue worry."

"Wish that were an option for us." The president reoriented his body, taking a step to the side to invite me in. "Ah, Mrs. Wargin. Does the governor need anything?"

"He's being well taken care of, thank you, Mr. President." I smiled and took a step into their sphere of influence. "Though I thought I might offer Director Clemons my assistance."

"Oh?" Clemons raised his brows as if he were baffled that I might have some use.

"If it would help, Elma and I have comparable spaceflight experience. I'm not 'The' Lady Astronaut, but I am 'a' Lady Astronaut." I gave a smile, calibrated to be warm but also acknowledging the somberness of the situation. "I'm available to do any publicity that would be useful for the corps."

"That's very kind of you, Nico—Mrs. Wargin." Clemons looked around to the door. "But Cristiano Zambrano is arriving shortly and was CAPCOM on this launch. I know how valuable you are to Governor Wargin and don't want you to split your attention."

"Of course." That sounded entirely reasonable, but I still wanted to scream. I could be useful if he'd let me. I was good at shaping public opinion and I was very good at press conferences. "Well, I'll let you two get back to it, then."

Turning, I thought that checking in with Kenneth would be the next intelligent thing. If nothing else, I could at least fetch coffee for him.

Behind me, Clemons murmured, "Honestly, if she were a bit younger it might not have been a bad idea, but the original six are old hat now."

The amount of self-control it took to keep walking instead of turning around and slapping him was a testament to my finishing school education. Old hat. Old hat?! Cristiano was a year older than I was, for crying out loud. But men apparently don't age in the same ways . . . *Old hat.*

By the time I got to Kenneth's side, I was able to keep most of my outrage behind my smile. I wrestled my fury back down into its usual spot, because despite the injustice of his words, the reasoning behind having the CAPCOM for the flight there was sound. I hadn't been on the base. I didn't have anything but the most cursory understanding of what had gone wrong. All I really knew was when it had occurred. Cristiano would have more current information.

Of course, if he didn't arrive, then there was still an opportunity for me. There are times when I am appallingly callous, because I was thinking about this near tragedy as an opportunity for advancement. It is hard, sometimes, to spot the line between a desire to help and ambition.

Kenneth gave me a tight smile as I approached. "Learn anything?"

"Cristiano Zambrano is coming in. He was CAPCOM."

Kenneth winced and pursed his lips for a fraction of a second. "He's a good man."

"But?"

"Oh, just wondering about the pros and cons of reminding the American public that this is an international partnership. I think it's probably the way to go, but . . ." He shrugged. "You know me. Always thinking about angles."

"Well, he's not here, so—"

Cristiano walked into the room. He could have been a movie star back home in Mexico, with a cleft chin and thick, glossy hair above eyes that naturally smoldered. I swear, all of the original male astronauts seemed to have been selected, at least in part, for their photogenic qualities. The same was true of us, which always bothered Elma. To me it seemed completely reasonable. We were symbols.

"Nicole . . . What we talked about in the car." Kenneth was going to ask me to stay here. In this goddamned room, doing nothing of any use. "Would you mind—" He stopped when Cristiano spotted me and made a beeline for us.

My fellow astronaut gave a weary smile. "Thank God. I thought I'd be the only astronaut here."

"Clemons says he doesn't need me." I delivered that line with a laugh—a cheery coating around my bitterness.

He snorted and glanced over his shoulder to where Clemons and the president were engaged in what looked like an intense conversation over a folder of papers. "That seems short-sighted, given the fact that you're in the next launch crew."

Behind me, Kenneth sucked in a breath. I had known where I was in rotation, but had not thought through to the fact that I would be in the next group to ride a Sirius IV.

I drew Cristiano away before he could say anything else

that would distress my husband. I'd flown a half-dozen missions as Cristiano's co-pilot back in the capsule days. This close, I could see the strain in the fine lines around his eyes. I murmured, "You okay?"

"I will need a martini of significant size at the end of the day." He glanced down and showed me his right hand. The tremor that had finally grounded him was much worse than usual, as if I needed a reminder about what happened to an astronaut who admitted that their health was less than perfect. Cristiano balled it into a fist and shoved it casually into his trouser pocket. "But everyone is alive. Search and rescue was right on top of them as they came down."

I heaved a sigh of relief at that confirmation. "Well, come over tonight and I'll mix up some martinis."

He winked, and a dimple flashed for a moment at the corner of his mouth. "Thank you. But I should go home to Giulia and the boys. Even though I wasn't up, she will worry."

"Of course. Who was the crew?"

"Randy Cleary was piloting. He had Isabel Sophia Dieppa Betancourt for Nav/Comp and—"

"Ladies and gentlemen!" One of the staffers stood by the door to the press room. "We're ready to begin. This way, please."

The press room at the Capitol building was built specifically for briefings and had a dais at one end of a square room. The walls were covered with heavy blue velvet drapes to muffle the sound in the room. They were green during Brannan's administration, but Denley tended toward more military trappings.

I did not go out on the dais. No, I stood in the gallery with the First Lady and some of the other politicians' wives. All of us had our practiced "supportive and attentive" expression engaged. It came in handy as a politician's wife and as an astronaut.

President Denley strode up to the podium and regarded the reporters. "Thank you all for coming. Let me answer first the question that is on everyone's mind. The Sirius IV rocket explosion this morning resulted in no loss of life. The passengers and crew aboard are now receiving medical treatment as a safety measure, but all appear to be in good health. We give thanks to God for their safe delivery. I've brought Director Clemons from the IAC out, and he will be available to answer your questions about that later."

He shifted a paper on the podium. "Of more immediate concern to most citizens in the capital are last night's riots. Let me say, right away, that we will not be cowed by terrorists."

And then he began a series of one-liners about the riots and civility. He had a half-dozen variations on the line "we will not be cowed by terrorists," which were disingenuous coming from a man who wanted to slash the United States's contribution to the IAC. Honestly, I tuned out, paying just enough attention to be able to nod appreciatively at the right spots in case one of the cameramen wanted a B-shot of the wives.

He droned on for a good fifteen minutes saying nothing of substance but promising an undefined "strong action" until he finally opened the floor for questions.

"Gerrard St. Ives of *The Times*." The British journalist was a portly white man in a rumpled gray suit. "Is there a link between the Sirius IV explosion and the riots last night? Specifically, was the explosion due to sabotage by the Earth Firsters?"

The president gestured to Clemons. "No, but I'll let Director Clemons explain why."

That caught my interest. He'd known this question was coming, which meant they had at least considered the possibility of sabotage.

Clemons sat forward, folds of his neck creasing over his collar. "The security at the IAC is very tight and reinforced by the UN. But setting aside the notion that someone might have been able to sneak onto the campus, there is no part of the rocket that a person could reach to damage. These spaceships are thirty-six stories tall as an example."

By dint of long practice, I did not react externally, but internally I sat up and stared. True, the Sirius was thirty-six stories tall once it was erected for launch. But there were ample opportunities for sabotage before that, to say nothing of the fact that it was surrounded by a gantry designed to allow you to climb it. If sabotage were actually not a concern, I might cite some evidence that was a bit more substantial than the height of the rocket.

The next reporter was a lanky blond man in the same rumpled gray suit they all wear. "Altus Oosthuizen of *Volksblad*. Given the ongoing trial of the Cygnus Six and the FBI's investigation into the possibility that Negro astronauts deliberately sabotaged that rocket, will the agency be involved in investigating this crash?"

This again. About two years ago, one of the Cygnus spaceships coming back from the *Lunetta* space station had misfired and come down way off course, in Alabama instead of Kansas. That was bad, but the pilots compensated and everyone was unharmed. The problem was that a group of six hunters—the so-called "Cygnus Six"—had decided to take advantage of the situation. They beat rescue and recovery to the ship and took everyone hostage. Including the famous Lady Astronaut, Elma York, which meant that it got even more press than it would have.

The even bigger problem was that they had been Black men and members of Earth First. Guess which one got more press? The allegations that Leonard Flannery, the only Black man on the First Mars Expedition, had been involved with the crash of the Cygnus rocket were founded on nothing more than the fact that he was a passenger and Black.

Director Clemons leaned into the microphone. "I'm unaware of any such plans."

"John Schwartz, *National Times*. This is the third failure of a rocket in the past two years. What about the danger to the capital residents of so many rocket crashes? Will the agency consider relocating the launch site?"

Rockets were as safe as the IAC could make them, but nothing changed the fact that every time we launched, we were sitting on top of a giant bomb.

You didn't need a saboteur to be at risk, you just needed an anomaly.

"I feel as if this is rather like asking, 'Governor, is it true that you stopped beating your wife?' With apologies to Governor Wargin." Director Clemons paused while the roomful of reporters chuckled. "Our flight paths are across the Kansas prairies and not over the capital, so there is no danger to Kansas City residents. As for relocation . . ."

My husband leaned into the microphone. "I should hope that the IAC does not relocate, because that would pull thousands of jobs away from hardworking Kansas citizens. I pray the protesters from last night come to realize that space is the biggest industry, by far, in Kansas and also in our neighbor Missouri. Losing that would be devastating to our economy at a time when we are just beginning to recover from the Meteor. Besides, if Kansans were the sort of people cowed by fear, they wouldn't live in tornado alley."

Inside, I applauded the way my husband had turned the question to his own ends. Otherwise, I stood there with the same smile of quiet support that all of the speakers received. The questions continued on, with one man in a rumpled gray suit after another asking about changes in safety measures—too soon to tell—about causes—too soon to know—about when launches would resume—too soon to know—a different version of wanting to know what happened—still too soon to tell.

It was not too soon to tell that these heels had been a mistake. Oh, I could stand in them. I could run in them if I needed to. But as the questions wore on, my feet slowly slid forward until the shoes' pointed toes squeezed my arthritic bones together. The balls of my feet burned, as the entire weight of my body pressed into the floor.

Did it hurt as badly as being upside down in the Neutral Buoyancy Lab at the end of a long day, with the fiberglass of my spacesuit digging into my clavicle? Maybe. Certainly, neither was pain that I could admit existed, but at least in the NBL, I had things to do to distract myself. Here I just stood and listened to men answer questions.

A reporter cut through my train of thoughts. "Governor, what about the ways in which your family, personally, profits from the space program? Your wife is an astronaut, which besides the federal paycheck, also puts her first in line for relocating to the Moon or Mars."

"To be clear, it's hard to live in the capital area without having a job that the government pays for directly or indirectly. My wife earned her astronaut wings as one of the first six women." Kenneth hesitated, with those weighted pauses that made him seem so thoughtful. The room leaned forward a little into that gap. "I'm proud of the work that my wife is doing to create a new home for humanity on the Moon, and she's doing so without any expectation of benefit to herself because we are *not* in line to permanently relocate. As you know, we have no children of our own so we have made the decision to stay here on Earth, until everyone is off the planet who can go. So yes, she's an astronaut, but the only benefit we derive from that is knowing that we are helping humanity."

My smile stayed steady and I nodded as if I agreed with him. As if we'd had this conversation. But the truth was that I had angled for a spot on the First Mars Expedition and was going to push to be seated on the second.

Director Clemons had already written me off as *old hat*. I didn't need Kenneth helping him decide that I was happy staying on Earth.

FOUR

FOOD FOR PEACE

KANSAS CITY, March 29, 1963—The United States
Post Office Department has merged the Federal "Food
for Peace" effort with the current "Freedom From
Hunger" campaign of the United Nations Food and
Agriculture Organization. The United States Stamp,
planned as a promotion for the American effort to aid
hungry people around the world, will begin with the
World Food Congress.

AFTER THE PRESS conference, my driver dropped me at
Building 3, where the astronaut offices were. Gritting my
teeth, I jogged inside, which I can still do in heels, thank
you very much, because I was just barely going to make
it for the training session I was scheduled to teach. I only
had ten minutes to change and get across campus. I kept
a change of clothes at the office—a couple of changes,
actually—so it took only a few minutes to strip out of my
stockings and into a pair of trousers and sneakers. The
joints at the balls of my feet throbbed, but standing flat
on the floor eased a lot of the pain. If I used one of the
ubiquitous bikes that dotted the campus, it would take

more of the strain off. I went outside, grabbed one from the rack, and cycled over to Building 9.

On the way, I passed four deer, a family of wild turkeys, and a duck. All of this wildlife had moved into the IAC campus as Kansas City had pushed outward. We had vast stretches of undeveloped land to keep clear flight paths for launches. No one bothered the animals, so they just made it their home. It was hard to see them and remember how bad things were outside of the IAC.

The humid air of an early summer coated me liberally with sweat. Among the things I do not miss on the Moon is humidity in summer. I do not miss it at all.

When I ran inside, the air-conditioning chilled the sweat and turned it clammy. Building 9, aka the Space Vehicle Mockup Facility, is a giant building the bulk of which was given over to one large open chamber filled with—and I know this is shocking—space vehicle mockups. Naturally, the IAC takes a perfectly descriptive name and turns it into an opaque acronym—SVMF.

As I rounded the enormous Cygnus 4 cockpit mockup by the door, I spotted Halim Malouf waiting for me under the great blue A-frame of the POGO zero-gravity simulator. I winced and slowed to a walk. It is always unnerving when the head astronaut turns up randomly.

He was studying a binder and squinting at the page. I wasn't sure if that was concern or if he'd forgotten his reading glasses. His shoulders were a little higher than usual, so I was betting on concern, but he smiled at me when he looked up from the binder. "I'm going to need to hijack part of your training session. Schedule changes."

"Understood." He and the other department heads had undoubtedly spent the morning in meetings, rejiggering the schedule after the accident. I hurried to the table where my harness was laid out and took a breath to slow down before donning it. Some things I could rush, some things I shouldn't. Slow is fast. "How's the crew?"

"Alive." He closed his binder. "But they did a ballistic reentry. Cleary said they pulled eight Gs coming in."

"Oof." I remembered that from the centrifuge. It was like your entire body was shoved into one of those new mammogram machines. "But everyone is okay?"

"Mm . . . mostly. A couple of fractures and more than one concussion. It was a hard landing. Like the old capsule days."

I winced. Parachutes only slowed you down so much. It still felt like a car crash when a capsule hit into the ground, even when everything was nominal.

The connectors on my harness all looked good, so I lifted it off the table and carried it over to the hydraulic lift.

Halim set his binder down. "Want a hand?"

"Sure thing."

He knelt on the floor, holding open the harness so I could step into it. "After you're done here, Clemons will want to talk to you."

I raised an eyebrow at that. "I just saw him at the press conference. He didn't say anything."

"Probably didn't want to risk a reporter hearing."

"That's it? Not even a hint?"

"Also a schedule change." Over the hum of the equipment and fans, the babble of a group of people talking inserted itself into the room. Halim cocked his head to the side. "Sounds like they're here."

Gah! Why did Clemons want to talk to me? In the best case, this meant a flight assignment. But it could also be a random drug screening. Schedule change, though . . . I wrangled my hopes back down to sit with my fury. They were not going to let me pilot one of the big rockets. And especially not after an accident like this. I squashed my curiosity and tried to drag my head back into the game. We had colonists approaching. "Aw. Sounds like the babies are excited."

Halim snorted. "Babies. Most of them have PhDs."

"Hell, I don't even have a Master's." If I applied to the IAC today, I wouldn't have qualified. Shit. What if Clemons was going to pull me from rotation? After all, I was *old hat*. "Besides, it's more endearing to think of them as babies than as rookies or stooges."

"You needed training too."

"And that's why I think of them as babies." I shrugged the black leather harness up to my shoulders. People think black leather harnesses are sexy, but this was like the ugliest apron you've ever seen. "Babies are smart and just need their hands held. And diapers."

He laughed and strapped the leg garter around my calf. "Hey, now. Astronauts don't wear diapers."

"We wear MAGs." Maximum Absorbency Garments. They're diapers, but no self-respecting fighter pilot could admit to wearing a diaper. They're such babies about their egos. I shifted my weight to allow him to strap the other garter around my thigh. "Speaking of training . . .

I'm happy to do any additional training you need, if that would benefit the corps." Like, for instance, if he wanted me to train on one of the new big rockets. I lifted the safety helmet and slid it over my pixie cut, which was another reason to give up on the bouffants.

"Noted. Thank you. Some of the other veterans balk at running training sessions, but I think it's good for the rookies to interact with the original corps."

"Oh—" I caught myself before I explained his mistake about my intention. I'd meant that I was happy to *take* additional training, not that I was willing to teach more classes, but . . . the secret to brown-nosing is to not push too hard for your objective in a single pass. I sidestepped into the gap he had offered. "I completely agree. And listen, if the boys are balking about doing any of the Sirius training, feel free to throw me in the simulator."

Someday, the IAC might let a woman fly one of the big rockets, but so far, the duty roster kept us firmly in the co-pilot or Nav/Comp roles. Apparently, my boobs got in the way of firing thrusters. I loved my job, but there was no possibility for advancement. Unless—

Unless Clemons wanted to ground me. Old hat. I wasn't that much past fifty. Old hat. Shit.

I bit my lower lip and forced my mind away from that gravity well. What were other possibilities? Halim had said there were multiple people with fractures and concussions. If any of them were pilots, maybe they actually needed to let one of the women fly. With Elma gone, I had the most flight time.

Oh . . . Oh shit. That was plausible. My heart had

kicked up in my chest and I would have been hosed if I'd had biomedical instrumentation attached to me. As it was, I had to consciously slow down my breathing. Plausible did not mean probable.

The crowd of young colonists rounded the corner of the Sirius IV mockup, led by their astronaut escort, Curtis Frye. The young American pilot was new to the corps and never saw a fact that he could pass by. That might have been his background on the Annapolis debate team or it might have been that he was a fighter pilot before the IAC. Either way, when he saw Halim with me, he immediately slowed the group. Curt recognized the change in routine and stopped them just outside the yellow caution lines painted on the floor around the POGO.

Halim nodded. "Good morning. I'll try to be brief, so you can get on to your training session today. Now, the first thing you'll want to know is about the incident this morning. Everyone aboard made it down safely, but I shall take this opportunity to remind you to review emergency procedures and to keep your arms tucked next to your body during launch and reentry. My second note . . . We're making changes to the schedule, which will involve asking some of you to launch on the next ship."

The young people standing opposite from us represented the best that Earth had to offer. They were all fit and smart and the product of rigorous testing criteria in their home countries. Black and white and every shade of brown mixed together with one common goal—getting off this doomed planet.

Even though they were part of the IAC, they were only

colonists, without full astronaut training, and I could see the beginning of fear as their eyes widened or their breathing quickened. I stepped in to be Halim's wingman. They would be frightened about the spaceship and I needed to redirect them. "I've had the chance to work with you over the past several weeks, and I would say something if you weren't ready to go. You are."

"Absolutely." Halim's smile was utterly charming. "We'll cover all of this in more detail later, but knowing how rumors fly, I wanted to make certain that you were aware that changes were coming. With the expansion into the Marius Hills cave habitats we'll need all hands to stay on schedule. If there are any issues, any at all, let me know and I will resolve them."

At one end of the group, Ruben du Preez, from South Africa, asked, "Any word on what happened to the rocket?"

"We won't know for certain what caused the explosion for months, but preliminary data suggests an overpressure event." He held up a soothing hand. "However, that was a Sirius IV. We're launching you in a Cygnus-class glider while we investigate this incident."

"Thank you, Halim. I know you've got a lot of work to do. We appreciate you stopping by." To keep him from being trapped by questions, I turned to the students with one of my prettiest smiles and patted the harness I wore. The world's ugliest apron was designed to support me as if I were in one-sixth of Earth's gravity. "Now, I'll be putting you through your paces with the POGO. That stands for Partial Gravity Simulator and, yes, I know. If the IAC were consistent it would be the PGS, but that's asking too much for an international governmental agency. This collection of servos, air bearings, and gimbals is not to be confused with Pogo oscillation. Any guesses on what that one is?"

A tan young woman with straight dark hair pulled back into a ponytail raised her hand. Aahana Kamal, of course. She was always fastest with answers in this group.

"Yes?"

Her voice sounded as plummily British as Clemons's did, which meant she'd done English-language schools, not Hindi, and ergo probably came from money. "Pogo oscillation is a self-excited vibration in liquid-propellant rocket engines due to combustion instability. The variations of engine thrust that result cause corresponding variations of acceleration on the vehicle, stressing the frame, and in severe cases can become critical."

"Well done." I smiled, while feeling outclassed by a rookie. "The similar names originate from the same concept. Has anyone been on a pogo stick?"

Halim had paused to watch us and raised his hand. "I have."

I didn't *quite* roll my eyes. "You named this thing, didn't you."

"I can neither confirm nor deny."

Laughing, I turned back to the colonists and gestured to the harness I wore. "You're going to use the POGO rig to run an obstacle course in simulated lunar gravity. I'll start by demonstrating what that looks like."

Another hand went up. Birgit Furst, from the Swiss contingent. "I had understood that the Neutral Buoyancy Lab was better at simulating zero-g."

"The NBL is better for spacewalks, yes, because we're simulating wearing a spacesuit. However, the water also generates drag so the POGO is better at giving you a sense of moving on the Moon."

It also didn't involve nearly the number of expensive resources as putting someone in the NBL.

Curt hooked the hydraulic line to the large swivel on the back of my harness. The line went up to the enormous A-frame that towered over us like a big blue Erector Set. "Ready?"

"Affirmative."

He grinned, stepping to the side, and powered up the POGO. The line tightened until it counterbalanced my weight. Even simulated lunar gravity made my feet happier.

"The first thing to know is that you weigh so little that it's hard to get traction. You'll note that when I start moving, I lean forward significantly. Walking is basically a controlled fall. Any questions so far?"

Another predictable hand shot into the air. Vicky Hsu, from the United States. "May I go first?"

Oh, clever girl. Going first makes you look eager and any mistakes you make are chalked up to being first. The middle of the pack disappears. The person to go last, if done right, can look polite, but most of the time they just look reluctant. Sure, this group was going to the Moon, but we all knew that if you wanted to go to Mars, you had to excel on the Moon. I winked at her. "Absolutely."

I stopped leaning and did a normal Earth walk. "Notice how much I'm bouncing?" My feet cleared the ground a little too much as all the force meant to support my body on Earth shoved me upward in the one-sixth gravity of the Moon. "When you lean forward, your force goes backward, transferring into momentum. But be careful. Your goal is precision and economy. It is not speed. In space, slow is fast. Moving quickly can cause you to overshoot your mark. Watch."

I got to the far side and turned to come back. Leaning nearly to forty-five degrees, I propelled myself into the lunar lope. I tightened my buttocks and legs to get a nice long, lean shape as I bounded across the floor. It helps with momentum but it also makes your ass look amazing. There's something very—

The floor slammed into me.

Forearms. Chin. Knees. Shoulders. I don't know what hit first, they all lit up with red alerts of pain. The air evacuated from my lungs. My vision went red and a roaring filled my ears like a rocket launching. What the hell?

"Nicole!" Curt was by my side, pulling the support crossbar off my back. If I hadn't been leaning forward in a lope, it would have slammed into my head. Helmet or no, that would have been . . . not a good day.

Beyond him, the babies looked horrified. Two of them had stepped forward, or maybe the rest had stepped back, because one of the hydraulic lines had breached and vented fluid all over the place. Some of it had soaked the front of my shirt.

My lungs burned as I dragged air into them. Wheezing is unglamorous, but I'd had the air knocked out of me before. "I'm fine."

At my back, Curt was undoing buckles on the harness.

"You've split your chin open."

Halim appeared with the first aid kit. "That is going to require stitches."

"Oh." I looked down as if I could see my own chin, and the front of my shirt was a vivid red. So, the dampness hadn't been hydraulic fluid. Noted. "Well. I suppose my modeling career is over."

FIVE

UN REFUGEE COMMISSIONER MAKES NEW APPEAL ON PANAMA

KANSAS CITY, March 29, 1963—(Reuters)—The United Nations High Commissioner for Refugees, Prince Sadruddin Aga Khan, made an appeal for nations to accept refugees from Panama. Prince Sadruddin said that 1,800 refugees had been accepted or were in the process of being accepted by twenty different countries. The majority of these refugees are Kuna, an indigenous people whose homelands in the Panama islands are flooding under rising sea levels.

THE FLIGHT SURGEON wanted me to go home. Can you imagine? Ha. As if one of the boys would do that after a little bump on the chin. I took the time to put on a clean shirt and headed to Clemons's office with all seven of my brand-new stitches. I held a clipboard in one hand because they fool people into thinking that you are serious and busy.

When I walked into the outer office, his secretary Mrs. Kare looked up with a smile that quickly went to shock. "Good heavens!"

"I was wrestling a goose." There's a game pilots play, where we never give a straight answer to an injury question to anyone except the flight surgeon and then only enough to get back to flying. "Is he in?"

She almost rolled her eyes at me, and I admired her professionalism that she managed to stop it. "Yes, he's expecting you."

In his office, Clemons had his feet up on his desk with a report propped on his expansive belly. A cloud of his ubiquitous cigar smoke surrounded him. I swear, the only place he didn't smoke was in the clean rooms. "Ah, Wargin. Can you—Lord. *That's* from the hydraulic failure?"

"Head-butted by a goat." The skin under the bandage pulled and stung with each syllable. "But I won. You wanted to see me?"

"Er . . . yes." He lowered his feet and stared at my chin. The floor supervisor at the SVMF would have called Clemons to let him know about the accident, but I was not going to let him dwell on the injury, which is why I'd brought the clipboard. I sat down as if nothing were untoward.

"Halim told my class about the new schedule. I've got their current assessments ready for when you need them."

"Ah . . . thank you." He shuffled some papers on his desk and pulled out a pair of stapled sheets. "I do apologize for not mentioning it at the press conference today. You know how those jackals are. But yes, we are accelerating the next launch."

"Absolutely." I swallowed and felt the bandage tighten on my skin. "When did you need us to launch?"

"Ten days."

"I see." On the one hand, I was delighted to head back to the Moon, where I had some use and where, honestly, life was simpler. On the other hand, I was supposed to have another month at home with Kenneth. I was furious with him for that comment at the press conference, but that didn't make me love him any less.

"Malouf thinks that's the absolute minimum time you need to prepare." He held out the paper. "Before you say yes, look this over. I'm shifting your role, and this lays out the revised crew schedule."

Please let it be pilot. Please let it be pilot. I took the sheet and clipped it to my board. Next to my name it said "secretarial staff." He had transferred me out of the astronaut department completely. It felt like I had been punched. It was one thing to have someone say you were *old hat* and another to be sent out to pasture. I suppose I should be grateful he was still letting me launch. "Secretarial . . . It's not my strength, but I'm happy to do what the IAC needs."

"Excellent." Clemons looked past me. "Ah, Malouf. Good."

"Sorry. I got caught by a colonist." Halim walked in carrying a file folder, and his expression was tight. He sat in the chair next to mine. "We've got one who doesn't want to launch despite it being a different class of rocket."

"I expect we'll get a few others, which will make . . . One moment." Grimacing, Clemons got up and went to the door of his office. "Mrs. Kare. No calls. Icarus program."

"Yes, sir." She glanced over her glasses at me and continued typing as if nothing unusual were happening.

The Icarus program? I spent six months out of the year on the Moon, and it was easy to lose track of Earthbound projects. I had no idea what Icarus was. Ship? Station? Training protocol?

Code phrase?

Clemons shut the door. He ran a hand over his hair and stared at me. At my chin. "Tell me about the accident."

"I . . ." Both of my bosses were in the room. Even if Halim hadn't seen the accident, this was not the time for games. "I was doing a POGO demonstration. While I was in the harness, the hydraulic sprang a leak."

In the chair next to me, Halim shifted and glanced at Clemons. I could feel an entire unspoken conversation between them, but the subject matter was beyond my guess. Finally, Clemons sighed and stared at the floor. "I've conferred with my security officer and am going to read you on information based on your security clearance and your new need to know. This is TS/SCI."

"I see." I stayed sitting calmly in my chair, but my insides tightened. For a variety of reasons, some due to being one of the first astronauts, some due to my work in the war, and a little bit due to my husband, I had Top Secret clearance. I had no idea which piece of my history Clemons was referring to from my file. With the IAC, my TS clearance had only ever been related to rocket details, and this did not feel like we were about to talk rocketry.

You have to be "read on" for each SCI—Sensitive Compartmented Information. The government does love its acronyms. . . . My voice was quiet and steady. My posture was perfect. Inside, was one long clenching of my guts. "May I assume there is no actual Icarus program?"

"You may." Clemons settled back in his chair. "If someone asks, the Icarus program is a theoretical project for navigating solo in space."

"I question that name choice for a space program."

"It makes perfect sense for referring to people who are trying to make us fall back to Earth." His face was haunted like I had never seen before. "I believe the launch was sabotaged and that it is not the only instance."

Years of practice at conversing with my husband's constituents allow me to sound calm even when I'm not. We had *just* had a press conference. People had asked about this. "Why aren't we telling the public? That would clear up the perception the IAC is at fault."

"The FBI has asked us not to, because they believe they are close to identifying the culprits. Publicizing this would, potentially, scare them off."

Internally, I made note of the fact that the FBI was involved, which meant they thought the sabotage was coming from a U.S. citizen. If not, it would be the CIA or the UN. "Scaring them off does not sound like a bad consequence."

"They would regroup and return with a different plan that we couldn't see coming."

A rocket had blown up this morning. I was not convinced they were seeing anything coming now. "So how are we handling it?"

Clemons cleared his throat and looked to Halim, who said, "Nicole . . . What are your thoughts on a Brazilian launch?"

"It depends on the context. In terms of this conversation, it makes me think the saboteurs are local. From an astronaut perspective, Brazil is farther from training facilities but has lower launch costs." Brazil primarily handled heavy lift cargo vehicles. Their equatorial placement gave them an advantage over Kansas, plus an ocean for rockets to ditch into instead of farm country. The only reason we launched from Kansas was that, at first, it's where the rocket industry was thanks to the Sunflower Armory. But now? Now it was because of politicians, like my husband, who were trying to keep jobs at home. The theory was that the training facilities for astronauts were already here, but truly it was about money.

And power.

I sighed because this wasn't really about my TS/SCI status. This was about the fact that I was married to the governor of Kansas. "You need me to talk to Kenneth about moving operations out of Kansas? Fine. I'll make sure he doesn't balk."

"Thank you, that would be appreciated. However, I did brief him this morning after the press conference." Clemons grimaced. "My apologies for not including you. I am trying to keep you out of the spotlight for anything related to Icarus."

In the back of my head, a signal alert went off. Was that part of why Kenneth had wanted me to sit out the press conference? Had he and Clemons talked about this and— Had my husband *known*? No. Wait. Wait . . . Clemons said he talked to Kenneth *after* the press conference. "What role do you want me to have?"

Halim nodded to the revised schedule Clemons had given me. "You'll be assigned to be the Lunar Colony Administrator's personal secretary so that you can interface directly with Otto Frisch."

I nodded and tried to quell the sense of relief that I wasn't being put out to pasture. We were talking about sabotage and terrorists and here I was feeling grateful that I still had a use. "Who else will I be working with?"

Clemons shook his head. "On the Moon, only the two of you. The FBI would prefer for it to be only the LCA, but . . . we have information to send to him that I cannot transmit. We believe they have someone in comms."

A shiver chased itself over my skin. A saboteur was bad, but someone who was actively inside the IAC was terrifying. "Here or off-planet?"

"We don't know." Clemons rolled his cigar between his fingers. "More accurately, I should say that the IAC does not know but I am not certain about the FBI."

"They aren't telling you everything?" I could understand limiting the information to need-to-know. News of a potential saboteur on the Moon could wreak havoc on the morale of a tiny, isolated community, but Clemons was the head of the agency. He needed to know. "They're asking you to work this problem without a full dataset?"

Halim rubbed the back of his neck. "I am attempting to believe that this is no different from a CAPCOM filtering the data a spacewalker gets so they can focus on mission critical work."

It was so hard not to yell. My voice was flat calm when I replied, "To continue that metaphor. When I've taken a rotation at the CAPCOM desk, my job is to parse and filter the information that the astronaut on orbit receives. But I don't hide failure points. And when they ask for more details, I damn well give it to them because they are the ones who are actually putting their lives on the line. I'm sitting at a desk." There is a look that my mother deploys when she is about to explain the errors of a man trying to chase her off a golf course. I could feel my nostrils pinch shut and hard lines form around my mouth. "What the FBI is doing right now is asking a group of astronauts to go to the Moon without giving them mission critical details. They're asking people to put their lives on the line without telling them that there is a potential failure point."

"I am in complete agreement." Clemons tapped the ash off the end of his cigar with more vigor than strictly necessary. "But my superior at the UN has informed me that the FBI has jurisdiction. So . . . I am authorized to read on one additional person. And that is you."

"To continue the briefing . . ." Halim pulled a piece of onionskin out of his folder. "This is a draft document intercepted from Earth First. The FBI calls it 'The Manifesto.'"

Exodus 32:27 And he said to them: Thus saith the Lord God of Israel: Put every man his sword upon his thigh: go, and return from gate to gate through the midst of the camp, and let every man kill his brother, and friend, and neighbour.

The planet Earth is recovering from the Meteor strike

but the United States is not. The needs of our fellow Americans are ignored in favor of an elite who pursue the false idol of living in space. Money that should rightfully be spent on infrastructure here on Earth goes instead to pay for complex programs that benefit other nations.

Revelation 16:21 And great hail, like a talent, came down from heaven upon men: and men blasphemed God for the plague of the hail: because it was exceeding great.

Representing every state and region, we have spoken to each other deeply, of our situation, of what God has done and is doing—in our world and in the unexplored frontiers which we now face. We might measure the world in terms of emergency, of the critical needs for money and manpower needed to keep the people alive in many areas. These needs are absolute, measurable, and commanding. It is our conviction, however, that to interpret the post-Meteor world only in those terms would be wrong. Those needs prove that the ideas we have of one another and of our common life are utterly obsolete and irrelevant to our actual situation.

We have attempted dialogue to change the course of human events. We have written letters. We have marched. We have begged and pleaded but still our children and wives are hungry. Still they do not have running water. Still they do not have electricity. We have been patient. We have waited.

But after eleven years, we are no longer content to

wait. Our pleas have fallen on infertile ground and so now we act. This serves as a notice that the lives of the astronauts and astronettes who started us on this fatal path are forfeit until the United States government withdraws from the International Aerospace Coalition.

Exodus 22:24 And my rage shall be enkindled, and I will strike you with the sword, and your wives shall be widows, and your children fatherless.

MY BRAIN CHURNED from the briefing with Clemons and Halim for the rest of the day. So much so that by the time I got home, I had almost forgotten the riot from the night before. Then it snapped into a new focus. Had that been just a riot or had that been Icarus?

There were extra security guards at our pied-à-terre when I arrived and charred places on the sidewalk. One of the lobby windows had chips in it where someone had thrown rocks—at least I hoped it had only been only rocks. Our building was built to post-Meteor standards and had bulletproof glass. It was stupid, because the chances of another asteroid slamming into the Earth were slim.

On the other hand, lightning also wasn't supposed to strike twice and my mother had been struck by lightning three times.

Of course, she also golfed and was stubborn about coming inside. The point being that the architectural overreaction meant it was as safe a place to put a governor as one could ask for.

I've got to say, it's a fascinating experience to have to

show ID to enter your own building. There was a small line next to the nice young security officer, and as I walked up, I realized that I recognized two of the men.

"Reynard! Nathaniel!" My heart twisted sideways in my chest, even though these men were both friends. They were also engineers at the IAC and Nathaniel was The Dr. Nathaniel York. If the lead engineer of the space program was here to brief my husband, then he must have turned up something new about the crash. "How are yo—"

"*Sacre bleu!*" Reynard gaped at me. "What have you done to yourself?"

"Ballet accident." I actually had kicked myself in the face once, but that was decades ago. I leaned in to kiss Reynard on both cheeks in the Parisian fashion and snuck a look at Nathaniel. The shadows lining his face did not come solely from his hat. "I'm surprised they could pry you out of the building."

Nathaniel looked at the sidewalk, hunching into his suit jacket, and I could see his shoulder bones poking through the fabric. He always ran to lean but he looked absolutely gaunt now in ways that were uncomfortably familiar. "Reynard turned the power off in my office."

"Clemons told me to!" He showed his passport to the security officer and stomped through the turnstile. "You would have stayed until dawn, and I have made promises to your wife."

"So have I!" I chirped and waved my ID at the guard, stepping through the turnstile when he nodded.

Nathaniel winced and pressed his hand to his side. "We lost a rocket today. I should be there, not playing poker."

Poker night. I had forgotten, but the relief that he wasn't there to brief Kenneth on some new and worse development made me ebullient. "Let the backrooms do their jobs. Come upstairs and I'll ply you with martinis."

He handed the guard his ID and followed us through the turnstile. Dark circles ringed Nathaniel's eyes and exhaustion dragged his face down. Today had been distressing, but he carried more than one day of fatigue. When we reached the elevator, he stood with his eyes half-closed as if he were dead on his feet.

I had been a terrible friend. I'd promised Elma that I'd keep an eye on her husband and I couldn't even remember the last time I'd seen him. And now I was going away and—oh. Oh. Nathaniel knew. He was one of the handful who knew about the saboteur because, as lead engineer, he had to know that the failures were not accidents.

We got in the elevator and I pushed the button for our floor. Here's the funny thing about our post-Meteor building. It extended down as far as it did up. The most expensive apartments were all the way down. Kenneth and I lived on the top floor because I was damned if I was going to spend my time on Earth buried under rock. I spent enough time living under regolith on the Moon, thank you very much.

Reynard leaned against the side of the elevator. "In the paper, I saw that you were caught in the riots last night." He gestured at my chin. "Is that . . . ?"

"No, no. We were fine." My ears popped as we arrived at the twenty-fourth floor. "We stayed with the Lindholms last night."

Nathaniel smiled, stretching the skin over his cheekbones. "They are good at taking in refugees."

"That they are." I led them down the hall to our apartment and nodded at the bodyguard who kept watch outside our door in the evenings when we were in town. "Will Eugene be here tonight?"

"No. He said something had come up." Reynard sighed. "Alas."

I had the new crew schedule Clemons had given me in my purse and it gave a likely reason. The Lindholms were headed back to the Moon with me and—oh, damn. Helen's name was on that list too, and Reynard clearly hadn't spoken to his wife yet. "How's Helen?"

"She is in Chicago at the Adler. No—wait." He looked at his wristwatch. "She should be landing at Sunflower shortly, if she is not already on the ground."

"You might want to skip tonight." I opened the door to the apartment and a wave of masculine voices swept out into the hall. Reynard's head came up and his shoulders tightened. I held up a hand to calm him. "She's fine."

"What is happening?"

If he didn't know about the sabotage, I couldn't tell him, but he should damn well know his wife's duty assignments. "Clemons is rotating us back to the Moon early. We launch from Brazil, which means they'll need to ship us out next week."

"*Merde!*"

Nathaniel closed his eyes for a moment, wincing. "Sorry." His voice was hoarse. "I argued for grounding everything. I didn't think Clemons would . . . I should have told you that was a possibility."

Reynard waved the apology away and looked back to the door. "Please give my regards to the governor."

I saw him out, and moments later, my husband appeared in the hall. "Nathaniel! I see you brought my wi— Nicole? What?"

I leaned in to kiss him on the cheek and whispered, "Training accident. It looks worse than it is. Tell you later."

The pressure of his lips against my cheek and the touch of his hand on my arm softened my shoulders just a touch. I wanted to sit with him and talk about everything, but we had company.

Pulling back, Kenneth turned to Nathaniel and extended his hand. I saw the moment when my husband really looked at Nathaniel and at the hollows of his cheeks. I tried not to see the following moment when his gaze turned to me and the specter of my past self. "How's Elma?"

"Good." Nathaniel cleared his throat. "She said she's reading *The Gods of Mars* and enjoying it."

"And yourself? How are you holding up with . . . everything?" Kenneth steered Nathaniel out of the foyer and into the living room of our apartment. "Don't take this the wrong way, but you look like hell."

Nathaniel laughed and the sound terrified me. It had a wheeze and tore at the edges like it was about to become sobbing that might not stop. "Clemons made me leave the building on the day of a rocket failure."

I followed them into the living room, which was filled with the men of the Astronauts' Husbands Club. It was still a small group and they tended to only come when their wives were away. Most of them were clustered around the dining room table, with cards dealt out, but a few were down in the sunken living room, sitting on the sofa or in an easy chair, talking.

"Come in. Do something social and we'll ply you with sandwiches and enough martinis that you'll get a good night's sleep."

"That would be nice." His voice was low and rough. "You know how it is."

"I do." Kenneth squeezed Nathaniel's shoulder and glanced at me again.

This fear was different. In that silent look, I saw boundless space reflected in his dark eyes and had a moment of clarity about what he goes through when I'm gone. All of the husbands worried. I saw that at every launch I attended as an astronaut escort. My job there was to make the family comfortable and to be their rock in case of a "contingency." Contingency. It's the IAC's way of referring to death. Kenneth and Nathaniel had been founding members of that club, which was built of equal parts pride and terror.

And this time it was going to be worse because Kenneth would know that someone might sabotage my launch.

"*La madre que te parió,* Ken. What did you do to your wife?" Florina Morales's husband stood next to the hors d'oeuvres set out on the sideboard.

"He finally showed her who was boss," Mandy Self's husband replied. "Am I right?"

"Hey, Nicole!" Deana Whitney's husband sloshed his martini as he gestured. "What'd you do to piss Ken off?"

"Now, Mr. Whitney." I laid a manicured finger along my bandage in a classic modeling pose. "Tell the truth. I got this head-butting you. I just forgot that I was wearing heels."

The men laughed and Mr. Whitney turned a little red. There's nothing wrong with being short, and under normal circumstances I wouldn't have hit an area that he was sensitive about, but let me tell you a joke that is not funny. When you see a woman with stitches in her chin and ask her what she did to make her husband angry.

There are two scenarios. The first is that she's happily married and you've insulted their relationship. The other is that her husband *is* abusive and she will not thank you for endangering her by drawing attention to it. In the range of possibilities in between, there's not a single one in which a joke about being a battered woman is funny.

I was done dealing with jokes about the stitches so I sashayed out of the living room and into the kitchen. I would pour a glass of scotch for myself and then have whatever our housekeeper had set out for dinner.

A few minutes later, Kenneth followed me into the kitchen. "Sorry about that."

"I'm fine." I picked up the sandwich she'd left for me and took a bite so he'd stop worrying about that at least. Ham and cheese with mustard. "Don't abandon Nathaniel."

He nodded and rubbed the back of his neck. "I got him set up with a sandwich, and Fernando Morales was making him a martini."

Setting the sandwich down, I opened the cabinet and pulled out the single malt we hid on poker night. A sixteen-year-old Abelour. I like the astronaut husbands, but not that much. I grabbed a rocks glass. "Want one?"

"I'll have a sip of yours." He leaned against the counter next to me. His tie was undone and his sleeves were rolled partway up to his elbows. "Want to tell me about the training accident?"

"I was demonstrating the POGO and the hydraulic line gave." I shrugged. Pulling off the cork released peat and the dark resin of heather on the heath. "Clemons checked my clearance level today and then he told me everything."

"Shit." Kenneth turned and grabbed a glass for himself after all. Given the sabotage implications, I was not surprised. "Did he show you the report from the lunar rocket misfiring two years ago?"

"He mentioned it." Myrtle had been coming back from the Moon and a thruster misfired during docking at *Lunetta*. No one had died, but it had done a fair bit of damage. I poured the beautiful amber liquid into my glass. "Told me to ask for your copy of the report. How long have you known?"

Kenneth sighed heavily. "This morning."

I poured a finger of whisky for him. "Did you have to yell to get them to brief you?"

"No. No . . . Clemons needed my help with dama—"

Someone shouted from the living room. "Oh God!"

The cries of alarm rippled from multiple male throats. Setting the glass on the counter, I ran into the living room. Men clustered near the sideboard, framing Nathaniel.

He was on his knees, half-doubled with blood streaking down the front of his shirt. For a moment, I thought he'd somehow split his chin open.

Howard Brown held his shoulders as Nathaniel vomited. Bright blood sprayed from his mouth. The husbands all stood frozen, with horror stretching their features. I ran toward them, as if I were on the triage team in a contingency procedure. On my way, I grabbed the ice bucket and dumped the ice and water on the carpet.

Kenneth followed me at a run. "Do you want the car or an ambulance?"

"The car. It's faster." Sliding to my knees next to Nathaniel, I shoved the ice bucket under his mouth in time to catch the next wave of retching.

A male voice said, "Jesus, Nicole. This isn't the time to worry about your damn carpet."

"Fuck you. The doctor might need to see the condition of the blood in his vomit." It was bright fresh red. He was bleeding inside.

SIX

DEVICE IS TESTED THAT SCANS SEAS

**Satellite Sensor Can Check for Plant Life
in Oceans**

By WALTER RUSSELL

Special to The National Times

BRUSSELS, March 30, 1963—Scientists of the International Aerospace Coalition have developed a method for aerially monitoring one of the most vital activities on Earth—the biological productivity of lakes and seas. The device watches for the telltale signs of chlorophyll. The drifting plant life of the oceans is vital not only because it feeds the fish eaten by man, but also because it replenishes the oxygen of the atmosphere.

HOSPITALS ALL HAVE the same smell of disinfectant and stale air barely masking old bandages. Kenneth and I sat in molded plastic chairs across from the waiting room's one phone booth, trying not to rush the happily weeping young man who was using it. He had been calling a list of family for the last hour to let them know about his new daughter.

I tried not to hate him, but I needed to make a call.

On the other hand, I wasn't sure what news I had. I looked up at the clock on the wall: 2 a.m. Nathaniel had been in surgery for five hours.

"He'll be fine." Kenneth rested his hand on my knee.

"I know." We were both lying to each other because it was anyone's guess how it would go, but you take your comfort where you can. "Have you given any more thought to the Moon trip?"

His bodyguard sat at the end of the row, ostensibly reading a book but really scanning the room for threats. Kenneth glanced to that end of the room before sighing. "I don't want you to go."

"Kenneth."

"You asked." He pulled his hand from my knee. "I don't want you to go. I know you will anyway."

I shouldn't have started the conversation in a place where neither of us could speak freely. "Brazil hasn't had any problems."

"Yet." He leaned forward. "Phone's about to be free."

A nurse entered the room, walking briskly toward the young man. He stepped out of the phone booth, blowing his nose on a handkerchief, and followed her off to see his new daughter.

I really did try to rejoice for him, but I just hoped that Nathaniel would escape the operating table with all of his internal organs intact.

Sliding out of my chair, I hurried to the phone before another patron could grab it. I had Elma's brother's number in my purse because I had been her family's astronaut escort when she launched for Mars. Slipping into the phone booth, I dialed 0 and waited for the operator so I could place a long-distance call. It was 2 a.m., which would be midnight in California.

"Operator."

"Long distance, please."

"Surely." In my ear, the sound changed subtly and a different woman said, "Long distance."

"Operator, I'd like to place a call to Los Angeles: Rockwell five-four-nine-seven-five."

"Please deposit one dollar and five cents for the first three minutes."

I shoved a series of quarters and a nickel into the slots at the top of the machine and waited, twisting the cord around my fingers as the operator connected the call.

It rang four times before a drowsy baritone answered, "Wexler residence, Hershel Wexler speaking."

"Hershel, hello. It's Nicole Wargin." I heard his intake of breath as keen as a knife cut. "Elma's fine."

He sighed. "Oh, thank God. Sorry. It's just that when you call—"

"I understand. Listen, I'm on a pay phone, so have to keep this short. Forgive me for bluntness. Nathaniel had a bleeding ulcer they couldn't stop and he's in emergency surgery now. I have your contact information, but I don't know his family at all." This was life after the Meteor. We never asked about people's families anymore, because of the hundreds of thousands of people who had died. "Does he . . . Who should I call?"

"Oh God."

"The doctor was confident going into surgery, I just don't have any news yet." Five hours and counting.

The phone rustled as he lowered it. "It's all right, Doris. Go back to sleep." Then he was back in my ear. "He doesn't have a lot of family. Only child. At the wedding, aside from a couple of cousins, there were mostly just college buddies or friends from work."

"Should I call one of them?"

"He . . . he worked out at Langley."

Langley. Langley didn't exist anymore. It hadn't been directly under the Meteor, but with the airblast and fires it might as well have been. "All right. I'll—"

The operator cut in. "Please deposit ten cents to continue the call."

I shoved a dime into the slot. "I'll round up folks from here to look after him."

"Thanks. Tell me the hospital? I'll book a flight as soon as I'm off the phone."

"Oh. I just didn't know who to call. You don't have to come out."

"He's family." He gave a half-laugh. "Besides, you've met my sister."

"Fair point." And honestly, it would be a relief to let someone else be responsible. If Hershel were here to manage Nathaniel's recovery, then I wouldn't have to feel guilty about going off to the Moon. Except, of course, that Hershel was a polio survivor and wore braces on both legs. "But . . . well, I mean. Will you be able— I'm sorry. That's a—"

"I can cook. I can clean. I can even change a diaper if it comes to that."

My face went hot with embarrassment that I'd even raised the question. "I have no doubt. But wait until he's out of surgery and we know what's what. They'll probably want to keep him for a couple of days."

"Sure. Okay. Sure, that makes sense."

The damned operator cut in again. "Please deposit ten cents to continue the call."

I scrabbled in my wallet for another dime and only came up with pennies. "Shoot. Out of change."

"Hospital?"

"Washington Memoria—" The operator cut us off. I wasn't sure if he heard the last syllable.

I hung the phone back on the hook and leaned against the wall for a moment before stepping out of the booth. The person I should have contacted immediately was nearly halfway to Mars right now. But to talk to her required a teletype with a twenty-minute roundtrip for messages.

And that's why I was waiting: because she would ask questions and I wouldn't be able to answer them. As soon as Nathaniel was out and we knew the score, I would go straight to the IAC and send her a message.

In the nature of things, as soon as I stepped out of the phone booth, the doctor walked into the waiting room. My husband straightened and stood to meet him, his calm politician's mask settling around him like a shroud. At the end of the room, his bodyguard stood as if he could protect us from this danger.

"He's in recovery and doing well." The doctor was a blond British man who looked as if he'd be more at home on the cricket pitch than in the operating room. He glanced at the bandage gracing my chin with professional interest, but mercifully said nothing about it. "Would Dr. York have had a recent diagnostic procedure?"

I looked at Kenneth, who shook his head and shrugged. "Not that I know of."

"That would have been too simple." He sighed heavily and ran a hand through his hair. "He appears to have ingested something radio-opaque. We want to figure out what's—"

"Radioactive?"

"Radio-opaque. It means X-rays can't pass through it. Sometimes that's radioactive. In this case, our top guesses were barium or thallium . . ." He trailed off, seeing our confusion. "We did an X-ray prior to surgery and his stomach is white. If he hasn't had a procedure . . . Have you any idea how he might have ingested rat poison?"

The bottom dropped out of the hospital room as if gravity had cut off. I am not normally one to go speechless, but I couldn't find my voice. Kenneth's jaw dropped.

He regained speech first. "Are you saying that someone poisoned Dr. York?"

"Unless you have reason to think that he would have ingested something intentionally." The doctor's face twisted with discomfort. "Thallium, as a rodenticide, is readily accessible and radio-opaque. Would Dr. York have had reason to . . . ?"

"No. Absolutely not." I rubbed my brow trying to wrap my mind around this. "Can you tell anything about when?"

"Based on its progress through the gut, no more than

three hours prior to his arrival." He shook his head and looked grave. "I will tell you that it is the only time, in my career, that I have been grateful for a bleeding ulcer. If not for vomiting blood, I suspect he would have ignored all symptoms of poisoning as he did the ulcer, and even then I'm not sure which was going to kill him first."

I had seen the ugly gauntness of Nathaniel. I knew what not eating could do, but surely if he'd been poisoned, that was the larger concern. "But it was just an ulcer."

"Just an ulcer?" The doctor turned serious blue eyes on me. "Let us say that he had not been poisoned so we were dealing, in fact, with 'just' an ulcer. In Dr. York's case, the ulcer had perforated his stomach, and had he not come in, we would have seen a severe infection of the abdominal cavity followed by peritonitis. We are fortunate that the perforation was new. Even so, he is now minus part of his stomach and still at risk of infection. So no, this was not 'just an ulcer,' this was an ulcer that had gone ignored and untreated for months."

"I see." When had we last invited Nathaniel over, aside from the poker nights? "And the poison?"

"We're waiting on the tests to confirm, but I have pumped him full of Prussian blue."

"The . . . the paint?" I didn't paint myself, but I ran the gallery on the Moon and couldn't quite make the connection.

"Ah. Close. The raw pigment. It will bind with whatever radio-opaque thing he's swallowed. He will have absorbed some." The doctor gave a helpless shrug. "We'll have to see. He may be fine. It may have long-term effects on his health."

"Thank you." That was such an inadequate phrase. "May we see him?"

"Room 220. He'll be groggy." The doctor leaned into me. "And let me be very clear about the importance of keeping him calm."

He was bordering on rude, and asking the impossible, but I nodded. "I shall do my best."

Clutching my handbag, with Kenneth and bodyguard in tow, I headed for 220. Outside the room, I stopped and opened my purse. Some people will find it absurd that I put on a fresh coat of lipstick before going in to see Nathaniel. Here's why I did. He needed to think that he had not inconvenienced anyone. If I looked well groomed, then it implied that I had not been sitting there for over five hours.

Beside me, Kenneth was straightening his tie for the same reason. He glanced at the bodyguard. "Wait here."

Kenneth held the door for me and I went in. I'd thought that Nathaniel couldn't look worse, but I was very wrong. He lay on the hospital bed under a thin white sheet that did nothing to hide how emaciated he'd become. The knobs of his knees made mounds under the sheet. Above the pale green hospital gown, his collarbones stuck out like brittle twigs.

His eyes were open at least. Nathaniel rolled his head to the side. "Sorry."

"Pish. You did me a favor." I walked to his side and smiled down at him. "I always have a devil of a time getting them to leave the house at a reasonable hour."

"Made a mess of your carpet."

"I hated that carpet."

Kenneth put his hand on my shoulder. "She's not lying. She's been after me to recarpet for months."

Nathaniel laughed and his face tightened with pain.

I pressed a hand to his in sympathy. "Sorry. I know the joys of abdominal surgery. No laughing."

"Noted." He slowly relaxed. "What was yours?"

"Lost a fencing match to a goose." Or an emergency hysterectomy, but that was decades ago and I hated sympathy. "We promised the doctor we wouldn't stay long. I just wanted to see for myself how you were doing before I wrote to Elma."

"Don't tell her." Nathaniel grabbed my wrist. "Don't."

"Nathaniel . . . She's your wife."

"She'll worry."

"She's not wrong to do so." Just looking at his face, with his skull practically visible through his skin, I wondered how we'd all let him go so long. "I'll start by letting her know that you're okay."

"No. Don't tell her. At all." His fingers pressed against my wrist with shocking strength. "Please. Please, promise me you won't tell her."

"I can't . . . She'll want to know. And I already called Hershel."

Nathaniel groaned and screwed his eyes shut. "You don't understand. Elma isn't—I work very hard to not worry her. This will make her anxious and there's nothing she can do. By the time she gets back, I'll be fine."

"You aren't fine now."

"For God's sake. She's got enough to worry about

without thinking that I'm sick." His hand was shaking and sweat beaded his brow.

"Nicole . . ." Kenneth stepped around me and rested a hand on Nathaniel's shoulder. "We won't tell her."

"Kenneth—"

"We won't tell her." My husband stared at me and I swear he was as angry as I'd ever seen him. "Nicole, will you give us a minute."

"I . . ." The doctor had told us to keep Nathaniel calm. "Yes, of course." I tucked my handbag under my arm and walked out to the hall with my head held high. Kenneth was right that it was not the time for this conversation.

To be fair, I could understand Nathaniel's hesitation. I knew about Elma's anxiety, but he couldn't keep this a secret from her forever. That wasn't reasonable. And we were going to have to tell Clemons.

Poisoned. Hell.

In the hall, the bodyguard looked around as I stepped out and then went back to waiting. I leaned against the wall opposite the door and glared at it. Not tell his wife. Ha. Men and their desperate need to protect us. It became infuriating, even with people I liked.

The door opened and Kenneth stepped out, straightening his tie. "I'll see you tomorrow. Get some rest." His smile dropped when the door shut and all the worry lined his face again. "Olvirsson, will you arrange for security for Dr. York?"

"Yes, sir."

I waited until the bodyguard had walked out of plausible earshot. "What did you tell Nathaniel?"

"That we wouldn't tell Elma."

"Kenneth. She has a right to know."

My husband wheeled on me and spoke with quiet rage. "No. She does not. When you leave, we have to carry on the best we can. We worry. We wait. And if not telling her makes his waiting easier? If it reduces his worry? Then that is exactly what we are going to do. There isn't a damn thing she can do from Mars so his right to make this decision about what is best for him is what we're going to honor."

I drew my head back. "Is that the way you act when I'm on the Moon?"

"Yes." He stalked down the hallway after his bodyguard. "But you'll go anyway."

I hurried after him and damned him for making me trot to catch up. "You would lie to me?"

"You don't have a problem with it when it's a lie you like."

All the rage I had squashed came boiling up. "Kenneth Talbot Wargin. I promised I would never lie to you again and I expect the same courtesy in return."

He stopped in the hall, flexing his fingers. "Did you eat today?"

"That is not—"

"Did you?"

I rolled my eyes. "Oh, for crying out loud. You saw me eat breakfast at the Lindholms'. You saw me eat a sandwich at home tonight."

"I saw you push your food around at the Lindholms', and one bite does not count as eating a sandwich."

Kenneth stared at the far end of the hall. "What did you have for lunch?"

"I . . ." Damn him. "I didn't have time. I went straight from the press conference to training and then to the flight surgeon and then talked to Clemons and then came home."

"Really? So that was a six-hour meeting with Clemons? Roughly?" Kenneth's hands clenched into fists. "Don't you dare chide me for lying to you when you're on the Moon. And don't you say a goddamned word to Elma York about Nathaniel."

"You wouldn't want someone to tell you, if I were in that shape? If I had actually stopped eating again, instead of just being busy because a goddamned rocket blew up today. You're really saying you wouldn't want to know?"

Kenneth shook his head. "What I'm saying is that Nathaniel York's life is out of control. His choice about when and how to tell his wife is a choice that we are going to respect."

"So . . . what. That's okay now? So I can just lie to you when I'm on the Moon?"

Kenneth looked at me, finally, and my heart cracked in two. "Oh, baby. I love you, but I don't expect you to tell me the truth. Not about food."

SEVEN

BRAZIL HELPS USA WITH
$322 MILLION CREDIT

BRASÍLIA, March 30, 1963—A $322,000,000 credit
package to help the United States meet a critical balance
of payments problem was announced today. Coupled
with $398,000,000 to Canada announced Monday,
it brought to more than $700,000,000 the amount of
financial assistance extended in a determined effort to
salvage political and economic stability for the North
American nations affected most directly by the Meteor.

THE ACOUSTIC TILE over the entrance to the IAC's conference
room had a pattern of dots that looked like a horse. I know
this because I had been slumped on a folding chair in the
hall for a good hour while the FBI talked to Kenneth. Any
hope that Nathaniel hadn't been poisoned dropped out of
orbit when Clemons sent us directly from the hospital to
speak to them.

Even so, I was exhausted and the only thing keeping
me awake was the fact that I sometimes drool when I fall
asleep. That and the fact that I couldn't stop thinking
about the fight with Kenneth. It takes me longer than I

like to stop being defensive and masking that with anger. Most of my life, even as a pampered only child, I've had to push to be allowed in the room. There are boxes that people want to put me in and I resent it.

The fact that Kenneth keeps me, still, in the anorexia nervosa box infuriates me.

Because he's right. Because there had been space in my schedule to eat. Because I had been just busy enough to justify skipping a meal. Because I'd been hospitalized twice for it over the course of our marriage. Because every time I came back from the Moon I felt heavy—which I know was just gravity but not all of me knew that and I had to fight to have an appetite.

I stood up and walked down the hall to the vending machine that was there for the night shift. No one was watching, so I let my stride shorten to keep from flexing my toes so much. The cafeteria was open, but even if I wanted to walk that far, I didn't think the FBI would take well to me wandering off to a different building. The Radio Chef Speedy Weeny vending machine was a source of constant jokes among the women astronauts, but it was protein and calories. Food was fuel.

And . . . I was out of coins. Well, shit. I'd pumped them all into the pay phone for the call to Hershel Wexler.

The door opened and my husband came out. His tie was askew and a photographer would make hay with the state of his hair. I hurried back down the hall toward him, even though I wanted to linger by the Speedy Weeny so he could see that I was at least trying.

His shoulders were slumped, not enough that someone

else would notice, but the fatigue weighed on him. It wasn't just the hour or Nathaniel or the FBI. It was worry about me, too.

I stopped in front of him and straightened his tie, fussing with the knot so I wouldn't have to meet his gaze. "I'm sorry."

Kenneth caught my hands and raised them to his lips. "Me, too."

"Mrs. Wargin?" Behind Kenneth, a painfully slender FBI agent pulled his gaze from my bandage to my eyes. He had cheekbones that made me both jealous of him and afraid of my jealousy. "I'm Agent Boone. We're ready for you now."

"Of course." I squeezed Kenneth's hands. "You go on. I'll grab breakfast in the cafeteria before I come home."

His eyes softened as he followed the unspoken parts of our conversation. "Thank you. And I . . . I need to go back to Topeka."

The capital of Kansas. Kansas City had been the right place for him to be this morning, but he was governor and needed to get back to governing.

"Go." I released his hands and stepped back. "I'll see you at home tonight."

I went into the conference room, which usually only held astronauts. The long, narrow room had only one other occupant, a generically attractive white man, whose only distinguishing feature was a fading scar across his forehead, just under his hairline. He sat at one end of the table scribbling on a notepad without looking up.

"My colleague, Agent Whitaker." Boone gestured

toward the seated man, who barely glanced up.

"Ah, yes. Good morning. Director Clemons mentioned the two of you yesterday." During my briefing on Icarus, he had mentioned that they had begun by investigating the Cygnus Six conspirators. Which reminded me that I hadn't had time to read Kenneth's copy of that report last night because of Nathaniel, which meant I wouldn't be able to ask intelligent questions today. "I'm not sure if he's had time to let you know that I was read on the Icarus project."

"I knew he was going to bring you on." The thin man walked toward the coffee pots along the back wall. "Coffee?"

"Thank you. I hope the IAC is treating you well." Clemons had said that the FBI was reluctant to share information, and here I had direct access to the agents in charge of the Icarus project. So it was time to get him into the pattern of saying yes to requests. To build rapport, I made an offer that I have never, ever made at the IAC. "Do you want me to make a fresh pot of coffee?"

He chuckled. "No, no . . . Director Clemons arranged for fresh coffee for us. Donuts, too, if you want one."

"Thank you." I didn't, but I walked to the back of the room anyway. As he poured a cup of coffee for me, I got a paper plate for a donut. I know some astronauts who love the damn things. Powdered. Chocolate covered. Cream stuffed. I picked up one of the plain cake donuts. "May I take it you see a link between the Cygnus crash and the one this week?"

Behind me, Whitaker's pencil hit the table with a snap.

"Let's clear something up. You are not an investigator. You were read on to be a courier, and this morning you're here as a witness. Period."

"Of course." Oh, they definitely saw a link. Were they still trying to connect the NAACP, the way the trial lawyers prosecuting the Cygnus Six were, or was the FBI concentrating on the Earth First protesters? I turned to him using my patented charitable concern smile. It signals openness and empathy at the same time and is useful for everything from meeting orphans to soothing FBI agents. I hoped. "I'm happy to cooperate fully."

Whitaker gave me a flat stare that offered nothing readable except that he was not impressed with me. He picked up his pencil and flipped back a page in his notes, drawing a line beneath a couple of words.

Next to me, Boone sighed. "How do you take your coffee?"

"With nothing but pure dark bitterness, like my soul."

That got a laugh from Boone at least. "I take mine with three sugars, so I'm not sure what that says about the state of my soul."

"Either you're sweet, or you're compensating for a bitterness as deep as mine. I'll let you decide which." I accepted the cup of coffee from him, allowing my fingers to brush his. It's not quite flirtation, but physical contact, even minor, can increase a sense of rapport. They teach this in finishing school and it has served me well.

"He's not sweet." Whitaker didn't look up from his page, but I had an internal moment of victory. I'd gotten him to engage, even a little.

Boone said, "Your mother thinks I am."

"My mother is easily swayed by flowers. Bastard."

"There's a lady in the room." Boone cleared his throat and offered me an apologetic smile. "Sorry."

I laughed, throwing my head back to show off my throat. "Please. I'm a goddamned pilot. That's a helluva lot milder than anything I've said in the cockpit."

Whitaker looked up and the corner of his mouth twitched as if he had almost remembered how to smile. I affected not to notice and walked to sit in one of the chairs that was slightly out from the table. The other one that was askew had a view of the door, so was probably where Boone had been sitting. Which meant that the one I chose was probably where they had put Kenneth.

The cushion was still a bit warm. It's funny the small things that can make your heart melt a little. "Now. How can I help?" I broke off a piece of donut. Crumbs clung to my fingertips.

Boone sat in the chair I'd marked as his and pulled a notepad from his jacket's interior breast pocket. He flipped through to a page covered with spiky black ink. "Do you keep rat poison in your home?"

"I honestly don't know." So, it *had* been thallium. The donut was crumbling into pieces beneath my fingers. "That would be a question for our housekeeper."

"And did she prepare the food last night?"

"Well, yes, but . . . it was a sandwich buffet." I put a bite of donut in my mouth to buy myself some time to think. The sugar coated my tongue with gummy sweetness. The doctor had thought that Nathaniel had ingested the radio-opaque substance within three hours of arrival at the hospital and—oh, shit. He hadn't eaten before he arrived.

He must have been poisoned at our apartment, and the FBI thought so too.

I chewed, scraping it away from the roof of my palate with my tongue. "Was anyone else poisoned?"

"Did you eat anything from the buffet?"

Of course he wasn't going to answer my questions. "Our housekeeper had left out a sandwich for me. Ham and cheese with mustard, if that helps."

I had eaten a single bite of that sandwich.

Agent Whitaker jotted something down on his notepad. "Have the team look at the mustard?"

Boone nodded. "I'll call them."

Two thoughts went through my head simultaneously. The first was that they didn't know the vector for the poison yet and were grasping at straws. The second was that Kenneth had said he had given Nathaniel a sandwich. These men were about to start investigating my husband for attempted murder. He hadn't poisoned Nathaniel, of course, but if the press got hold of it that would dominate the news.

"He also had a martini." If there was a hell, I was about to go to it because I was going to try to steer them away from my husband to someone else. "Kenneth said that he left Nathaniel with Fernando Morales. He was making a martini for Dr. York, I think?—I'm not sure, of course, I was in the kitchen by that point."

"What can you tell us about Fernando Morales?"

"He is . . . an engineer? Or a dance instructor." I

frowned, realizing that I couldn't remember which one. "One of the husbands is a dance instructor. Wait—that's Howard Brown, because he always has perfect ballet hands when he gestures and stands with his feet in third position. Right. Mr. Morales is the engineer."

I was shifting into bubbling socialite mode because I wanted to pull their attention as far away from Kenneth as possible. It would diminish their trust in me for the Icarus project, but that was clearly already doomed.

I smiled at the men. "He's Florina Morales's husband and the newest member of the club. He just joined last year when she went up for final training. She's on the Moon now as a suit tech. I expect you'll want to know about all the husbands. Mr. Whitney is a naval officer and was on a submarine during the war, but I only remember that because he brags about how being short is an advantage. His wife is Deana Whitney. She's a Native American astronaut of Cherokee descent. Her little boy loves dinosaurs and she always takes one of his drawings with her to the Moon. Isn't that delightful? I can't believe that one of them brought rat poison into our home just to kill Nathaniel York—"

My babbling stopped dead.

"I'm sorry . . . But are we sure that Nathaniel was the target?" The building blocks of last night rearranged themselves in my head. "What if someone had been trying to kill Kenneth?"

Agent Whitaker didn't even look up from his notepad. Agent Boone sipped his coffee and set the mug down on the table. "Have there been any threats?"

"He's the governor of the state. Of course there are threats. He got threats when he was a mayor because of begonias." I leaned forward in my chair to try to engage them both. "Night before last there were riots outside his fundraiser. And now poison in our home?"

"Those are two very different things."

My rage shifted. They weren't even going to entertain the idea. And then a vacuum sucked all the rage away, leaving me cold. "We left his bodyguard with Nathaniel."

"That was very kind of you." Agent Boone's mouth stretched in a rictus of a smile. "We've sent men to watch Dr. York's room, so there's no need to worry about him."

I dialed my voice into its most patrician form. "While I'm worried about Nathaniel, I am also concerned that we may have left my husband exposed by focusing on the wrong threat. What are you going to do with regards to Governor Wargin?"

Agent Whitaker stopped scribbling and lifted his head from his notepad. "We're going to keep doing our job, which involves investigating credible threats and actual crimes." He drew a line on the page. "You mentioned that Mr. Morales was an engineer. With what department?"

They weren't going to do anything. The room went red with the heat of my rage. I would murder anyone who touched Kenneth. So help me—I'd been angry about what had happened to Nathaniel, but if Kenneth had been the target there was not a rocket large enough to escape me.

* * *

BY THE TIME I finally bailed out from the clutches of Whitaker and Boone, I had squashed so much rage that I was shaking. They didn't want to talk to me about Icarus and they didn't want me to worry my pretty little head over Kenneth. But if I was correct, he was on a train right now, sans bodyguard.

I got out of the room and ran for the second floor. I had a choice—elevator, which was slower, or stairs, which hurt my feet. Speed took priority today and I could jog up them in heels and a skirt, even if it cost me. Each step felt like someone was trying to slice off my toes.

There was a phone in one of the briefing rooms. I shouldered the door open and—

Clemons and Halim looked up at me. Clemons lowered his cigar. "Oh, Wargin. Excellent. How did everything go with the FBI?"

"All right." The phone was sitting on the table next to Halim. "Any update on Dr. York?"

"He's trying to get someone to bring him things from his office." Clemons shook his head. "We shut that down. Poisoned! It's an ugly business."

"Yes." I took a step back, trying to think of where the next closest phone was.

Halim held out a hand. "A moment, Nicole . . . Are you still willing to fill an empty chair in a Sirius sim? Al-Zaman's wife went into labor early so he had to hop out. It's the middle seater."

The middle seat. Copilot.

Clemons raised his eyebrows. "You can't just throw her in without any orientation."

"Nicole reads manuals for fun. And this is their first run."

Moments like this are why I'm certain that there is not a God. Or if there is one, he's mercurial and cruel. "When?"

"Now, if you're up for it." Halim nodded, like he was trying to reassure me.

I'd been in the Sirius simulator, not because I'd ever been assigned but because I wanted to be ready. Just in case. And here was the just-in-case moment. "I need to make a call first. Do I have time?"

"Of course." Clemons studied me through a cloud of cigar smoke. "But, Halim . . . She was up all night at the hospital. Even if she knows the manuals, she must be exhausted."

"I'm fine." I was rumpled. I had a spot of blood on one cuff. I also had perfect posture and impeccable lipstick, both of which cover a multitude of sins. "I just need to make that call."

"And she can't do the simulator in heels."

Honestly, I could, but this wasn't the time to shock them with that revelation. "I have a change in my office. Just . . . phone. Please? I need to—" Some little warning bell went off in the back of my head. If I told Clemons that I was worried about Kenneth and why, he'd never let me sit in the simulator. He'd write me off as being distracted. "Actually, I have a phone in my office. I'll call from there while I change. I can be at the SVMF in half an hour."

"What about your chin?"

"Gentlemen. I'm fine. So, here's the order of operations. I'm going to my office. I will change and make my phone call at the same time. While I'm doing that, Halim will call the SVMF and apprise them of the staff change. By the time I arrive, they should be ready for me." I gave a swift nod to Halim. "Thank you for the opportunity. I'll get going so they aren't kept waiting."

I fled before they could stop me. I ran back down the stairs, grabbed one of the ubiquitous campus bikes, hiked my skirt up, and peddled to the astronaut office building. I ran up the stairs to my office and pretended the pain in my feet was a training exercise. I could do that maybe one more time, before limping visibly.

By the time I got to my office, my shirt was stuck to my back with sweat. I kicked my office door shut and grabbed the phone. Sandwiching the receiver between my ear and shoulder, I dialed with one hand and opened my locker with the other.

The phone rang once, and Kenneth's secretary picked up. "Governor Wargin's office. How may I help you?"

I kicked off my shoes. "This is Mrs. Wargin. Is the governor in?"

"No, ma'am, not yet. We're expecting him in on the 10:30 train. His driver has just gone to fetch him, in fact."

Shit. Did I wait for him or go to the SVMF? "Is Medgar Davis in?"

"Yes. One moment, I'll transfer you."

My hands were shaking as I undid the buttons on my skirt. I shucked it off and pulled a pair of trousers out of my locker. I was hopping on one foot with the other partway down a pant leg when his chief of staff picked up.

"Mrs. Wargin, how are you?"

"I think someone might be trying to kill the governor." I didn't have time to be gentle. "You know about Dr. York?"

"Yes. The governor called to brief me before he got on the train." Mr. Davis's voice was always calm. I adored him.

"There is a possibility that the poison might have been administered at our apartment during the poker party." I was being an alarmist, but I would rather do that than ignore a possible danger to my husband. "Then there was a riot the night before. I don't know that there's a link, but can you take precautions, just in case?"

"Of course, ma'am."

I peeled my sweaty blood-speckled shirt off. "Thank you. And have him call me when he gets in? Just so I know he's safe."

"Absolutely. Is there anything else?"

"That's it." I grabbed my clean shirt and the hanger tumbled to the floor. "Thank you!"

As soon as I got off the phone, I pulled on the clean shirt, which stuck to the existing sweat on my torso. *Please let me be wrong about someone targeting Kenneth. Please let me be wrong.* I shoved on my sneakers and sprinted out the door again.

All the way down the stairs, I was trying to pull my mind away from thoughts of Kenneth's train derailed or an assassin coming at him with a knife. I needed to switch back to astronaut mind and concentrate on the Sirius. There was nothing I could do about Kenneth that I hadn't already done.

I ran outside and— "Shit."

Someone had taken my bike. That's the trouble with ubiquitous bikes, they are ever present so you can just grab any of them. All right. I'd be sweatier when I got to the SVMF, but I was wearing sneakers and sometimes you just had to suck it up and ignore the pain.

The SVMF was only a half-mile away, and I ran farther than that for training. I set off at a steady jog through the lovely humidity of Kansas. The first steps hurt as my bones shifted and ground against each other, but then they loosened up. By the time I got to the SVMF, my feet felt no worse than being on a ballroom floor and I was soaked with sweat, which would be oh so very pleasant for everyone in the sim with me.

I shoved open the door to the building, figuring that I had time to stop by the bathroom and towel off a little, or at least wipe out my pits. The blessed air-conditioning smacked me in the face with welcome cold air.

And I fainted.

EIGHT

BIG SAVINGS SEEN IN NUCLEAR POWER

AEC Study Calls Atomic Electricity Plants Vital

CHICAGO, March 30, 1963—(UPI)—The director of the Atomic Energy Commission's division of reactor development said today that peaceful nuclear power can lead to savings in the cost of electricity to American consumers of "between four and five billion a year by the year 2000." The commission determined that if no supplementary forms of energy were used, the rate of IAC rocket launches and ongoing recovery efforts from the Meteor would cause the nation to exhaust its "readily available, low-cost reserves of fossil fuels in 40 to 60 years."

I CAME TO moments after I hit the ground. I know this, because people were still running toward me when I sat up. The SVMF circled around me so I didn't try to stand yet, just waved jauntily from the ground.

Curt was in the lead and slid to his knees in front of me,

blue eyes tight with concern. "How do you feel?"

"Like a fool. This is the second time in twenty-four hours you've seen me on the floor here." I sat up and winked at him. "Let's not make a habit of it, hm?"

Rachel Gutin, one of the new Nav/Comps, jogged up. "Is everything—What happened to your chin?"

"She had a training accident yesterday. The POGO failed."

"I didn't hit my head. I just ran over from the office and the cold came as a shock. That's all." I got to my knees, moving carefully just in case I fainted again. "I'm sorry to keep you waiting, but I'm fine now."

"You're sweating a lot." Curt followed me as I stood, hands out as if I were going to topple over again.

"I did say that I had run over here. As in actual running." The room held steady, but Curt was right. Sweat drenched me and my heart was racing faster than it should, even with the run. Because I hadn't eaten. "I had a long night, which Halim knows about. He sent me anyway, so shall we get on with it?"

Now more people were gathering around. It looked like everyone associated with the sim, trainees, trainers, technicians, had all decided to come and gawk at the lady who had fainted. From the side of the Sirius mockup, where the monitoring stations were, Ana Teresa Almeida Brandão jogged toward me with her medic kit.

Crap. A flight surgeon. Ana Teresa had the power to ground me. She shouted, "Curt! Get her a chair."

"Honestly, I'm fine." If I could have a few minutes to compose myself, and maybe grab something from the vending machine, I'd be as good as new.

Ana Teresa glared up at me as if our height difference pissed her off. "Sit down."

"I'm fi—"

"Sit. If you do not sit, then I will assume that you cannot comprehend basic instructions and that you are unsafe to fly." She took a step closer. "Now sit. Down."

"Yes, ma'am." I sat in the chair that Curt had produced. "But I really am—"

"You could be decapitated and you would still be insisting that you are 'just fine.' Please. I am well familiar with the ways of pilots. Do not think me an easy fool." She produced a pen light from somewhere and shone it in my eyes. "When did you hit your head?"

"It's not—" I bit my lips before I moved to a full shout. Taking a short breath, I forced a smile. "May I speak to you privately for a moment?"

She glared at me, which honestly she'd never stopped doing. I liked Ana Teresa, but her bedside manner was that of an angry terrier. She turned her glare on the men surrounding us. "Hey! Go! Each monkey on your own branch."

Watching a half-dozen men slink away as if she were going to bite their balls off was one of the only delights of my day. When they were gone, she said, "If you are going to tell me that you are pregnant—"

A laugh startled out of me. "God, no. Not actually possible." I held up my hand to stop any questions. "I forgot to eat breakfast. I was up all night with a friend who had to go to the emergency room—which Halim knows about—and I forgot to eat, and then the air-conditioning hit me like a ton of bricks. Let me grab something from the vending machine and that'll sort me."

"Sudden exposure to cold should not cause a faint." She crossed her arms and glared harder at me. "When was the last time you ate?"

I hate this question. "A full meal?" Day before yesterday. "I had part of a sandwich last night. And a donut this morning."

"And a head injury yesterday."

"It's my chin. My brain is not in my chin."

"Whiplash concussion doesn't need a direct blow to the head."

I sat forward, resting my elbows on my knees, and focused on her, because if I didn't, I was going to burst into tears, and I am not a woman who cries. "Please. This is just a sim. They're letting me sit in the copilot seat. They've never let a woman even pretend to fly a Sirius. Please. Please let me do this."

She pursed her lips, then winced and looked away. "No. I'm sorry."

"For the love of—"

"No. Because fainting out here I can explain as a temporary concern. A day off, you'll be fit. But if you faint in there? Then it is that flying the Sirius is too hard for a woman." Ana Teresa looked back at me and I could see every lick she'd had to take to get through med school. "Tell me I'm wrong."

She wasn't wrong. Goddamn it.

* * *

I SAT DOWN at my desk with a tray from the cafeteria. Following my usual overreaction, I had filled it with mounds of mashed potatoes, boiled greens, curried lentils, chicken parmesan, and two types of cake. Recognizing a cycle and being able to stop said cycle are not the same thing.

I rubbed my forehead, trying to massage the ache out. It would probably go away once I ate something. I ground the heels of both palms into my eyes. I had been so close to that cockpit. Even if it was just a sim, it had still been the copilot seat in one of the big rockets, and it was my own damn fault that I wasn't there now.

Letting out a sigh, I lowered my hands. I was over fifty years old and I had fought for the knowledge of how to manage myself. I unlocked the right-hand drawer of my desk and pulled out the pill bottle there. Miltown.

I no longer took it often, but there were days when using something to calm me made more sense than trying to fight through the day on my own. My stomach clenched at the thought of eating. But a pill? Some water? That I could handle. At least we were long past the days of my Miltinis . . .

It wouldn't really kick in for another twenty minutes or so, but just exerting some control over myself relaxed me. For my next demonstration of control, I would eat a reasonable amount of food.

"Food is fuel." I took a bite of greens and reached for my in-box.

I'd had one call while I was out. Kenneth's chief of staff. My husband had arrived safely on the train and was in his office at the Kansas capital.

I let out a breath like a rocket venting. I am rarely grateful to be wrong, but this was a good example of such an instance. Of course, it made today's activity worse, because that meant I had definitely had time to eat breakfast. I had assumed that Nathaniel hadn't eaten anything at work, because, well . . . because I hadn't and he looked like he'd been starving himself. I picked up a little bit of mashed potatoes, which, even in my current state, tasted infinitely superior to the dehydrated potato flakes on the Moon. They tasted fresh and earthy.

Earthy. It takes on a whole new meaning in the lunar colony.

Had Nathaniel eaten anything before arriving at our place? Grabbing the phone, I dialed the hospital and asked for Nathaniel's room.

The phone rang three times, and then rattled against the cradle as if it were being dragged off. I had a moment of terror that I had woken him.

"Hello?" His voice, even in those two syllables, sounded stronger than earlier this morning.

"Nathaniel, hi. It's Nicole. How are you feeling?"

"Like someone sliced me open and pulled my guts out."

"That seems like a legitimate way to feel after someone slices you open and pulls your guts out."

He snorted and then hissed. "This whole not laughing thing is a problem."

He was making jokes, which was a good sign. But . . . he would still be groggy and out of it for days. The doctor had said not to stress him, which was making me second-guess my call. I stirred my mashed potatoes with my fork. "What did the doctor say?"

I'd structured that as an open-ended question and how

he chose to answer it would tell me a lot. Nathaniel sighed. "You mean about the rat poison? Asked me if I came into contact with thallium at work."

"Do you?"

"No." Waiting for him to speak, I pressed the phone harder against my ear and heard his small sigh. "I just . . . I don't understand why."

"You've been the face of the program since President Brannan said we had to get off the planet. People are . . ." I caught myself before I made some sort of excuse for the person who had done this to him. "I don't know. It's awful."

"No one has told Elma, have they?"

"Not to the best of my knowledge." I hesitated, setting my fork down, and then picking it up again. "I think you should tell her."

"It's . . . It's not a good time."

I barked a laugh that bounced off the walls of my tiny office. "When is it ever a good time to hear that one's husband has been poisoned *and* has a peptic ulcer?" I took a bite of potatoes and slid the phone receiver away from my mouth so the mic wouldn't pick up the grotesque sound of chewing.

"Technically, I no longer have a peptic ulcer." He sighed again. "I'll tell her, just . . . just not now."

"Listen . . . Nathaniel. Did you eat anything before coming to our apartment?"

"You've been talking to the FBI men." The phone rustled as he shifted. "Coffee. Probably a donut at some point yesterday. I honestly don't remember. The rocket . . . I was pretty focused."

"Sure."

"And to save you from asking the same questions they did, I take my coffee with a cube of sugar and a little cream."

"Thanks." I wet my lips and remembered my own sojourns in a hospital bed. "Do you need anything? I can run by your apartment if you'd like."

"Actually . . . This is a silly thing, but would you mind stopping by the teletype room to see if there's any mail from Elma?"

"That's not silly."

"The next part is. You know how the transmissions have garbage at both ends? Could you bring that, too? It's . . . I know it's ridiculous, but it starts transmitting as soon as she turns it on, and even if it's garbage—it's garbage she touched?"

Weird, but he was also understandably on a lot of drugs. "Sure. No problem."

"And . . ." He swallowed audibly. "If it's not too much to ask, there's a copy of *Just So Stories* on my desk. Would you mind?"

I laughed. "When Clemons said you were trying to get people to bring you stuff from your office, I was expecting it to be schematics. A book? Gladly."

"Oh, well, I wanted those, too, but he hung up on me before I finished getting the request out. I don't suppose . . ."

"Don't make me hang up on you."

He laughed and hissed again. "There's no rush, if you're working—"

"I'm not." I should be in a sim. "I'll be right over. I just need to finish lunch."

*   *   *

PICKING UP ELMA'S most recent letter was easy. Not reading it took a valiant effort that most people would not appreciate. I stuck that teletype paper into an envelope and stuck the envelope in my purse and though it burned with the fire of the sun, I did not give in to my curiosity and read it.

I wish this were a thing to actually be proud of.

Letter in hand, I headed for Nathaniel's office, which was one building over from Mission Control. There were a lot of black cars parked outside the engineering building. Some engineers milled around on the sidewalk, talking in small knots or shuffling papers in their hands. Periodically, one of them would glance toward the building, where a man in a plain black suit stood in front of the door.

As I walked up the sidewalk, the man held out his hand before I got to the door. Even behind the sunglasses, I could see him study the bandage under my chin and assign me to a lineup. He was obviously with the FBI, but I pretended not to notice his lack of subtlety. Instead, I stopped and raised an eyebrow. "Can I help you?"

"I'm afraid I can't allow you entry to this building at this time."

That explained the engineers milling about, but I wanted to know why. "I have ID. And I'm running an errand for Dr. York. Dr. *Nathaniel* York."

There was a slight hitch to his shoulders when I said Nathaniel's name. Enough to make it clear that my hunch was right. The FBI was searching his office.

"I'm sorry, ma'am. I can't allow you in." He spread his

feet a little as if he were prepared to fight me.

This was not a man that I would be able to bluster past, so I skipped all of the tactics I might have deployed on him and went straight for escalating. "I understand. May I speak to Agent Boone then? He'll understand the nature of my errand, I'm sure."

"He's not available."

"Agent Whitaker?" Who would probably be as unyielding as this oaf, but he might be persuaded to at least fetch the book.

"He's not available."

I ground my teeth behind a smile. "Then perhaps you could tell me who is in charge."

"I'm sorry, ma'am. I'm going to have to ask you to move on." He tilted his head down and returned a smile as flat as my own. "I can't allow you in at this time."

"Well. I certainly thank you for your service. I'm sure everyone feels much safer knowing that you are on the job."

Sarcasm is not always a useful response, and the man took a step toward me. "What is the nature of your business?"

"I was collecting a children's book for a sick friend." I turned on my heel and stalked away, because it suddenly occurred to me that I did not want to provoke this man into searching me, not while I had Elma's letter to Nathaniel. These bastards would probably confiscate the letter for their investigation. Nathaniel had few enough comforts without losing that.

But my pride still fired a parting shot over my shoulder. "I'll let Dr. York know that his book is not available at this time."

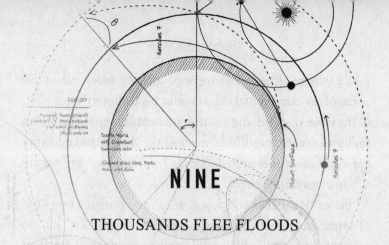

NINE

THOUSANDS FLEE FLOODS

3 States Ravaged by Rain and Tornadoes
Call on President for Aid

HARLAN, Ky., March 30, 1963—(AP)—Rain-swollen streams swirled out of the southeastern Kentucky mountains today, leavings thousands homeless and causing millions of dollars in property damage in a 20-county area. The increase in tornadoes and flooding has been blamed by meteorologists on climate change caused by the Meteor's strike 11 years ago. The floods, which struck severely in neighboring Tennessee, Virginia, and West Virginia, came in the wake of tornadoes that left a trail of death and destruction in parts of Mississippi, Alabama, and Georgia.

WHEN I WALKED into Nathaniel's hospital room, I thought he was asleep. I rose onto my toes, to keep my heels from clicking against the linoleum. I also paused for a moment and watched his chest to be certain he was breathing.

His jaw was slack and his head tilted to one side. Strands of his straw-blond hair straggled across his forehead. He didn't look any better than he had before, but being asleep meant that some of the tension had ebbed out of his features.

The door snapped shut behind me and his eyes opened. They really were shockingly blue, the way the sky used to look on a clear day. Nathaniel smiled. "Hey."

"How are you feeling?"

"Better." He shifted on the bed, which was propped up a little. "I'm not sure if that's the morphine or the surgery."

"In my experience, the morphine is pretty good." I set down the bags I'd brought and pulled up a chair to sit next to him. If I weren't scheduled to leave for Brazil and then the Moon, I might have waited, but there were things I needed to say to the man, and I needed to say them in person. And, frankly, if I had waited, I probably would have found a reason not to say anything. "Look . . . Nathaniel."

"Uh-oh."

I raised my eyebrows. "That transparent, am I?"

"You're going to make me pay for having the carpet cleaned, aren't you?"

"Worse." I smiled, glad that he could joke. Then I sighed and slid my chair closer. "I stopped by your apartment on the way here, to pick up some things for you."

"Thanks." His brows came together. "How'd you get in?"

"Please. The day I can't talk your landlord into unlocking a door as a favor is the day I have to turn in my socialite card. But honestly, your spare key is still under the brick in the courtyard." I shrugged. "I remembered from when I was watering your window boxes."

"So why am I in trouble?"

"Nathaniel . . . there's no food in your apartment."

He stopped moving, even his breath stilled for a moment. "You went through my kitchen?"

"I did and I won't apologize for it." He hadn't even had canned beans on the shelf. "The only thing I found was a half-bottle of milk that looks as if it's been there since Elma left and a packet of matzo crackers."

He swallowed and looked out the window. There wasn't anything to see except another building. "I just moved in."

"Weeks ago."

"It doesn't make sense to cook for one. Especially not with the cafeteria at the IAC."

"Your life feels out of control, doesn't it. With her gone? You can't do anything for her that you haven't already done, so—"

"Do you have a point?"

I sighed and rubbed my hand across my face. A different angle was necessary, and this was a conversation I didn't want to have. Ever. But I had to get him to hear me. "Abdominal surgery."

"What?" He was curious enough to look at me.

"I had an emergency hysterectomy after my fifth miscarriage." I wound my fingers together and stared at the wedding ring with the big diamond that Kenneth had given me all those years ago. "I was far enough along with that one that we thought I might actually come to term, so technically, she was a stillbirth. Evelyn Marie Wargin. I . . . I still looked pregnant. After. So I stopped eating."

"I didn't—"

"I hated my body and I hated feeling powerless and this gave me one thing—one tiny thing—that I had complete control over. Kenneth had to have me committed." My fingers ached from clutching them. "After the Meteor, I did it again. There have been other times, but those two landed me in the hospital."

Beyond the windows, a streetcar clanged past. In the hall, someone pushed a cart with a squeaking wheel. I swallowed and swallowed again before I could look up. His face wore the look of pity and horror that I dreaded.

I lifted my chin and took a breath. "You have to eat. You don't have to like it, but you have to eat."

"I do. I just . . . I just get busy." He plucked at the edge of his blanket as if rearranging it would hide how thin he had gotten. "And I was poisoned, remember."

"Sure." The poison was not even remotely all that was going on. "So you won't mind if Myrtle and I stock your pantry."

"Yes. Actually. I would resent being treated like a child."

I wet my lips and looked out the window at the wing of the hospital opposite us. The windows there reflected pale silver sky. Pushing him would do exactly as much good as pushing me did. I flipped on my hostess mask and bent down to my bag with a smile. "I picked up Elma's letter for you. And the garbage! Silly boy."

"Thank you." He rose on an elbow to take it. "And the book?"

I shook my head, digging into my bag. "The FBI wouldn't let me into your office building, so I grabbed the one sitting on the coffee table in the living room."

Nathaniel took the paperback of *The Mile-Long Spaceship* by Kate Wilhelm and his face fell. "Thanks. I was just . . . Do you think if I called, they might let you have it?"

"Ah-ha!" With a flourish, I produced a copy of *Just So Stories* from my bag. "I also stopped at a bookstore on my way here. Ta-da!"

His shoulders slumped and I didn't believe his smile for a

second. "Thank you. That's . . . that's very kind."

"Was . . . was I wrong? It was Kipling, wasn't it?"

"Yes." He accepted the book and flipped through the pages. "It's just a different edition. I—I liked the illustrations in ours."

Disparate pieces came together in my head. Garbage from a teletype. Specific edition. Disappointment. "Are you and Elma sending messages with a book code?"

Nathaniel fumbled the copy of *Just So Stories* and it fell off the side of the bed. Honestly, I don't know how he survived poker night. "That's—I mean. Shit." He dropped his head back to the pillow and rolled his eyes to the ceiling. "Yes. Please don't tell Clemons."

"Darling. I think that's brilliant."

He laughed and pressed a hand to his side. "How did you know?"

"I dated a fellow in intelligence during the war." More than one, actually, but that was beside the point. "So, you can't read the stuff in the garbage without that copy?"

"I can brute force it." Nathaniel squinted at the page. "Usually."

"But a book code . . ." I trailed off, because the garbage had been mostly letters and a book code would have had numbers. Page, line, and word.

"It's not a true book code. It's a keyed Caesar." He rubbed his forehead, staring at the paper, and lines etched themselves back into his skin as I watched. "We use the book to pick a different keyword each time. So the letters of the alphabet are jumbled to put the keyword at the front of—"

"I know how keyed Caesars work, Nathaniel." I stood and reached for the paper. "Give me that."

"What?"

I waggled my fingers. "I'll crack it for you."

His face turned red, which was good since that meant he had enough blood for blushing. "Oh. Um. These are . . . they're kinda personal."

"Believe it or not, your wife and I talk about a good number of things. I hope you don't think I am so delicate as to be shocked or offended by innuendo involving rockets, thrusters, or orbital insertions." I straightened my arm. "Or do you really think that you're able to crack a code while on morphine the day after being poisoned and after having major surgery?"

Nathaniel cleared his throat. "I . . . um."

"Will Elma notice if you don't write back and refer to the contents in the 'garbage'?"

Nathaniel made an aggravated sigh and handed the letter to me. "But if you breathe a word of this to anyone . . ."

"You'll die of mortification. I know." I sat down in my chair and pulled a pencil out of my bag. "Men can be such delicate wilting flowers."

(In answer to your question, I read your last letter in the garden module. While your hands were occupied with attaining maximum thrust back at home, I was concerned with calculating the appropriate angle of entry. I look forward to comparing these figures with you upon my return. Go for landing cannot come soon enough.)

Dear Nathaniel,

It's hard to believe that we're halfway to Mars. My biggest problem is that every time someone says that we're "halfway" I think for a moment that it means we're halfway through the mission, but it's still years before I get to see you. Everything here is going as well as can be expected.

Terrazas is making noises about doing another radio play just for something to break the routine. It's funny how much I miss hearing the radio broadcasts from Earth. Florence thinks that on a future mission we could potentially create a large array by linking the three ships in some way. It would still have the delay, of course, but it would be nice to be able to hear voices from home.

I miss you.

Love,

Elma

(I continue to be worried about Florence and Leonard. All I can see when Parker posts a duty roster is that they only get cleaning and maintenance shifts. That's not strictly true, I suppose, since Florence does have comms, but it's been ages since either of them rotated to any of the science parts of the mission. I would chalk it up to the FBI still causing problems for Leonard, except it's affecting Florence, too. She wasn't on the Cygnus with us, but they're both members of the NAACP. What on Earth— literally—is the FBI thinking?)

When I finished cracking the code, the key appeared to be "armadillo." I handed the translated letter to Nathaniel without a word. His face went beet red at the first part, as well it should. Not because of the content, but honestly their rocketry innuendo was embarrassing. They were married. Just say "dick" and "masturbate" like an adult. Poor innocent dears. I remember when I showed Elma my vibrator on the Moon and I thought she'd melt her spacesuit with the heat of her embarrassment. She's adorable.

But the second piece of translated garbage made Nathaniel's face crease into a frown. He gnawed on his lower lip and finally cleared his throat. "Say . . . Since you know, would you be willing to send her a message for me? I can reuse her code."

I had been waiting for this opening since I began to translate the text. Oh, that wasn't my initial thinking. Then, I had just wanted the man to stop trying to work. Fortunately, or unfortunately, I can't stop looking for angles and opportunities. A kinder person would have said yes without hesitating. But he had offered me a lever and I intended to use it. If I hadn't been to his apartment, I probably would have used that lever to insist he tell Elma about what was happening with his health, but . . . I wanted him to be alive to meet her when she got home.

I sat up straighter. "On one condition."

"I'm not telling her. Not now."

"Lucky for you, that's not my condition." Crossing my legs, I sat back in my chair as if I had nothing at stake. "I'll send your messages and pick up your mail until they ship me to Brazil, if and only if you agree to let Hershel come out *and* promise to eat on a regular and regimented schedule."

"That's two conditions."

I tilted my head and delivered a death glare with mildly pursed lips.

Nathaniel shrank a little in his pillow. "The hospital has control of my meal schedule."

My expression stayed flat and I blinked at him. Once. Silently, I counted in my head, making a bet that he would crumble by the time I got to five. He lasted until four.

"By the time I'm out, it'll be Passover. Hershel shouldn't be away from his family."

"Hershel is your family." I stood up, collecting my bag. "You can stop pretending to be a bastion unto yourself, just because Elma is away. These are my conditions. Do you want to write to your wife? Or do you want me to write to her."

It wasn't fair. It wasn't nice. I cared too much to be bothered by either.

Nathaniel wiped a hand down his face. "You're a cruel woman."

"Yes. I am." From my purse, I drew out a pair of white gloves in order to dramatically tug them on and delay the moment at which I actually departed.

"Fine. Yes. Hershel can come—but only if he volunteers. You can't ask him to."

"He already volunteered." I sat down and shoved my gloves back into my bag, swapping them for my IAC notebook. "I'll even do the cipher for you."

The sigh he gave sounded more pained than anything the surgery had triggered. "You're not going to let me do any work, are you."

"I'll be generous enough to let you write the plain text yourself." I handed him the pencil and my notepad. "But only because I'm worried about the strain all that blushing is going to put on your circulatory system."

He caught his laugh with a grunt and a small wince.

While he wrote, I pulled out my IAC binder and studied up on the mascons between the main lunar base and the new mining locations. Mass Concentrations of gravity could throw navigation off if you weren't prepared for them. It was not quite like knowing how thermal updrafts affected an airplane, but similar enough that I was happier to do the work before I got into the cockpit of my spacecraft.

When Nathaniel finished, it wasn't a long letter.

(30 7 4 I cleverly left Kipling at the office, so I'm reusing your code tonight. Sorry about that. I understand your concerns about the duty rosters, but Mission Control has reasons for making the assignments that they do. You don't realize how bad it is here. I'm glad of that, but we're sending the rosiest possible news to keep morale up. Trust me when I say that this isn't something we should push right now.)

Dear Elma,

You'll be proud of me. I actually left the office early on Friday in order to go to the Wargins' for poker night. Don't ask me how I did, it's best not discussed. And yes, I am well aware that I should not be working on a Friday night anyway. As I have reminded you on more than one occasion, you knew when you married me that I was a terrible Jew.

The exciting thing is that the lunar team has figured out a way to cast lunar dust into machine parts. We think. We're sending a prototype up on the next launch to be sure, since things never work quite the same way in lunar gravity as they do on Earth, even with vomit comet testing.

I'm rambling about work after starting off by bragging that I had taken an evening off. I can hear you laughing from a million kilometers away. Did you do anything on the ship to celebrate the halfway point?

All my love,

Nathaniel

(I'm not sure that there's an hour in which I don't think about you. What I want most is to curl up in bed with you and ignore the rest of the world. I don't need a launch. I just want to be in the same orbit again.)

I'll give him this. Every word Nathaniel sent to Elma was true. It's amazing how many lies one can tell with the truth.

TEN

CYCLONE IN ALGIERS KILLS 43

ALGIERS, March 30, 1963—(AP)—Forty-three persons were reported killed today by a cyclone that ravaged the town of Mascara in western Algeria. Officials said that over a hundred people were injured and much of the historic town center was destroyed.

THE GOVERNOR'S MANSION in Topeka used to be an old pile of a Victorian, but after the Meteor, it had been replaced by a bunker with ballrooms. That was before Kenneth was governor, or he would have stopped that foolishness. But people were so scared of another Meteor they just buried everything. It wasn't entirely underground, but built into the side of a hill to create safe zones.

The exterior had a porticoed facade that led down a few steps to the front door. It was a terrible design that had all the grace of a fart and collected water on the landing when it rained, which it was doing now. My driver came around to my side with an umbrella, which did little to help as the wind kicked up and snuck water under the shield.

As I came down the stairs, I tugged off my gloves, glad to be free of them in the humidity. Tu Guanyu Chu, our butler, opened the front door to greet me. As always, his tuxedo was impeccable, and the starched white collar set off his polished tan complexion beautifully. His gaze flicked to the bandage on my chin and then straight up to my eyes. "Good evening, madam. The governor is just sitting down in the dining room."

He stepped back to let me enter, and my driver retreated up the stairs to take the car off to the garage.

"Very good, thank you, Chu." I handed him my bag and kicked off my shoes, sighing with relief.

From the stairs, a small dark streak bounded up, tail held high. Marlowe meeped as he trotted to me.

I crouched to greet my cat. "Well, hello, handsome."

He meeped again and shoved his head against my hand.

"Yes, I know. The state of the world is worrisome." I scooped him up. "What should we do?"

"Mrroo? Mrrp. Mrrrrooo." He shoved his head under my chin and mixed purring in with his meeps. He doesn't meow so much as monologue.

"That's a very sound plan." I rubbed his dark ears as his golden eyes closed with pleasure, and then I turned back to Chu. "Sorry. Is there anything that I should attend to before dinner?"

"No, madam. The correspondence that requires your personal attention is on your desk, and Mrs. Pelletier would like your approval on the menu for next week. She's concerned about creating The Garden Club tea within the ration book stricture."

I winced and shifted Marlowe to my left arm. He balanced, paws holding on to my shoulder like a baby as

I unpinned my hat. Next week I would be getting ready to go to Brazil and thence the Moon. "I'm sorry . . . I'll talk to her, but I'm afraid I have to cancel the tea."

His brows twitched up, but that was all the reaction he gave beyond: "Of course, madam."

I sighed and closed my eyes, resting my head against the warm body of my cat for a moment. I had not given myself time to react to Nathaniel's collapse last night nor to my own stupidity this morning. I was still so angry at myself that I could cry.

At minimum, I needed a few moments to myself. I am fortunate in that I can often delay my reactions to intense events. For instance, when Kenneth had nearly severed his finger in a car door, I was completely calm. There are sounds you never want to hear your husband make, but I was cool and businesslike through the whole thing. The next day, I came apart.

I opened my eyes and smiled at our butler. "Right. Thank you, Chu. Will you let the governor know that I've run down to change and will be in—"

"Darling, I was beginning to wonder if you'd make it." Kenneth appeared from the dining room, dressed in his tuxedo. We're old school that way, still dress for dinner and all. But honestly, you never know when some diplomat is going to turn up. In any event, Kenneth always looks so dapper that I enjoy our little ritual.

I let Marlowe hop down and crossed the marble floor to kiss Kenneth on the cheek. "I'm so sorry I'm late. I went by the hospital to see Nathaniel after work today."

"I was wondering what had kept you." The concern

in his gaze was for me, but his posture and tone was unruffled for our staff. "Thank you for the message, by the way. It had not occurred to me."

"I'm glad it was a false alarm." I needed to get away before I fractured. I'd curl up with Marlowe on the bed, weep a little, and then come in for dinner. "I'll just run change."

"Nicole, it's all right. You don't need to dress for dinner on my account."

"Nonsense, dear. We aren't heathens."

He caught my arm before I could turn away and opened his mouth. Forming on his lips, I could see some version of the question, *"Are you trying to skip dinner?"* But Kenneth closed his mouth, smiled, and nodded. He squeezed my arm. "Then I'm glad I took the trouble of putting on the tux."

If he had pressed, I would have dug my heels in. As it was, I blurted, "I blew it today." I stared down at Marlowe as if I had never seen a cat before. "Halim asked me to sit in on a Sirius sim, in the middle seat, and I—I hadn't . . ." My throat was raw with longing. "I hadn't eaten. I fainted and—"

Kenneth pulled me into an embrace. The world vanished in the deep black wool of a well-crafted tuxedo. Beyond the circle of his arms, quiet footsteps exited the room. Kenneth murmured into my ear, "We're alone."

"Oh, hell. I was so close and—" I clung to that wool and sobbed. It had just been a sim, but if I had done well, then maybe next time they would have scheduled me on purpose and maybe one day I'd get to fly one of the big rockets. I had known when my hands were shaking what the problem was. I fainted because of a series of choices that I had made. As often as I railed against the system that kept women from advancing, when the opportunity finally came . . . "I blew it."

He held me tight and swayed with me as if we were dancing and the band had just begun to play, neither of us sure of the rhythm yet. Kenneth pressed his cheek against my head, breathing slowly and steadily. He smelled of citrus and cloves.

My outburst did not last long. I am not a woman who cries except under certain very specific conditions. Funerals. Weddings. A properly executed play. The right kiss in a novel. Other people's grief and other people's joy can tip me over into cathartic weeping.

Anger. When it is self-directed. And tonight's bout of weeping was almost entirely anger at myself with a modicum of rage-infused tears directed at the IAC for creating new inner sanctums of a boy's club modeled upon centuries of boy's clubs. I know the system. I can work the system. That doesn't mean I don't loathe it.

I had been so close and I wouldn't need to push so hard if they hadn't put up those damn barriers in the first place. Well, screw them. Next time I would be ready. I sniffled and lifted my head. "Thank you. I'm just so mad at myself."

He withdrew his pocket square and wiped the skin under my eyes. "I'm sorry that happened."

I kept waiting for the "I told you so" even though I knew he wouldn't say that. Hell, he wasn't even dragging me into the dining room or asking questions about when

I ate last. I straightened and ran my hands down the satin of his lapels. "Shall we have dinner?"

Kenneth smiled at me, but there was a heartbreak behind his gaze. "Whenever you're ready."

It's the small things that make me love him and damn it all if I didn't start crying again.

THE SMELL OF coffee burrowed into my dreams and dragged me back toward the surface. Marlowe purred in a warm puddle between my shoulder blades.

Kenneth kissed my cheek before he sat up in bed next to me to greet our housekeeper. "Morning, Thelma."

"Morning, Governor. Morning, Miss Nicole."

I grunted. They were lucky to get that much. All I wanted to do was to sleep until the end of time. I shoved my face against the cool satin of the pillowcase. There was a damp spot where I'd drooled. Grimacing, I opened my eyes and glared at the pillow.

"I think she's awake." Kenneth tugged on my earlobe.

"Well, I let y'all sleep as long as I could." Thelma came around the bed carrying a breakfast tray for Kenneth. "Be right back with your tray, Miss Nico— Good lord."

Clenching my fists in the fabric, I dragged the covers over my face. "Juggling accident."

"All . . . all right. I'll be back with your tray."

"Maybe later."

"You should . . ." Kenneth rested a hand on my shoulder. "We need to leave for church in about forty-five minutes."

I groaned. The thought of going to church and pretending to a piety I did not possess felt like a zipper waiting to peel down my spine. "I'd forgotten it was Sunday." Beneath the covers, I squeezed my eyes shut as if that would save me and mumbled into the pillow. "I can't get up, it would bother Marlowe."

Kenneth clinked some porcelain with his fork and the bed shifted. "Marlowe. Want some eggs?"

My cat vanished, mrowing as he hopped across the bed.

"Traitor." I hauled myself up to sit slumped against the headboard. New aches presented themselves from my fall. My knees. My shoulders. Those I could mask, but I wasn't sure I could handle an entire congregation of people asking about my chin. "Can we just pretend that I'm still at the IAC?"

With my cat next to him, nibbling on a bit of egg from his saucer, Kenneth scritched Marlowe's ear. "I'm sorry, baby. I need you to go."

"Even with this?" I tapped the bandage.

He hesitated and for a moment I thought I'd found an out, but Kenneth shook his head. "I'm afraid so."

I sighed and screwed my eyes shut, thunking my head back against the mahogany headboard. I knew how this worked. If I was home from the Moon and he went to church without me, it would send a message that our marriage was in trouble. If not for that, I would skip it every single chance. Instead, I went to church with my husband as faithfully as anyone in the congregation. "Tell me, at least, that Linda Salvatore isn't doing a solo this week."

To his credit, he did not respond to me like the whiny teenager I sounded like. Kenneth's knife rasped against toast as he spread butter on it. "I wish I could."

"Ugh. Her vibrato sounds like she's using a jackhammer as a dildo." I threw the covers back and slid out of bed. "If I'd remembered, I would have stayed in Kansas City last night."

His knife clinked against the plate as he set it down. "People are already looking for signs that our marriage is in trouble because of how much you're gone."

I stopped, with one hand on my dressing gown, trying to review our conversation from last night. I'd been so caught up in my own upset that I had missed something. Kenneth picked up his creamer and carefully added some to his coffee. His expression was so mild that it felt like a slap, because he was giving me his public face.

"Are we?"

He picked up his spoon and stirred the coffee. "Are we what?"

"Are we in trouble?"

Thelma walked in, carrying the second breakfast tray. The last thing I wanted was food. Scrambled eggs glistened on the plate. I clenched my jaw against the surge of bitter saliva that filled my mouth. Swallowing, I smiled at Thelma. "Thank you." I scooped Marlowe up and carried him to the table at the foot of our bed. "I'll eat here, if you don't mind."

"Of course." With a practiced economy of motion, she folded the tray legs under and set it on the white lace tablecloth.

I sank onto the chair and settled Marlowe on my lap. He squirmed and jumped down, which was no wonder. My posture was so upright that my back came nowhere near the white lacquer chair. Picking up a piece of toast, I turned it over until Thelma had left. The clink of Kenneth's cutlery seemed to fill the room. I took a bite of the toast and my teeth crunched through layers of sandpaper greased with butter.

I swallowed that bite. Ate another. I was very conscious of Kenneth watching me from the head of the bed, and it took everything I had to not wave the toast at him. For crying out loud, he'd seen me eat dinner last night.

He cleared his throat. "Do you think we are in trouble?"

"I didn't." I did not want to cry. It would be hellishly manipulative if I did. "Is that why you don't want me to go to the Moon?"

He snorted. "An active saboteur isn't enough?"

That wasn't an answer to my question. That was a sidestep. I took a bite of the eggs I did not want before I spoke again. When I was certain that I was calm, I set my cup down and faced Kenneth. His mild face was still on and I lifted my chin to greet it. "Is it the saboteur or politics that's the problem? Or is it me?"

He opened his mouth and then closed it around whatever his first response had been. Kenneth sighed, rubbing the back of his neck, then set his tray aside and pushed the covers back.

"Nicole . . . It's not just one thing." When he got out of bed, his back was to me. He drew on his purple tapestry dressing gown and belted it around his waist. "Am I worried about the political implications of nepotism? I wouldn't be doing my job if I weren't, but in this case politics and my own fears overlap. What would have happened if you had been on that rocket?"

"The LES worked. If I'd been on that rocket, I would still be alive and you would have crafted a message—"

"Yes!" His gown flared as he turned, and the mild face had dropped away. He pointed a shaking hand to the sitting room. "Publicly, it would have been something I could have managed. Hell, my staff already has a statement drafted in case you die up there. But that's not—that's . . . That's not what will happen to *me*."

My throat tightened. I pushed back my chair and went to Kenneth, wrapping my arms around him. I'd seen what that seed of potential mourning did to the members of the Astronauts' Husbands Club—hell, I'd visited a founding member in the hospital yesterday—but it was easy to forget the toll it took on Kenneth because he hid it so well.

Ah . . . The lies that I liked. I snuggled my head into his shoulder as we held each other. What I should say was that I would drop out of the program and stay home and be the politician's wife that I used to be. My skin tightened across my bones thinking about trying to fit back into that box. More than that, I knew what it would do to the program if I dropped out right after the rocket failure.

I was too high profile: the wife of Governor Wargin, one of the original six women astronauts. Even if I was "old hat" people would notice and speculate that I had dropped out because the program was too dangerous. Or were those lies I was telling myself because I didn't want to drop out? I tightened my fingers in the tapestry folds of his gown. "I'm sorry."

He held me tighter and kissed me on the forehead. "Thank you."

"You know, I'd . . ." I stopped the lie before I could go on. *I'd quit if you asked me.* He had asked me.

Kenneth winced before I'd even finished and looked away, shaking his head. "We'd better get going or we'll be late for church."

"Kenneth . . ."

He picked up his worn Bible and thumbed through the pages with a quiet riffle of onionskin. I don't think he saw the book—

Book. I blinked. "There's a way I can send you private messages. Just for you. Would that help?"

"What do you mean?"

I chewed on my lower lip for a moment, because I'd surprised the secret out of Nathaniel, but it was still his secret. "Another astronaut and her husband are sending coded messages hidden in the teletype garbage—"

His jaw fell open. "Nathaniel and Elma are sending coded messages?"

I shouldn't have been surprised that he guessed. "Don't tell. We could use a code if it would help reassure you."

"Reassure— For the love of God, Nicole." Kenneth swiped his hand through his hair, leaving it in disarray. "People think there's a conspiracy at the highest level of the IAC and now it turns out that the lead engineer is sending coded messages to the First Mars Expedition."

My veins curled up and shriveled into knots. "Well,

shit." I closed my eyes, remembering the FBI crawling all over Nathaniel's office. "We may have a situation."

Kenneth groaned and sat in a rustle of fabric and the clatter of porcelain. "What."

I forced my eyes open. Kenneth sat crumpled against the headboard, his coffee cup tipped over on the tray. I wet my lips. "I sent a message for Nathaniel." I was such a fool. I should have spotted this vulnerability. God, I wanted to explain it away—that Nathaniel had been worried. That I'd bargained him into letting Hershel come out. None of that was germane to the issue at hand. "After I visited the hospital, I went back to the IAC and sent a coded message on the teletype using his passcodes. I should also note that the FBI was still on campus, specifically searching Nathaniel's office."

"You do remember that you're the First Lady of Kansas, don't you? You know how that's going to look."

"You were the one who was wanting to help Nathaniel lie to Elma."

Kenneth tensed and his face went completely blank. Rising from the bed, he undid the belt of his dressing gown. "We'd better hurry or we'll be late for church."

"I don't care about the damn church."

"I'm well aware of that, Nicole." He held up a tie and laid it against his suit. "It would be nice if you cared about me more than you do the Moon."

"Jesus Christ. Do you have any more cheap shots you want to take?"

"No. But if you keep pushing me, I will." Kenneth opened his closet door and dug around looking for a pocket square. "I'm angry, and right now, both of us need to put on a good face when we step out."

I wanted to scream at him. I wanted to be petty and ask him to coordinate my wardrobe. I wanted to storm out of the room. But I am a goddamned adult. My voice was clipped and formal, but it beat my other choices. "I'm sorry. I didn't think. I'll brief Mr. Davis as soon as we get home."

"Thank you. I'm also sorry." Kenneth bent his head as if he were praying, and then turned to face me. "I know yesterday was difficult. I should have taken that into account when I responded, and I would appreciate a conversation later."

We're diplomats, both of us. I dressed and put on a tasteful shade of red lipstick to go with my practiced Sunday-best smile. God forbid that someone at church think our marriage was in trouble.

ELEVEN

THE MOON-DOGGLE:
Domestic and International Implications
of the Space Race
By AMITAI ETZIONI

Meg Greenfield reported from The National Times to The Reporter: "The Moon program was worked out over a hectic weekend in May of 1953 at the Bunker following the Meteor strike on Washington, D.C. It was a political response to the tidal waves and the fires of the disaster, among other things. Reportedly, President Brannan, Dr. Nathaniel York, one of the remnants of the NACA, and a few others met around the clock starting Friday evening and worked out the crash program that was presented to the UN for a decision the following Monday. 'We have been told,' as one of the participants puts it, 'not to fool around.'"

Never has a more important peacetime decision been based on less research and deliberation. On May 25, 1953, the UN proclaimed the establishment of a colony on the Moon as a major international goal and the highest-ranking space project.

KENNETH AND I belong to the Topeka First United Methodist Church, which has the distinction of being older than the state of Kansas. When we joined, I had not noticed that the congregation was exclusively white. Now, after years of working at the International Aerospace Coalition, I found the church disquieting in the sameness of the flock.

As we approached the vestibule, I lined up my script for running the gauntlet to the sanctuary. Kenneth does not get to stop being a politician, even on his day of rest. My usual set was:

"So good to see you!"

"What a charming hat/coat/brooch."

"I would love to talk longer, but I need to keep Kenneth moving . . ."

But today I had a bandage on my chin and that was going to be its own set of fun. As Jane Austen might have said, it is a truth universally acknowledged, that a woman with a bandage upon her chin must be the subject of gossip. It began the moment we hit the vestibule. Oh, they were all too well bred to openly gawk, but the number of people who suddenly needed to contemplate the stained glass windows just on the other side of me was impressive.

Kenneth squeezed my hand in a quick double beat that meant trouble was incoming. A bulldog of a man stumped up to us, the empty left sleeve of his coat pinned up in its customary place.

I slid between Kenneth and him. "Mr. Salvatore. So good to see you!"

"Good lord!" Mr. Salvatore did a double take at my chin. "Were you on that rocket?"

"Not at all, we were breakfasting with some friends." I smiled with the warmth of a pre-Meteor sun. "What a charming lapel pin."

"Thank you." He glanced down as if he'd forgotten he put it on.

In his moment of inattention, I tried to steer Kenneth around him before Mr. Salvatore could start complaining about my husband's policies. "I would love to talk longer, but I need to keep Kenneth moving . . ."

"See here, Governor. What are you going to do about those blasted rockets?"

Well, I'd tried to deflect him. His war injury meant that he'd never be declared fit for space travel and as far as he was concerned, if we couldn't get everybody off the planet then no one should go. He didn't seem to understand that the Earth was like the *Titanic*. It was going to go down. We didn't have enough lifeboats for everybody, but that didn't mean we shouldn't try to save as many people as we could.

Kenneth's voice was genial with a layer of ice beneath it. "Come by the office and I'll be happy to talk. But let me have my day of rest and leave the politics at the door."

As if we ever, ever got to do that. I put my hand on Mr. Salvatore's upper arm to build rapport and smiled at him. "So good to see you— Oh! I think the prelude is starting."

It was, and that marks the only time I've been happy to hear his wife's amorous vibrato.

As Kenneth and I made a break for it, he leaned down to whisper, "Thank you."

We made it to our customary pew and I sank onto the padded bench. The ritual sequence of sitting and standing gave me space in which to calm myself. This is the value of ritual and repetition, be it in a cockpit or in a church pew. Familiarity gives us room to breathe and to think.

Our marriage was in trouble, because the warning bells had been ringing and I hadn't been paying attention. Kenneth was focused on politics. I was focused on space. I could not remember the last time we had gone somewhere without an agenda.

The Methodist mumble took me mindlessly through the Gloria Patri and into the Lord's Prayer. At times, I have felt hypocritical reciting these words, but in truth, even when I was one of the faithful, I rarely paid attention to what I was actually saying. Ironically, after parting from God, I often found resonance in the words of the service. Of course, I can also find resonance in lyrics sung by Ella Fitzgerald, so take that as you will.

But when I said, "forgive us our trespasses, as we forgive those who trespass against us," I took Kenneth's hand. I hate it when we quarrel. It worried me that I hadn't seen this one coming. He looked down and squeezed my hand. This unspoken conversation was not a lot, but it gave me faith that he and I could work the problem.

AFTER CHURCH, WE escaped the gauntlet of the Fellowship Hall and slid into the back seat of our waiting car. Kenneth took my hand. "Maybe we could go out for brunch?"

"That sounds lovel— Oh. Wait." I ran my gloved thumb

around the end of his fingers feeling the warm blunt shape of them. "I'm sorry. I promised Myrtle I would help her prep for a check ride. A late lunch?"

He grimaced and kissed the cotton of my glove. "I have an afternoon meeting."

Our driver got into the front seat and that was it for our private conversation. I made a promise of my smile. "All right, I'll make sure I'm back in plenty of time for dinner."

He gave me a funny look, before lowering my hand to hold it on his thigh. "Did you remember that we have opera tickets tonight?"

I let my head drop back against the seat. "No." Beyond the rear window, the sky was a high, clear overcast. "Should we skip it? Or no—wait. I forgot. We need to schmooze with the Fergusons. It's *Idomeneo*, right?"

"Yes." He sighed. "I'm sorry."

I shrugged and left my hand in his, watching the tree branches pass as we drove down the street. "Me, too."

KENNETH HAS HIS church and I have mine. The incense is the heady aroma of petroleum products in the form of fuel and tarmac. We have our catechism of call signs and the high holy language of acronyms. In the temple that is the hangar, we store our artifacts, relics, and holy vessels.

I got out of my car, and my fellow priestesses of the sky looked around, waving. Myrtle Lindholm was sitting with the group at the picnic table by the hangar doors laughing with Imogene.

"Myrtle! Sorry to keep you waiting." I slammed the

door of the car, shoving my keys in my pocket.

"Gave me a chance to catch up." She shrugged. "I haven't been to a 99s meeting in over a ye— What in the world did you do?"

"Whatever do you mean?"

Helen Carmouche pulled her head out of the engine of her Beechcraft Staggerwing. When we'd started, she'd been the only astronaut from Taiwan and now we had six. Today, she had a smudge of grease on her forehead and winked. "Don't tell us, you cut it shaving."

Across the table from her, Betty looked up from a newspaper. "My bet is a gardening accident."

"Don't be silly. She sliced it on her own wit." Imogene ducked under the wing of her Mustang and stared at the bandage. "How many stitches you got under there?"

"Seven. And I'm stealing all of those explanations." I bent over to grab a cookie from the picnic table. I didn't want it, but I'd skipped lunch to get out here on time. It was deep brown and coated with sugar crystals.

Imogene laughed. "Question. Helen said your trip was bumped up?"

"Why, were you hoping to borrow my plane?" The Beechcraft Debonair, with its five seats, is perfect for taking visiting dignitaries up and allowing my husband to woo them with unsurpassed views of the great state of Kansas. That impresses them.

What impresses them more, is when I take the plane up above the cloud cover and remind them what a blue sky looks like. As the golden light of unfiltered sun floods the cabin, I've seen senators weep.

Imogene shook her head. "Just wondering if there was anything I should know before the Monday-morning staff meeting?"

Some of the newer members drifted toward us with that question. Alyshondra Meacham casually picked up a cookie. Birgit Furst just happened to need to get a rag near us. Rehema Njambi didn't even pretend to be subtle about listening to my answer.

I rolled my eyes. "You can't possibly believe that Clemons would pre-brief any woman. Monday will be a surprise for all of us."

The subtle art of not lying while lying. I hated keeping the secret about Icarus from this group, but I'd handled sensitive information before and knew how to compartmentalize. At the same time . . . Myrtle and Helen were two of my closest friends. The FBI was visibly on campus so I could at least alert them about that. I kept my voice light and breezy. "Hey, Helen. Come up with us and you can help Myrtle reorient to Earth."

Helen cocked her head for a moment before nodding. "Sounds good."

She knew something was up. The challenge with having very smart friends who knew you well was that they could tell when you were redirecting them. Keeping the Icarus project a secret was going to be a challenge.

I LOVE THE ritual of a preflight check. The order and rhythm fill my brain and push the fragmented list of things-that-must-be-done away. Hobbs and squawks . . .

CHECKED. Exterior preflight . . . COMPLETE. Fuel . . . MEASURED. All electric . . . OFF. Avionics master . . . OFF. Front seat belts . . .

"How's your seat belt?" I turned to Myrtle, who sat in the copilot seat beside me.

"Secured." Her voice carried a slight edge of nerves. Which was fair, since I was clearly up to something. That or the fact that I was about to let her fly my Debonair. After we were up, I mean. I wanted to see how she handled the stick before I let her do a takeoff or landing.

From behind us, Helen confirmed that her belt was secured. I hadn't had doubts, but we go through these checklists with faith that they will keep us safe.

I opened the window and yelled, "Clear prop!"

No one was anywhere near it, because the 99s have sense, but you never know when some random stranger is going to wander onto the field. I pulled the starter and fastened the window.

It muffles the sound, but not usually enough to carry on a real conversation. Fortunately, Kenneth and I had invested in upgrading the comms on the plane. The voice-operated exchange was a miracle of technology, since VOX meant I could talk to my husband without having to release the controls.

In my ear, Myrtle activated her mic as we rolled onto the runway. "Don't be gentle."

"Darling. I had no intention of it." I hurtled us down the runway and did the shortest takeoff I could. G-forces pressed us back into our seats with more suddenness than a rocket launch, even if nowhere near the power.

Beside me, she laughed with delighted abandon.

We had to wait until we climbed to nine hundred meters before I could indulge in any real aerobatics—oh, I was rated at four hundred and sixty, but I wouldn't with passengers—which meant we had time for conversation. "Imogene asked about what you should know before tomorrow's meeting. As briefly as I can . . . The FBI is on campus because Nathaniel was poisoned this weekend. He was—" My ears filled with startled exclamations.

"Poison!"

Myrtle's voice snapped over the comm. "What— What the heck, Nicole."

"I know. We thought it was an ulcer at first and—"

"I mean, why didn't you call us?"

"Oh."

"Reynard is one of his best friends." Helen's voice was quieter but edged with bitter anger. "Why were we not told?"

"I'm sorry. After the FBI questioned us they asked us to be quiet about it."

"We are his *friends*." Helen's diction always becomes very crisp when she is angry. Excited? Then her native Taiwanese syntax comes out a little. At the moment, she sounded like old New England money. "We should have been there for him."

"Yes. I'm sorry. That was a mistake. I called Hershel Wexler, so Nathaniel does have family coming in, but you're right. I should have called you, too."

Myrtle's voice was calmer. "You said the FBI was investigating?"

"Yes, and they're the same ones who were looking into the Cygnus Six." That was a matter of public record, so not breaching any clearance issues.

We crossed nine hundred meters and still had plenty of room before the cloud ceiling. I set the plane level and waited for Myrtle or Helen to respond. I wanted to tell them about the sabotage. Hell. Clemons should tell everyone. But I also knew the realities of situations like these. The only way to keep secrets was to not tell anyone, and if they were trying to catch a saboteur without tipping their hand, the fewer people who knew, the better.

Helen asked, "Do you think there is a link between Nathaniel and the Cygnus Six?"

"I don't know." That would be completely true if I didn't know about the sabotage. "But the FBI will almost certainly still be there on Monday and I'm betting Clemons will let them start questioning people."

"Again?" Myrtle's sigh was loud over the VOX. "Eugene got pulled in for questioning when the Mars team was prepping for launch."

Helen said, "You should do some tricks. People will wonder why we're flying in a straight line."

I did not need more prompting than that. I started with the basics, just a simple wing over. Technically, it was a move that allowed one to convert speed to height, but really it was just fun. I pulled up into the steepest climb I could and then rolled while banking, maintaining my back pressure to keep the Debonair's nose over the horizon while we pushed into that turn. Dropping the nose into a dive was better than a roller coaster.

I ran us through a chandelle followed by a dip into a lazy 8 topped off with a couple of steep turns. For the last of the turns, I did a sixty-degree, so we pulled 2 g as I kept the plane level, partly to see how Myrtle handled gravity—she'd been living in 1/6 g for over a year—but mostly because I loved being pressed into my seat and feeling the plane's response.

The maneuvers weren't enough to clear my head. I was too conscious of the other women in the cabin. I could feel them thinking through the causal chains and possibilities.

After I had played for a while, I leveled out. "Myrtle, do you want control?"

"Yes," she groaned. "I really do have to prep for this check ride."

Here's the interesting thing about the IAC. It's an international organization, with astronauts from different countries. They allocate seats based on how much money each country contributes to the effort, with America getting some additional "hardship" seats because the Meteor had hit us. So the IAC has their criteria for who can qualify, but each country also has its own criteria for who can apply.

The United States still has on the books that you need a pilot's license to qualify as an astronaut candidate. Mind you, the number of people who actually fly in space are a tiny proportion of those of us who go up. Why, might you ask, would a nation restrict who can apply by some archaic rule?

Well . . . if you want to limit the application pool to people with disposable income and a certain background, then a rule like this would be very useful. Hell. The 99s used to have an unspoken rule that they didn't accept Negroes, which is why there were so many Negro aeronautic clubs in the United States. Funny, that. I can't imagine the correlation . . .

At least the IAC proper had gotten rid of the pilot rules. You had to pass a physical and a battery of tests, because no one wanted to kill an astronaut with the forces of launch, but otherwise getting a seat was open to anyone.

I trimmed the craft so we were flying level and waited until Myrtle had her hands on the yoke. I said, "You have the aircraft."

Myrtle gave the response, "I have the aircraft."

I let go and let her fly. I waited until I saw the muscle in her jaw relax and her shoulders lower. And then I waited until she had done a turn to the left, then to the right, getting a feel for the plane. She pulled back the yoke for a climb, which was a little rough and sloppy, as if she weren't using enough rudder to keep the turns coordinated. I very consciously kept my own shoulders down.

Oh, she's a fine pilot, but flying on the Moon was not at all like flying in atmosphere. Her reaction times were a little off. You have to anticipate with a spacecraft in very different ways than an aircraft, because there's no air to slow down your forward inertia.

When she leveled out again, I finally asked them. "All right. What, if anything, do you want me to do? About the FBI, I mean."

"Honestly, I'm thinking more about Nathaniel." She opened up to full throttle, pulling up so our feet were on the horizon, and then took us into a smooth roll to the right. "The NAACP put together a checklist for responding to police or the feds years ago. You should hear Eugene's bullet points sometime. He sounds white as marshmallows in Jell-O."

I blinked. "Wouldn't that make them less white?"

"Oh, honey . . ." Myrtle laughed at me. "Why do white people hate food so much?"

That was not a question I could answer or refute. But it also raised another issue. "Nathaniel's pantry was empty. What do you think about a phone list asking for casseroles so we can stock his freezer?"

Myrtle's eyeroll was almost audible. "Elma was always after him when they were with us. I swear, that man can get so lost in a problem I think he'd starve before he remembered to eat."

I wanted to tell her that it wasn't about remembering. "His brother-in-law is coming out to help with convalescence."

"Hershel's a good man and—" The engine changed pitch.

The prop sputtered and became visible as the engine died. Whatever Myrtle was going to say dropped away. She turned the plane back toward the airfield, while climbing to convert airspeed into altitude. That was exactly right. She'd be set up well to take us into a glide if we couldn't get the engine back.

It coughed. The prop fluttered and caught, spinning back up to speed. It was over so fast it might not have happened. Maybe water in the line.

She let out a shaky breath. "Well, they'll do a simulated emergency in the check ride. So, thanks for—"

The engine cut out again.

Myrtle kept the plane level and optimized its configuration for best glide, feathering the prop. Behind us, Helen went completely silent—not out of fear, but to keep the lines of communication clear. We were eight to nine kilometers from the landing strip and, critically, it was behind us. At the Debonair's best glide speed, we were not going to make the turn and get back, no matter how much altitude Myrtle exchanged for speed. I leaned to the side, scanning for fields in which to set down. I'd scouted this on previous flights out of habit, but you never knew when someone was going to add irrigation or a barn.

And then the engine caught again. Shit. This was, believe it or not, worse than a complete engine failure. An intermittent partial engine failure meant that Myrtle would be caught between thinking she could make it back to the airport and the very real possibility that it would cut out again.

Which it did.

I glanced at her. Her face was tight and her entire body was focused on working the problem. I did not want her trying to make the airfield in order to spare my plane a rough landing. "There's a cornfield at ten o'clock."

She nodded. "Copy."

Since she was task-saturated, I took the radio. "Tower, Debonair one zero declaring an emergency. We have an engine failure and are setting down in a cornfield approximately eight kilometers northwest of the landing field."

Myrtle had her lower lip firmly between her teeth. She

was used to flying in vacuum.

I reached forward and took the yoke. "I have control."

"You have control." She recited the litany and let go.

I pointed our nose down a little from where Myrtle had it to get our speed up to L/D-max. Lift over drag . . . Lift is maximized, drag is minimized. Once I got us there, I set the trim, and aimed us toward the cornfield. Besides being nicely in front of us, our angle of approach would be into the wind. I needed our touchdown speed to be as low as possible.

With one hand, I released the latch to crack the door. At my side, Myrtle did the same. It wasn't in danger of flying open, because the wind was keeping it shut, but if we bent the airframe with the landing, this would allow us to get out of the plane. In case it caught fire or something.

Opening doors is not a thing you do in vacuum, by the way.

I could feel the drag on the plane as I went full flaps to get us even slower. The field grew more detailed and I kept my focus shifting between the instruments and looking live at the corn. These landings always looked like they were going to be so smooth and then—

The new corn caught at the landing gear, filling the cabin with the harsh pop, pop, pop of stalks striking the metal frame. The plane hissed and bucked as we came down on furrowed ground. The windows became a chaos of green that shook and rattled us like the Jolly Green Giant was playing craps.

I slammed forward against my belt as we stopped.

"Nice landing," Helen said, and she wasn't being ironic.

The plane rested neat and level amid a sea of young cornstalks.

Myrtle picked up the mic. "Tower, Debonair one zero emergency down northwest of the field. All safe."

I looked over at her. "Feel ready for your check ride?"

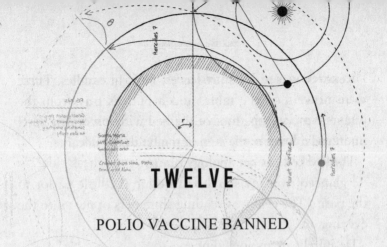

TWELVE

POLIO VACCINE BANNED

Special to The National Times

CHICAGO, March 31, 1963—Tests of a new anti-polio vaccine developed under the auspices of the National Foundation for Infantile Paralysis have been banned temporarily in Illinois, Dr. Roland R. Cross, State Health Director, disclosed yesterday in Springfield. It was learned that Dr. Cross ruled against using the vaccine in Illinois on the advice of a technical advisory committee that consulted with him in Chicago yesterday. Dr. Cross said that he had written the foundation asking for further evidence that the vaccine was safe before his office would permit it to be tested as part of national field trials the foundation will start May 8.

DEALING WITH ARRANGEMENTS to get the plane back to the hangar had made me run horrifically late. I ran into our bedroom, nearly tripping over Marlowe, who tried to twine between my legs. Dancing around my cat, I tossed my handbag on the bed. "Sorry I'm late but—" My sentence sublimated in my mouth.

Kenneth was in his shirtsleeves. He'd lit candles. There were flowers on the table, and a butler's tray from the kitchen stood at the foot of the bed with a wooden bowl on it and a wine bottle standing next to the decanter.

This looked like an apology dinner.

I glanced over my shoulder through the little parlor to the patio. The grill was sending shimmers of heat into the evening air.

Definitely an apology dinner.

Kenneth had that furrow between his brows that he gets when he's been concentrating all day. It takes hours to smooth it out. He crossed the room in a rush. "Are you all right?"

"What . . . ?" I looked at the butler's tray. It had the ingredients to make a Caesar salad lined up. Very, very much an apology dinner. When I am in one of my "states" the only food that seems remotely appetizing is a Caesar salad and a rare steak. "Don't we have the opera tonight?"

"Hang the opera." He rubbed his forehead as if the furrow were going to dig its way through his skull. "You could have been killed."

I blinked at him. He clearly knew about the plane coming down. I'll admit that I'd entertained thoughts of not telling him. Not for long. Just maybe not before the opera. "How did you know?"

He waved his hand toward the phone. "Medgar Davis called."

"And how did he know?"

To my astonishment, Kenneth blushed. "I . . . I have someone monitor air traffic when you're up."

"Excuse me." I'm not sure that I've heard something so sweet and so infuriating at the same time. "Well. I'm not sure what to think about that. Definitely not flattered by your confidence in my skill."

He winced. "Baby, you know it's not that."

I did. He was a worrier. It drove him to try to fix things and make the world a better place, but it also kept him up at night fretting about all the things that he couldn't fix and— "Wait. Do you do this when I'm on the Moon, too?"

Kenneth turned and walked to the butler's tray. "You know, in the early days, they gave everyone a squawk box, so we could hear you."

It was a rite of passage back in the day. The IAC would bring in a box wired directly from Mission Control so the families could hear their loved ones on a mission. There are too many of us now. "Do you still get one?"

"Not personally, no." He picked up the decanter and held it in front of the candle to check for sediment. "But I will admit that, as the governor of Kansas, it seemed prudent to have a squawk box installed at my office in case there's anything we need to know for public relations. It's in the press office and they have instructions to contact me if there are any anomalies."

"Kenneth Talbot Wargin. You are a crafty son of a bitch."

"Wine? It's a right bank Bordeaux from . . ." He tilted the bottle so he could see the label, which told me that Chu had picked it out for him. "It's a Lafleur. Forty-nine."

"Yes, please." Right bank Bordeaux. Not only had

Kenneth remembered that I liked Merlot, whatever he'd said to Chu had caused him to pick a stunning pre-Meteor vintage.

I kicked my heels off and let my aching feet sink into the carpet. Sometimes I don't realize how much they hurt until I stop. With a sigh, I sank into the green brocade chair and took the rest of the weight off my feet. Marlowe hopped into my lap the moment it presented itself and began making biscuits on my thigh. "Well, now you know I'm fine. I've set planes down without power before, so there's no need to skip the opera."

He pulled the cork out and set it on the table, aligning it with the edge. "There is, actually."

I straightened in my chair. "Now you're concerning me."

Kenneth didn't answer immediately, concentrating on pouring wine into the goblets we'd picked up in Venice on our honeymoon. He carried one over and sat down facing me. "There are two reasons." He sighed, turning the stem of the glass in his hand. "I'm not sure where to start."

This was so unlike him that a chill seemed to invade my veins. "Darling . . ."

He took a sip of wine and sat for a moment staring at the floor. "I looked at the calendar."

This was a daily activity for a public servant, so I waited to find out what he'd seen. My throat was as dry as if I were breathing pure oxygen. Swallowing, I lifted the wineglass and took a sip. It was lavender and wet clay and fig.

And Kenneth was still staring at the floor.

"I counted how many days there are till you leave for the Moon and it's not a lot. Six days, to be precise."

"I know. And I'm sorry."

He shook his head, running his hand through his hair. "I've been thinking about our conversation concerning Nathaniel and how we both got angry at the other one for hiding things. And then the plane coming down today . . ."

"I was going to tell you." I sat forward. "After the opera, I'll admit, but I would have told you."

"That's the thing. We wait until the right time, but I looked at the calendar and realized that there isn't a right time. So . . . so I'm not going to wait any longer."

Oh God. I could see where this was going and set the wine down. *People will think our marriage is in trouble.* What had he been hiding? The air in the room seemed to grow attenuated. Hypoxia was possible on Earth, but not likely in our bedroom.

"On your last trip, I . . . I had a heart attack."

"A . . . a heart attack." I reached for my glass of wine and nearly knocked it over. I had been so afraid of another end to that sentence and this was worse. "Jesus. Were you ever going to tell me?"

"I just did."

"Yes, but—" I squeezed my eyes shut. "When? I mean, when did it happen?"

He wet his lips. "About two weeks after launch."

"I could have come home!" One day to *Lunetta*. Three there to acclimate and transfer supplies to the trans-lunar shuttle. Three to fly to the Moon. A week on the Moon for refitting . . . The trans-lunar shuttle would still have been docked and I could have gone back on it. "Why didn't you . . . Oh. Because I would have come home."

"There was nothing you could do. And I couldn't tell you in the clear without risking someone hearing and that would sink any hope of my presidential run and—" He swallowed. "But it's why I didn't want you to go . . . I'm fine. All right? It wasn't a major heart attack. But I'm not rated for spaceflight anymore. Ever."

I stared at him. "I feel like there is a dichotomy here. How can you be simultaneously fine and also not rated to fly?"

Kenneth cleared his throat and stood. "The IAC's goal is to establish a base for humanity off the planet. Their threshold for risk, relating to health, is more conservative than—"

"So you *are* at risk for another one?"

He drummed his fingers on the butler's tray and picked up a clove of garlic, peeling the paper from it. "Yes."

"And still planning on running for president, which is not known as a job without stress." I picked up my wine and took a healthy drink from it. "I'll tell Clemons I can't go."

Kenneth threw the garlic clove into the bowl. "No. I want you to go."

"Are you serious? After you've been complaining you *didn't* want me to go for the past several days. After you told the press that we were going to live here on the Earth." Which made sudden sense now. "*After you had a goddamned heart attack and didn't tell me?*"

"And after someone sabotaged your plane."

"For pity's sake." I slammed the glass back onto the table. Marlowe lifted his head and stared at me with wide golden eyes. I ran a hand down his spine, but I couldn't tell you if that was to reassure him, or me. "It was a partial engine failure. These happen. I was trained to—"

"The mechanic called." Kenneth gripped the edge of the bowl. "While you were driving back from the airfield. The mechanic called, which would have been a helluva way to find out that you'd had a crash, I have to say."

"It was a controlled landing." Not that my status as a pilot was my chief concern, but it was easier to correct him there. "And you're changing the subject away from your heart attack by manufacturing a crisis."

"So you put engine oil in your gas tank."

I stopped with my mouth open. Engine oil? That would be consistent with the intermittent engine failure. It would go through in bits and foul up the engine completely. Only the oil pan and the fuel tank were nowhere near each other. "How much was in there?"

"Three or four liters. No telling how much at the beginning." He measured salt into the bowl and started mashing the garlic with a pair of forks. "He tried to tell me that 'the little lady' probably didn't know any better. Apparently, your species gets confused easily."

I could not think of any reason for oil to be in my gas tank. Even if someone had a reason to touch my plane while I wasn't there, all of the women in the 99s were accomplished pilots who would never make a mistake like that. "You're thinking of Icarus."

The muscles in Kenneth's forearms flexed as he tore and pressed the garlic in the bowl. "Airplane. Training 'accident.' Manifesto." He looked up at me. "I'm thinking Nathaniel wasn't the target."

"I thought it might have been aimed at you."

"The Manifesto talks about 'astronettes.' Of those, you're the wife of the governor. An original astronaut. If I wanted to take down the IAC, then targeting you wouldn't be a bad strategy while discrediting the program as a whole through accidental deaths." Kenneth dumped an anchovy fillet into the bowl and began mashing it into the garlic paste.

"Poison is an outlier."

"Yes. But I am one of the most vocal advocates for the space program. If you died . . ." Kenneth reached for an egg and stood there, holding it without moving for a long minute. He cleared his throat. "Leaving aside the question of how it would affect me, if you were poisoned in our own home, the press would raise the question of if I had done it."

People will think our marriage is in trouble . . .

Marlowe squawked and jumped out of my lap. Wisps of his fur clung to the sweat on my clenched fists. "Shit."

"True." Kenneth lifted the egg and cracked it against the bowl. The brittle snap of the shell was shockingly loud. "Everything the FBI identifies as Icarus has happened in Kansas City. You'll be safer on the Moon than you are here."

"You can't possibly think I'll leave you, not after telling me that you've had a heart attack."

"Nicole." Kenneth set the fork down and wiped his hands on a clean white towel. "Nicole, if I hadn't told you about the heart attack and just said that I'd changed my mind, would you argue with me about going?"

"That's neither here nor there." I would have been relieved. But he had told me about the heart attack and that changed everything. I wasn't going to abandon him here, and especially not to save my own skin.

"I am trying—I want you to understand that I could have 'managed' you. And I didn't. You want me to be honest with you and this is the price for that." He shrugged. "You want me to not protect you? Here we are. I had a heart attack *months* ago. You were on the Moon and I'm fine. The fact that you weren't here? It changed nothing. I'm fine."

It changed nothing. And that was the problem, wasn't it? I wiped my hands on my trousers, brushing the sweat and cat fur off on them. "So, just to sum up for clarity: you want me to go to the Moon because I will be safer and have no Earthly use."

He rolled his eyes. "Come on . . ."

I winced. "No. You're right. I'm sorry." I rubbed my forehead and turned my grimace to the floor. "I know you were trying to reassure me. But without my sass, that's essentially the shape of things. In this context, I'm more useful on the Moon than here. And if I go, it will provide an illusion of normalcy, as a side effect, which is politically advantageous right now."

"Yes." He shook his head. "I thought about not telling you. About the heart attack. And I know it seems unfair to tell you now, but if I didn't do it tonight . . . I've put it off for months, waiting for the right time. There's not going to be a right time and—the lie was filling my brain constantly. I'm sorry."

"I'm not sure if I should thank you for telling me or yell at you for not telling me."

He cocked a finger at me. "You already yelled."

Not enough. But I also understood. I had planned to wait to tell him about my unpowered landing. If the right time had never come . . . I sighed. "Thank you for telling me."

"So you'll go?"

I didn't feel relief or delight or anything except despair. "I'll go." I leveled my own finger at him. "I'll go, if you promise to tell me if it happens again."

"I promise I'll tell you."

"And you won't wait." I glared at him with all the formidable power of a Swiss finishing school education coupled with lessons from my mother. It is a glare that tells the viewer that I am not planning on murdering them, but that they are already dead and I'm trying to find their next of kin. "I know your feelings about private codes right now, but if you aren't willing to tell me in the clear, I want a code."

Kenneth inhaled as if he were going to start an impassioned address to the senate. He held it. It escaped in a long, slow sigh and I knew I'd won. "Fine. But not for exchanging letters. I'll . . . if it happens again, I'll send a message telling you that the 'flowers are blooming.'"

I wanted to push for more, so help me, but this would do. For now.

PART II

THIRTEEN

RIOTERS SEIZE BUILDING

KANSAS CITY, April 9, 1963—Demonstrators ended a seven-hour invasion of the United States Capitol today after a personal appeal by Kansas's governor, Kenneth T. Wargin. About 100 demonstrators had holed up in the building, some threatening to burn themselves and the building if police tried to evict them. The rioters said at first that they would not leave until the president agreed to use emergency powers to reallocate resources to states still impoverished by the effects of the Meteor. But the demonstration came to a surprising end with the arrival of the governor. He spent time praying with individual protesters and making handwritten notes of their concerns. One by one they walked out of the building, although one demonstrator said afterward that the group would meet with the governor later and would try to return to the building if the meeting was unsatisfactory. Governor Wargin is widely discussed as a possible front-runner for the presidential races in 1964, although he has not yet declared if he will run for office.

THE ENTIRE TIME we were in Brazil, I kept waiting for something to go wrong. Nothing did. Our team had been drastically reconfigured, with the thinnest of public rationales, to remove anyone who might be a potential "bad actor." I was used to teams that had worked together for months before a launch. Now I had a mixed bag. I had known some of the new team members for years, others were going to the Moon for their first time.

The night before we launched, I slid into the phone booth for my scheduled call with Kenneth. The Brazilian astronaut quarters had substantially better views than the Kansas center. It was a three-story home, with stairs leading down to a private beach. Outside the phone booth, the waters of the Atlantic lapped against steep ruddy cliffs. In the distance, a sailboat cut through the waves with its yellow-and-red sail taut in the wind.

The phone barely rang once before Kenneth picked up. "Hello?"

I melted a little at the sound of his voice, but even in those two innocuous syllables, I could hear the strain. "Hello, love. Everything down here is going swimmingly. How's life at home?"

"Good. Good. I've got Marlowe sitting on my lap. He misses you."

"Scratch his ears for me?"

"Already there. Here . . ." The phone fumbled and shushed as the receiver brushed against something and then a steady purring filled my ear.

I closed my eyes and put my hand over my mouth to keep the weeping inside.

The purr faded and my husband's voice returned. "Could you hear that?"

"Yeah." I wiped the skin under my eyes and sniffed to clear my nose. "I miss you so much."

"Me, too." I could picture him sitting in his wingback chair in his study, head leaning against the side, with Marlowe curled in his lap. In one hand, he held the phone, eyes half-closed, while the other hand made circles through dense black fur. All of the unsaid things crackled on the phone lines between us. Kenneth cleared his throat. "How are things in Hell?"

I laughed. For unknown reasons, the Brazilian spaceport was called *Barreira do Inferno*—literally, the Barrier to Hell. "I had a mango daiquiri yesterday. Truly my life is so difficult here."

He chuckled as if this were a normal conversation and not my last night on Earth. "Ready for launch tomorrow?"

"Yes. Everyone has been great about all the changes and we've really pulled together as a team, I think." All of that was true, but it was the flat surface of the situation. Everyone was tense and stressed about the changes because they didn't understand what was happening, but they had guesses. You can't send a group of terrifyingly brilliant people in to talk to the FBI, make changes to the launch schedule and staffing, and expect them to think that everything was nominal. "How about you? Any flowers in the garden?"

"No. Everything is a healthy, verdant green, but nothing is blooming." He cleared his throat. "You don't have to ask me every day, you know."

"When I'm on the Moon, I promise to only ask once a week."

He laughed. "You only get one phone call a week."

"But there's teletype. I could ask you every day in the mail, so count your blessings."

"I do. Every day, I do." He didn't tell me that he was praying for my safe return, but I could hear it in his voice. "In other news, Nathaniel is out of the hospital. I stopped by with Reynard and we played some poker. Hershel, by the way, is a wicked player. I'm convinced he counts cards."

"If he has half of his sister's math skills, he probably just intuits the probabilities without thinking about it."

"Well, he now has a very nice jar of cocktail onions to show for it." He sighed into the receiver. "Keeping up with the news down there?"

I grimaced. "The situation at the Capitol? Yes . . . Is the news making it sound better or worse than it really was?"

"A mix. It was mostly peaceful, but the contingent that turned violent was very effective at their mayhem. I think Denley is going to set a curfew. I think that's going to make things worse, but . . . but it's also easier to police if there are fewer people on the streets."

"Are you mostly staying in Topeka?"

"It's been a lot of back and forth. Honestly, I'm home tonight to take your call." He shifted the phone. "Would you . . . I think I might need to publicly declare for office before you come back. Is that . . . is that all right?"

The room went cold. I'd been there for every opening rally. When he ran for mayor, and state senator, and then for senator of the new post-Meteor government, and governor. If I wasn't there, it would be remarked upon in the news cycle. He would be going in burdened by speculation that our marriage was in trouble. That I wouldn't be able to fulfill my duties as the First Lady if I was on the Moon.

But I also understood why.

"You need to shift the news." Things were going to shit, and once he declared, his voice would be amplified beyond Kansas. I closed my eyes, blocking out the ocean and the beach. "Would it help if I did a broadcast from—"

Someone banged on the door, and then Birgit threw it open. "Nicole! The sun is out."

Beyond the window, a rare break in the perpetual clouds had formed. Golden light bathed a patch of the coast, turning the water from silver to a painful azure. Astronauts and technicians flooded out of the house. Michael Lin pulled his shirt off and fell back on the grass. Curtis Frye sank to his knees lifting his face to the sky in what looked like prayer. Eugene spun Myrtle, laughing, in a circle.

"Oh, I—"

In the phone, Kenneth said, "I heard. Go. Quick. Before the clouds close."

"I love you!" What a world we live in, that sunshine was rarer than being able to talk to my husband from the Moon.

I'm SURE IT will surprise no one that I am happiest when I am in control. I've become accustomed to being a passenger when we launch on the big rockets, but I don't enjoy it. I miss the days when it was just three people in a capsule and I had an actual job. Today, I was lying on my back, strapped securely into my launch couch and listening to the comms piped in from the pilot compartment up above. This was our fourth attempt to launch. We'd been scrubbed thus far by a lightning strike, a wayward plane invading the IAC's airspace, and a stuck relay switch.

At least I had an aisle seat.

Eugene's voice crackled over the speakers. "Two minutes downstairs; flight attendants stop beverage service and prepare for launch."

Laughter rippled through the cabin. There were no flight attendants. Just twenty-eight astronauts and colonists, strapped into couches with our feet in the air and a desperate need to pee. I reached up to close my visor, the polycarbonate hissing against the rubber seals. It clicked into place, leaving me with the metallic tang of bottled air, the hum of my suit fan, and the crackle-pops of rookies triggering their VOXs with excited breaths.

Imelda Alva Corona lay to my right, her long dark hair pulled tight beneath her "Snoopy cap." She stared out the window at the ocean and sighed.

"You okay?"

"Oh. Yeah." She jumped, probably startled that I could hear her sigh with her helmet closed, but it had triggered her VOX. She gave me a little shrug. "The ocean is just . . . I grew up in the plains. I saw the space station before I went to the beach."

Across the aisle from us, Luther Sanchez said, "Even for

oceans, Brazil's coast is pretty impressive. I grew up with long flat beaches. This whole jungle, then cliff, then water thing is disorienting."

No one asked him where he was from originally. Post-Meteor, a lot of people didn't talk about home anymore, because it was a reminder of too many dead friends. From going through all the files with Clemons, I knew that Luther had been from Florida. The panhandle was still fine, mostly, but tidal waves had been hard on the coast. His hometown was just gone. He'd been in Europe with the Air Force when the Meteor hit. First person in his family to graduate from college and leave town.

"I grew up in Detroit and we'd vacation at the Great Lakes." We had a vacation house where we'd escaped the summer heat. "I thought I knew surf, until the first time I went to California. So wrong. I was so, so wrong."

Behind me, Faustino Albino Rios said, "I am not sure I ever heard you say you were wrong about anything."

"I was wrong about liking you."

At the starboard window seat of our row, Imelda said, "Oh! There goes the LOX arm."

Much as some people might wish that it meant they'd loaded the ship with smoked salmon, it was the liquid oxygen supply arm retracting. I couldn't see it from my vantage point. A faint mechanical whir reverberated through the cabin, and at the port window of our row, Aahana flinched in her seat.

There are things that no amount of simulation can prepare you for. I leaned toward her, but my voice would carry over crew comms to the rest of the people in the cabin. "That's the yarmulke cap being pulled."

Nathaniel had made a joke about that early on, and it stuck as official nomenclature for the cap that kept the rocket stable on the pad until right before launch. I hoped he would be all right. Hershel said he was still having trouble keeping food down.

"Thanks." Aahana smiled, and it was a little tight. "I should have known."

"Someday, they'll make a simulator that includes everything. Until then . . . Think of them as delightful surprises." I wished, not for the first time, that we hadn't needed to take new people up to the colony on this trip. If Clemons had cut all the first-timers, people would have noticed. People would have lost even more confidence in the program.

Outside the window, a huge gust of white haze vented, wiping away the ocean. Conversation vanished underneath the harsh hiss. From somewhere in the cabin, a man yelped, "Mother of God!"

"Liquid oxygen vent," I murmured to Aahana. "Totally normal."

"This is your captain speaking. Please make sure your seat belts are fastened and your tray tables stowed." Eugene was such a ham. "One minute. I repeat. One minute, downstairs."

Luther Sanchez tugged on his harness, which was adorable. "Upstairs" in the command module, they would be doing final checks while those of us "downstairs" in the passenger module had been locked into our seats for the better part of two hours.

"Cabin pressure is probably going to give us an alarm." Eugene had barely finished speaking before a klaxon blared through the cabin.

I heard multiple people gasp—the problem with the colonists is that their training time was significantly shorter than ours. I say that, but I am also lying. Every noise, every alarm made me tense in ways that they normally did not during a launch. With each one, I was certain that something that looked like a routine problem was about to kill us all.

Myrtle raised her voice to cut through the buzz on the comms. "Folks, this is a pretty routine alarm during prelaunch."

"Sorry about that . . ." Eugene sounded utterly calm. Of course, I've also heard him sound that calm when he was flying a plane literally on fire, so take that as you will. "The alarm looks good."

Which meant our cabin pressure was acceptable. Clemons had flown down for this launch and I knew he was in the Firing Room. Even if no one else in the launch center knew about the larger concerns, he wouldn't let us fly if anything was off-nominal.

"Ullage pressures are up." Curtis Frye's voice carried over the comm from the copilot seat. "And the right engine helium tank is just a little bit low."

"It was yesterday, too . . ." Under normal circumstances, being a little low on helium wouldn't slow us at all. "Can we get confirmation that we're Go for launch?"

The comms were silent for a moment. Then our CAPCOM said, "We're stopping the clock at forty-three seconds."

A groan went through the cabin. Beside me, Imelda said, "My kid asked me what time our scrub was today."

From somewhere else in the cabin, a British man said, "Bloody hell. Starting to wonder if we'll ever launch."

"No kidding," a woman replied—Midwestern American, so maybe Sarah Holtermann or Vicky Hsu. "If my husband had this much trouble getting it up, I'd have left him years ago."

"Makes me understand the Earth Firsters." That voice was low and male and American and could have been one of a handful of people. If we had stuck with our original team, I would know everyone's voice, but some of these people I'd only met when we arrived in Brazil.

"We were scrubbed six times on my first mission." I stretched as much as I could in my seat, but the pace of my heart would have given the flight surgeon some concern back in the old days when we'd all worn telemetry hookups for vital signs. "Everyone can calm down. This isn't a scrub; they're just pausing the clock."

"Thanks, *Mamãe*." Faustino was lucky that he was right behind me, because if I could reach that man, he would not have appreciated the consequences.

"Just let me know if you need help with your diap—"

The comm crackled and I shut up as our CAPCOM said, "The right helium tank looks good. Restarting the clock at forty-three seconds."

Across the aisle, Luther crossed his fingers in his lap. Aahana leaned toward the window, lower lip between her teeth. I closed my eyes, wondering if Kenneth was listening to the squawk box in his office.

What was I thinking? I know my husband. Of course he was. I opened my eyes and said, as clearly as I could, to the colonists, to him, "Everything will be fine. Don't worry."

Faustino said, "Thank you, *Mamãe*."

I rolled my eyes. "Don't make me come back there."

"Thirty seconds downstairs."

Inside my boots, my toes curled as if I could get better traction and do something. I tucked my arms in by my sides, and stared straight up, past three rows of helmets and launch couches.

"Fifteen."

From somewhere in the cabin, one of the new kids started the chant and a few others joined in like they were tourists. "Ten. Nine. Eight. Seven. Six—"

The main engines ignited and the entire ship shuddered. It swayed back as the engines began to push against the bolts tethering us to the ground. The chant faltered into nervous laughter.

"Three at a hundred." Eugene reported that we had one hundred percent thrust level for all three engines.

Curtis Frye said, "Here we go."

And we had liftoff. Nothing went wrong. All systems nominal.

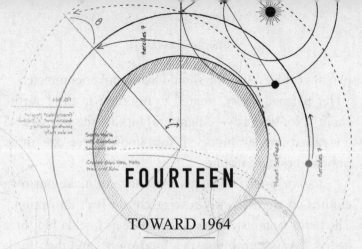

FOURTEEN

TOWARD 1964

TOPEKA, Kan., April 12, 1963—Gov. Kenneth T. Wargin's unavowed campaign for the 1964 Democratic Presidential nomination seemed to be moving into higher gear last week. He met in Kansas City with Elbert Simmons, the head of the party, who called him the "front-running" contender. To this, Mr. Wargin replied, "The important thing now is to create unity. It is still too early to crystallize on a single candidate."

I FLOATED NEAR the ceiling of the translunar shuttle with a foot hooked under one of the guide rails and glanced over my magnetic cards again. Imelda sat to my left in the "south" chair—even though there's neither "north" nor a "chair" when playing bridge in zero-g. From the "east" chair, I had a good view of my seat and my crew preference kit. My CPK had a package from Clemons to the Lunar Colony Administrator. I would much rather have had it on my person, but when we'd tried it on Earth, it had interfered with closing my suit. That is not nominal in space.

Chewing her lower lip, Imelda stared at her cards. It was a bad tell that she needed to break if she was going to keep playing bridge. And she should avoid poker completely.

Her partner, Vicky, floated to my right in the "north" chair. "No, seriously—Angora rabbits are the way to go."

I raised my eyebrows. "You know there are other hobbies besides knitting."

"At some point, we're going to have to make our own clothes on the Moon. Growing cotton isn't an option." The petite botanist wrinkled her nose as Imelda bid three hearts. "Angora rabbits are a food source and their fur is a dream to spin."

The last member of our group, Myrtle, sat in the "west" chair opposite me. "What about goats? Mohair is a great fiber and then we'd have dairy."

Vicky tilted her head, considering. "Transporting them would be a challenge, though."

We get some work done on the three-day transit to the Moon, but for the most part, it is the closest thing we get to a vacation. The transfer at *Lunetta* exists so we can switch from a launch vehicle to a lunar shuttle, designed to fly only in vacuum. One of the nice side effects was that it gave the rookies time to acclimate to microgravity and learn to use a zero-*g* toilet, so we didn't get a lot of vomiting and floating poop on the flight to the Moon. Down the length of the ship, people read, or played cards, or chatted as if they had always been in space. I doubled Imelda's preempt. "What about bringing baby goats up?"

"Kids." Myrtle glanced at the choice I had made and reconsidered her cards. "Baby goats are called 'kids,' city girl."

I stuck my tongue out at her like the grownup I am.

Vicky made an SOS redouble. "Oo! Have you seen Cameroon dwarf goats? So tiny! Better for composting, too. Although I don't know about their fur as a fiber source . . ."

Aahana floated up to our group, grabbing a handrail to stop herself by Myrtle. She leaned in and whispered something that made Myrtle look sharply toward the command module. "Thank you." She swallowed and then turned to us. "Ladies, if you'll excuse me."

I've played bridge with Myrtle and Eugene long enough to know their subtle reactions, and this was not a subtle reaction. Something was wrong with Eugene.

AN HOUR LATER, I hung in my couch, pretending to read while I watched the activity at the front of the ship. Ana Teresa floated in and out of the command module, so I could safely guess that Eugene was ill. He'd seemed fine at breakfast. But based on the number of cleaning supplies that I saw Helen and Myrtle haul into the CM, I could also make a guess that he'd vomited.

I wanted to help, and it took enormous restraint to stay put and out of the way.

But . . . but I couldn't stop thinking about Nathaniel.

Mind you, I couldn't imagine how someone could get rat poison into a dehydrated meal, but that didn't mean it was impossible. I also didn't know if the symptoms of that sort of poison would show up immediately, or if Nathaniel had vomited because of the ulcer.

None of that kept me from fretting. I worried the inside of my cheek and read the same page over and over.

Curt emerged from the CM, guiding the feet of a sleeping bag. Everyone in the main cabin stilled, watching as Ana Teresa followed, guiding Eugene's head. Inside the sleeping bag, he was half-curled into a fetal position. One arm was out, clutching an emesis bag, so I'd been right about the vomit. His eyes were closed and his brow creased with concentration as if he were working very hard not to throw up again.

Myrtle followed after them as they pulled him into a corner. She glanced down the length of the main cabin and found me with her gaze, beckoning. I released my couch's footrail, stowing my book in the net bag attached to the chairback in front of me. It only took two pushes to "superman" up to the front, where I snagged a guiderail and stopped by Myrtle.

"What can I do?"

"Honestly . . . I don't know." She rested a hand on her husband's shoulder. "He's going to lie to you and tell you he's fine."

"No." Eugene cracked an eye. "But I promise I can manage an emesis bag. Just tether me here and—"

His face twisted and he yanked the bag up to his mouth. The fact that he was vomiting was bad. The fact that a pilot had just admitted he was ill was terrifying.

Ana Teresa put a hand on Eugene's shoulders to steady him, while Curt braced his feet. I turned and grabbed some tethers from one of the stowage bags. Here was one small thing I could do.

I secured the right shoulder of the sleeping bag to the corner of the cabin, aware of all the people watching us. Eugene finished and lay limp and gasping inside the restraints as if he'd just wrung out his insides. Ana Teresa gently took the bag from him and slid an empty into his hand.

From down the cabin, Faustino pulled a little closer. "What's wrong with him?"

Ana Teresa slid the used bag into a larger trash bag. "I believe this is food poisoning contracted before departure and that he will be recovered as soon as it works its way through his system. Nothing contagious, so no need for anyone to be alarmed."

"But he'll be fine in time to land us. Right, doc?" Curt still held Eugene's feet. Sweat beaded his brow and I realized that, as copilot, if Eugene wasn't better, Curt would take over the landing. It would be his first time landing on the Moon.

"Oh . . ." Ana Teresa glanced past Curt to the rest of the cabin and I could see the lie form in that hesitation. "I'm sure he will be."

I kept thinking about Nathaniel. For that matter, I was wondering if the illness that had hit the Mars Expedition was really just simple food poisoning. "Is there . . . Are you sure it's food poisoning?"

She snorted at me. "It is not 'space germs,' if that is what you are asking."

I rolled my eyes. "Please grant me a modicum of intelligence." The newspapers had grabbed hold of that as if it were a real thing, but no one who actually worked in the aerospace industry believed in weird mutant diseases from Outer Space. "I'm wondering if this could be an ulcer, or stomach flu, or any number of things that can cause vomiting."

She shook her head. "There is a reason that we call medicine a 'practice.' I have nothing in this tube with which to do any real testing. So. Let us make him comfortable so he can recover soonest."

I slid down to where Curt was. "I'll finish tethering him so you can get back to the CM."

He nodded, squeezing Eugene's foot. "Don't you dare leave me to land this thing solo. Sir."

Eugene managed a smile. "The way you jockey? Wouldn't dream of it."

THERE'S REALLY ONLY so much you can do to contain vomit in space. Even with the most exquisite care, there's always some liquid that gets past containment. From near the back of the cabin, Guillermo Reyes Munoz recoiled suddenly. "Gah!"

He swiped at the air and then immediately looked like he regretted his choice.

"On it." Imelda kicked over to him with a wipe. "Who knew that having a five-year-old would be so helpful in space."

Eugene cracked his eyes and rasped. "I'm buying everyone a beer."

"Easy promise." Myrtle looked up from her crochet. "No beer on the Moon."

"Not yet. But I know for a fact that Ken Harrison packed hops in his personal allowance. There's— Shit." He clapped a bag to his mouth again and retched.

Ana Teresa watched him, and the line between her brows got deeper.

I floated over to hover beside her. "You look worried."

The corner of her mouth twitched. "I don't have any way to keep him hydrated. It is concerning." She glanced at Eugene and spoke quietly. "I do not see any way he will be capable of flying tomorrow."

Eugene lowered the bag. "Heard that. Ask MC for a replacement now. Even if a miracle occurs, it's better to have a backup ready to go."

My goddamned ambition perked up and waved its hands. *Pick me! I'm the most senior astronaut on this crew. Pick me!* But I kept my mouth shut, even though I had more flight time than anyone on this crew except Eugene, even though I'd landed on the Moon before, because Eugene wasn't the one to make that call. The IAC knew my qualifications. If Clemons wanted me to fly, he would pick me.

As THE DEORBIT burn kicked in and gave us gravity for the first time in three days, my seat slapped against my back. That was a little rougher than necessary.

I slid side to side in my seat as we oscillated around in yaw. Before I had time to tense, it settled out and then the burn vanished. I bit the inside of my lip and stared past Imelda to the window. There was nothing in view to give me a sense of pace or altitude.

It was just a subtle sense of wrong. Don't misunderstand, the approach to the Moon is always a little different, based on where we are in orbital cycles, but there are still rhythms and patterns. An oscillation wasn't completely out of the ordinary—in fact, Jacira's ship had experienced severe oscillation on her first landing. It could be anything from a little debris to a cranky thruster to a gauge to pilot error.

If Eugene had been flying, I wouldn't have worried.

But he was strapped into a couch at the front of the cabin, with cracked lips and an unhealthy gray pallor.

The IAC bumped Curt up to pilot and tapped Michael Lin to copilot. Two rookies to bring us in, because God forbid that they let me fly it.

At least Helen had stayed put in the Nav/Comp seat so they had a veteran up there. She'd keep them on course and could compensate for burn errors.

"Artemis. Translunar Shuttle 1093." Curt's call to Lunar Mission Control sounded as calm as if this weren't his first landing.

"TLS-1093, Artemis. This is Deana Whitney on CAPCOM." Good. I liked her. She was level-headed and wicked smart—and then I remembered that her husband had been at the Astronauts' Husbands Club the night that Nathaniel was poisoned. "How do you read?"

"Loud and clear. Horizon checklist right on time. Our radar checks indicate 15200 meters perilune. Our visual altitude checks steadying out at about 16100."

"TLS-1093, your state vector is good. Perfect ground track. You are Go to proceed with landing."

"Roger. Downstairs, we're making our final approach," Curt said. "Flight attendants, stop your beverage service and prepare for landing."

No one laughed. I wanted to yell at him to concentrate on flying. Eugene cracked jokes when we were sitting on the launchpad waiting, not during actual flight. I tightened my grip on my harness. Curt was so young.

A moment later, Mikey said, "AELD control circuit breakers. DECA GIMBAL AC—closed. GIMBAL enabled. RATE SCALE—25."

I shifted in my seat, picturing the cockpit. I'd done five moon missions back when the corps was small enough that they had to let women fly sometimes. It would be fine. Everything would be fine. On my first landing, we'd had no problems and there was no reason to think the new kids would either.

Helen said, "Your alignment is Go on the AGS. On my mark, 3:30 until ignition."

Curt responded, "Roger."

"Mark."

Those three minutes and thirty seconds stretched out to fill the black void of space. Across the aisle, Aahana had her fingers dug into the knees of her spacesuit and I couldn't think of anything to reassure her. I kept finding myself pointing my toes, like I was about to go on pointe, and had to force my feet to relax over and over.

It felt like longer than three minutes and thirty seconds. It always feels like longer.

"Thrust translation—four jets—Balance couple—ON. TTCA throttle—MINIMUM. Throttle—AUTO CDR. Standing by for . . ."

The engines kicked the seats against us. Somewhere in the cabin, one of the Algerian contingent murmured a string of Arabic that sounded like prayer.

Helen said, "Pitch 212, yaw 37."

I waited for the sideways thrust of the yaw maneuver and it didn't come.

Her voice sounded a little more urgent. "Curt—pitch 212, yaw 37."

"TLS-1093, we're showing you coming in high."

"I'm . . . The controller is not responding." His voice still sounded dead calm. "I've lost attitude hold. I'm having to manually maintain all of my rotational input."

Even the rookies understood enough that the cabin filled with tension. None of us spoke. Even though we weren't in the CM, keeping lines of communication clear was paramount. The control failure meant a lot more mental overhead in keeping the vehicle aligned.

Up at the front, Eugene reached for his shoulder straps and stopped, clinging to the webbing. I knew the feeling. I wanted to unbuckle and superman to the front to help. There were ways to compensate for failures in the control system. Curt and Michael had both been pilots before joining the IAC. They'd had the years of additional astronaut training that our colonists hadn't. They could handle this.

Assuming the ship hadn't been sabotaged, of course. Assuming this was a recoverable error.

From the front of the ship, Eugene's voice was ragged, but calm. "Crew, seal helmets and check your restraints."

Around me, dozens of helmets clicked shut. I slid my visor down, sealing me into suit air. If there was a breach, we'd be protected from vacuum. If there was an explosion, well . . .

In the comms, our collective breaths hissed and popped

as we triggered the VOX at different intervals. As long as people were breathing calmly, the voice-activated channels would stay quiet, but I didn't bet on many of the colonists breathing easily.

Gravity seemed to come from our left as Curt used two thrusters to spin the ship to the correct position. He'd burn through a lot of fuel doing it this way, which made the margins for landing uncomfortably close, but he'd get us down.

Mikey said, "After yaw around, angles: S band pitch, minus 9, yaw plus 18."

"Copy. Looking good."

I let out a little breath in relief, but just a little.

"Beta ARM. Altitudes are a little high." Mikey sounded as if this weren't any more exciting than a Methodist mumble. "I'm getting a little fluctuation in the AC voltage now."

"Roger."

"Might be our meter?"

That would be an easy way to crash a rocket. You wouldn't even have to damage an engine, just cause the instrumentation to fail. But that was okay, we'd trained to fly with visual only. They knew how to do this.

Helen confirmed. "Stand by . . . Our position checks downrange show us to be a little long."

"Compensating." A moment after Curt spoke, a quick burn kicked our seats against us and stopped.

"Good." Now I could hear the relief in Mikey's voice. "We got good lock-on. Altitude lights OUT. DELTA-H is minus 2 900."

"Artemis Base, are you looking at our DELTA-H?"

"TLS-1093, that's affirmative. It's looking good to us."

Helen said, "6 plus 25, throttle down—"

"Roger. Copy. 6 plus 25."

I looked down, surreptitiously checking my Omega watch strapped to the outside of my suit. Imelda caught the motion and raised her brows in question. I shook my head at first, then turned off my mic and leaned over to press my helmet against hers. "Tracking the burns. They're doing great."

Right on time, we lurched forward as Curt throttled down. We yawed a little, but it felt as if the course held mostly steady.

Mikey said, "AGS and PGNCS look real close."

"Manual attitude control is good. That thruster came back online."

No. No. No . . . don't trust it. Intermittent engine failure. Sure, maybe that thruster was back online for good or maybe it was going to fail again. I curled my fists inside my gloves and only a good manicure kept me from digging through the tips.

"Six hundred meters. Six hundred meters. Into the AGS, forty-seven degrees." As Mikey spoke, I turned to look out the starboard window.

The horizon of the Moon filled the starboard side. I reached across the aisle and nudged Aahana. She jumped at my touch. I pointed toward the window and her mouth rounded in astonishment.

"35 degrees. 35 degrees. 230. Coming down to 7."

The stark beautiful craters and shadows scrolled past.

Scale was impossible to tell without an atmosphere to soften the distance. In photos, the Moon always looks gray, but the color fluctuates to include tans and bright whites depending on where you look.

"165 meters, down at—9. Down at 5."

In the distance, Brannen Crater rolled into view. In the shadow of its rim, an artificial light shone with the presence of humanity—the entry dome at the Marius Hills outpost, where they were building a massive habitat inside a forty-kilometer lava tube.

"We're pegged on horizontal velocity. 91 meters, down 1.06, 14 forward."

We were coming in a little fast for my taste, but still within parameters.

"On 1 a minute, .45 down."

Beyond the windows, our shadow came into view, fluttering over the rocky surface. People gasped in unison, as if we had rehearsed it. Honestly, it didn't matter how many times I flew home, that first view of shadow made my chest loosen in wonder.

"15.25, down at .76, 6 forward."

I lifted my arm to point as the first dome of the Artemis Base slid into view, glowing with life on the surface of the Moon. Aahana was already leaning forward against her restraints to see.

The ship kicked sideways, snapping my arm against the side of my seat. We changed vectors again, restraints gouging into my chest so hard it knocked the breath out of me. I wheezed, staring out the window as dust billowed past it.

The ship slammed down. Even through my helmet, metal groaned as the entire ship torqued way out of specifications. Bundles and CPK bags tumbled past in an avalanche accompanied by disembodied yelps of pain. Over it all was the persistent blare of the decompression alarm.

We stopped moving. One-sixth gravity settled us in our couches. "T-touchdown." Curt swallowed audibly on the microphone. "We have touchdown."

The depress alarm still sounded. We were in our pressure suits for exactly this reason. It would be all right. We would need to evacuate. Normally, I wouldn't worry about my luggage, but I had a package to deliver and—

It was gone.

My entire CPK bag was missing. It must have been jarred loose on impact, taking the package of codebooks with it. Well, shit. I shook my head inside my helmet. Worry about that later. Get everyone off the ship first.

Someone was trying not to cry, a disembodied breath catching and failing to stay silent.

My arm ached like fire, but I dragged in breath, trying to project calm. "It's okay, people. That was rough, but we're down. Just stay put while they shut down the—"

The rocket lurched violently.

Adrenaline flooded my system. We were down, so why were we still moving? I looked out the window and the horizon tipped sideways. With a scream of metal I could feel through my seat and hear in my teeth, the entire vehicle slowly, slowly canted sideways. In one-sixth gravity, there's a lot of time to fall.

FIFTEEN

DEATH TOLL REPORTED AT 2,300 AS PAKISTANI FLOODING SPREADS

Special to The National Times

KARACHI, Pakistan, April 13, 1963—The death toll in the Pakistani floods was reported today to be more than 2,300 as the swollen Indus River coursed southward through heavily populated districts. More than 15 million people have been made homeless since the river waters started overflowing their banks in Punjab and Sind Provinces two weeks ago after unseasonably heavy rains. Climatologists warn that more such flooding can be expected due to post-Meteor changes in weather patterns.

WE FELL TEN degrees off vertical and jarred to a halt. Metal ground and we dropped again. Fifteen degrees.

Despite hours spent in sims, I tensed and grabbed for my chair arms, making the pain in my left wrist flare. Everyone was breathing heavily, including me. The oxygen dried my tongue. One-sixth *g*, after three days without gravity, felt more significant than it had any right to.

The ship swayed, pulsing as if a strong wind were buffeting it. Or as if someone were using reaction thrusters to keep it upright.

"Everyone stay put." Eugene's voice cut through the chaos of breath, sounding stronger over the comm than it had for the past two days. He wasn't piloting the ship, but he was still the mission commander. "Keep the comm lines clear. Frye, give me the command module status report."

The pause while we waited for Curt's response almost killed me. The ship kept settling, then rocking back up to vertical. But he answered as calmly as if this were a sim. "We've lost a landing strut and I'm compensating with thrusters."

Mikey took over the report, leaving Curt to concentrate on keeping us upright. "CM pressure reads good . . . We've got a dP/DT alarm in the passenger compartment. Evaluating the loss of pressure rate."

"Frye, vent the main tanks." Eugene loosened his shoulder straps. "Do not vent the ATC tanks."

"Copy."

When the ship fell the rest of the way over, it would be subjected to lateral stress far outside its design parameters. We would almost certainly rupture the main fuel tanks, which would, in the words of our SimSup back in training, lead to "a bad day."

On the starboard side of the ship, Aerozine vented in a plume, freezing instantly as the toxic chemical spewed across the lunar landscape. On the port side, out of my line of sight, the oxidizer would be creating another plume counterbalancing the thrust generated from venting.

That solved one problem. It left another. An experienced pilot could use the thrusters in the nose to keep the ship upright. But with a broken landing strut? When the thruster tanks emptied, the ship would fall over. Someone was going to have to stay aboard and keep it vertical until everyone was off.

"All crew, prep for emergency egress, but stay in your seats." Eugene reached for the emergency oxygen supply canister stowed beneath his seat. "Helen, patch me into the Big Loop with LGC."

Of course, Lunar Ground Control wouldn't be able to hear him from the passenger module.

"Copy. Stand by." Helen's voice was as cool as ice.

While we waited, the rattle of breaths started to drop away as the act of prepping for egress focused people and they stopped accidentally triggering their VOX. Or maybe they were like me, filled with adrenaline that had nowhere to go and working very hard on breathing with a closed mouth in order to keep comms clear.

I turned the rotary buckle on my seat restraint and started to work my left shoulder free. The strap caught on my wrist and sent a jolt up through my elbow, directly into my brain.

Tears flooded my eyes. I couldn't breathe for a moment.

Goddammit. If I had sprained my wrist by pointing like a rookie during landing, I was going to be so pissed. Trying not to flex the wrist, I drew it through with only the throbbing it had been doing since I'd hit it. So foolish.

I almost jumped when Helen cut back in. "LGC, lunar shuttle, Mission Commander Eugene Lindholm is on comm. Go ahead."

"LGC, Lindholm. Can you get the gantry to us in this position?"

The comms went dead silent as if we had all simultaneously held our breath.

On Earth, we had to land kilometers from Ground Control, to keep the soundwaves from shredding people. In a vacuum, you didn't have to worry about soundwaves or a transfer of heat, so on the Moon, we touched down by the base.

"Negative."

Without the gantry . . . the egress from the shuttle was nearly five stories off the ground.

"Understood. Can you get someone to us with rovers? I'm calling Hatch Jettison Mode V Slide egress."

Mode V meant we'd be dropping down a five-story inflatable tube threaded with a constant rate rappel line to control our fall. In training, it's actually fun. On Earth. From a stationary space vehicle mockup.

I reached forward and grabbed the egress cue card from the seatback. Yes, I had trained colonists on how to egress, but cue cards keep you from making mistakes in the moment.

Beneath the lunar surface, dozens of men and women would be scrambling to get us to safety. Back on Earth, after a 1.3-second delay, the entirety of the IAC would be mobilizing to ready to work unexpected problems.

And in his office, my husband would be listening to the squawk box. His team would be setting up their own battle stations, ready with talking points and press releases. I wanted to speak, to let him know that I was all right, and I bit down hard on my tongue.

Instead, I slapped the emergency egress card onto my wrist Velcro. My fingers were clumsy as my gloves stiffened as the cabin pressure bled into vacuum. The suit pressurized to compensate, tightening around my sore arm with painful insistency. That was going to be a helluva bruise.

"Lindholm, a mining team is going out the Dewey dome airlock and will drive around to meet your people. The backroom would like to know how much propellant remains in the thrusters?"

Helen answered, "At current use, we have fifteen minutes of thrust."

Out of habit, I glanced at my watch and marked the time. For the astronauts, that was plenty. We'd done multiple sims, rappelling down the sides of various classes of ships. We could do an evac in 6.5 minutes.

Our colonists had taken one three-hour class.

"Copy." Deana didn't sign off, so the LGC was still listening to everything in the ship.

"All right. Mode V. Mode V. Mode V. Curt, I'm coming up to take control."

Across the aisle, Myrtle reached for Eugene, as if she could stop him, but drew her hand back without completing the gesture.

The price she paid for being in the astronaut corps with her husband was being willing to accept that he would be on the rocket when it fell over. This wasn't just about the captain going down with the ship. Eugene was the more experienced pilot in vacuum. The ship would still sway, but the oscillation would be minimal compared to the ride Curt was giving us. None of his instincts had been built in vacuum.

Above me, Eugene was attaching his emergency oxygen supply. "Myrtle, position 1 for hatch jettison. Carmouche, position 2 for slide deployment. Wargin. Position 3 for Sky Genie distribution. All crew, prep for hard vacuum. Do not unplug from the ship's hardline communications until calle—" His comm cut off. Eugene's head and shoulders twisted to the side. Ana Teresa put a hand on his back to steady him.

The ship swayed with each pulse of the thruster while Curt fought gravity.

Myrtle dropped down the ladder, heading to the hatch at the base of the passenger compartment. Above us, Helen emerged from the command module. She put her feet on either side of the ladder and slid down it like a double fire pole.

I grabbed my emergency oxygen supply canister with my good hand. My left hurt with a cold, bone-deep ache like ice distorting my arm, but I didn't have time to baby it. I'd been forced to use my right back in finishing school and it would have to suffice.

"Pyro safing pin removed." Below us, Myrtle was standing at the airlock, tethered to the top handrail. "Hatch jettison on three. One. Two. Three." The thump of the pyro bolts firing resonated through the frame of the ship, not quite to the level of sound in the airless cabin. "Hatch clear."

At the new angle of his body, I could just see Eugene raise

his hand to his chest and toggle his mic on. He'd been using manual control of his microphone and not VOX this whole time, to keep the voice activation from being triggered when he retched. When he spoke, his voice sounded strained. "Wargin . . . Can you take the controls?"

He hadn't issued it as a command, because he wasn't just asking me to keep the ship vertical. He was asking me to ride it down when it fell. And he was asking, because if he threw up while trying to keep the ship upright, it would be a Bad Day.

"Yes. Absolutely." Kenneth would be listening to this. "Who knows, maybe I can lay the ship down on its side."

"Aft and forward hinge pip pins removed." At position 2, Helen worked, connected to the ship by the emergency umbilicals beside the airlock. "Slide assembly locked, black on black. Standby inflation."

Helen pulled the inflation lanyard. Nothing happened. She braced with one hand against the ship and pulled again in a motion like a gardener trying to start a lawn mower.

Was there anything I could do to help her? No. And focusing on things I couldn't affect could cause me to miss something important on the tasks I was assigned. Tethering the bottled O_2 to my suit, I pulled the "green apple" to activate it. As soon as I had green on the oxygen indicator, I disconnected my suit from the ship. Without hardline communications, the ship was eerily silent. Only the sound of my own breath and the fans were audible.

I swung my legs out of my couch and grabbed for the ladder. The angle was tilting off-true, and with pressurized gloves, it was going to be an unpleasant climb. I tightened my left hand on the rail and pulled up.

Inside my arm, alarms went bright red, full alert. Failure state.

I gasped and closed my eyes. This wasn't a sprain. My arm was broken.

There were not enough curses in the world for this. Even if I wanted to endanger my crewmates by hiding a serious injury, my left arm wouldn't support my weight for the climb up to the CM. I crawled back into my couch and plugged into the comms.

"—lide is no Go. The argon tank is drained. From impact?"

"Copy. Switch to Mode V.a. Free rappel."

On the comm, someone moaned, and I couldn't blame them. We had trained to keep the rocket vertical with manual inputs. We had trained to egress via a rappel line without the slide. We had trained to have a depress. But this was a lot of failures deep . . .

And the situation was worse.

"Lindholm, Wargin." Theoretically, I could pilot, but we didn't have time to figure out how to get me there. "We have a problem. I think I broke my left arm in the landing."

"Copy." He might as well have cursed. In the sound of breath and fans, I could feel him evaluating the other astronaut-pilots on the ship. Myrtle. Helen. Curt. Mikey. The women flew in vacuum but not with this ship. The men knew the rocket, but not vacuum. That left himself. Any wiggle had the potential to slam the person on the rappel line into the side of the ship. "I'll take the controls."

On the comms, someone made a sharp intake of breath. No one spoke, but I was willing to lay money on that being Myrtle.

"Frye and Lin, prep for handover and then assist Carmouche at position 2. Myrtle, you're first down the line to stabilize it. Ana Teresa, assist Wargin with her injury."

Eugene unplugged and climbed to the CM.

In sims, I'd played the injured crew member more than once to give my crewmates a sense of what it would be like to have to evacuate someone who was incapacitated. I'd be sent down as the first of the astronauts after the colonists. The best thing I could do was to stay out of the way until they were ready for me. I wasn't going to be moving fast.

Unseen, in the CM above us, Eugene said, "I have the controls."

Curt's liturgical response followed. "You have the controls."

In their spacesuits, my crewmates were distinguishable only by general body type and quality of movement. It was obvious when Curt and Mikey came down the ladder from the CM, because they moved with a surety that the colonists lacked.

Except for the ones who had been up before, like Faustino or Rose Barlow, the colonists had experienced a pressurized IVP suit only once, in a vacuum chamber on Earth.

The rocket swayed upright and stayed close to still, oscillating only a little.

"Vertical. You are Go for egress."

We'd stopped hearing the LGC. Either they were keeping

our lines of communication clear for the evac, or Eugene had taken the cabin out of the Big Loop now that he was in the command module. I was betting on the latter.

I swung to the side, to let Aahana out of our row. Her concern was clear through her visor, but she stuck with training and didn't pause, moving like she was a full astronaut. I was so proud. I uncovered the harness carabiner on my left shoulder and opened it, so I would be prepped when I reached the hatch. Ana Teresa got off the ladder next to me and tethered herself, bracing her feet on the chair back below me.

At the hatch, five stories above the ground, Myrtle sat on the edge of the airlock clipped onto the rappelling line hanging over her left shoulder from a support bar that extended a meter from the ship. Curt leaned out of the hatch, tethered to the ship with a safety and a local tether, to watch the ground and act as a spotter. He gave her a thumbs-up.

Myrtle leaned forward, swinging out with the motion of the ship, and vanished in a controlled rapid descent down the side.

From the hatch, Curt said, "She's on the ground. Rappel off. Hand signals indicate line secured."

"Copy that. Ten minutes fuel remaining."

Helen replied, "We're sending the colonists down."

Ana Teresa leaned forward for helmet-to-helmet communication. "Do you need the egress sling? And don't be a pilot when you answer."

I toggled my mic off, holding in my urge to make a snappy comeback. "I can rappel one-handed." I'd practiced that carrying "incapacitated" crew members in a sim. "But I may need a spotter on the ladder and with landing."

She nodded. "I'll go down first and wait for you at the bottom."

I could feel the quick pulses of the attitude thrusters through the frame of the ship as Eugene kept us upright with an elegant economy of thrust. Below us, Curt, Helen, and Mikey helped colonists attach their carabiners to the Sky Genie and egress. Some of them hesitated on the threshold, before slipping off the edge and out of sight. Most of them moved, if not smoothly, then with purpose.

I glanced at my watch. By my mark, we had about five minutes of fuel left.

As soon as the ladder was clear, Ana Teresa nudged me. I unplugged into silence, and swung my legs out to join her on the ladder. She positioned herself two rungs below me, with her hands on the outer rails. I could feel her helmet pressing against my lower back.

Climbing down one-handed was slower than I liked, but rushing had the potential to knock us both off the ladder.

Ana Teresa led me to the hatch, as if the broken arm somehow affected my other senses. Two more colonists went out the door, directed by Helen with precise hand signals. When the last left, Ana Teresa clipped onto the rope and went out the hatch on signal.

As soon as Curt gave the thumbs-up that she was on the ground, Mikey wrapped the line quickly once around the shaft of my Sky Genie, which was all the friction we needed in lunar gravity, and fit the cover cylinder back in place with the thumbscrew. Helen clipped it to my harness carabiner as if I were a child. That was the correct procedure for an injured crew member, but I dislike being out of control enough that it still rankled a little.

It felt weird to sling the rope to my right, but I gripped it and tucked it behind my back to apply full tension to the line before sitting on the edge of the hatch.

Below me, Myrtle held the end of the line to try to guide rappellers clear of the teetering ship. Leaning forward, I fell away from the airlock as I brought my right arm out from my body. I hung from my left shoulder, and my rate of descent was so slow that I thought, for a moment, my Sky Genie was malfunctioning.

But with all my Earthside training, I had never rappelled in one-sixth gravity. Line fed through the Sky Genie at a fraction of the speed I expected, even though we'd discussed this in class, and I gently fell down the side of the rocket.

Until my back slammed into the ship with all the mass I'd brought from home. My arm flared into red-hot anger again. I spun back out, twirling on the end of the line, as the ship oscillated forward. The moonscape swung past in blacks and whites. Above me, on the far side of the ship, the rocket's attitude thrusters fired a white plume across the dark sky as Eugene pushed the rocket back to vertical. I careened into the ship again, barely catching myself with one foot.

Banging into the side, I was unstable coming down and would have fallen in my stiff suit, if Ana Teresa and Myrtle hadn't been there to steady me.

They helped me unclip my snap shackle. I backed away,

clearing the line as Mikey egressed. Silhouetted against the side, I only knew it was him because they would be coming out in order of seniority.

Across the landscape, a mining rover trundled around the mounded regolith of the lunar colony. Gray dust sprayed up in a rooster tail behind them, arcing back to the ground with perfect trajectories unmarred by breezes. I headed with Ana Teresa toward the gantry to wait for our rescuers, fighting the suit for every step.

Even with that, it was easier to move than any other time I'd been out on the surface. I could feel the heat radiating from the sun and started to sweat inside my IVP suit.

Intravehicular pressure suit. This was never designed to be worn on the surface of the Moon. I had air, but no cooling system. My boots were not rated to handle the sharp glass grains of lunar soil.

I veered, clear of the pad, into the shadow of the gantry. Turning, I was in time to see Helen sliding down the ship. I started counting, in my head. She would have told Eugene that she was last out before unplugging. He'd give her thirty seconds to get clear.

Helen touched down as lightly as possible in an IVP suit. Curt and Mikey stepped in, helping her unclip.

The moment she was free, Myrtle pointed to the gantry. They all turned and ran in the awkward skip-hop it took to fight a pressurized suit on the surface.

Behind them, the thrusters stopped firing, letting the rocket slowly list away from us.

I moved on an intercept course to Myrtle, who should not be alone to watch her husband . . . fall. She hit the edge of the landing pad and turned to face the ship, staring up at it as if she could see into the command module at the very top. Helen stopped by Myrtle, offering her gloved hand. I got to them as the thrusters on the far side fired a series of quick noiseless bursts.

The rocket kept falling.

I grabbed Myrtle's hand with my right. She clung to it so tightly that I could feel her palm even through the pressurized layers of rubber and fabric. Inside her helmet, her mouth was moving in constant silent prayer.

She was still in the sun. I dragged them both into the shadow and out of the 173-degree-Celsius heat, heart tight in my chest.

The massive, quiescent landing engines were facing us now as the rocket dropped below forty-five degrees. White plumes kicked out, just visible past the sides of the ship. In the shadow, the lunar surface was cold and sucked heat out of the soles of my feet, but I stayed put, bearing witness as the rocket continued its inexorable path to the ground. No jets. Had he run out of fuel or was he saving it?

The rocket seemed to reach for the surface. Sharp, quick bursts fired in sequence. Dust swirled up in wild spirals, dropping straight the moment the thrusters stopped. Eugene fired them again, in a single long sustained thrust, spraying dust away from the spacecraft as . . .

it . . .

landed. It stopped moving, at rest on its side. Then it rolled, settling with the edge of the damaged landing strut digging into the ground, silent and still.

SIXTEEN

DISASTER ON THE MOON

ARTEMIS BASE, Moon, April 13, 1963—(AP)—Earlier today, a flight from *Lunetta* to the Artemis Base here on the Moon crashed on landing, contaminating the landing field with Aerozine, the highly toxic propellant used by lunar landers. Though no lives were lost, Mrs. Kenneth T. Wargin, wife of Gov. Wargin (Kansas), suffered a broken arm. This crash was apparently due to the same retro-thruster which stuck on Lunar Shuttle 1063 two years ago. This is the first rocket to the Moon since last month's failed Sirius IV launch. The resulting explosion of that rocket cast debris over a wide field close to the nation's capital. Officials at the IAC say that the fact that neither incident resulted in a loss of life is a testament to the systems and training they have implemented. Critics of the program, however, point to the increase in aerospace disasters as a sign that the space program has pushed too hard and too fast. It is only a matter of time, they say, before the IAC loses the passengers with the rocket.

EVEN ON THE Moon, with the same recycled air that circulated through the rest of the colony, the sickbay's filters could not mask the hospital smell of disinfectant and sickness.

My left arm felt unnaturally heavy with the weight of the cast. Ironic that it felt heavier on the Moon than it did on Earth. I sat in one of the plastic chairs that populated the colony. Lightweight, easy to assemble, and generic gray.

Myrtle sat in one next to Eugene's bed.

He lay on his side, knees drawn up under a thin white sheet. Eugene wet his lips and asked, "So . . . Does anyone besides me think the ship was sabotaged?"

"That's a frightening proposition." I wanted to shout that it had definitely been sabotaged. I had a coded letter to Kenneth burning a hole in the thigh pocket of my trousers until I could get to the teletype machine. "What are you thinking?"

"Besides the thruster? The argon cannister for the egress slide was empty. It wasn't when we launched."

I inhaled sharply. "Not just damaged in the crash?"

"Helen said the seal was broken and it had been drained." The corner of his jaw tensed. "I checked it as part of my prelaunch walk-through."

The FBI's restriction to keep the Lindholms in the dark was foolish. But . . . but Eugene had brought sabotage up on his own. If I didn't mention Icarus or share classified information that I'd learned from my briefing, then maybe we could still work the problem. "Do you think it's linked to the rocket that crashed?"

"Yeah . . . You're supposed to be the secretary for LCA Frisch?" Eugene rubbed his forehead, as if just the thought of the Lunar Colony Administrator was enough to give him a headache. "I tried to tell him that I wanted to speak to him privately, but with the rest of the staff around it was hard to push."

"And you should rest." Myrtle ran her hand over his brow, drawing circles at his temple as Eugene let his hand drop away. "You don't have to be a hero all the time."

"There's an active saboteur on the Moon."

"We don't know that." She pulled her hand away and smoothed the fabric of her trousers as if she were straightening a skirt.

"Drained argon tank. Thruster? Nathaniel was poisoned—"

"That was on Earth." She stood and walked around the bed to check Eugene's IV drip.

"Yes, but . . ." I looked at Eugene on the hospital bed. His face was ashen and tight with discomfort. "I think we can argue that Eugene *was also poisoned*."

"It's food poisoning." Eugene cut a glance to Myrtle and then back to me.

He wanted me to keep quiet about the fact that someone had very probably poisoned him so that Myrtle wouldn't worry? We were so far past that, it wasn't even worth trying. "Food poisoning can be deliberate. The fact that you got sick and no one else did is telling."

Myrtle moved to the foot of his bed, smoothing the thin blanket over him as she went. "That could have happened in Brazil."

She wasn't wrong, and it was the preferable scenario. "So you're saying I shouldn't talk to Frisch?"

"I'm saying that . . ." She sighed. Yanking on an end of the blanket, she made a neat corner and tucked it under the mattress. "I'm saying that I don't want to suspect the people I live with up here."

"I don't want to suspect the people at the IAC, either."

"That's just— It's different for us. For the full-timers, I mean. The trip home for our son's graduation was the first time we've been back on Earth in over a year. There are only about three hundred people on the Moon. We're too small a community to start suspecting everyone."

Suspicion and paranoia were never good, and in a group this small, they would be meteorically bad. People would turn on each other. Divide into groups. Things would get personal real fast. "All right. I take your point. So what's your suggestion?"

"Talk to Frisch. There's not a lot—" Eugene shifted on the bed, closing his eyes.

I jumped up, too high, and had to catch myself on the ceiling. My cast thunked against the plastic, sending a dull jolt through my arm. Myrtle rounded the end, moving in lunar gravity with grace, and scooped up a bin to hold for Eugene.

He opened his eyes and waved her away. "Cramp." Straightening out, he said, "At least I'm done with the barfing phase. Be glad when the shitting is—"

"Eugene! You watch your language."

"Woman, Nicole is a damn pilot. The day I shock her with my language is the day I invent a new word."

"What about me?"

"You?" He snorted. "You're supposed to be nice to me on my sickbed."

"I cleaned your ass. I don't know what else you want."

He laughed and it sounded so good. "Here you were complaining about *my* language."

Laughing with them, relieved for a moment to have something to laugh at, I said, "I'll leave you two lovebirds to your ass-wiping. I've got an appointment with the LCA."

"Thanks for that." Eugene let his head drop back onto the pillow. "See you in church tomorrow?"

I stopped in the doorway, raising an eyebrow. Putting aside all other questions . . . "Do you honestly think you'll be out of here?"

"It's Easter." He shrugged as best he could, lying on his side with an IV in his arm. Damn pilots. "I'll be fine."

"Lord save me from having to wrangle this man." Myrtle looked at the ceiling. "Lord, give me strength to survive his obstinance and—"

"*My* obstinance?"

I escaped the crossfire and stepped out into the hall. It was empty and quiet save for the Lindholms' cheerful argument and the distant whir of the centrifuge room. For a moment, I was alone.

The wave of emotions that I needed to manage rose up, grief and rage and terror pressing against the backs of my eyes and crowding the soft palate of my mouth. Kenneth would have been in a room like that, months ago, and he would have been alone.

I closed my eyes. My hands tightened into fists, nails pressing against the plaster cast. I did not have time for this.

* * *

WITH A CLIPBOARD under my good arm, I bounded through the newest corridor of the Moon Artemis Base in the forward-leaning lunar walk that was the most efficient way of travel. My first couple of hours back on the Moon were always a little awkward as my body recalibrated to the presence of gravity after days without it. You could spot the experienced lunar dwellers by their walk.

I stopped at the entrance to the small tube buried in the regolith that served as the outer office for Lunar Colony Administrator Frisch. Dull gray plastic created a wall for the LCA's inner office decorated with an outdated calendar on one side and a star chart for a trans-Earth orbit on the other.

Through the translucent plastic sheeting of the "door," I could hear Curt's voice. "With respect, sir, I was the pilot."

"I am aware of that, Lieutenant Frye. However, the IAC's policies are quite clear." Frisch was Swiss but had learned English from a Brit so always said things like "Leftenant." It sounded like an affectation every time. "This is not a permanent state."

"It is not fair. Carmouche, in particular, was nowhere near the controls."

"Did she, or did she not, provide you with the calculations for the landing?"

"Her calculations have nothing to do with the hand controller failing. Come on, you know that. And Mikey? If he wasn't giving me good instrumentation readings, I wouldn't have been able to set us down at all."

They had grounded all of them. I clenched my teeth and patted the sheeting in what passed for a knock on the Moon.

"Yes?"

I slid the plastic aside. "Sorry to bother you . . ."

"Ah, Mrs. Wargin." LCA Frisch hunched over his desk like an anemic stork. His Swiss pallor was even more pronounced on the Moon than it had been on Earth. The man needed to spend more time in the sunlamp room.

Curt was standing in front of his desk, arms crossed, and had that extremely neutral expression of someone who is trying not to scowl. "Oh good. You can back me up. They're grounding Helen and Mikey. I get needing to do that with me, but for Pete's sake, it shouldn't affect anyone else."

I winced. He wasn't going to win this argument, and as a rookie, he wouldn't know that. Frisch was a rule-bound bureaucrat through and through.

"I'm grounded too." I waved my cast. While I agreed with him, I also needed Curt to go away so that I could talk to Frisch. "It's not unreasonable for them to want to examine Helen and Mikey's involvement."

He took a deep breath as if he were going to yell and then sighed, fingers tightening on his biceps. He did have nice biceps, but I digress.

Frisch nodded. "It is only until after the investigation, which we will conduct as efficaciously as possible."

Curt stared at the floor, mouth compressed. "So, do we have any active pilots right now?"

"Yes. Of course." The administrator of the Moon lunar colony swept his dishwater-blond hair back from his high, peaked forehead. "This will put us on a tighter rotation, but nothing unmanageable."

It's funny how the brain will draw connections. Eugene was down for the count with the food poisoning. I was out. Curt, Mikey, and Helen were out. Now, there were some pilots already up here, but when they rotated back to Earth in two weeks, that would make us severely short-staffed. In fact, Frisch might have to schedule some of the rookies who had flight as a secondary qualification.

Was the intention to activate a pilot who otherwise wouldn't have had access to a ship? Or was it just a side effect of trying to kill us all on landing?

And then, because I am very good at manipulating people, my brain went one better. Could I have faked that thruster failing? If I had been piloting, could I have done a controlled landing that looked like a crash? Probably. Yes. Curt was being awfully pushy for a rookie on the Moon. Did he really care about his copilot and Nav/Comp this much or was he just trying to "prove" that he was one of the good guys?

There are times when I hate my brain. But it serves me well, so I made a note to myself to keep an eye on Curt.

I held out my clipboard, which had random paper on it, to LCA Frisch. "Would now be a good time to speak with you about the Icarus program?"

His eyelids fluttered several times in rapid succession. Why were all of these men so terrible at poker faces?

"Y—yeeasss . . ." He swallowed, and his smile would have fooled no one. "Would you excuse us, Lieutenant Frye?"

"Of course. Sir." Curt turned on his heel, overbalancing in the light gravity of the Moon. I reached out to catch him as he compensated badly. He shot me a strained look and nodded his thanks. Moving more cautiously, he fumbled with the plastic sheeting and left the administrator's office.

Frisch met my gaze with a thin smile, glancing at the door. We both waited, in silence, for the sound of footsteps bounding off rubber to fade down the hall. "Forgive me, but I was unaware that you were involved in the Icarus program."

"Director Clemons read me on before we left." I gestured to the chair. "May I sit?"

"Of course." He stood carefully in the tiny space. "May I offer you some tea? I have a new pressure kettle so I can get boiling water that's hot now."

"Thank you." I sat on the chair and rested the clipboard in my lap. "Director Clemons sent me with a package for you, which is unfortunately still on the ship."

"Ah. The engineers tell me that we have to wait for the propellent to sublimate off the surface before they can stabilize the spacecraft enough to unload the cargo."

"I see." It would take a full lunar day, which was nearly two weeks, for the sun to crawl across the surface and reach into all the shadows. "I can give you a verbal report when you're ready."

He turned so his beak of a nose was in profile. "Go ahead with your report."

I told him about the Sirius IV crash. I told him about my plane. About the POGO's hydraulic lines. The other small "accidents" that had happened around the IAC, like shorts, propellant leaks, and sticky valves. I told him about the argon tank for the slide.

When the kettle boiled, Frisch poured water into a teacup for me. "Sugar or cream?"

"No, thank you."

"Hm . . ." He handed me the cup and sat down. "And you say that Major Lindholm asked you to speak with me?"

I nodded. "Independently, he suspects sabotage. I would strongly recommend reading him on."

The LCA dropped a pair of sugar cubes into his cup and shook his head. "Not at this time. I'll confer with Director Clemons."

"Which brings us back around to the problem that the codebooks are still on the ship." I pulled a sheet from under the random ones on my clipboard and held it out to him. "May I offer a possible solution for that? I'll be expected to send a letter to Kenneth after the crash and no one will look twice at it."

He reached across the table to take it, frowning. The ever-present fans stirred the air as he read it, and even though I'd handed it to him, I tensed a little at sharing a letter to my husband. Frisch sipped his tea, still frowning.

I finally set my cup down on the table and said, "The first letter of each sentence." I'd worried that it was blatant, as codes went, but I wasn't sure how else to signal to Kenneth that it was there.

"Ah!" He held the cup to the side and nodded. "Very good. I would not have spotted the code, without your hint. Do you think he'll catch it?"

"I don't know." I took the page back and secured it to the clipboard until I could get to the teletype machine. "Kenneth won't be looking for one."

Although my question about the flowers was also code. I was hoping that if Kenneth didn't see the first letter signal, that my reference to Nathaniel would make him take another look, but I couldn't tell Frisch about either of those. Secrets upon secrets.

"Do you want me to adjust the message to ask about Major Lindholm?"

"Not at this time." Frisch set his cup in its saucer. "We've not had problems here, so I think it can wait until we retrieve the codebooks."

Wait? He thought it could wait? I pressed the clipboard against my knees and remembered to speak as a subordinate because LCA Frisch valued hierarchy. "I'm so sorry, sir. I think my verbal report may not have been clear . . . The indications are that Icarus has come to the Moon."

"Correction. It is *possible* that Icarus entered your ship at some point. Whether or not he is on the Moon is another question." He picked up his cup and smiled at me over it. "I am certain it is very exciting to be involved, but let's not allow our imaginations to run away with us, hm?"

I have so much practice at smothering rage that I could let the wave of heat wash over me without driving the clipboard into his forehead. But only just.

13 April 1963

Dear Kenneth,

First letter home and I'm already reporting trouble.

This isn't going to become a habit, I promise, but I am going to presume that you are already aware of the events surrounding our landing. Everyone here is talking about the fact that Eugene pulled off a miracle, although I doubt the papers back home will report his exact words, which were "Holy shit, that worked." Love, I trust that you weren't so concerned that you felt the need to buy me flowers. Like I could stop you.

Clearly, you are going to be distressed because my arm is broken. Luckily, it is only a hairline fracture. Even so, the medical staff here are—if you'll forgive me—over the Moon to have an actual break to study. My first break, too, which is surprising given that there are plenty of skinned knees and sprains in my past. One surprising side effect is that I will apparently make it into the history books as the first broken arm on the Moon. Needless to say, I find this a dubious honor. Still, I am strangely thrilled to have a cast for people to sign.

Perhaps less thrilling is Ana Teresa's prescription for daily centrifuge chamber treatments. A weekly X-ray study to monitor how I heal is also in order. Centrifuges will be necessary for our long-term survival on the Moon, but they are evil. Kinetically, it's quite interesting. As I have just learned, for a break to heal properly you need to put stress on the bone. Gravity should help more here than in a microgravity environment like the early space station, before they added the centrifugal ring. Everyone is going on and on about how all they've had thus far have been rodent studies to the point that you would think they are happy I'm injured.

Luckily, our team is settling in nicely and I should be able to continue with their training without interruption. Oh—may I ask you to do me a small favor? Someone here mentioned Kipling's *Just So Stories* and it is bothering all of us that we can't remember the name of the story with the armadillo. The library here doesn't have a copy, so could you look at home or ask Nathaniel, since I know he has one.

Love,

Nicole

SEVENTEEN

IAC AIDE BRIEFED ON MARS EXPEDITION DEATH

Secret Report to Be Given to UN Leaders in the Capital

KANSAS CITY, April 14, 1963—A top International Aerospace Coalition official received today the first preliminary but secret report on results of the investigation into the tragic accident this past November, just one month into the three-year First Mars Expedition. Norman Clemons, director of the space agency, spent all day with a nine-man board of inquiry and then shared the details of that report with the diplomats representing the eight member nations of the IAC. Director Clemons declined to make any statements before or after the meeting.

WHEN I WAS little, Easter Sunday involved a new dress and a bonnet. Bright white gloves. My nanny polished my shoes to a mirror gloss. After church, the extended family would gather on the sweeping front lawn of Cousin Walter's house for an Easter egg hunt. As a teen, I dyed eggs and hid them for my younger cousins, imagining the day when my child would toddle after them.

When I got married people kept asking when we would have children. And then . . . we stopped going.

There are no children on the Moon to hide eggs for. Hell, we got our first chickens in the last six months and their eggs had only just made it into the food rotation. I couldn't imagine convincing the IAC to let us dye them for fun.

I did not have a new dress—or any dress, for that matter. Bonnets and hats were beyond silly up here. I had a delicate pomona green silk scarf to tie around my neck and a white linen blouse, which I'd brought up to celebrate the lunar colony's move to a "shirtsleeve" environment after years of wearing flight suits and carrying a safety helmet. With that I gussied myself up as best I could and went to church.

Not because it was Easter, but because Eugene and Myrtle were my friends and this was important to them. We didn't have ministers or rabbis or imams—not formally—but we did have members of all of those faiths who found ways to have worship services. There was no church. No mosque. No sacred space, unless you counted Lunar Ground Control.

"Church," in this instance, met in the restaurant in Midtown. Le Restaurant, because the Moon has only one and it is run by a French couple who are beautiful cooks and not terribly original with names. I stepped through the airlock from the "Baker Street" gerbil tube into Midtown and had to resist the urge to latch it shut behind me. The lunar colony now had electromagnetic latches that would let the doors swing shut in case of a breach.

My chest expanded a little as I crossed into the large, open dome of Midtown. The light is always the first thing that catches me. Even with filters to make the dome translucent, Midtown is flooded with vivid white light during lunar day. It caught on the edges of the cubicles and silvered the rubber walls. Midtown used to be our only habitat, with everything crammed into it. Now, the upper floor functioned primarily as a recreation space with a running track circling the living quarters that lined the walls.

Even on Sunday, people loped along the track, getting in their hour of IAC-mandated exercise. Guitar music floated through the "streets" formed of storage containers. In the middle of it all was Central Park. Coming from Earth, the pathetic patch of green was unworthy of the word "park." Six raised beds grew a collection of weeds.

But I still had my Earth lenses on. By next week, this would seem to be a paradise of living matter. The weeds made sense in nutrition-poor soil. I had enjoyed more than one delicious meal involving dandelion greens or roasted prickly pear.

"Nicole!" Myrtle stood with Helen near the dandelion bed.

"You can settle an argument for us." Helen beamed at the flowers as if we hadn't just left the lushness of Brazil. "Does communion wine need to be grapes or would dandelion wine work?"

I held up my hands. "You are asking the wrong person. I nearly stayed in bed this morning."

"I was going to say . . ." Helen wore a smart salmon-pink linen top with a deep turquoise rhinestone peacock that was probably the only peacock in space. "I don't think I have ever seen you in church."

"Eugene invited her yesterday." Myrtle laughed. "This might be our Easter miracle."

I tried not to stare at the empty space where Eugene should be. "I suspect the miracle is that you convinced your husband to stay put."

Myrtle rolled her eyes. "He's already in there."

"Ah . . ." I glanced at Le Restaurant, which was a cubicle facing onto Central Park. "Didn't want people to see how shaky he was?"

"Remind me why I married a pilot?" She wore a navy blouse, nipped in at the waist with a broad white patent leather belt, over a pair of matching navy "moon" trousers. The ankles were snugged tight beneath the soft drape with matching navy buttons. Somehow, she'd brought a beautiful navy toque up with her. On her, the hat wasn't silly; its veil and flower details were glorious and made me reconsider my wardrobe choices. "That man . . . Lord help me, I love him, but he's going to be the death of me."

As we walked toward Le Restaurant, I lowered my voice. "How is he?"

"Better. But I'm not sure how much of that is just gravity."

"He is definitely better than he was in the CM." Worry pinched Helen's brows. "I thought we were going to run out of emesis bags."

The trouble with zero-*g* is that there's nothing to hold food down in the stomach. So if you have gas, it doesn't rise above the solid matter, it pushes it out. Burping is likely to lead to some form of upchuck. So intestinal distress? It gets messy, fast. Even 1/6 *g* was enough to let gas rise and help food stay down.

I held the door for Myrtle and Helen. It looked like the Arnauds had painted Le Restaurant since the last time I was up. The plastic floor had a wood-grain pattern, scuffed in places to reveal battleship gray. Blue-and-white braided pads, made from uniform discards, somehow made the ubiquitous gray chairs look like garden furniture.

At the front of the room, Eugene was looking better, but then scrubbing vomit out of your hair will do that. He sat, talking with a couple of people and nodding earnestly. For all the world, he reminded me of Kenneth talking to constituents.

"We should talk about husbands sometime."

"Why? What did yours do?" Myrtle stepped into the tiny six-table restaurant and oriented immediately to Eugene the way a solar panel aligns to the sun.

I opened my mouth to brush her off, but all of my fear crowded my throat. I had to swallow before I spoke. "Noth—"

"Don't nothing me." She held up a hand. "If it's none of my business, say so. But don't lie. Not on Easter."

Biting the inside of my lip, I sighed. Fixing my gaze on the faux wood floor, I gave a small shrug. "He had a . . . health issue while I was gone last time. And did not tell me."

"Oh, for the love of—" Myrtle pinched the space between her brows. "Men are . . . How do they survive to adulthood?"

"It is one of the great mysteries of the universe." Helen clucked her tongue. "Reynard had never understood that one must sweep under the bed. I will not describe to you the horrors . . ."

I laughed with the women, although to be honest, I hadn't known that either. I'd grown up with a maid and a housekeeper. I hung my own clothes up, and some of my society friends thought I was progressive for doing that.

More of the small congregation was filling the space. "I'm going to grab a chair before they're all gone."

Myrtle gestured to the front of the room. "Come sit with us. He'll be up in a minute and you can have his seat."

"I'm more comfortable in the back, if you don't mind." I winked. "Besides. Just in case . . . I don't want to be in the spatter zone."

She snorted. "I tried telling him . . ."

Squeezing my arm, Helen turned to walk to the front of the little room with Myrtle. I settled in a chair in the back corner, where I could see the door and count who came and went. Whoever had written the Manifesto was Christian.

And this was Easter Sunday.

When Deana Whitney started to sing the communion hymn, I'll admit that my mouth dropped open. She had a clear, high soprano that seemed to float as if free of gravity's lightest touch. I'd trained with her and had no idea she had a voice like that.

There is a fountain filled with blood, Drawn from
Emmanuel's veins;
And sinners, plunged beneath that flood, Lose all
their guilty stains;

One by one, the small rows of congregants stood to file to the front. Aldrin had used part of his personal allotment to bring wafers and wine to the Moon.

I sat in the back corner and made notes of everyone who attended. Those who stood and those who, like me, stayed seated. I'm not sure how many lunar citizens were Christian, but fifty-three came to the church service.

Eleven people from our rocket attended, not counting the Lindholms, Helen, and me. It was more than I expected, honestly, but I suppose a near-death experience coupled with a major religious holiday would instill piety in the most doubting of souls.

> The dying thief rejoiced to see That fountain in his day;
> And there may I, though vile as he, Wash all my sins away;

From that list of eleven, I set aside the people Clemons had rotated onto our team. Ana Teresa, Ingram, Tierra, and Faustino. My reasoning was that they had gone through additional screening and had all been on the Moon more than once. If they wanted to cause trouble, they had prior opportunity.

Unless, of course, they were a recent recruit or this was all timed to coincide with activity on Earth.

That left me with a list of eight.

1. Kadyn Murphy
2. Imelda Corona

3. Vicky Hsu
4. Ruben du Preez
5. Danika du Preez
6. Curtis Frye
7. Luther Sanchez
8. Catalina Suarez Gallego

"Not going up?" Faustino sidled into the row in front of me.

At my husband's church, I would have taken communion because to not do so would have invited questions. Here . . . It felt disrespectful. I shook my head. "Thank you, no."

"I know he's not a real priest, but I promise you won't burst into flames." Faustino cocked his head. "Wait. I forgot who I was talking to."

"I'm kicking your chair through the rest of the service."

He smirked and tipped his chair back, which is dead simple in light gravity. And still just as annoying. I kicked his chair.

Even with my accurate warning, he jumped and overcompensated badly. Faustino's chair fell backward. I reached for him and his chair back cracked against my cast.

I gasped as a lightning bolt went off in my arm. But I caught him. Granted, he didn't weigh much more than ten kilos. Still, the moment I pushed his chair upright, I tucked my arm against my body, pressing my right hand to the wrist as if I could stop the throbbing.

"Nicole!" "Are you okay?" "What happened?"

And just like that, my discreet corner in the back became

a cluster of people. Luther held out a drinkbag of water, as if that would help.

"Hey! She kicked my chair over." Faustino wasn't serious, but I had left my sense of humor somewhere outside the lunar sphere of influence.

"It was that or your balls." The moment the words were out of my mouth, I regretted them. Makeshift though this was, it was still a sacred space to the people here. "Sorry—I'm sorry. That was inappropriate."

"Aw . . ." Faustino gave a one-sided shrug. "No. I'm the one that's sorry. I shouldn't have been messing with you, being hurt and all."

I drew myself up straight. "I'm fine. I caught you, didn't I?"

"Pilots . . ." Myrtle stood in the aisle and shook her head at me as if I were a child. "Always the same."

At the front of the room, Aldrin held up his hands. "Did everyone get communion who wanted it?" He waited a beat. "Great. I guess that's it, then."

Curt jumped up. "Um. Friends? Before we go. I'm . . . I'm new up here, but my family always had an egg hunt, so—so I brought some candy eggs and hid them in the park out there."

There was nearly a mass exodus, including me, but Faustino waved his hands. "Wait! Closing prayer at least."

So close. As people settled back into their chairs, Vicky held out my little notebook, which was scuffed from being underfoot. "I think you dropped this."

"Thanks." I took it back and tried to appear attentive as Faustino moved to the front.

"Let us close today with a prayer of Thanksgiving."

The rustle of clothes accompanied his words as the small congregation bowed their heads. "O Lord, our Heavenly Father, we most humbly beseech You to grant Your forgiveness through the merits and death of Your Son, Jesus Christ, and through faith in His blood . . ."

I ducked my head, not to pray, but to update my notes on who had taken communion.

The page was gone.

I riffled through the little book. It was scuffed and pages were bent, but only one was torn out. Around me the rest of the congregation stood up.

"Easter eggs in the park!" Curt's voice sounded impossibly young and energetic. "And I have a prize for the one who collects the most."

I knelt, looking on the floor. The page wouldn't be there, but I wanted it to be. There wasn't anything terribly incriminating on it, was there? Just a list of names. Not as though I'd written "MY LIST OF SUSPECTS" at the top or anything.

"Everything okay?" Curt stood at the end of the row of chairs.

I sat back on my heels. "Oh, yes. Thank you. I just dropped something in all the hubbub earlier."

"Can I help?"

I waved him away. "Thanks, it's fine. Besides you should be out looking for eggs, right?"

He glanced over his shoulder, corner of his mouth dimpling. "That's the problem with hiding them. I know where they are." His smile deepened and the damn man got down on his knees. "But hey! You've lost something, so that's kind of like hunting for Easter eggs, right? What are we looking for?"

On Earth, the easy lie would have been that I'd dropped an earring. I didn't wear them up here. So I went with an almost truth, just in case he actually found it. "A list. I was going to set up a bridge night and had started making a list of potential players."

"Neat." He slid chairs aside, peering across the floor. "Am I on there?"

THE MONDAY AFTER our arrival, which would normally have had me doing a refresher flight on a BusyBee instead had me fighting a typewriter. I pulled the paper out from the glossy black behemoth and glared at it. Somehow, I'd managed to insert the carbon paper backwards. Again.

In theory, acting as Frisch's secretary made sense . . .

In practice, even if my arm hadn't been broken, I was a hunt-and-peck typist. On Earth I had a private secretary. Why would I need to know how to type? Or use carbon paper?

Down the corridor, Danika and Ruben du Preez skip-walked toward my tiny desk with the overconfident speed of new lunar residents. Day one, people went very, very slowly. Day two, they thought they had it figured out. Warning them didn't make a difference, so now I waited for—

Ruben's head hit the roof of the tunnel after he pushed off with too much force. The white South African electrician flinched and overcompensated, coming down at an angle against the gently curved wall. Danika was going too fast to avoid him and the couple fell in a tangle of limbs.

I pushed off from my desk, moving with a low lunar lope. When I got to them, I pitched back on my heels to counterbalance and stopped as neatly as if I'd never lived on Earth.

"Are you okay?" I offered my hand to help them up.

Danika rose to her knees, leaning forward to check on her husband. "Well, thank you. At least falling is here softer."

"Talk for yourself." Ruben kissed his wife on the cheek and ignored my hand. "There is not an angel who crashed on you."

"If I were an angel, surely I would have flown."

"Are we not in the heavens now?" Ruben clambered, carefully, to his feet. He smiled as he helped his wife up. "But we're doing really well."

"I'm glad to hear it." Angels. Heaven. They'd been in church yesterday . . . Might they have written a manifesto filled with scripture?

Danika checked the bobby pins holding her long blond plaits in a crown around her head. "It's not like the POGO?"

I laughed, shaking my head, and tried to dial my suspicious brain down as I led them back to my desk. "Not so much. This happens to everyone. Just remember that slow is—"

"Fast." Danika rolled her eyes. "Slow is fast. I know. I keep telling him, but—"

"But I am so excited to here be." Ruben grinned and then his smile faded. He cleared his throat. "Is the administrator in?"

"I'm sorry, the LCA's not available right now." I can't type, but I know what a secretary sounds like. "Is there something I can help with?"

Ruben chewed his lower lip and shifted his weight. "It's truly nothing."

"Then it will be easy to resolve." I sank into my chair, pulling a notepad close. "Let me guess. You've just realized that it's the fifteenth and you forgot to pay your taxes."

"What?" Ruben looked completely baffled.

"Taxes in the United States are due today . . ." I shook my head. The FBI thought that Icarus was American and these two were South African. "Never mind. How can I help?"

Twining her fingers together, Danika winced. "I hate to do this, but . . ."

"But our country has these regulations. Understand that we don't have a problem." Ruben held his hand out. "Truly. But we have to—"

"We have to file a complaint." Danika swallowed. "The married couple sleeping module is not segregated."

"We like Myrtle and Eugene. But the South African Aerospace Administration stipulates that we—"

I put my hand flat on my desk and barely avoided slapping it. "There is no segregation on the Moon. This is an international colony and local regulations do not apply here."

Ruben sighed with relief. "Thank God for that. We just have to . . ." He waved his hand in frustration.

"We have to make the complaint." Danika's cheeks were pink with a blush. "Can you file it so we don't get in trouble at home?"

I had no idea how to file a complaint. There was probably a form for that. The IAC always had forms and this one undoubtedly had an acronym. "I'll see what I can—"

The lights went out. Aside from the luminescent glow of my Omega wristwatch, the corridor was as dark as a mausoleum.

In the silence, Danika's voice sounded piercing. "Is this . . ."

The lights came back on.

I winced against the sudden glare. Emergency lights. I'd managed to be staring directly at one when it came on. The battery-powered light was an attenuated yellow and gave a jaundiced tint to Danika's fair skin.

Ruben laughed uneasily, looking over his shoulder at the light. "Solar power isn't usually—"

"Shh . . ." I closed my eyes, as if returning to darkness was useful, and I listened. In the distance, I could hear a murmur of other voices as people tried to figure out what was going on. I could hear them clearly. I shouldn't have been able to. The constant hum of fans usually masked that with white noise.

We'd lost all power.

EIGHTEEN

NEGROES AND WHITES REJECT
INTERPRETATION FOR KINLOCH

ST. LOUIS, MO, April 15, 1963—White and Negro leaders here are concerned because the disorders in suburban Kinloch this week have been widely misinterpreted as race riots. They are particularly disturbed because St. Louis, especially in the decade since the Meteor, has made rapid progress in race relationships. Continued success in this field, they believe, will be important to the city's prosperity in the coming years. In retrospect, responsible residents of the community attribute the disorders to pent-up frustrations of underprivileged youths who feel that they will be denied the opportunity to leave the planet Earth.

IT HAD ONLY been fifteen minutes. As power failures go, this was nothing. It wasn't enough time for the temperature to change or the air to become toxic with carbon dioxide, or for me to run out of lighthearted banter designed to distract two new lunar residents.

"Bridge parties give you a lovely chance to get to know people outside of your graduating IAC class."

Danika was chewing on the quick of her thumb. She blinked when I stopped talking. "Oh. That's . . . that sounds pleasant."

I would bet she hadn't heard a thing I said and was responding only to the pause. I kept going, as carefree as I could. "Shall we plan for Friday night? I can round up some other couples."

Ruben looked down the hall at the emergency lights again. "I should try to help."

I shook my head. "The airlocks will be sealed." If there had been a breach, there would be a depress alarm. Ergo, there wasn't a breach, but I felt the absence of my emergency mask keenly. "The electrical engineers on shift will have this under control."

Danika shifted to picking at her nailbed. "Is there something we should be doing?"

I didn't even know if the outage was base-wide or just the admin module. Once upon a time, I would have opened procedure manual 49.a and turned to section 137.c, ready to troubleshoot with my teammates. Now . . . now we had a crew to handle power fluctuations.

Not that we'd had a power failure since very, very early in the colony's history. This wasn't a coincidence.

"We are doing exactly what we're supposed to. Stay put. Don't panic." They should know this. It had been covered in their training. "The less we move, the less oxygen we consume."

"Should we be talking?" Danika's eyes had grown wide again.

"Why don't we—"

The lights came back on. The air stirred with a gentle hum. A sigh of relief escaped me, because I had been pretty firmly convinced that someone had taken out the entire power module. I checked my Omega. Sixteen minutes.

What mischief could someone do in sixteen minutes without power?

I stood from behind my desk. "Come on. We can do the airlock check."

I led them down the hall to the airlock, but Aahana had beaten us there. She was snugging the door against the electromagnet that held it open. She smiled brightly and gestured at the airlock. "Look! My first power restoration. I checked the Delta-v pressure and did a visual confirmation. How did I do?"

"It looks great, Aahana." I examined the airlock door with false enthusiasm, because the question in my mind was . . . why was she here? Aahana was a geologist and had no reason to be in the AdminMod. She should be prepping to head out to the South Pole mining outpost. "What brings you here?"

"I was coming to see you. Curt said you were putting together a bridge party, and, well . . . if it's not too presumptuous, I adore bridge."

"Perfect! I'll add you to the list." I smiled back at her, wondering if she'd had as much practice as I had at looking sincere. Most people hadn't. Fishing in my pocket, I dug out a pen. "Oh! Here. Want to sign my cast? In fact, you all should. First broken arm on the Moon. We can all go into the history books together."

Through this process, I learned that Aahana and Danika

were both right-handed. Ruben was a lefty, like me.

And that Aahana had dirt under her nails. As a geologist, that was probably normal.

April 16th

Dear Nicole,

First letters are a mysterious and wonderful thing.

Despite the number of times you have gone to the Moon, without issue, I find myself worrying about every launch as if it were the first. Of course, the fact that this one resulted in an injury is troubling, but I try to console myself with the notion that it is an example of the success of the IAC's systems. No loss of life occurred, which is surely a miracle given the harshness of the environment. Every possible precaution had been taken and the training of the team paid off when a malfunction occurred—would that those were truly preventable.

Tediously, I must ask you once again to please be careful. Even from here, I can feel you rolling your eyes at me, but please, dearest, I do not want to have to buy flowers for your grave. Listen to the doctors and do as they tell you. Likely, you'll ignore this plea of mine, so I will keep it short and simply say that I wish you loved yourself as much as I do.

Friday, I'm going ahead with that task we were discussing, which I wish I could delay but some of our friends are suggesting rather strongly that the time is right to do it now. Rather strongly is an understatement. I have received no less than five phone calls this afternoon, urging me to move ahead. So, I'm afraid that I need to ask a favor of you. Can you forgive me for having company when you call home this week? He is quite enamored with what he perceives as the romantic quality of receiving a call from the Moon, so I hope you'll be willing to talk to him for a bit.

Can you forgive me for that? Home seems quite empty without you. Even Marlowe seems to miss you and wanders from room to room crying. Cats are not as inscrutable as they might seem. Kitten season is starting here and I'll admit to being tempted to bring one home to keep Marlowe company.

But you will be wanting other news from home. Let me catch you up on Nathaniel's health. At our last visit, he was in much better shape and spirits, which I attribute entirely to the good care that Hershel has been taking of him. Some of the Astronauts' Husbands Club members wanted to put together a gift basket for him, but I suggested that we leave his diet to the doctors at this time. They grumbled, of course, but saw the sense in it. I am trying to stop by every time I am in Kansas City. Nathaniel tells me that the doctor has given him permission to return to work for half days after Passover. Good luck keeping him to half days . . .

Speaking of people who work too hard, and I am not speaking of myself here, did I hear that Eugene was sick during the flight? Tell him that I send my regards and hopes for a quick recovery. Oh, I don't expect him to slow down, any more than you would. Really, you astronauts are supposed to be the best and brightest, but I find it impossible to believe any of you has a care for your own health. Every night, I look at the clouds and find the glow

of the Moon through them and think of you. Sending you
all my love . . .
    Kenneth

SIXTEEN MINUTES. IT had been more than twenty-four hours
since the power outage and nothing else had happened.
But I couldn't stop thinking about how much mischief I
could do in sixteen minutes.

I could have poisoned the water supply in that time. I
could have fouled the CO_2 scrubbers in that time. I could
have vented the oxygen tanks in that time.

I leaned over Frisch's desk and placed Kenneth's letter on
it. "Clemons wants you to check the explosives stores."

He lifted his beak of a nose beneath brows raised as if
for flight. "At the mining outposts?"

"Do we keep them elsewhere?"

Frisch snorted and lowered his head, looking at the
letter. He rubbed his forehead as if it hurt. "Does he say
why?"

"Not in this." I glanced at the wall calendar. Four days
since we had landed. "Any word on getting my package
off the ship?"

"They're still putting the scaffolding in place." He
lowered his hand, reaching for his tea. "I'll put in an order
to have the explosives inventoried."

"By whom?"

He's naïve, but he's not an idiot. If Icarus was on the
Moon, and we didn't know who they were, then they could
very easily lie about the inventory. I saw the realization

go through his face and into his limbs as he sagged. Leaning forward, Frisch rested his head on his hands. "All right . . . The two of us will conduct the inventory." He sat back and looked at the cast on my arm. "Can you pilot a BusyBee with that?"

"Fortunately, yes. The controls are designed for right-handed pilots." My control would not have as much finesse as I would like, but it would be acceptable. "When would you like to depart?"

Frisch pulled his calendar toward him and flipped through some pages. Days. He was turning the calendar days into the future. "The rest of this week is packed with meetings and . . . *Gott im Himmel*. I think Saturday the twenty-seventh is my next unscheduled day."

Today was the sixteenth. "With all due respect, there is enough urgency here that clearing your schedule might be warranted."

"With all due respect, I have never found that English idiom to convey respect of any sort." He pushed his limp blond hair back. "I did not say I would wait until the twenty-seventh only that it was my next free day. It is too late to depart today. Tomorrow I have meetings that I cannot put off."

"Sir—"

He held up his hand to stop me. "I am responsible for the health and safety of three hundred and twenty-eight people. The main spaceport is blocked by a downed rocket and contaminated with propellant. The supplies that were on your ship are still, in fact, aboard it. When I say that I cannot reschedule tomorrow I am not being an obstructionist. I am prioritizing because I am the administrator for this colony. Are we clear?"

I had to borrow a trick from Elma and count to ten in my head before I could answer him calmly. "Yes, thank you. Please let me know when you would like to go and I will make the arrangements for the BusyBee."

"Two days. The nineteenth." He turned the calendar around to face me. "And since you're supposed to be my secretary . . . Clear these appointments, will you?"

NINETEEN

100 LEADERS ASK FOR END OF VIOLENCE

Mississippians Appeal for Prosecutions in Rioting

JACKSON, Miss., April 17, 1963—Continuing clashes between Meteor refugees evacuated from New York and residents of Jackson have spilled out of the city into the surrounding suburbs. More than 100 business, industrial, and professional leaders of Mississippi appealed today for an end to violence in the state and prosecution of those responsible for mob rioting.

WAITING IN THE communications module for my call to Kenneth, I sat in one of the ubiquitous plastic chairs suspecting everyone. It had been two days since the power outage and nothing had happened.

I sat next to Wafiyyah Zinat Abbasi. The young botanist was on her third lunar rotation and had been on our shuttle as a replacement. Theoretically, Clemons had swapped her in because she was trustworthy, but I barely knew her. Until this trip, we'd been on alternate rotations.

"Have you been out to the caves yet this trip?" Framed

by her headscarf, her skin had a youthful glow that I achieved only by dint of a healthy layer of cold cream every night. "They finished wiring the grow lights since the last time I was up. Oh! It is so exciting."

I held up my cast, winking. "They're keeping me pretty close to the main base right now."

"Oh, of course." Wafiyyah's face grew serious and I regretted the joke. "How is your arm?"

"Good, thanks." Honestly, the cast was worse than the chin bandage. That, at least, I had been able to have fun lying about. "Wish me luck reassuring my husband. Who are you calling today?"

"My lab partner. Huda. Her asthma is very bad, so she is not rated for spaceflight, but is the smartest person I know regarding amelioration of soil. I wanted to run some numbers past her."

"You shouldn't use your personal call for that! Come by the administrator's office and I can let you use his line."

"Oh, no . . . This is something I should be able to work out on my own."

"It's still work." I dug into the thigh pocket of my trousers—by the way, the best thing about life on the Moon is all the pockets—and pulled out my little notebook. "You get one personal call a week. Don't throw that away on business."

She flushed. "Well, it is. I mean. We are . . . we are very good friends and so it is mostly a social call. The numbers are just an excuse."

I smiled to myself as I pieced things together. Holding the little pen out to her, I gave her the courtesy of pretending not to notice that this was probably a romantic call. "You haven't signed my cast yet, have you?"

There were probably better ways to track who I had spoken with, but I was in no danger of losing this set of notes. Wafiyyah was right-handed and had a small, elegant signature.

"Nicole Wargin." Faustino beckoned me.

"Faustino . . . What's got you working in comms?"

He shrugged. "Birgit has a cold so I offered to cover."

"Not . . . not food poisoning?"

"No. Only achy, from what she said." He shrugged again, which was apparently how he communicated. "You're in booth five."

The phone booths were not much different from ones on Earth. They were little boxes, just big enough for a stool with a phone mounted to the wall except they are made of plastic and aluminum rather than wood and glass. Murmuring snippets of conversation snuck between the thin walls.

". . . couldn't make your recital . . ."

". . . see what the doctor says . . ."

". . . two sticks of butter, a cup of . . ."

". . . you said Mrs. Which did what?"

I pushed the door open and settled on the plastic chair. It was still warm to the touch from the last caller. The receiver is the same plain black form as on Earth, so when you pick it up, the lightness surprises you.

"Operator." The voice on the other end of the line was a young woman on *Lunetta* orbital station.

"Earth, Kansas long distance, please."

"Surely." In my ear, the sound changed subtly, as if the gravity well of Earth were audible, and a different woman said, "Long distance."

"Operator, I'd like to place a call to Topeka: Oldfield three-seven-two-three-four."

There was a pause, as my voice transmitted across space to her. Not long, but enough to feel the difference. "Surely."

She didn't ask me to deposit coins. The IAC paid for these weekly calls and I was deeply grateful every time I called home.

The phone rang, cutting off mid-bell. "Hello, Kenneth Wargin speaking."

I sagged against the side of the booth because part of me had been convinced that his letter to me had been someone else writing to mask another heart attack. My voice shook with relief. "Hello, love."

A gap, just enough to make me think the line had cut out, even though I know it takes 1.3 seconds for my voice to get to Earth and another 1.3 seconds for his voice to return to me.

"Nicole." His voice went rough, just on the shape of my name. His next breath caught against the receiver. "I have been . . . worried."

"I'm sorry. I'm okay, really." I glanced down at the cast, wondering if his "company" was already in the room. It was our code for a reporter. If he'd said "guest" it would have been a diplomat of some sort. Just in case he wasn't alone, I was circumspect with my reply. "It's more annoying than anything."

"I'm glad to hear that."

"Did you buy me flowers?"

He chuckled. "No. I hope that doesn't distress you."

I wrapped the cord around my knuckles. "Not in the slightest. What would I do with flowers on the Moon, anyway?"

"Well . . . maybe you'd like a book instead? Nathaniel caught me up on what he's been reading lately."

I wanted to just talk to him, freely, but our private conversation was now about to be in service to the Icarus project. And people wondered why our marriage was in trouble. When did we get time for ourselves? But I know my job and I kept my voice light. "Did you have a book in mind?"

"I did. *The Long Tomorrow,* by Leigh Brackett. And since I can't deliver it to you, I checked to see if there's a copy in the lunar library. Got myself a copy to match, so I can imagine us reading together. Just the two of us."

"You are the most romantic thing . . ." That was unexpected. If I understood him correctly, he wanted to use a book code for *us,* not for IAC business. I had two simultaneous reactions. One was that I was delighted to have some form of privacy with him. The other was fear about what had gone wrong that he needed a code to talk about. "I'll check it out as soon as I'm done here."

"We'll talk about it in our next letter, hm?"

I nestled the phone against my cheek and something made a *boing* almost like a comic book spring being struck. "Did you hear that?"

"The spring sound?"

"Yes . . ." In the silent space between us lay a question:

Was it just a sound, or was someone intercepting the call? Clemons had said that Icarus had someone in comms. Sending radio waves from the Earth to the Moon required the Outer Space Tracking Network. Back when we'd started, the IAC had just had a single radio dish and the rotation of the Earth had caused loss of signal except when Kansas was pointed at the Moon. Now, the OSTN had three large-array radio dishes on Earth coupled with satellites. None of them should have sent a sound back into our call. "How odd."

"It's likely from the apparatus that the reporter set up in the office." Kenneth sighed heavily and his speech slowed down, distress building pauses between his words. "I . . . should bring them in. I'm sorry, Nicole. It's just that the political pressure to announce is significant. Denley imposed the curfew and it's not . . . good. I think . . . Being a formal candidate will give me the ability to cut through the noise. A little."

"I understand." There was a time when we talked about the opera on these calls. "Any new talking points in your platform?"

"The usual. Emphasizing, perhaps, that the distress of Earthbound citizens is real, while drawing a line between peaceful protests and the extremism of the Earth Firsters. Only don't mention the—"

"Don't mention the Earth First movement by name. I know . . ." I sighed and closed my eyes. "I know my job. I'll be the loving and supportive space wife."

"Nicole . . ."

"It's all right." I sniffled and sat up a little straighter

in the booth, as if the person on the other end of the line would be able to see me. We had the technology to do a visual conference, but that was something only the engineers and flight controllers used. I had no access to it for private business. "Let me talk to the reporter."

THE NICE THING about working in Frisch's office was that I had easy access to personnel files. I consulted my cast to see who I was still missing and pulled Kadyn Murphy's file from the cabinet. According to his file, he had listed chess as his recreational activity.

So I headed to the cafeteria where our chess club met. It is a long, low room that occupies half of the main floor of the Habitation Module. The curving walls glow during the two-week lunar day thanks to lightwells from the surface. Tomorrow, the light would drop abruptly as we shifted to night and fewer people would find reason to congregate here.

Amid the scent of cabbage and rehydrated beans, pairs of men and women huddled over chessboards along one wall. Some of the games had spectators, chatting quietly. Helen's was one of those, unsurprisingly. She was leaning back in her chair with an incipient smile waiting for her partner to realize that he had already lost. Oh, occasionally someone beat her, but the woman had been a chess champion in Taiwan before joining the IAC.

She glanced up as I crossed the cafeteria and waved. "Nicole! What brings you here?"

So much for being discreet. Half of the club turned around to look at me. "Just grabbing some lunch."

One of the guys raised his eyebrows. "Isn't it a little late for lunch?"

"I was busy and forgot to eat." I shrugged. "You know how it is . . . Call it an early dinner if it makes you more comfortable."

"They have cabbage!" One of the long-timers grinned. "And lettuce from The Garden!"

"I'll check it out." To look as though I had a legitimate reason to be there, I wandered over to the food stations to see if there was anything palatable. Kadyn Murphy should have been easy to spot. At nearly two meters, he was one of the taller colonists. I had loved talking to him in training, because his accent shifted from Caribbean to a painfully sterile, but beautifully posh Queen's English in this gorgeous baritone. I caught him singing once. Just once, and I was determined to get him to sing again.

I stopped by Helen's table and waited until her turn was over. Chess is not my game, but Helen was playing white and there were not a lot of black pieces left on the board. "Have you seen Kadyn?"

She shook her head. "Not since yesterday for his rover checkout."

"They have you doing rover training?" Teaching people to drive on the Moon wasn't the worst job, but it was so far below her skill set as to be laughable.

"At least it gets me out of the habitat." She glanced around the room, frowning. "But I am surprised that Kadyn isn't here. We played a couple of times on Earth and he is not terrible."

One of the long-timers whistled. "Whew. Remind me

not to play him if the Abbess thinks he's not terrible. That translates as damn good. Begging your pardon."

"The Abbess?"

Her partner reached for a pawn and sat there, resting his fingers on it and frowning. "Like a girl bishop. The bishop is one of the most powerful pieces on the board, but is underrated because folks focus on the queen. People never see Helen coming."

Two tables down, one of the women from the computing department leaned forward. "Kadyn is sick."

"Oh ho! And how do you know that, Garnet?" Another computer nudged her. "Got your hooks into him already?"

"No! It's nothing like that." Garnet's blush said that it was exactly like that. "We're just friends is all. I knew Kadyn on Earth but I deployed first. We played chess together. That's all."

My brain circled back to his absence. "I'm sorry to hear he's not feeling well. He didn't look like he had space sickness on the flight out."

She wrinkled her nose. "Just a stomach bug. He thought he might have come down with the same thing Major Lindholm had."

"Oh, that's too bad." Was someone up here deliberately tainting food? My veins chilled. "He was one of my trainees, so I'll go look in on him. Is he in his berth?"

"I'll go with you." Helen slid her chair back.

Her partner moved the pawn forward a square. "Does that mean you forfeit?"

"No. That's check and mate in two." She slid her bishop

across the board and took out his remaining tower. "Your move."

As it happened, Kadyn was not in his berth. He was in the men's lavatory audibly retching. It was, shall we say, not an appropriate time to question him.

Crossing the hall from the West Bay men's quarters, I kept thinking about how sick Eugene had been on the ship. Was this the same thing? Or had someone poisoned him the way they had Nathaniel? And if so, why would someone target Kadyn? He was a botanist.

In the corridor between the men and women's quarters, Helen touched my arm gently and stopped next to the spiral stairs in the center of the module. "What is going on?"

"What do you mean?"

Her mouth twitched. "After you told me about Nathaniel and FBI, you had several meetings with Clemons before launch. He put you in secretarial. You cannot type. The IAC has made a number of schedule changes, specifically swapping out personnel. All of this points to something larger being off-nominal."

"There was a rocket crash." I tried to laugh it off, but Helen is smart enough that she could fill in the gaps. "Are you missing a favorite chess partner?"

She gave an aggrieved sigh. "I respect secrets, but I would rather have you tell me that something is off-limits than have you give me misinformation. A hole in the data, I can work with."

It is harder to lie when I don't want to. "A hole in the data sounds like one of Elma's absurd double entendres."

"I want you to appreciate that I am not pushing you

for more information." She drummed her fingers on the curving banister surrounding the stairs. "My curiosity is very strong."

"I appreciate it more than you know." And I could relate to it. If I had been in her shoes, I would have chipped away at the edges of the secret until I could pull it out into the open. I had to get her off this topic and, hoping a location change would help, walked to the door of the East Bay women's quarters.

"At least we've confirmed that Kadyn is really sick." Helen followed me into the "lobby" of EBW, which was a small semi-circular common area that served as a buffer to the crew quarters ringing it. When the base was new, we'd slept in bunks, but with the expansion had come private rooms. Tiny private closets, really.

I shrugged, shifting the focus of the conversation further from the Icarus project. "True. It's hard to get men to give a health report accurately under the best of circumstances. For all I know, 'under the weather' actually means dying. They all think they can out-macho a germ."

"Do you want to tell me what is going on with Kenneth?" Helen kicked her shoes off and set them by the door to her cubby. In the middle of our common room, a giant braided rug softened the gray floor. The blues and whites of cast-off uniform fabric had been pushed to lilacs, lavenders, and deep purples thanks to dye that someone had brought up.

I glanced at the closed cubby doors. Even if we had the common room to ourselves at the moment, there was no guarantee that people weren't in their rooms. From experience, I knew exactly how little sound the plastic "doors" kept out. "Oh, he was just so . . . typical. He was sick and didn't tell me." But I made eye contact with her and mouthed "heart attack."

Her eyes widened. "Is he . . . is he all right now?"

I spread my hands wide as if I could encompass all of my frustrations. "That's what he tells me."

Helen stared at me for a moment. I am honestly not sure what she saw, or if she simply played through the possible scenarios the way she ran chess moves in her mind. What I know is that she crossed the small room and folded me into a hug.

I did not mean to weep. But at least I was silent.

TWENTY

FIRST LADY OF THE MOON?

By Julie Holderman, Special to The National Times

TOPEKA, Kan., April 19, 1963—After Gov. Wargin became the first in his party today to announce his candidacy for the Democratic nomination for president, many noted the absence of his wife from the activities. This reporter reached Mrs. Wargin at her residence on the lunar colony to inquire about her ability to perform her duties as First Lady from the Moon, should her husband achieve his goals. "Naturally," she said, "the needs of our great nation come first. While I love serving my planet through my work here, I look forward to coming home to Kansas."

Mrs. Wargin told me that she was wearing a simple blue pantsuit, with a brooch given to her by her mother, and had her hair trimmed in a fashionable "lunar" cut.

FRIDAY MORNING, I carried my bag to the #3 airlock, which just accommodated lunar buses or BusyBees. I was pretty confident that my cast wouldn't be a problem, but the smart thing to do was to run myself through a sim to make sure I understood the limitations in my range of motion in the context of the cockpit.

BusyBees were basically just a tube with an engine, and on other trips I flew them multiple times a day, running construction workers, miners, or geologists out to different sites. Elma described it as being a glorified bus driver.

And yet . . . there was a joy in flight, regardless of the craft. Flying in vacuum is so unlike flight on Earth. Some of it is the lack of wind, sure, but the rest is the way your relationship with mass and velocity takes on the purest expression of each. And flying in space is different than flying over the Moon. Both are vacuum, yes, but the clarity of the lunar landscape gave a sense of speed that you did not get in true space.

And then, of course, night flights when the stars come out. I remember seeing stars from the surface of Earth, but I've always been a city girl, so they have been muted pale things that fluttered against a sky lit by sodium vapor lamps. On the Moon, when I'm flying at night, it is as if someone has spilled diamonds on black velvet. I would kill for a gown that looked like the stars in space.

I'd also kill for a chance to launch one of the big rockets, but I wasn't holding my breath on that.

FRISCH DUCKED HIS head into the cabin. "Oh, good. You're here." He slung his Crew Preference Kit off his shoulder and headed for one of the lockers. "As soon as you're finished with precheck, we can suit up."

I tucked the log back into its elastic holder and stood up. "Ready."

"I find myself unsurprised." He pushed his CPK into the locker, efficiently securing the bag with temp-stow tethers. "I was thinking to start with the South Pole outpost, since it is further, and then work our way back."

"That sounds sensible." I followed him out of the BusyBee to the donning room adjacent to the airlocks.

The room hummed as the morning shift prepped for a day of work. Some were heading out to do construction at the habitat being constructed in the Marius Hills lava tube and others to do prospecting for water at the South Pole. When the base was new, the donning room had been coed to conserve space. I think at some point the original plan had been to split it the way they had the crew quarters, but that never rose to the top of the priority list. The fact was that getting into an intravehicular pressure suit didn't require being naked.

If we were going to be donning a full extravehicular mobility unit, that would be different, but the IVP suits we wore in transit were just meant to protect us in case of depressurization. We didn't need a liquid cooling and ventilation garment or a battery pack, just an umbilical to connect us to the main ship for air, power, and comms.

On my first trips to the Moon, we had helped each other change in tiny spacecraft crowded with instrumentation. These days astronauts had the luxury of having suit techs on the Moon. This was an unexpected benefit of the fact that the colonists weren't as highly trained as full astronauts. Having someone else check and prep the suits was safer.

My assigned IVP suit hung in place on the 6B donning stand with several others, prepped for surface work as I'd requested on the work order. Florina Morales smiled as I walked over and held out a pair of under-gloves. "Good morning. How was Earth?"

"Hectic." I took the thin, warm wool, which would protect my hands inside the suit, and answered the question she was really asking. "I saw your husband at the Astronauts' Husbands Club. He's doing well."

"He got a promotion!" She smiled, cheeks glowing with pride. "Project lead."

"Splendid!" Her husband had been there the night Nathaniel was poisoned. Did that mean I needed to suspect her, too? Mr. Morales was an engineer with access to the rockets. Potentially, he had fallen in with the wrong crowd because he wanted his wife home. Or perhaps I could go an hour without suspecting the entire Moon. "You're heading downplanet on the next rocket, aren't you?"

"Depends on how quickly they decontaminate the spaceport." She glanced across the room to where Frisch was pulling on his own set of gloves. "Have you heard anything?"

So many things. "Not really." The fabric glove was snug going on over my cast. Fortunately, the IVP gloves and boots were modular so you could swap them out depending on activity. "Did you put the extra-large glove on the left?"

"Yes, why did you—" She did a double take at my cast and beckoned for the under-gloves. "No. Absolutely not."

"It's the same connector."

"No." Stepping forward, Florina took my cast in hand and worked the cloth glove backwards as if I were a child. "First of all, did you clear flying with medical?"

I had not, but neither had they told me that I was grounded. "I'm flying with LCA Frisch."

"Mm-hm. Second. The suit is not rated to have hard plaster inside it."

"There will be wool between me and the suit."

"No. It's not rated to have anything rigid inside it. At all. No. Absolutely not." She stepped between me and the suit, arms crossed, as if I were going to push her down and get into it anyway.

I pivoted, looking for Frisch. The BusyBees were rated as a shirtsleeve environment for passengers. Even the pilots flew with helmets open, so perhaps I could go without a suit. Even as I thought that, the smarter, more professional part of my brain told me that this wasn't a problem that I could solve. Space was dangerous. It was easy to get complacent with shirtsleeves and cafeterias and movie nights, but we were still in space.

Vacuum was just outside these walls.

Frisch had zipped the front of his suit. His tech stood by with outer gloves ready. Taking the gloves, Frisch looked past the tech to me. He cocked his head to the side in question.

Grimacing, I lifted my cast. His gaze went from it to the suit to the gloves. His head dropped back to stare at the ceiling. With a sigh, he handed his gloves back to the suit tech and beckoned me.

Swallowing, I arrived at his station as he undid the outer zipper on his suit. My cheeks felt like a plasma field on reentry. "I'm sorry, I'll find another pilot for you."

He undid the inner zipper, looking over my shoulder at the clock on the wall. "I'm going to my office. If they can get someone suited up by noon, then we'll reverse the planned order, starting with the near outpost first." Shrugging the suit off his shoulders, he squinted at the floor. "Failing that, we'll reschedule for Monday."

That was three days away. "Perhaps tomorrow would—"

"I have explained my restrictions and am uninterested in discussing this here." Frisch stepped out of his suit, leaving the tech to gather the heavy thing from the floor. "If going today is advisable, then find me a pilot who can actually fly."

I CLIMBED THE spiral stairs into the common area of the married couples quarters. It had fewer doors, as each cubby was a double-wide. The floor outside the Lindholms' had a welcome mat that Myrtle had crocheted from strips of discarded crewlock bags. I stood on it, raised my hand to pat the plastic sheeting, and hesitated. It was so early. They might still be asleep.

I patted the door. Through the thin plastic, Eugene said, "Who is it?"

"It's Nicole."

Myrtle murmured, "Isn't she supposed to be flying?"

I heard cloth rustle and the bed creak. A moment later, belting a bathrobe, Eugene pulled the sheeting open and looked out. "What's wrong?"

Holding up my cast, I tried to be as clear and direct as possible. "I can't wear a suit. Frisch needs another pilot by noon."

He straightened, pulling his head back with understanding. "I'm cleared to return to duty, but medical won't clear me to fly until next week."

"Sorry—I wanted to know if Myrtle was available."

Inside their cubby, the bed creaked again and a pair of feet slapped against the plastic floor. Myrtle rose to stand behind Eugene, a scarf knotted around her hair. "What do you need?"

"Frisch needs a pilot to take him out to the mining outposts."

She shrugged and nodded. "Sure. Give me a minute."

Eugene frowned and put his hand on her shoulder. "There are other pilots on the roster . . . What are you asking her to do, really?"

She raised her brows at him. "Are you trying to make a decision for me?"

"I'm just asking a question."

Myrtle snorted and glared at him, tugging the strap of her negligee up on her shoulder. Pursing her lips, she still wore the remnants of that glare when she faced me and I nearly took a step back. Honestly, I was surprised that Eugene hadn't been incinerated.

"Give us a minute." Myrtle pulled the plastic sheeting closed.

Through the door, I could hear furious, hissing whispers.

I stepped back, crossing the room to one of the plastic chairs on the far side. Sitting down, I looked at my cast, running my fingers over the plaster. Names covered it in loops of cursive Roman alphabet, flourishes of Arabic, and intricate hashmarks of Chinese. I still needed to talk to Kadyn, Imelda, and Luther. Maybe I really should throw a bridge party. I could ask Myrtle if she'd host with me. We could use one of the common rooms or perhaps I could host a small fête at the gallery.

The plastic sheeting slid open. I stood, and walked back, meeting Myrtle as she stepped out into the common room. She carried a CPK bag in one hand, and shook her head, lowering her gaze to the floor. "I have guesses about why you're asking and I resent the hell out of you for not telling us. But I acknowledge the necessity."

"We haven't finished discussing this." Eugene stepped out, zipping up a flight suit as if he were going to fly in her place. "Who wears the pants in this family?"

"On the Moon?" Myrtle shouldered her CPK bag. "We both do."

I HURRIED DOWN the corridor in the AdminMod and dashed through Frisch's outer office. "I've got a pilot for you— Sorry." I stopped just inside his door. Ana Teresa sat in the chair opposite Frisch's desk and her shoulders were turned down as if she were exhausted. "Myrtle Lindholm is heading to the airlock to meet you."

Frisch looked up from his desk, where he was reading a sheet of paper. He checked his watch and sighed.

"Dr. Brandão, I'm sorry but I have another engagement."

Ana Teresa lifted her head, eyes narrowing. "This cannot wait."

"I understand that." Frisch drummed his fingers on the desk next to a stack of teletype pages still in their accordion fold. "You have my approval to proceed as necessary, but use quarantine protocols as the last resort. The short-timers whose tour is up are already delayed because of the crash. Wargin will help you with requisitions and deconflicting the schedule."

Quarantine? I knew there were some people who were under the weather, but I had no idea that it was something serious. "Certainly. We can sit down and go over that after the administrator leaves."

Ana Teresa's nose pinched with displeasure. "This needs to take priority."

Sliding his chair back, Frisch stood with the careful grace of a long-timer. "I should be back from the outposts Sunday, but will be in radio contact if anything needs my immediate attention."

I stepped back, out of the tiny office, to give him space to exit. "I will keep you informed."

"Stop." Ana Teresa stood, more awkwardly than Frisch, pushing off just a little too much and rising onto her toes with the force of acceleration. "You're going to the outposts?"

"Yes . . . Are you thinking the flu is coming from there?"

"No. Did you not read— Flu-like symptoms, not the flu. High fever. Stiff neck, cramps in the legs." She leaned over the desk and flipped to a page deeper in the report Frisch had been reading when I arrived. "There is a significant chance that this is polio."

The room seemed to flash hot and cold. Polio. The numbers rose every year. What had been a childhood disease now took older and older people. Everyone knew someone who had been hit by it. Except . . . "We were vaccinated."

Scowling, Frisch sat back at his desk, scanning the page. "Not those of us on the Moon."

"No one? How is that possible?"

"For accuracy: fourteen people on the Moon have been vaccinated." Ana Teresa's exhaustion seemed to deepen. "Dr. Sabin's vaccine is so new, supplies are limited, we were vaccinating based on launch schedule—the original launch schedule. The new hires have not been vaccinated yet and the vaccines intended for lunar residents were on the rocket that we lost."

"Have you—Tell me that they at least vaccinated the medical staff."

Even her scowl was tired. "I was vaccinated before we left. The other medical staff up here . . . It is a problem."

Frisch turned another page of the document. "You say the early cases were all people who were on your ship followed by people who had contact with them?"

"Correct. The virus is spread through the alimentary tract—the gut—and with Eugene's illness on the ship, our containment was not as good as it should have been."

"Wait. I thought you said Eugene had food poisoning." I had been so certain that someone had poisoned him. If he had been ill with polio, that changed the navigating conditions.

Ana Teresa stared at the pages in Frisch's hand and looked uncertain for the first time, possibly ever. "Illnesses express differently in zero-g, so I might be wrong, but . . . the larger issue is that Dr. Sabin's vaccine uses a live virus. It sometimes—rarely—stays alive in the gut for two weeks. If we had stuck with the original launch schedule, that would have all happened on Earth."

I wanted another chair to appear in the office so I could drop into it. "So, anyone who got the vaccine might infect people?"

She held up her hand. "No. The vomit created the potential vector. My actual concern is with unvaccinated individuals, like the LCA, who had direct contact with Eugene after landing."

Frisch pulled his head back like a stork that had eaten something distasteful. "Me? But I'm not sick."

"You don't have to be sick to be a carrier." Ana Teresa spread her hands. "In fact, you're at your most contagious before symptoms express."

Slumping in his chair, Frisch stared at the doctor. "*Mein Gott . . .*" The pages seemed to wilt in his hands. The administrator licked his lips and lowered his gaze to the report. "There have been no cases at the outposts?"

"Not yet."

He nodded, and I knew what was coming before he said it. I couldn't even argue with him. "Then I cannot go."

TWENTY-ONE

NEW APPROACH TO HOUSING IS WEIGHED IN CAPITOL

Subsidies for Rehabilitation of Rundown Buildings and for Rent Proposed

KANSAS CITY, April 19, 1963—President Denley's housing advisers are studying two significant departures from past Meteor-relocation policy in the continuing effort to help needy families find decent homes.

COMMS WAS PART of the admin module, housed down the hall from Frisch's tiny office. While they could patch through, they couldn't guarantee a secure line into his office, which meant that we had to go to them. The small chamber at the front of comms had a few people waiting in chairs for a call home. Most of them were from one of the European contingents, since the time zones for that worked out best for a day call by Kansas time.

Frisch walked to the receptionist's desk and loomed over her. "I need the IAC secure line, stat."

She didn't blink. "Yes, sir."

"Two headsets." I ignored Frisch's double take; I was not

letting him do this call alone because he would minimize everything.

"Yes." He folded his arms over his chest. "Two headsets, please."

"Of course. And Mrs. Wargin, there's a letter for you in your box." Turning to her roster, she drew her finger down the list. "That booth is in use. One moment while I clear it."

While she went to boot someone out of the secure booth, I could feel the room behind me shift as people realized that something was up. The last thing we needed was for news about polio to get around the colony without being pitched correctly. It could cause panic. I kept my body language as relaxed as I could, but Frisch's shoulders were hunched around his long neck. As much as I wanted to retrieve the letter from my box, I did not want to leave him unattended.

While we waited, I murmured, "What if Eugene goes with Myrtle? They could stay suited."

He pursed his lips and shook his head, voice as low as mine. "I want to speak to the director and see how urgent the matter is."

A scream of frustration built in the back of my throat, but we were going to have Clemons on the line in the next five minutes. I could wait that long. Assuming he was in the office. My smile was placid and encouraging. "That's a prudent course."

"LCA Frisch?" The receptionist reappeared with a group of engineers trailing her. "Your booth is ready."

I followed Frisch to the booth, hearing bits of conversation in French, Swiss-German, and Spanish as we went down the little hall. Regardless of language, the patterns sounded like any call home. Recipes, birthdays, and expressions of longing.

Frisch opened the door and stepped into the secure booth. It was larger than the others, designed to have room for key personnel to make conference calls with the IAC on Earth. I shut the door—an actual door—sealing out sounds of the colony except for the ever-present hum of the fans. I picked up the second receiver and waited with Frisch as we were patched through *Lunetta* to Earth to Clemons's secretary and finally to him.

"Otto." Clemons's British accent rounded the o's in the director's name into baubles. "Is this about the inventory I asked you to carry out?"

No beating around the bush when an off-schedule call came in. Frisch tucked his chin into his chest. "I'm afraid I have not had an opportunity to do that yet."

"That is disappointing."

I could have kissed Clemons, but I held my tongue and did not mouth "see" at Frisch.

"I was going this morning, but we have a developing situation. In brief . . . In brief, we have a possible polio outbreak."

The silence stretched like the kilometers between the Earth and the Moon. I wrapped my fingers in the cord of the handset, pressing the earpiece against my head as if I would be able to wring anything more from the silence. I could imagine the words reaching the director and threads of cigar smoke curling up in shocked exclamation points.

Clemons's gasp reached back through space. "How many cases?"

"Five in hospital, plus another three people who have had fevers. Dr. Brandão is requesting that we isolate the SciMod and quarantine the outposts to contain the illness."

"But she's not sure it's polio?"

"Correct. There have been no instances of paralysis. It may, in fact, be the flu rather than polio." Frisch referred to Ana Teresa's report. "The larger problem is that we don't have the facilities to care for this many sick. I'd like to request bumping the construction supplies from the next launch in favor of a relief package."

"Send the list via teletype and I'll make arrangements . . . It will still be two weeks at the earliest, you realize."

"I do. We shall carry on here the best we can until then." Frisch rubbed his brow. "What are your thoughts on quarantine protocols? It will bring expansion to a halt."

"Have Dr. Brandão confer with the flight surgeons here and we'll do what they advise."

Something on the phone made a noise like a struck spring. Frisch pulled it away from his ear for a moment. "What was that?"

Two different thoughts connected in my head. Clemons had said that comms was compromised and that was the same spring I'd heard when Kenneth and I spoke with the reporter.

I scrawled on my notepad *ICARUS*.

Frisch raised his brows, mouthing the word. He should never play poker.

But I was dead certain we were being recorded. I made

my voice light and unconcerned. "Oh, that was just the satellites doing a handover."

A moment later, Clemons's voice reached us. "Good lord! Wargin is on the line?"

Frisch cleared his throat. "Yes, sir, I thought it advisable to have her here to take notes in case you had anything to add to the polio question."

"Ah . . . Very good." Clemons was a smart man and I could feel him putting the pieces together on the other end of the line. Finally, he said, "And I think she's quite correct about the satellite. The heat of the sun causes things to expand, et cetera."

Frisch's gaze dropped to the word "ICARUS" scrawled on my notepad.

"I agree." The LCA straightened his pages. "I'll talk to Dr. Brandão about quarantine and send you that list ASAP."

Frisch was getting ready to sign off, and they'd dropped the question of the inventory. It was harder to discuss with Icarus listening, but not impossible. I cut in as gracefully as I could. "Director Clemons, it occurs to me that we could still arrange that inventory you requested if the team stays suited."

"Hm. Yes . . . Please make that so. Especially if we are changing what we send, it would be advisable to have a precise inventory. They can take supply drops to the outposts as well." Clemons sighed and I could imagine the exhalation of cigar smoke wreathing him. "Otto. Your hands will be full with this outbreak, so I'm going to delegate everything related to the inventory management to Nicole."

The administrator's nostrils flared. He stared at the booth wall as if meeting Clemons's gaze. "I trust that you are aware her arm is broken."

"Which doesn't affect my ability to reason and delegate." I smiled at him as triumph surged below the surface of my skin. "I'm happy to take that off your plate. Director, I thought I'd send the Lindholms, since they are both vaccinated. Have I your permission to brief them on the goals of the inventory?"

The silence stretched like clouds of smoke reaching for the ceiling.

"Don't trouble them with the details, just what they need to know to do good work."

"Of course." So, I would be able to tell them a little about the saboteur, even if I couldn't read them on fully. That was still something. "Thank you. That will simplify matters. And may I also note that a quarantine would stop movement between modules. You might consider it as a preventative safety measure."

We waited longer than the 2.6 seconds it took for voices to make the round trip to Earth. I hoped, desperately, that it was because Clemons had understood and was considering my suggestion that he proceed with quarantine to keep Icarus contained.

"Yes . . . Yes, we do want to be safe. Proceed with quarantine procedures while Dr. Brandão speaks with the flight surgeons here."

"Very good, sir. I'll do that as soon as we've had an opportunity to prepare appropriately. And I'll send you that supply list. Good day." Frisch ended the call and wheeled on me. "Do not ever undercut me in that manner again."

"I only asked a question."

"Please." He stood, pushing past me. "I know you better than that. You never simply ask a question."

THE LETTER I'D picked up in comms was burning a hole in my pocket. All I wanted to do was read Kenneth's words, and instead, I hurried down the corridor to the port with a Lindholm on either side of me.

Myrtle shook her head with a constant stream of muttering. "And you've known how long? I swear to God you're lucky I don't bend you over my knee and try to knock the sense your mama gave you back into place."

I couldn't even blame her for feeling betrayed. I'd been careful not to say a word of untruth to them, but I had deliberately lied by omission.

"Myrtle." Eugene put his hand on her arm, slowing a little. "You know I had to keep secrets from you during the war. Nicole wasn't doing any different."

"Those secrets didn't endanger me. These did."

I sighed. "It probably doesn't help that I agree with you, but I do." We rounded the corner toward the port. "For the moment, do you feel like you have everything you—Curt?"

He half-knelt, legs at awkward angles on the ground. Sweat drenched his shirt. He had both hands on the guide rails that lined the tunnel, trying to pull himself up.

"Shit." Eugene dropped his bag and bounded forward.

"Oh." Curt smiled at us, that goddamned pilot. "Hi, guys."

"Hey, buddy." Eugene knelt by him. "What's going on?"

"Just doing a new pull-up form." He lifted his upper body a few degrees, and one of his legs almost moved. "See?"

"Curt." I put a hand on his forehead. Heat radiated off his skin as if he'd laid his head against an engine. "Can you move your legs at all?"

His smile faltered. "I could . . . They were cramping. I thought I could walk it off, but . . ." Curt grimaced, looking down at his legs. "I'm in a bit of a pickle."

I exchanged glances with Eugene and Myrtle over his head. Polio hit fast. When I was a kid, there had been a family in my town that had been fine in the morning. In the afternoon, the eldest daughter got a fever. She was dead by nightfall. One after another, all nine of their children got sick. Three of them lived. Two of them paralyzed below the waist. Resting my hand on Curt's shoulder, I asked, "How long has this been going on?"

"I don't know . . ." He shook his head, trying for another smile. "I was walking this morning."

Myrtle had her hands clasped together and her lips were moving, shaping the silent words of a prayer.

"Well, let's get you to sickbay and Dr. Brandão can tell us what's going on." I wet my lips and looked at Eugene. "You and Myrtle go on to the BusyBee. You can call sickbay from there."

Myrtle started. "We can't leave this boy here."

"I'm fine!" Curt waved at her. "They're just pins and needles is all."

"Right." I squeezed his shoulder and stood, letting him

have his denial a while longer. Leaning into Myrtle, I murmured, "Frisch thinks quarantine is just a precaution. He was dragging his heels, but as soon as he hears about this, he won't let you take off. You know I'm right."

"And you know we can't just leave him." She looked down at Curt, who was still reaching for the handrails as if he could pull himself up.

"I'll get him to sickbay. Just go."

In SICKBAY, A miasma of illness escaped the filters. All five beds were full. In my years on the Moon, I had never seen anyone be sick enough for hospitalization. Sprains. Cuts. Bruises. The occasional rookie with a bad case of space sickness. Sometimes a cold. But we went through quarantine before coming up for a reason. The lunar colony was the cleanest, healthiest place that money could make it.

Today, though . . . Imelda was bent over, vomiting. Kadyn had a damp cloth covering his eyes. Birgit from communications. Hans from the mining crew that had helped us out of the ship. Curt . . . All of the beds were full of people moaning or shivering under blankets.

Curt. Kadyn. Imelda. Three of my "suspects" knocked down by polio. Behind me, I heard the click-buzz of the intercom button. "Administrator Frisch? Dr. Brandão here."

Frisch's voice was tinny and buzzed against the walls. "Go ahead."

"I have a patient with paralysis of the left leg and severe weakness in the right." Ana Teresa inhaled and I could feel the weight of what was coming next, even though I already knew it. "I no longer doubt. This is paralytic poliomyelitis."

"Who?" Frisch could have gone straight into procedural, but for all his faults, the man cared about the individuals who were under his care.

"Curtis Frye, sir."

From the bed, Curt murmured, "Ask him if I'm still grounded."

I bit down hard to stifle a moan. He was joking at a time when it was likely he would never fly again.

Frisch's voice shook a little but steadied as he spoke. "I heard that, Captain. Let's get you well first, hm?"

"Yes, sir."

A shiver ran through me.

The rocket that exploded was carrying the vaccines for the colony. Was that the plan? To leave the majority of the lunar colony unprotected and to deliberately introduce polio?

Kadyn's bed was next to the door and I went to him, keeping my voice low and soothing. "Hey, Kadyn, it's Nicole. Garnet at the chess club was really worried about you." He was sick. He was also on the list of people who might be Icarus. If Icarus wasn't acting alone on the Moon, then knowing who he associated with would be useful information. "You know, it would probably help the medical staff if they had a list of everyone you had contact with."

Was I really questioning a kid with polio? What kind of monster was I?

He raised a hand and pushed the cloth back so he could squint at me, brown skin gone ashen. "Garnet's not sick, is she?"

"No, no." But if she had picked it up from him, she wouldn't have been sick yet. It took between seven to fourteen days after exposure for the first symptoms to occur. It would look like a mild flu. She'd get better, and then three days later, the extreme symptoms would hit. For all I knew, she might be running a fever right now. "I saw her last night."

"Tell her that I'm all right. It's just a headache."

Ana Teresa's voice caught my attention. "—recommending immediate isolation. Close the airlocks. Inform everyone to shelter in place until we can get a medical history."

If I was in here when they closed the airlocks, I would be on hospital duty for the duration. And that would also leave Icarus free to operate unsupervised. Frisch sighed into the microphone. "You are correct. I'll do a station-wide announcement."

"Kadyn, I'll go tell Garnet that you're all right." I walked calmly to the door, but as soon as I crossed the threshold, I ran for Midtown. To move from one module to another, you pretty much had to pass through Midtown.

But if I were Icarus, I'd be much more interested in the fact that Lunar Ground Control was housed in Midtown. From there, you could control everything.

FEELING MORE BATTERED than I had since my early days of training, a part of me fully expected the Midtown airlock to slam shut behind me. It didn't. The LCA and Ana Teresa must still be talking. How long did I have before Frisch closed the doors?

Drumming the fingers of my good hand against my thigh made paper crackle.

Kenneth's letter. With everything happening this morning, I'd only had time to glance at it, but that had been enough to know he'd sent me a coded message as promised in our phone call. I needed the book he had mentioned, which gave me my order of operations. I would go to the library, retrieve *The Long Tomorrow*, and then let Frisch know where I was.

The library was built into the outer curve of Midtown. Unlike Le Restaurant or my little gallery, this had been purpose built by the IAC for morale. Every month, we received a small shipment of books to add to the library.

I pushed through the plastic door and the smell of paper, ink, and glue made my shoulders relax. The walls were lined with shelves filled with thin paperback books printed on flimsy onionskin paper. Since my last rotation, someone had added a new bookcase in the middle of the room, built from plastic panels and support strut discards from the habitat expansion.

Catalina Suarez Gallego sat at a folding table, working a crossword. She was on my list of possibles, but I hadn't been able to catch her for conversation yet. Across the little room, Danika was flipping through the card catalog with her lip tucked between her teeth.

Their unruffled calm would vanish the moment Frisch made his announcement.

Heading to the fiction shelves, I waved at the other women. The shelves were wire mesh aluminum attached to the long curve of the outer wall. I ran my finger along the shelf under the books. Bates, Bouzerous, Brackett . . . Tipping my head to my side, I read the titles and . . . *The Long Tomorrow* wasn't there. I stepped back, staring at the shelf as if that would make the book appear. To be fair, sometimes distance helped, as my eyes aged.

I checked the shelves above and below it. I scanned the ones to either side.

No book.

There was no librarian on duty. Checking things out was on the honor system and so was returning them. Although not to the shelves. Oh, originally, we had put the books back ourselves, but a couple of years ago the IAC hired a comms operator who also had a degree in library science. You could have launched rockets with her rage at the way cataloging was done. Now we had a small returns cart.

I went to the cart and flipped through every book on it. Nothing. I kept telling myself that *The Long Tomorrow* was a popular book, that someone else just had it checked out, that the spring sound on the phone had been a coincidence.

I kept up that interior litany as my stomach tightened. The other women glanced at me as I searched, but even on the Moon, even without a librarian, none of us would talk in the library. Trying not to look frantic, I went to the catalog and flipped through the cards of books that had been checked out, looking for *The Long Tomorrow*.

I found that. My eyes ached from trying to focus on

the tiny letters, but there was no mistake. It had been checked out day before yesterday—the day I had talked to Kenneth.

By Vicky Hsu.

Coincidences did happen sometimes, but this seemed unlikely. At the same time, why would she as good as announce that she had taken it by writing down her own name—Writing. I rotated my cast, looking for Vicky's signature.

She had signed back near the elbow. I laid the card next to it. Even accounting for the differences in surface and writing utensil, the signature on the card was not Vicky's handwriting.

So whose was it? I slid the card over my cast, looking for a match. I couldn't see them all well and some had been written across. Catalina and Danika were both staring at me. To be fair, that was not necessarily suspicious, because I *was* acting odd. Looking embarrassed was not hard as I showed them my cast and whispered, "It itches."

Danika closed the card catalog drawer and walked toward me. In the distance, a metallic clang sounded, followed by three others, one on top of another. The airlocks closing. Danika and Catalina both turned to look out the library door. Hell, I did too. Even knowing it was coming, that sound sent chills down my spine.

Three chimes sounded as the public-address system activated. "All station, all station, all station." Frisch's voice was crisp, but unhurried. "This is not a drill. I repeat. This is not a drill. We are beginning immediate isolation procedures and have moved to temporary lockdown mode. Please refer to section 141.a in the emergency manuals for the full protocol."

Danika put her hand over her mouth, eyes widening. Catalina's expression did not change.

"The colony is experiencing an outbreak of polio and, as a precaution, we are limiting travel between modules while we assess the scope. If any member of the colony experiences fever, aches, vomiting, or a stiff neck, they are to report immediately to sickbay via intercom for instructions."

"Ruben is sick." Danika hurried toward me. "He threw up all night last night. Does he have polio?"

Catalina took a step back from Danika, and I couldn't blame her. If Danika had been with her husband, she was very likely a carrier right now. I caught Danika's shoulders. "Where is Ruben?"

"In our quarters." She sagged at the knees, and I honestly thought she was going to faint. "The airlocks are closed."

"It's all right . . ." It wasn't all right, but I guided her to a chair. "Danika, look at me. Hey. Hey, look at me. Breathe."

"He doesn't like being babied. He told me to go."

I knelt in front of her. "Are you an expert in polio?"

She shook her head. "We barely have any cases in South Africa."

"Exactly. We'll report to sickbay that he needs attention, but there's nothing you could do for him even if you were there." My heart tore into pieces as I spoke, because these were exactly the arguments Kenneth had used on me about his heart attack. "The best thing you can do is to stay here and do your job."

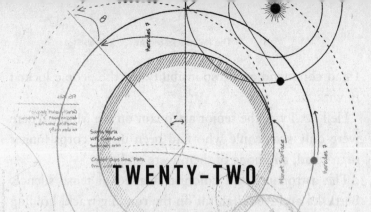

TWENTY-TWO

FAMINE SAID TO IMPERIL LIVES OF THOUSANDS IN JAVA AREA

SEMARANG, Indonesia, April 19, 1963—(UPI)— Famine is threatening the lives of people in the overpopulated regions of central Java, according to reports here. About 12,000 people are being treated for starvation in hospitals overflowing with patients and in emergency camps set up by the Indonesian government. Thousands of refugees have been displaced by rising ocean levels and are streaming into central Java after having bartered their meager possessions to get food. These already overcrowded cities and towns had been stretched thin after absorbing an earlier wave of refugees during the Meteor Winter and the new influx of refugees has pushed them to breaking. Officials said 50 victims are known to have died while under medical treatment. Official estimates of deaths caused by food shortages range as high as 500 a month.

PEOPLE WERE CLUSTERED around me as I stood at the intercom by the Baker Street airlock as per item 47 in lockdown procedure 12, subsection 3.a—Isolation. As the senior astronaut in Midtown when the airlocks shut,

I had command and responsibility for the people locked in with me.

Hell . . . I was the senior astronaut on the Moon. There were only six people who had been in the corps longer than I had, and none of them were up here.

The astronauts and colonists waited in tense silence. Bertuska and Abdullah sat on the running track, holding hands so hard that their hands must ache. Chaffee twiddled his thumbs, leaning against the wall of the airlock. There was a cluster of people who had flown up with me, standing at the top of the stairs leading down to Lunar Ground Control.

I stood with the relaxed posture and alert, calm expression that I had perfected as the wife of a politician. I knew how to stand on a stage and look as though I could be useful while doing absolutely nothing. It was its own form of helpful, even in this circumstance.

I would prefer to have talked to Frisch from one of the cubicles erected for offices or my little gallery, but per protocol the LCA would buzz this intercom because it was centrally located in the hab.

The intercom's buzz, when it came, made me tense inside my skin. "Midtown station, Frisch. Report."

"This is Nicole Wargin reporting for Midtown station." The grill of the intercom was shiny brass and had bits of dust caught on the edges. "I have taken roll call, as per protocol. We have thirty-seven people here. Let me know when you are ready for the list of personnel."

LGC would have done their own roll call, locked into the floor beneath us. Below them, the computer department would have done the same. There were probably sixty people in the Midtown dome right now, isolated from each other as if we were in separate ships.

"Any fevers?"

Behind me, the crowd shifted uneasily, and I could see people tucking their hands under their arms as if that would keep them from touching someone with the disease. "None presently, but Garnet Cunningham and Vihaan Bhatrami report having had a fever within the last week. We also have fourteen people who have had community contact with known patients within the last seven days."

"Understood. When you set up sleeping quarters, separate the community contact individuals from the rest of the group." He continued, oblivious to how people shifted away from each other with unconscious tension.

Wait—I was wrong. The fourteen people with community contact were finding each other and stepping to stand apart from the rest.

"Isolate Cunningham and Bhatrami for the time being and monitor them."

Other colonists clustered, gesturing as if they were working on sleeping arrangements. I was so proud of these people. They were terrified and still starting to work the problem. With my finger back on the buzzer, I said, "We're making arrangements now."

"Can you accommodate five additional people?"

I ran through the available space, thinking about how to isolate groups. I could rig old-school hammocks the way Midtown used to be kitted out. "That should be fine."

My finger was still on the talk button when a lone man

muttered, "Then what the hell's the point of quarantine?"

I turned, looking for him. Brooklyn. Tenor. A slight nasal buzz.

"The point is to minimize risk." Frisch's voice was as cold as the shadow of the Moon. "The people who were training on the lunar rover will be safer if we are not asking them to shelter in an airlock or a vehicle parked on the surface. I trust that no one takes issue with this."

The crowd was silent.

"Happy to welcome in the rover team. As you heard, I've got a bit of an audience here and some people are wondering about their colleagues. Any word from the outposts?"

That wasn't something that would have been on my normal set of responses in this scenario, but I wanted to know if Eugene and Myrtle had reported in.

"Yes, I've spoken to them and to the pilots who were en route. They report that everything is nominal."

Nominal, which in this context I took to mean that the Lindholms had completed their inventory at the first stop and that nothing was missing. I was deeply relieved, but it also made me wonder if I had been jumping at shadows.

On the other hand, there were two more outposts to check.

Dear Nicole,

I was privileged to attend the birthday celebrations for Mrs. Denley at the Mayflower Room in Kansas City, although I believe that I was invited in your honor as I was one of the few unaccompanied gentlemen in attendance.

President Denley was courteous, although he did tease me about entering the race so soon, and said that he would try not to take it as a personal affront. Then he asked where you were, as if the fact that you are on the Moon were not a matter of public record.

Red Skelton performed, appearing out of a large gift box, to do his routine and amused us all with something like a hundred and two really good quips. He invited Mrs. Denley to join him on stage, which I think startled her, so she took three ladies with her. It was hard not to watch and imagine you in her place up there. The whole affair was quite grand, with a band that I'm guessing had at least nine trumpets. You would have liked her gown, I think, which avoided the floral motif so common these days. I inquired for you and am told it was French brocade.

Which reminds me . . . I was going over the accounts with Chu and there were some charges that I was uncertain about. I do hate to ask you to do something so tedious, but could you look over these numbers and tell me what they were for? Gowns? Hats? Gloves? The vagaries of keeping you dressed on Earth continue to elude me. Please tell me that you understand my puzzlement at least.

$191.14 on the 6th

$47.19 on the 1st

$10.01 on the 3rd

$215.20 on the 12th

$73.09 on the 10th

In other news, I have succumbed to the kitten temptation. One of my staffers brought a box of the fuzzballs into the office in a display of ruthless strategy. I have brought home a bundle of gray fluff with iridescent eyes like one of your brooches. Her current name is Tiny Monster, although I will try to think of something more elegant for her. Your suggestions are welcome. Marlowe is baffled by her and tolerates her clumsy pouncing.

I can't wait to introduce you to her.

All my love,

Kenneth

I HAD SPENT the day organizing sleeping arrangements, coordinating meal pack distribution, getting instruction from medical about what early symptoms to watch for, but the people in the Midtown quarantine zone were so professional and focused that once I had delegated tasks, I had nothing to do except brood. I needed to do something concrete.

Hanging a picture in the gallery was an inconsequential act, but I wanted to accomplish one damn thing when everything else was out of my control. Using a Pistol Grip Tool with my right hand was annoying, but it was something I could do.

The door to the gallery opened and a figure stepped in. She paused as her eyes adjusted to the dim room. Aside from the skylight and five gallery lights, which I'd brought up one at a time in my personal weight allotment, I kept the gallery dark. "I thought I might find you here."

"Helen?" Relief flooded through me at the sound of her voice. I stepped down from the bench I'd been standing on and lowered the PGT. "You were in the rover training group?"

"Correct. So . . . why aren't you in the AdminMod?"

"Oops." I gave a half-smile and shrugged. "I just happened to need to run an errand and it's a compleeeeeeete accident that I somehow didn't make it back to the AdminMod before the airlocks closed."

"Mm-hm . . ." She dropped onto the bench. "New exhibit?"

"It's overdue. Work built up while I was away." Plus, my broker on Earth had managed to fetch some good prices for Ariela Housman's calligraphic series of astronaut portraits. I wiped my hand over my face and sat down, with the world held at bay in shielded darkness. "What the hell are we going to do?"

"Hire a curatorial assistant?"

I lowered my hand. "You know what I mean."

"Yes. That is why this was called a joke." She sighed and rested her head against the wall. "I don't think this is a problem we can solve."

We sat on the small bench in the gallery and stared at the sculpture in the middle of the tiny room. Fernando Botero had chiseled a smooth, haunting figure out of lunar basalt. It had the rounded curves of a fertility figure but represented a spacewalker, seated. He'd come up from a residency in Paris, because France is still civilized and had spent the resources to send an artist to the Moon.

The rest of his sculptures had been sent down to Earth to fetch prices that were literally astronomical. I'd bought this one. There were other pieces in the gallery that I loved, but none of them made me feel as at rest as this did.

I needed that rest, desperately.

But I didn't get to have it. I pulled the letter from Kenneth out of my pocket and passed it to Helen. A code from my husband was not restricted by the Icarus project. "What do you see?"

She tilted the thin paper into the nearest beam of light and frowned at it. "Is it . . . a book code?"

"Yeah."

Do you know what it is like to hold a letter from your husband and know, *know,* that there is a hidden message in it that you can't read? That string of accounting he'd asked me for gave me the page, line, and word position of text. He'd sent a six-word message.

"What's the book?"

"The Long Tomorrow." This wasn't as simple as the Yorks' code. They had used their book to pick a key for a Caesar cipher. You couldn't brute-force a true book code. Without the book, it was just a string of random numbers. "It looks like Vicky checked it out of the library."

"Oh no."

"'Looks like.' It's not her handwriting." Something was wrong on Earth, something was deeply and seriously wrong in my husband's life and I didn't know what it was. I was willing to bet that it wasn't directly related to Icarus, because when we'd spoken on the phone, he'd made a point that this was a conversation for just the two of us. In the letter itself, Kenneth had made certain that I knew he hadn't had another heart attack, by mentioning the lack of a floral motif, albeit that left a whole host of other potential health issues.

I fished out the card, which I'd taken from the library,

and handed it to Helen. "Can you see if any of the other handwriting is a match? The angle is bad for me."

"Other handwriting . . ." She trailed off as I held my cast out to her. Nodding, she took the card and bent her head to the task.

I let my eye rest on the sculpture and traced the lines of the arm, where the soft beam from the skylight seemed to strike stars into the dark basalt. I say "skylight" and what I mean is "translucent panel" that I'd had placed in the top of the storage cubicle. At this time of the lunar month, it was artificial light, but in context it felt like the outside world was brushing the room with silver.

What was happening on Earth? I had stared at the letter, trying to will some extra meaning out of it. What I was left with were the absences. The more I thought about it, the more I felt one absence keenly.

He had not mentioned Nathaniel.

Helen sighed. "It is, perhaps, Curtis Frye or Imelda Corona. But neither of them include any common letters except the C and I."

"And they are both sick with polio." Was it possible to fake being sick? How would one fake the fever and the sweating and the vomiting?

Although that last one I knew the answer to.

Helen shook her head, staring at the cast. "The other possibility is that it is one of the people who signed in Arabic or Chinese."

"Or someone I haven't talked to yet." I grimaced and let the cast drop back into my lap. "So, I need to interview more people and we need English writing in longer samples." If I were in the AdminMod, ironically, I could have opened up their files and would have had no shortage of writing in various reports and documentation. I was going to need to find another rationale to get people to write things down. "What about doing an invento—"

The lights went out. The fans stopped. "Shit. Not again."

TWENTY-THREE

ISRAELI TRANSLUNAR LINER
DEDICATED IN FRANCE

TEL AVIV, April 19, 1963—The translunar liner *Shalom*,
which is under construction in a French shipyard, is being
designed to offer passengers a choice between kosher
and nonkosher meals. It will be part of the fleet carrying
colonists to the Moon when construction at the Marius Hills
settlement is completed next year. The ship will be lifted
into orbit aboard Sirius IV rockets and assembled in space.
The Israeli Rabbinate has been involved in the design and
construction, hoping to establish guidelines in approving
and maintaining a kosher section on spacefaring vessels
for a future journey to Mars while also accommodating
non-Jewish passengers on interplanetary voyages.

OUTSIDE THE GALLERY, conversation stuttered to a halt.
The emergency lights kicked in, but the gallery itself was
nearly full dark. I snatched the Pistol Grip Tool from the
side of the bench and flicked it to drive. The guide light
under the barrel came on, giving us a flashlight.

Helen was already on her feet, brow furrowed in
concentration. "Do you think it's station-wide again?"

"Assume it is." I went to the door and stopped with my hand on the knob. Helen hadn't been read in, but I needed an extra body. I gave instructions without context and trusted her brilliance to connect the dots. "Head to the Baker Street airlock. Tell me if anyone comes through."

She stared at me for a moment, then nodded. "You're looking for someone coming from the OpsMod."

"Yep." I opened the door, and the PGT's light made a circle of brightness on the floor. "I'll check the LGC."

Once upon a time, when everything was in Midtown, it housed all the controls. Lunar Ground Control was the only operations still housed here, with their "backrooms" in the operations module. The people in either place could control the colony.

"Wargin, what's going on?" Faustino stepped into the path in front of me.

"That's what I'm going to find out." I sidestepped and he pivoted with me. "You know the protocol for a power outage."

He grabbed my arm and dropped his voice. "It would help to know if there was something else going on."

"Later." I wrenched my arm out of his grip, pushing past him.

Behind me, I heard Faustino sigh and then shout, "Okay, people. This isn't your first outage, so stop whining like babies. Stay where you are and let the power team do their work."

Leaning forward, each thrust of my legs propelled me, leading with my head and shoulders. As I ran, I dipped in and out of pools of light from the emergency grid with the PGT's light bobbing ahead of me. People stood at intersections and stepped back as I passed.

Until a door opened in front of me. I tried to swerve, but my foot seized as if I'd stepped on a nail. On the Moon it's easy to forget that I have arthritis in my feet because I only weigh a sixth of what I do on Earth, but my mass is exactly the same.

It carried me forward and I slammed into the door.

It knocked me on my ass. What little wind remained after the initial impact got knocked out as I slapped into the floor.

"Holy Mother of God—" Luther dropped to a knee next to me. "Are you all right?"

I nodded, trying to drag a breath into my empty lungs.

He put a hand on my back. "I am so sorry. I was coming out to see . . . Are you sure you're okay?"

The wheeze of my lungs reinflating burned my throat and felt like my chest had been filled with a thousand tiny knives. "Fine," I croaked.

"You don't sound fine."

He was on my list. Luther was on my list and just happened to step out when I was running. Suspicious, yes, but realistically, how would he have known to be waiting for me?

Easy, if Icarus were more than one person. That would just take a wireless radio.

"Just winded." I had dropped the PGT and it lay at an angle, its light careening across the floor. I put my good hand in his and let him help me up. Acting suspicious of him would be one of the worst things I could do. I smiled and grabbed the PGT. "Thanks. It's really fine."

He looked unconvinced, or maybe he was wishing he'd hit me harder. I don't know. I headed down the stairs to Lunar Ground Control, slower this time. The mantra "slow is fast" existed for a reason that I'd totally ignored when I'd been running.

The door to the LGC was shut, as it should be, which was a relief. The chances of someone working in the LGC being able to turn off the power without anyone noticing was slim. I'd be able to get a list of everyone who was on duty and we could go over the logs in a debrief.

I bounded back up the stairs and went to the module directly above the LGC. Smaller than my bunk, the Remote Power Control Module was a legacy system that used to house the fuses and breakers for the colony. It was still here because the IAC believed in redundancy.

I opened the door, which moved easily. I'd never wanted padlocks on the Moon before this point. Inside, only my PGT offered any light. Racks filled the little chamber with thick vines of wiring. It had been designed to allow for the expansion of the colony by routing to a new breaker board in the OpsMod.

But cutting something in here would have the same effect as blowing a fuse or flipping one of the new breakers.

Gnawing on the inside of my lip, I ran the light of my PGT over the racks, squinting at the cramped labels. In its dim glow, I had trouble getting my eyes to focus. Moving my head back didn't help because the writing was so tiny. I turned old memories over, trying to find the main power.

Command and control, communications, lighting, life support . . .

From the pathway outside, a flashlight lit up the interior with a white glare, blinding me. "Nicole?" A young woman's voice. Cultured. British but rounder—

"Aahana?" I raised my hand to block the light.

"What are you doing?" She lowered the flashlight so it wasn't pointing directly at me.

What an excellent question. Give as much truth as I could and it would probably fly. "Legacy systems. I was part of the installation team when the colony was new." I stepped out to join her, gesturing to the interior because shutting the door would make it look like I was hiding something. "I thought I'd see if I could spot a problem."

"That's not protocol . . ."

"Hey! Good job remembering your training. Makes me proud . . . In truth, since protocol didn't spot the problem the first time we lost power, I was moving on to second-level troubleshooting." I gestured to the flashlight. "What about you?"

"Faustino told me to check the old RPCM . . ." She stared at the module and then back at me and then down at the drill. "What were you doing with a drill in there?"

"Flashlight." I held it up, pointing to the PGT's light. But I could also see how it would look to her. I needed to segue her away from thinking about me, and one of the best ways to do that was to make her an ally. "I came from the gallery and it was the best option, but not great. Give me a hand?"

She hesitated, looking at the entrance to the little room. "What are we looking for?"

"We start with the obvious first and eliminate that."

I stepped back in, hoping that she was just a pawn of Faustino and further hoping that he was just being officious. "Want to bring your light in and help me read these labels?"

Aahana squeezed into a space that would have been too small for two on Earth, but on the Moon your ideas of personal space change dramatically. She shone the light on the racks and it helped, but I still had to squint.

Running my finger along the rack, I glanced sideways at her and tried to steer the conversation even further away from my activities. "By the way . . . if you don't want to sound like a rookie, call it a PGT."

She sighed and it softened her. "I know . . . I know. Pistol Grip Tool, but it's still a drill."

"My dear, are you questioning the wisdom of the IAC and their love for acronyms? Be thankful that you didn't have to memorize the fifty pages of acronyms we did back when I started." I laughed with my best finishing school sparkle. "Elma had the worst time with them. I can't remember, did you have a chance to meet Dr. York before she left?"

"At the reception when our class was accepted." Her eyes glowed with the fervor they all had when they were talking about The Famous Lady Astronaut. "She was so nice."

"Elma is that, indeed. Why, one time—" The lights came on. Blinking, I lifted my arm to check my watch. "Sixteen minutes?"

Like last time. What was Icarus doing in those sixteen-minute chunks? And when would the next one come?

* * *

DAY TWO OF the quarantine. Everyone was nervous and tense, and that was without knowing about a saboteur, so I decided to try to kill two birds with a single stone. The bridge party that I'd been going on about was under way. I sat across from Danika in Le Restaurant. She kept rubbing the back of her neck, and I couldn't decide if it was a nervous habit or if her neck hurt.

"Claiming," Danika said, "all trumps." We all passed and she noted the contract on her scoresheet, giving me a brief example of her handwriting, which was not a match for "Vicky."

To my right, Luther stared at his cards waiting for his turn to come around again. "The question, in my mind, is if the lunar caves are really a better model for post-Boil Earth caves than actual Earth."

"Well, is a more hard environment, no?" Catalina looked over her cards. "The Earth has microorganisms and a breathable atmosphere. If we accept the Earth is going to heat to the point the oceans boil, then we also have to accept the loss of both."

"If we accept?" I raised my eyebrows. The best minds had spent the decade since the Meteor slammed into the Chesapeake Bay trying to find a way out of the runaway greenhouse we found ourselves in. So, was she an Earth Firster or just using a turn of phrase? "Do you have new insight into the data?"

Catalina shrugged, still studying her cards. "I mean, the oceans they are going to boil, unless a miracle happens, that's why I believe the lack of microbes here is beneficial. It gives us an idea of what we will have to do in the depths of the Earth."

Danika frowned. "Wait. I think I have something missed. Why have we a need for caves on Earth?"

Catalina lifted her head, staring at Danika as if she had grown an extra hand. "For people who can't leave. No matter how successful we have here or the First Mars Expedition, there are people who will never survive launch."

Like Kenneth.

"Right. Sorry . . ." Danika rubbed the back of her neck. "Sorry. I am today a little vague."

Around us, small murmurs of conversation made it sound as if everyone was having a lovely time. We were all so good at sounding as if nothing were wrong, and yet . . . I folded my cards. "Sweetheart . . . is your neck stiff?"

Her shoulders sank and she looked down at the table. Luther pulled his head back, nostrils flaring as he understood. A stiff neck was one of the first symptoms of polio.

Catalina looked at the cards as if she could get polio from them and set them down on the table. "Why do we quarantine on Earth if we would come here to get sick?"

"I figured it was just a ruse." Luther stared at Danika as if she were a piece of unexploded ordnance during the war. "Quarantine wasn't on the original schedule. Neither was Brazil."

I slid my chair back. "The original schedule went up with the rocket that exploded."

"Brazil, though? Understand, I was happy to be home, but . . ." Catalina scowled. "You might wonder if the IAC is covering up anything."

"Such as?" I wanted to keep this conversation going, but I also had a responsibility to isolate Danika.

"There've been many failures recently, that's all." She wiped her hands off on her trousers. "What if they know something is wrong with a piece and ignore it for convenience?"

Luther tossed his cards on the table and shook his head. "If you're going to believe in conspiracies, may as well go whole hog and start mining for green cheese."

"I'm not saying what I believe, only I'm saying I understand why people ask themselves." She shrugged. "Or maybe there are really space germs."

I snorted. "Please. That's something the press latched hold of which has no bearing in reality."

Luther tipped back in his chair, tapping his chin. "Actually . . . The increased radiation could account for this . . ." He waved a hand as if encompassing the entire quarantine situation. "That might be why the vaccine reverted from the attenuated version."

"That happens on Earth, too." Two days ago, I hadn't known that the virus could revert, but after reading Ana Teresa's report, I did. "It's infrequent, but it has been known to happen."

"Sure, but maybe the likelihood is increased here. It's worth investigating so that people can plan for it, if that turns out to be the case."

Putting my hand on Danika's shoulder, I bent down. "Come on, Danika. Let's find a spot for you to rest."

She hunched in on herself and rose. I put one hand on her back to steer her and she flinched. Sensitive skin or just nervous? As we walked out of Le Restaurant, people stared at us as if Danika would kill them just with proximity. Ironically, there was a chance that everyone here was infected with polio.

Apparently, 95 percent of people developed no symptoms. Isn't that fun? A bunch of walking disease vectors and only 4 or 5 percent would get noticeably sick. On the Moon, that meant, statistically, sixteen people. Not bad as epidemics go, except for two things.

1.   The lunar sickbay wasn't set up to handle sixteen sick people.
2.   It was polio, and you could be fine in the morning and dead by night.

Outside, Danika stopped next to Central Park and brushed her hand across the dandelions. "Do you think the LCA would now let me join Ruben? Since we are both sick."

"I'll ask. For the moment, we're going to take you to lie down and I'll give him a call."

People could be infectious up to ten days before they showed any symptoms *and* after they recovered, they could keep shitting out polio virus for six weeks. This quarantine wasn't going to end any time soon.

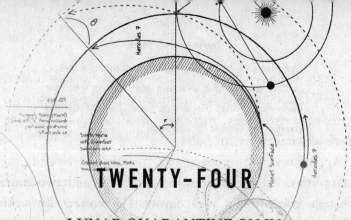

TWENTY-FOUR

LUNAR QUARANTINE ON IN "POLIO" EPIDEMIC

Special to The National Times

ARTEMIS BASE, Moon, April 21, 1963—An outbreak of paralytic poliomyelitis has stopped all traffic to and from the Moon. Declaring that the disease has reached an epidemic stage here in Artemis Base, the Lunar Colony Administrator, after conferring with the director of the International Aerospace Coalition, ordered a drastic quarantine. There have been nineteen cases reported in Artemis Base. So far, the disease has not spread to the three outposts, but Dr. Ana Teresa Almeida Brandão asked the IAC on Friday for authority to impose the quarantine. LCA Frisch said last night, "I would like to reassure the families back on Earth that we are doing everything in our power to keep the lunar residents safe and healthy."

According to the IAC, plans are under way to procure enough of the new polio vaccine to send to the Moon on the next available ship. Even with all urgency, it will be weeks before the supply ship reaches the Moon.

Opponents of the space program point to the outbreak, and the severity of it, as a sign that germs in space are more virulent than they are on Earth. The IAC did not respond to a request for comment.

DAY THREE OF the quarantine and we'd had two more people come down with fevers. I'd packed Wafiyyah Zinat Abbasi and Eric Wright off to sickbay. I'd caught Todd Sanders washing his hands with disinfectant until the knuckles were cracked.

I bent over a table in Midtown, with my good arm nearly up to my shoulder trying to snake an RF antenna cable back into place. To think, I'd been pleased when I realized that I couldn't clean the toilets because of my cast. But that was before I realized that Helen and I were the only ones qualified to do spacesuit maintenance among the people quartered in Midtown. With the quarantine in place, we were the ones responsible for doing the full wipe-down and cleaning of the suits after use.

Fascinating thing about a quarantine where you have spacesuits. Unvaccinated people in critical roles could still go through the airlocks to their regular shifts, provided there was a suit for them. Was a spacesuit overkill? Yes. Polio wasn't airborne. You could only get it from ingesting fecal matter or spittle, and yet . . . We worked for the IAC, which believed in redundancies and taking every precaution, so people who had not been immunized wore spacesuits if they had to leave their holding area.

A foil meal pack bounced off my shoulder, spinning as it dropped slowly toward the floor. I made a grab for it, but the packet ricocheted off my cast and tumbled down.

"Nice catch." Helen saluted with her own packet and came to sit beside me on the table. "You're allowed meal breaks, you know."

"I just want to finish this cable routing." The access for the cables was a pain and I didn't want to start over. "I'll eat later."

She watched me, and I have never felt so silently judged by someone drinking cold tomato soup through a straw. "I have a question that you may not be able to answer."

"All right . . ." I straightened up, so I could give her my full attention, wincing as my back popped like the Fourth of July. "Try me."

Helen nudged my meal pack across the floor with her foot. "Which outpost did Eugene and Myrtle head to?"

"They started at Marius Hills and then they were going to The Garden, finishing at the South Pole today." I picked up the foil packet and nearly set it to the side, but I could feel Helen watching me. When was the last time I ate something? I couldn't remember, which was never a good sign. Food was fuel. I peeled back the foil and extracted a square lump of date cake.

"Did they report anything unusual at The Garden?"

"This is an alarming train of questioning. And I don't know. My call with Frisch isn't until end-of-shift." I gnawed on the brown block and my mouth flooded with saliva. The brick of congealed cardboard didn't even taste good, but I was apparently hungry. "Why do you ask?"

"According to Luther Sanchez, who has been in touch with the miners at The Garden because of the work they are doing on 'his' plant beds—"

"His?" He was on my list. "Got to love some proprietary stakes."

She nodded but didn't smile. "The selenologist on-site recorded a seismic event that was either a blast or a meteorite impact."

I lowered the brick of food. "But . . ."

"But they had no blasting scheduled. And it happened during our blackout, so they couldn't tell exactly where it occurred."

It took me a moment to put the pieces together. With the main colony offline, they would have received telemetry information only from their sensors and been unable to triangulate the location. "You think it was a blast, timed for the blackout."

"Or it was a meteorite and we're jumping at shadows." Helen crossed her arms over her chest. "Can you tell me why they really went there?"

"They were doing an inventory of mining supplies."

"During a quarantine." Helen rolled her eyes. "What did I say about misinformation?"

I clenched my jaw. "That was a true statement." Could I tell her more? She knew about Nathaniel. She knew about the FBI. She knew we potentially had a bad actor on the Moon. She did not know about the Manifesto. "The inventory would include blasting supplies, so Eugene and Myrtle should be able to tell us if anything is—"

At the end of the "street" leading away from the airlock, Faustino rounded the corner, talking to Paulo Mendes da Rocha, one of the architects on the Moon. Each of them carried a launch/reentry suit that they'd used to venture into other parts of the colony.

"—necessary for another bridge party." I smiled at Faustino and Paulo. "Do either of you play bridge?"

Faustino looked offended at the mention of the game and laid his suit on the table next to the one I was working on. "You still are talking about it?"

"Morale is important in times of stress."

"So why suggest more time with the most boring game on any world? Why not a talent show?" He flexed his biceps and struck a pose with his chest out. "I could be a strongman."

"Please." I wrapped the remaining food back in its foil. "On the Moon, anyone can pretend they're strongmen."

He shrugged. "Music and comedy could be better than a bunch of ninnies sitting around card tables."

"Ninny?" Carefully, I tucked the meal pack into a hip pocket so I couldn't throw it at him. "It's nice to know where we stand in your assessment."

He leaned back on his heels, brows coming together, and held up his hands. "Wait—does 'ninny' not mean 'quiet person'?"

I sighed. "It means a fool."

To my surprise, he blushed. "I am very sorry." He glanced at the intercom on the wall. "Further, I have just told Frisch that he is too much of a ninny."

Of course, he wasn't blushing about calling bridge players fools; still, he had apologized. "Well, if it makes you feel any better, Frisch isn't a native English speaker either, so probably just assumed he had the definition wrong."

"Mm . . ." He shook his head, and tapped Paulo on the shoulder, switching to Portuguese. *"Do jeito que conversamos?"*

"Eu ainda acho que você está sendo uma 'ninny,' *mas, para você, eu digo."* Paulo rolled his eyes and turned to Helen. "I have been told my chess game is shameful and harangued into asking for help. Can I take you away?"

Helen was quiet for a fraction of a second longer than she needed to be before she answered. "Can you spare me, Nicole?"

Tempting though it was to tell her no, I was curious to see what Faustino wanted. I was fluent in French and German but had only "space Portuguese." When we were launching from Brazil, I could talk about rockets but all I had caught with these guys was something about a conversation. And, of course, ninny. "Absolutely. You're due for your fifteen-minute break anyway."

As if she hadn't just come back from a lunch break. "Thanks." She turned to Paulo. "Let's go to Central Park. There's a board set up there."

Faustino watched them go, chewing on his lower lip. As soon as Paulo and Helen rounded the curve of the "street," Faustino stepped closer to me and lowered his voice. "Frisch wants to see you."

I raised my eyebrows and looked at the intercom. "And yet, he didn't call for me."

"He says that this is simply convenient. You are his secretary, et cetera." Faustino looked over his shoulder and lowered his voice. "When the power went out, you knew something that the rest of us didn't. You said you would tell me 'later' and you still owe me an explanation."

God, I wanted to snap that I didn't owe him a damn thing, but I needed to deescalate this and redirect him. I sighed and loosened my body language, tilting my head so the rod up my ass wasn't as visible. "I had a hunch it might be related to the legacy system." I shrugged. "I was wrong. I'm sorry, but I don't know why we lost power."

God, I wished that weren't true.

GOING BETWEEN MODULES, even as someone who had been vaccinated, had required a meteoric level of antiviral scrubs. My hands still stung by the time I got to Frisch's office. I clapped my hand against the plastic sheeting of his door.

"Enter." Frisch's voice creaked with fatigue.

I pushed the sheeting aside and stepped in. The air in his cubby stank of sweat and old breath as if the scrubbers had failed. Frisch had pale stubble on his cheeks and sat hunched in his chair. Stacks of reports cluttered his desk, held in place by uneaten meal packs. A blanket was wadded in one corner.

He looked up as I came in and his eyes were deeply bloodshot. "Nicole. Have a seat."

I picked up the blanket and shook it out. "Have you been sleeping here?"

He gestured vaguely at the intercom. "If someone calls and I'm unavailable . . ."

"You could delegate that, you know."

The corner of his mouth quirked as he watched me fold

the blanket. "Yes, well. My secretary has been overseeing Midtown."

"There's the secretarial pool."

His skin had a jaundiced cast to it. "Staffing is not a high priority at the moment. Do sit down and let's get on with our discussion, shall we?"

"Maybe we can troubleshoot the problem together?"

Frisch closed his eyes and pinched the bridge of his nose. "No."

"Excuse me?"

"I said 'no.' Whatever the problem is, simply tell me and I will handle it, but *you* will not be involved in troubleshooting of any sort."

"Now, now . . ." I waggled my finger at him. "Clemons specifically asked me to work on—"

"Shut up!" Frisch slapped his hands on the table, shocking me into silence. "I tolerated your bullying and grandstanding for years and finally—"

"Bullying and grandstanding? You mean fighting to be heard. If I were Stetson Parker, tell me a single thing I've done that would be cast as anything less than desirable."

"You have overstepped—" Frisch cut off and straightened the pages on his desk. His nostrils were constricted and his mouth pinched into a hard, flat line. After a moment, he took a breath and continued in the sort of calm upper-crust voice I'd heard from British officers during the war. "Please sit down. I regret raising my voice. I invited you here as a matter of courtesy and I was discourteous. We are colleagues and I am aware that this will not be an easy conversation for you." He pushed back from the desk and turned to his kettle. "Please sit. I'll make some tea."

The first thought that went through my head was that something had happened to Kenneth. I sank into the chair while my heart tried to fill my throat and suffocate me. The part of my brain that puts pieces together pointed to Frisch saying that I had "overstepped." This would be job related.

It *had* to be job related. That was acceptable. I could talk my way out of a problem there. I couldn't "bully" a heart attack.

Frisch puttered with his kettle, slowly releasing the valve to bleed off pressure. Steam whispered out. Frowning, he opened the spout and poured hot water into two cups. "Do you take anything?"

"No. Thank you." A knot of tension formed below my right shoulder blade as I waited for him to clip the tea bags into each cup.

A part of me did not want to accept anything from him, but I also needed to deescalate the situation. In the moment, his disdain for me was not as time sensitive as either the polio outbreak or Icarus.

I did not give a full smile when I took the cup, but I made sure my expression was soft. "Thank you. Have you heard from Eugene and Myrtle?"

Frisch settled in his chair, hunching over his cup. "I will be succinct and then answer any follow-up questions I can. I must remind you, the subject of this discussion is Classified Top Secret." He blew on his tea and then set it aside, looking directly at me. "You have been accused of sending coded messages."

My brows came together. "Yes . . . you know I have. Clemons sent me to the Moon with codebooks—can we retrieve those yet?"

"I'm not speaking of the sanctioned use of codes. It has since come to light that these are not the only coded messages you've sent or received."

I took a sip of my tea, which was still mostly just hot water, and considered my options before I spoke. "My husband and I have a code to exchange private messages related to his political career, yes."

"Those are a concern, but I was referring to the messages you sent to the First Mars Expedition using Dr. Nathaniel York's passkey. Those have been leaked to the press, which is lending credence to the conspiracy theories of Earth First." Frisch steepled his fingers together and stared at me over them. "To counter that, the moment quarantine is lifted, you will be placed on the next ship back to Earth. Until then, you are suspended without pay and confined to quarters."

The room seemed to fade around me, leaving only the heat of the ceramic mug in my hands. A webwork of responses sprang out, each pulling for my attention. I lifted my chin. "We're being played for a fool."

"Are you denying you sent the messages?" He settled back in his chair and picked up his tea.

I was married to a politician, and that meant never directly admitting guilt. "I am pointing out that this question coming up now is meant to hamper our investigations. The timing is suspect."

"Be that as it may, the press has picked up the story and

run with it. Do you have any idea how much damage you have caused?" He sipped his tea again and shrugged as if all of this were out of his hands. "I have instructions from Clemons. You are to be confined to quarters."

I sipped my tea back at him. "How many people do we have who are immunized against polio and can do suit maintenance?"

Frisch stared at me, steam curling out of his cup. He blinked and looked down at the papers on his desk, as if counting through a roster. He probably was.

I already knew the answer because I'd helped him come up with duty rosters via intercom. "There are five of us. Just to refresh your memory." Leaning forward, I set my cup on his desk. "Wherever you confine me, I suggest my quarters is not the appropriate place. With all due respect."

TWENTY-FIVE

SECRET MESSAGES IN SPACE—
WARGIN SEEN AS TARGET OF PLOT

KANSAS CITY, April 26, 1963—The wife of Governor Wargin, of Kansas, appears to have been sending coded messages to the First Mars Expedition. Documents shared with The National Times by a source within the IAC reveal an internal investigation into Mrs. Wargin's activities.

However, William J. Reed, Democratic State Senate majority leader, charged on the floor of the Legislature today that this leak came from the Denley Administration with the intention of embarrassing Governor Wargin's administration. The Governor is considered the front-running opponent of President Denley in the 1964 election.

Mr. Reed said agents of the Federal Bureau of Investigation were "honeycombing" the state "under the guise of a conspiracy investigation." He said the work of the agents involved "wiretaps galore" and "willful misinterpretation of what are clearly love letters."

"The ruthlessness of the Federal Administration is

beyond all believing." The purpose, Mr. Reed said, was "to embarrass a great American." He said the Denley Administration was afraid of Mr. Wargin.

I WAS NOT confined to quarters, but I was confined to the science module, which isolated the polio patients from the rest of the colony. Near the door of the repurposed biology lab, I knelt by Guillermo's bed, holding his left foot in my right hand. My plaster cast was shrouded in a giant black rubber machinists' glove, since I could wash that. It was hygienic, but I looked like a comic book villain and had to keep resisting the urge to laugh maniacally. "Push against my hand . . ." Nothing happened, but I said, "Good."

Guiding his knee with my cast laid gently against it, I pushed his leg up the way Ana Teresa had shown me. My back ached from bending over beds, helping exercise the patients in the men's ward. The lingering musk of rabbits underlay the smell of sweat and vomit. The rabbits were in Midtown now, along with our flock of lunar chickens, and in their place were six of the polio patients.

Some of them only had a little muscle weakness. Others were . . . worse. "Now pull. That's right . . ." A muscle twitched under my hand. "Good!"

Across the aisle from us, Kadyn watched me, mimicking the exercises. Fear tightened his face, but beneath the blanket his left knee drew up a little. He'd been getting function back in his legs as the fever dropped.

Guillermo grunted, fists clenching his blanket. "Pathetic, huh?"

"Better than yesterday." I looked up as Ana Teresa came

into the ward and went to the crate I'd set on the counter earlier. "Let's see what the actual doctor thinks, hm?"

"Thanks . . . Hey, doc! You remember about the game?"

She nodded to Guillermo, beckoning to me. "If you stop griping about your exercises, I get a radio so you can listen to the game."

It would be more than just a radio. It wasn't like a regular radio could pick up a station from the Earth, especially not when we were buried in regolith. We had a selection of five stations broadcast up from the ground via our satellite system. To get the game, Ana Teresa would have to send down a request to the IAC for them to add a new station. But the boys had nothing else to do with their time. I had no doubt Clemons would approve it. The IAC took care of their own.

"Nothing will be sweeter than listening to France lose. Brazil will trounce them." He plucked at the blanket covering his limp legs.

"That is definitely something to work for." Patting his leg, I stood and walked back to Ana Teresa.

She dug through the crate and pulled out a strip of torn insulation, scowling. "Well, we'll make it work."

I looked into the crate, worried that I'd screwed up the instructions. "You wanted ten-centimeter strips, didn't you?"

"Yes, yes. They're fine." She waved her hand to clear the air, before lifting the crate. "I just want wool, which I can't have. Thick *and* absorbent. One layer. Here, I have to do two."

"Can I do anything to help?"

"Hot water? With you in a plaster cast?" She made a loud raspberry of a snort. "Use the centrifuge room. When was the last time you were on there?"

"I meant with the wraps?"

She gave me a look my mother would have been proud of. "When. Was the last time. You used. The centrifuge room?"

"I . . . I don't remember."

The terrier of space was about to grab me in her teeth and shake me. "Go. The last thing I need right now is to reset a malformed bone."

The thing is, running in Earth gravity hurts my feet. Oh, on the Moon, the arthritis is still there, but it takes so much less effort to move that my toes don't flex as much or take as much weight or . . . If I said any of this to Ana Teresa, she would put it in my file that I had arthritis. Clemons already thought I was old hat. I didn't need my body proving it to him, not if I wanted to get back into space after this suspension. I smiled at her like a good little girl scout. "I'll do that now."

"Good." She carried the crate back to Guillermo's bed. "All right . . . ready for some more torture?"

From another bed, someone laughed. "I think you're enjoying this."

"I am." Ana Teresa set the crate by Guillermo and threw the blankets back.

I stepped into the hall and leaned against the smooth rubber wall for a moment. At the other end of the hall, just outside sickbay proper, one of the nutritionists rested his head against the wall. He'd had polio as a boy, recovered completely, but lost his kid sister. Got lifelong immunity, though, so, like me, was assigned to helping with the sick.

He raised his head and wiped his hand across his face. "Wargin. How goes it?"

"Oh, you know." I pretended not to notice that his eyes were red and that his cheeks were damp as I lifted my cast. "I've just been told to go jog in the centrifuge room."

He snorted. "Have fun with that."

"Right . . ." I walked past him to the supply closet where my gear was stashed. I'd rigged a hammock from the ceiling and had the relative privacy of a room filled with blankets, saline, and scalpels. I didn't have running gear here so much as I had my flight suit. Not that it mattered. Everyone in the science module was so exhausted, I could have jogged naked and it would have gone unnoticed.

I WALKED ALONG the centrifuge track and the floor curved up in front of me like a hill I would never climb. I was supposed to be jogging, but no one was in the centrifuge room and I wanted to spare my feet. It is a hateful thing to weigh Earth normal for an hour. Usually, there would be people jogging up the curve and out of sight "above" me, but it was a week into the outbreak and no one else was visible. Even if there were a nurse or doctor exercising, the curve of the room and the faint thrum of the motor and flywheel gave me the illusion of privacy.

If I were lucky, maybe I could get through my entire hour without having to run.

Ahead of me, a pair of feet came into view, standing on

the curved floor. Swell. Grimacing, I stepped into a slow jog. Each footfall ground my bones together. Another meter forward and I could tell that there were three people standing. Two women and a man. Eugene crouched down to peer past the curve of the ceiling. He waved at me and stood up, waiting for me to reach them.

Myrtle and Helen stood with him, talking in a tight group. I slowed down, feeling simultaneous relief and dread. Being told that they had returned safely from the inventory trip was different than seeing them in the flesh.

"Fancy meeting you here." I stopped next to them, waiting for the other shoe to drop. I could not imagine a benign coincidence that would lead to the four of us having the centrifuge room to ourselves. "What's going on?"

Helen gave me a quick hug. "Are you all right?"

"Tired and currently worried." And my feet were throbbing in time with my pulse. I cocked my head at them. "How did you get this cleared and why?"

Eugene's grin was not innocent. "As some of the people immunized, it made sense to help with delivery of supplies to sickbay. And while here, it's only sensible to get in our exercise routine."

"Speaking of . . ." Myrtle gestured to the track. "Let's go."

I gawked at her. "You want me to jog when you clearly have news."

Myrtle shook her head, pointing at my cast. "That needs to heal right and this is the deal we made with Ana Teresa."

"So, she knows . . ." Before I could finish, Myrtle began a slow jog away from me. Helen and Eugene paced her, forcing me to follow. "All right. So Ana Teresa knows . . . what, exactly?"

"I implied it was related to Kenneth and our concern for you as friends meant that we wanted to talk to you privately." Myrtle had a scrape near her hairline and a little bruising on her cheek. "And while that's true, I'm deferring it."

"I'll give you the quick brief." Eugene jogged along easily as if he weren't getting ready to tell me that something had gone wrong on their inventory trip. "Then we have questions."

"Shoot." My brain slowly caught up and wondered why Helen was here and who they were worried about overhearing us.

"First, the item we were tasked with, inventorying the blasting stores at the outposts. Everything was present and accounted for. It all matched the inventory lists we had been given, which also matched the on-site lists. However . . ." Eugene glanced at Myrtle. "My brilliant wife raised a question."

"I used to be a computer at a chemical company. We made beauty products mostly, hair-straighteners, lightening creams, and the like, but some of the supplies had to be carefully tracked because they had explosive or corrosive properties. I wondered if someone who was interested in blasting stores might not have an easier time masking their tracks with other components."

"So we inventoried the fertilizers and oxidizers at each site." Eugene took a deeper breath. "Those numbers did not match."

Myrtle added, "The chemistry lab here is also missing an entire bottle of perchloric acid."

"Shit." With those, Icarus would have no trouble making a bomb. Multiple bombs, in fact. "What else?"

"En route to our first stop at Marius Hills, the right-hand controller failed. Eugene used the copilot controls to set us down at one of the emergency way stations."

"Frisch didn't report that."

Eugene said, "It happened during the blackout here. We thought we'd lost comms as well, and by the time we realized that wasn't the case, we had also developed reason to delay reporting. Myrtle's hand controller had been hastily and clumsily damaged." Eugene's mouth set in a grim, tight line. He took a breath and slowed to a walk. "Hell. You should see this."

My heart was pounding too quickly for the five minutes of running we had done. Helen's arms crossed over her chest.

Eugene fished in his pocket and drew out a handkerchief wrapped around an oblong. He unfolded it carefully. "This had fallen into the underdeck beneath the control console. I only found it because I had the panel off to do repairs."

He held a battered Swiss Army knife, one of the ones with pliers and screwdrivers. In the end, inlaid in silver, was a beautifully monogramed "F."

Helen said, "I found *The Long Tomorrow*. It was in Frisch's office."

If we had still been running, I probably would have tripped over my feet and taken a header. Frisch had been resistant to the idea of doing the inventory or even the notion of Icarus being on the Moon at all. But he'd also been living and working on the Moon for years. I could not wrap my head around why he would have aligned with Earth First.

I wet my lips. "I see. Where in Frisch's office? Just out and easy to see or did you go in and toss it?"

"Toss?"

"Search." Eugene glanced at me for a moment and then continued the explanation. "She wants to know if you had to search the room or if it was someplace obvious."

"Ah. I 'tossed' it." She pointed at the knife. "There were three people with this initial who had access to the BusyBee that morning. Faustino, Curtis Frye, and Otto Frisch. I checked all three quarters to see if there were any correlating items as well as Frisch's office while he was in the LGC. The book was the only item that, to my eye, had significance, but I am acting with incomplete data."

Sighing, I nodded. "I know. Thank you."

"The book had fallen under his desk and had a copy of Kenneth's letter to you tucked inside."

I turned to her so quickly that the Coriolis effect of the centrifuge room nearly made me fall over.

Myrtle caught me as I staggered. "Maybe we should let you sit down before we tell you the rest."

"There's more?" I put my hand on her shoulder. "Of course there is . . . You're about to tell me what the letter said."

"Do you want to sit down?" Helen asked.

"Heck, I want to sit." Myrtle lowered herself to the curved track. "I live on the Moon because I don't like 1 g anymore."

Eugene laughed, but dropped to sit next to her. "You were the one insisting we make her run."

"And we did. She can run after."

I was going to strangle all of them for drawing the answer out like this. I sat with my knees drawn up and bit the inside of my cheek to keep from screaming at them.

Helen knelt in front of me, resting her hands on her thighs, with a beautifully straight spine. "POISON AT HOME GOVERNMENT INVESTIGATING ME."

"My God. How many vectors are they covering?" I closed my eyes. Whoever Icarus was had shown incredible foresight to plant rat poison at our home, even though I was, by now, doubting that Nathaniel had been poisoned there. It would have been hard to guarantee his arrival, unless Reynard had deliberately lured him there. Even if I granted that, there were easier ways to get poison into the man at work.

"Who are 'they,' Nicole?" Helen asked.

I wiped my hand down my face, trying to order my thoughts. If it was Frisch, why was he acting now instead of before we arrived? "I think we have to consider the possibility that Frisch was framed and we're being played."

Eugene pursed his lips and studied me. "Because both items were easy to find? I have to tell you the knife was not."

"It's also the timing. Creating dissension in the ranks is an effective way to cause disruption. Making us suspect Frisch would fit that nicely." I ticked points off on my fingers as I went. "Alternately, there could be two culprits and Frisch was a sleeper agent who was waiting on his accomplice to arrive on our ship."

Eugene stared at me as if I were a problem in a sim he was going to break apart. "Why exactly did the FBI send you?"

Furrowing my brow, I tilted my head and laughed, almost by reflex. Inside, I had gone cold, though, because while Clemons had talked to me about going, and he was clearly cooperating with the FBI, I had not mentioned that to anyone here. "You just told me the FBI was investigating my husband. Why would they send me to the Moon?"

"Kenneth said 'government.'"

"I hardly think 'FBI' is in our key book." A part of me wanted to stop dodging and tell them everything. Another, completely hateful part of my brain pointed out that if Earth First could recruit a sleeper agent like Frisch, then why not my friends? The Lindholms and Helen had been everywhere Icarus had acted. It was unbelievable, but then that was what sleeper agents did. And I knew Eugene was sympathetic to some of Earth First's motivations. "All of this is a distraction. Let's look at opportunity for each of the people you've identified, without worrying about motivations. Those are rarely useful as predictors, anyway."

Eugene turned to Myrtle and Helen. "Will you give me a moment alone with Nicole?"

Myrtle opened her mouth and turned to Eugene. I don't know what nuances she read in the set of his jaw or the line of his shoulders, but she closed her mouth and stood. "Come on, Helen."

With only one backwards glance, Helen followed her, leaving me alone with Eugene. He waited until they were nearly around the bend and leaned forward, voice low. "What did you do during the war?"

"I was a WASP. You know this." The bright finishing school laugh would not serve me here, so I settled for concern.

"Come on . . ." Eugene pulled back a little, studying me. "The thing I keep coming back to is why Clemons sent *you*. Why he told you to investigate whatever this is and not me. The easy answer? The easy answer is that you're white. You have seniority over me. But neither of those get you a security clearance for Top Secret, Classified intel. They don't teach you words like 'toss,' 'operative,' or 'sleeper agent.' They don't teach you strategies for disrupting a group. So . . ."

"You've forgotten who my husband is."

"I haven't. The first lady of a state doesn't automatically get clearance." Eugene wet his lips. "I dropped a 'bird' during the war, you know. Only once, because they kept the Tuskegee Airmen segregated, but it's not the sort of thing a fellow forgets. Bird didn't look like a spy, which is their job, right? Little slip of a white girl. Blonde and blue-eyed. Very upper-class. Knew German. Knew how to use a parachute. Knew how to send and break codes. Guess where she said she learned it?"

My throat was dry, and swallowing didn't help. There was nothing I could say here that would fix anything.

His smile was almost sad. "Swiss finishing school."

TWENTY-SIX

AFGHAN FLOOD TOLL IS NOW 107

KABUL, Afghanistan, April 26, 1963—(AP)—
The death toll from the flood in Herat, in western
Afghanistan, has risen to 107, the Afghan Red Crescent
Society announced today. The flooding is likely to
worsen, as reports from the meteorologists aboard the
IAC weather space station report that another storm
system is bearing down on the battered region. Rainfalls
this year are double their previous record.

THERE ARE POINTS in your life where you have to make a
choice between two loyalties. Sometimes it is seemingly
innocuous, like choosing between attending a baby
shower or a graduation. Sometimes it is between your
husband and your job.

It comes down to value and harm.

When Eugene asked me if I was a spy—when he knew
that I was, I had a choice. I could have kept the secrets I
had promised to keep and sacrificed his friendship. He
was a military man. He would have understood if I'd just
said, "I can't tell you that."

But I valued him. What harm came from telling the

secret? Potentially my career. Potentially Kenneth's.

What harm came from keeping the secret of the Icarus project? Potentially the lives of everyone on the Moon. If I'd been able to really talk to Clemons, I might have made a different decision.

I TOLD EUGENE to call Myrtle and Helen back and then I took that thin permission Clemons had given me to tell them what "they need to know to do good work" and told them everything. Forty-five minutes later, I felt as wrung out as if I'd been vomiting the entire time. In a way, I had. The floor of the centrifuge room rumbled under me as I sat, knees bent and arms wrapped around them. My audience of three stayed silent after I finished talking.

I truly had been a WASP. I'd been recruited there. And Swiss finishing school . . . I went to two. One in my teens as a good wealthy socialite. And then a second that was not Swiss and taught very different skills.

Myrtle spoke first, "Does Kenneth know?"

I lifted my head and stared at her. "Of course he does."

"Some women never told their husbands . . ."

I shrugged. "I trust him." Our marriage was strained and compromised in every direction, but the one thing I knew with absolute certainty was that Kenneth had my back. "So . . . now you know I was a spy. You know about Icarus. What else can I tell you?"

Eugene rubbed both hands over his head. "I'm thinking Icarus has effectively sidelined you—and Kenneth, for that matter. They haven't done jack shit to us."

With one hand, Myrtle smacked his shoulder. "What part of 'visible sabotage' are you forgetting?"

"If Nicole had been allowed to wear her spacesuit, that would have been her and Frisch."

"Also, food poisoning."

Eugene rolled his eyes and then straightened. "No. You're right. When specific people have been targeted there's a strategic reason behind it. Nicole and Kenneth to sideline them. The BusyBee sabotage to stop the inventory. Nathaniel because it would have scuttled the program to lose him. So why hit me with food poisoning?"

Helen lifted her hand and ticked off some options. "Deliberate spread of polio. Cancel flight to the Moon. Get specific pilot in place."

There were easier ways to spread polio and for that matter better diseases to hit us with. The flu was more contagious and had a higher fatality rate. I chewed on the inside of my lip, thinking. "That last one . . . Why do you think Mission Control picked Michael Lin to step up to copilot?"

"You mean instead of you or Myrtle?" Eugene tugged on his ear, thinking. "Well . . . she would have been distracted worrying about me."

Myrtle sniffed. "As if that's not every day of my life married to a pilot . . ."

"You're a pilot too!"

"No. I know how to fly. There's a big difference." She shook her head. "What are you thinking about Mikey?"

I squeezed my eyes shut and pinched the bridge of my nose where a headache was forming. "Do we really need to have this conversation in 1 g?"

"If you're going to complain about gravity . . ." Myrtle hauled herself up and stretched her arms over her head, brushing her fingers against the low curved ceiling. "Let's run and talk. Is it possible that Mikey made Eugene sick so he could get into the cockpit?"

Her voice faded a little as she jogged away from us.

"I hate you." But I got to my feet and followed. Admit that my feet hurt, even to my friends? I'm still a pilot. "Maybe Curt needed to get into the command seat."

Helen jogged easily on my right. "To what purpose?"

"I keep wondering if I could have made it look like the thruster was malfunctioning." I looked over at Eugene as he paced us on Myrtle's far side. "Could you?"

Eugene cocked his head and nodded slowly. "I could have. Pretty sure."

"Did it misfire when you were in there?"

He shook his head. "No, but it was also not in a position to help me keep the vehicle stable and I was consciously avoiding it."

"Damn good flying."

"Technically, not flying. Grounding?" He shrugged. "But yes, I could have faked that. You?"

I nodded. "Hey, Helen. You were actually in the CM with Curt. What do you think?"

"I was focused on numbers." As Nav/Comp she would have been working double-time as soon as the trajectories started changing. Her feet hit the track at an even pace while she considered. "Nothing I heard over comms or saw on instrumentation made me doubt that the thruster was misfiring. And then there's the broken landing strut.

That was definitely real."

"True . . . But a hard landing could do that." I tried to picture bringing the craft down in a way that would deliberately break the landing strut. "I don't think I could do that on purpose. Not reliably."

Eugene shook his head. "No. Faking a thruster misfiring in vacuum is possible. The moment you touch down . . . There are too many variables. You're more likely to tear a hole in the side of the rocket than you are to crumple the strut. And how would you even practice it?"

Grunting in response, I ran next to them feeling every jolt of my feet against the floor through my too-heavy flesh. "If Curt is Icarus, then our problems might have solved themselves, since he's down with polio."

Myrtle side-eyed me. "That's a cold thing to say."

"She's right, though," Helen said. "There has not been an incident in the week since Curt got sick."

Myrtle said, "There was a power outage."

"It could have been a timer," Helen said.

I'd had the same thought myself about the outages and the odd length.

"So maybe his plans are toast, unless he had deliberately infected himself to spread it among—" A sudden memory of candy Easter eggs in dandelions went through me. "Oh, shit. Curt brought those candy Easter eggs up and gave them to people at the church service. What if that was the vector for the polio virus?"

"Is that possible?" Helen slowed for a moment. "If that's so, then the initial cases would be people who ate the eggs."

"Not necessarily." I had learned more about polio in the past week than I had any interest in knowing. "Some people might have been symptom-free carriers. I can ask Ana Teresa . . . I think I can do that without being too overt."

"But wouldn't Curt have vaccinated himself before coming up, if that was his plan?"

She had a good point. If the eggs were the vector, why would he be among the sick? "So maybe it's not Curt. Maybe the quarantine is stopping Icarus. Trapped in the wrong module for mischief."

"If that's the case, when it's lifted, we're back in trouble again."

Our footsteps pounded against the unending hill of the centrifuge room. Eugene slowed a little and then caught up. "You said that document was filled with Bible verses. Which ones?"

"Exodus 32:27, Revelation 16:21, and Exodus 22:24." I grimaced, remembering the bloodshed and violence of the verses.

"Oof." Eugene sounded as though he knew exactly what those were, which I suppose wasn't surprising given that he and Myrtle led a Bible class up here. "Any chance you remember the specific edition it was from?"

"No. Sorry. What are you thinking?"

"I figure the FBI has already thought about this, but the edition can tell you what denomination a person is likely to be and a little about their relationship with God."

Myrtle looked up at him with a fond smile and then turned to me. "My husband was in seminary before the war and would have made a fine preacher."

Eugene gave a little smile. "But then I met an airplane. Closer to God than any church gets me."

"Amen." I worshiped at that altar myself. Sighing, I said, "Clemons sent a copy of the Manifesto up along with a set of codebooks. But it's in my CPK bag, which is still on the shuttle, so I don't know how—"

"The shuttle was unloaded. Day before yesterday." Helen frowned, probably wondering the same thing I was. Why hadn't anyone told me? "The luggage is in the port until people can claim it."

"Frisch knows that the codebooks are in my bag, so I would assume he's grabbed it." I jogged, heels jarring against the curving floor. "It will probably be in his office. Can you get it, Helen?"

She shook her head. "Challenging. He's begun sleeping there."

"I can get it," Myrtle said.

"How?" I raised my brows. "No offense, but I used to do this and when someone is present it's—"

"I've got a tool you don't." She held up her hand and shifted her inflections just a little, softening the *t*'s to *d*'s and adding a touch of lilt. "Put a vacuum in this hand and no one will blink that I've pulled a cleaning shift."

IT TOOK NEARLY two days to catch Ana Teresa alone. I finally had to deploy the same trick Helen had played on me. I tossed a meal pack at the doctor. "Come on."

She fumbled it and nearly upended the bin of fabric scraps she was sorting on the counter of sickbay. Snatching the spinning brick out of the air, she stared at it with a vague expression as if she'd never seen one before, which worried me. "Come where?"

"We're taking a break." I held up my own meal and waggled it. "Follow me."

"I need to finish . . ." She gestured at the fabric.

"No, actually, you don't." This was a script I knew all too well, although I usually played the other side. Today, I played Kenneth's part and walked over, looping my arm through Ana Teresa's. "That is something you can delegate. In fact, delegating is something you can delegate. But mostly, you need to put food in your body so when you need to be smart, you are not fuzzy from hunger."

"It will not take long, and I can eat while I work." But she was letting me steer her away from the fabric at least.

"Point of diminishing returns." I had her nearly to the sink, but her feet were slowing as we passed the beds set up here. "For example, you're talking about eating while sorting unwashed clothes that have been wrapped around polio patients' bodies. Sweat. Feces. Ointment."

"The ointment is nontoxic."

"Don't believe her," Garnet rasped from one of the beds. She was flat on her back but still managed to pull a grin out of somewhere. "Stuff stings like the dickens."

"And it stinks." Birgit was sitting up in bed and lowered the book she was reading. "Polio is one thing, but that ointment makes me doubt your judgment."

"Yeah, doc. Take a break." Wafiyyah rolled her head on the pillow. "We aren't going anywhere."

"Wash your hands." I stopped Ana Teresa in front of

the sink. "And your face. We're going to sit down. Fifteen minutes. That's all, and then you can come back and sort if that still seems like the best use of your time."

It helped that she knew, really, that I was right. She scrubbed her hands, and the outside of the meal pack, splashed water on her face, and then stayed bent over the sink. Water dripped off her chin and nose back into the reclaimer.

It would get whisked through tubes and pipes to one of the water recyclers, which would filter, irradiate, and reprocess the hell out of it. That would be a good target for Icarus. Break all of them and it would shut down the lunar colony. Not from polio, mind you, but just from simple dehydration. The South Pole outpost mined lunar ice, but it wasn't like you could just melt a block and drink it.

I watched the water drip off of Ana Teresa's nose and thought about how much damage I could do in sixteen minutes to the water reclamation system.

She drew in a breath and straightened, turning to the air dryer. Wiping her hands briskly under the heated air, she looked like she was trying to form a to-do list behind her eyes.

I poked her in the arm with my plastic block of food. "Favorite song?"

Ana Teresa's teeth bared as if she were going to bite me. "What?"

"We're taking a break. What's your favorite song?"

As she snatched the meal pack off the counter, there was a fair chance she might murder me with it. I was probably only saved because Birgit said, "Mine's 'When the Roll Is Called Up Yonder,' which is more on point than I'd like . . ."

"Mine will fix that." Garnet laughed breathlessly. "Chattanooga Choo Choo."

Over on her bed, Wafiyyah said, "Hymne à l'amour."

From around the room, song titles sang out from a chorus of women's voices. I grinned at them. "I'll see if we can get some of that in here for you ladies." I leveled the meal pack at Ana Teresa. "You?"

"I don't know." She looked down at the meal pack. "Can we go eat now?"

I did not push the song issue, because it wasn't the battle I needed to win. I got her into the hall. She started to sit down on the floor, but I caught her arm. "Come on. Actual break. Upstairs."

Either she realized it would be faster to stop arguing with me, or some small part of her mind knew a real break would help more than anything. I was using it as an excuse to get her alone, but I also wasn't wrong. She followed me to the stairs and we went up.

Each of the large lunar modules is built using the same plan, which is the most efficient way to do it, but there are variations because they were manufactured at different times, applying lessons learned from previous modules. Midtown was dug into the surface of the Moon, with a large translucent dome. The science module rested on the surface of the Moon, and we had pushed lunar regolith over it to mostly bury the thing. It did not get Midtown's translucent dome, to make it easier to control the temperature for various science experiments.

It got windows. The very top of the module was a lounge, ringed with windows looking out across the lunar landscape. It was night and the Earth cast silver-blue light across the Apennines mountain range.

Ana Teresa stopped, staring at the soft, rounded slopes of the Apennines, which rose from the Mare Imbrium cloaked in black velvet. During the two-week night, by earthlight, the Moon is a fairy landscape filled with blues and silvers and a black that rivals space. It occurred to me that Ana Teresa had been a flight surgeon on both Earth and *Lunetta*, but she was a first-timer on the Moon. She'd seen the lounge before, but we'd arrived during the day and had been in crisis mode since. There was every chance she had never seen the Moon at night.

She dropped into one of the chairs and let out a sigh that told me I'd been every kind of right to pull her out of sickbay. For that matter, my own sigh was not much shallower.

Gazing out at the undulating hills, Ana Teresa tore the meal open and took a bite. I followed suit and the square coated my tongue with waxy residue. I let her sit and stare. I say "I let" as if I wanted to do anything else myself. I will never get tired of looking at the Moon.

She swallowed. "Thank you. This is . . ." She gestured at the landscape with all the eloquence I think any of us can muster the first time.

"It is." I sighed and let myself settle back in the chair.

"How's your arm?" She glanced at the cast.

"I was in the centrifuge yesterday and this morning before my shift started." This was true. Since Myrtle had forced me, I had been reminded of how good exercise was for me, even when it hurt. It was twenty minutes where I had direct control. And now that Ana Teresa had started talking, I needed to exert control and swing the conversation over to my question. I gnawed off another bite of whatever. "Enjoying your meal?"

Ana Teresa snorted. "The only compliment I will give it is that it is better than my mother's cooking."

"Oh dear. I thought all mothers were supposed to be paragons of virtue in the kitchen."

"Mm. Alas. After the war, she became fascinated with Italian food and collected Italian cookbooks and magazines." She rolled her eyes with a fond smile. "She does not speak Italian."

"How . . . How does that work?"

"She tried to make food that looked like the pictures. I thought I did not like pasta." She held up the bar. "This, at least, is not pretending to be something else."

"True. At least you survived it." I wrinkled my nose. "Some of the early meals in tubes . . . Some things should never be pureed. I thought they were trying to poison us."

"Nutritionally complete does not signify good."

"Speaking of poisoned food . . . Do we need to watch out for contamination? As in, could polio taint food somehow?"

"No. Unless that you were ingesting feces or spit. Polio does not survive outside the human body and certainly would not survive the requirements of food processing of the IAC."

"Sure, I can see that. But people bring treats up to the Moon in their CPKs, like . . ." I snapped my fingers as if it had just occurred to me. "Like, Curt brought candy Easter eggs up to share with people. He just picked those up at a five-and-dime. Maybe something like that got tainted."

Ana Teresa laughed in my face. "Candy eggs?" She laughed harder, in that way people do when they are overtired and something isn't really funny. "*Viajar na maionese* . . . It is not like this how polio works. Candy eggs . . . Ahahaha . . ."

I laughed with her, holding up my hands in surrender. "I just asked. Pilot! Not a doctor!"

"Very clear!" She wiped her eyes, still chuckling. Taking a deep breath, she stretched. "Thank you for this. But I should stop putting smoke in a bag and delegate sorting fabric to one of the people who recovered."

The tricky thing about polio was that even after people felt better, they could still be shedding virus, so we were keeping them isolated for safety. I nodded and took a last bite before folding the wrapper around my waxy square. "Before you go . . ."

"More candy egg hypotheses?" She stood, and her posture was a little less dragged down than it had been.

I did not see fit to answer such impertinence, I just walked to the long curve of windows that had been at our back and beckoned to her. She followed and I heard the moment when she came close enough to the glass to see Earth.

A soft gasp behind me. "*Mãe do Céu* . . ."

I flicked off the light switch. Hanging over the dark edge of the Moon, the waning gibbous jewel of our home planet hung in a field of crystal stars. I looked over my shoulder at Ana Teresa. The blue-silver earthlight traced the tears on her cheeks like rivers from home.

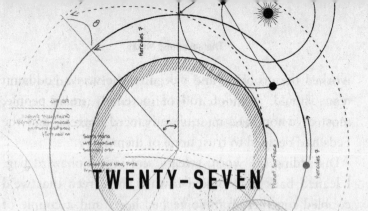

TWENTY-SEVEN

ALGERIA PLANS SALES TO CANADA
OF WHEAT WORTH $500 MILLION

OTTAWA, April 30, 1963—Algeria is on the brink of concluding a $500,000,000 foreign aid wheat deal—the biggest in her history—with Canada. An official announcement is expected early next week that an agreement has been signed with the Canadian delegation for the sale of 250,000,000 bushels of wheat to make up for shortfalls after repeated hailstorms devastated crops last autumn. The agreement would cover a period of three years, with most of the grain for delivery in the next twelve months.

THE LAMP I'D clipped to the side of the worktable gleamed on the helmet I was working on. In case anyone thought that I had only one job in the science module, they would be wrong. Suits still needed to be reconditioned, and I was the only person in the SciMod who was trained and certified in that and in good health.

For all that, I was humming as I replaced a helmet seal.

Since I had talked to Helen and the Lindholms, I'd felt . . . lighter, and not just because we had gotten out of the centrifuge room. We had a plan. We had talked, and worked the problem, and delegated the way a goddamn team should. A moon full of incredibly smart people, most of whom had multiple advanced degrees, and the Feds had decided to trust none of them.

Discarding the worn, sweaty seal in a biohazard bag, I leaned back and looked toward the screen that we'd cobbled together from some bedsheets and a couple of tethers. A sign warned people to do a verbal check before coming into the area where I was working, ostensibly so we could avoid contaminating a suit that I'd just cleaned.

But really, it was so I could have a little privacy. Closing my eyes, I listened. Fans. The regular creak and pops of metal as cooling fluids were pumped along pipes in the ceiling. Way down the corridor, I could just make out a murmur of human voice, but not enough to tell who was talking.

Satisfied, I opened my eyes and pulled the helmet toward me. I tipped it back and pulled the pad out of the back of it. I'd need to launder it before putting it back in. That was important for hygiene. More important, in this moment, was not a question of hygiene but rather the piece of paper tucked in behind the pad.

N—

I'm not sure how I got designated secretary, but here's what we've learned.

Checked the port first and your CPK was still there. We have the contents.

E. says the translation they used for the verses is the Douay-Rheims 1899 edition. It's a Catholic text.

H. says that of the people on your original list, only three are Catholic: Imelda Corona, Curtis Frye, and Catalina Suarez Gallego.

H. made a list of people who have F initials who would have had access to the BusyBee and were on our flight. That adds Faustino Albino Rios as a possibility and reinforces Curt's potential.

On my last shift in LGC, I worked my way through the flight logs, looking for people on either list who would have gone to The Garden since our arrival to see if any of them could have stolen the fertilizers. Besides us, no one from our ship has gone out there.

We've been thinking. We found Curt on our way to the port, which means he could have been coming from it. The sabotage on our BusyBee was clumsy and hasty, which would be consistent with being sick.

We think Curt is probably our man. He's in there with you. Got any ideas?

Meanwhile, go use the centrifuge room. Eat something. Get some rest.

M—

OF THE POSSIBLE outcomes for the codebooks, I had not expected them to just be sitting in a hangar. The fact that they were made me think that maybe they actually had slipped under the radar the way Clemons and I had hoped. The problem was . . . Frisch knew they existed. That the Lunar Colony Administrator hadn't retrieved them was extremely concerning. He had an opportunity to send secure reports to Clemons and wasn't.

I didn't understand why.

The radio was playing when I walked into the men's ward. Guillermo was sitting on the edge of his bed, which was a tremendous improvement. "Come on! Comparing Eusébio with that new kid Pelé? You watch. His ten goals were a fluke and that's—Oh." He saw me and suddenly didn't know where to look. "Hi, Nicole."

"Hello." I smiled at him, pretending not to notice the way all the men were either staring at me or studiously finding Anything Else to look at. "How was the game?"

"Oh, it was great. Real good." He glanced at Kadyn, who gestured at him with a sort of "go on" gesture. Guillermo shook his head. "Do you ever go to football—soccer?"

"Not usually, no." I carried a clipboard in one hand. It doesn't matter if you're on Earth or the Moon, it makes you look so official. I flipped a page on it, as if checking a note. I truly did need to do therapy with the boys, but I could start with anyone. I didn't want Curt to be Icarus, but I couldn't think of anyone on the Moon I would want it to be. There were things on Earth he couldn't have done, but those could have been done by a collaborator.

He didn't have a way to retrieve the fertilizer material. But neither did anyone else on our list. I laid the clipboard on the end of Curt's bed and smiled at him. "How are you today?"

Behind me, I heard a whispered, "Ask her," and "No, you ask her."

"Finer than froghair." But Curt frowned, glancing toward the voices, so there was no pretending that I hadn't heard.

"Ask me what, boys?" I pulled on my ridiculous black rubber glove and peeled the covers back from Curt's legs. Nearly two weeks in and they were starting to lose their muscle.

Curt rolled his eyes. "The news was on right before you came in." His voice sounded stronger today, which was good, since we had no capacity at all to deal with breathing paralysis. "The coded messages? I told them it was none of their business."

Ah . . . Frisch had said it had made it into the news. I had been wondering how long it would take to work its way through the community. This was the downside of providing radio for the boys.

"It's our business if the IAC is sending her up to spy on us!" Guillermo sputtered.

In the far corner, Hans was sitting on Kadyn's bed, playing cards. "You know, when I started coming up, we had to wear health monitors so they were getting telemetry on everything we did."

Thank heavens for Hans. He hadn't been coming to the Moon as long as I had, but long enough. I winked at him as I took hold of Curt's foot in my good hand and rested my rubber-clad cast against his knee. "Don't forget the hot mics. Nothing like having the IAC listen to, and record, everything you say. And do. Potty time was extra fun. Being on CAPCOM I once heard a male astronaut close the pee valve too early and—"

The collective gasp of horror from the men in the room as they all simultaneously imagined pinching their manhood in the vacuum valve was deeply satisfying.

I flexed Curt's foot. "Push against my hand."

"But that's not the same as coded messages." Kadyn looked at me as if I'd betrayed him personally. Although the betrayal might have been from the pee story. But probably not.

I sighed, because the fact of the matter was that I *had* been sent to spy on them. As I pushed Curt's leg to bend the knee, I used the same line I'd used on Frisch. "It's true. My husband and I have a private code that we use to talk about his political career."

"They say you sent a message to the Mars Expedition." Guillermo leaned forward, resting his elbows on his knees. "How is that about politics?"

Kenneth must be having to work hard to thread this needle at home. If we could talk, I would tell him to feed me to the wolves. It was the smart thing to do, because, as a woman, I could plead foolishness in ways he could not. I could do that on Earth as the wife of Governor Wargin. I could not do that on the Moon.

"In that instance, I sent a message for Dr. York, since he was in the hospital. We have similar strategies to deal with long separations from our spouses, so he felt comfortable asking for my help." I left out the part where I had bullied Nathaniel to let me help. I looked away from Curt for a minute and gave Guillermo a sad smile. "There's someone you miss at home, right?"

"Yes! Of course, but I don't send coded messages."

"Do reporters follow you when you're back home? Do people go through your trash? Do they write about you in opinion columns and judge you by the clothes you wear?"

In the widening of his eyes, I could see that no, of course they did not. That had not happened to anyone in the way it happened to the original astronauts and the first six "astronettes." I was also the wife of a politician. And here was the truest thing I would say to Guillermo. "There is not a moment of my life in which I'm not subject to public scrutiny. Don't begrudge me a way to talk to my husband with some semblance of privacy. Do not begrudge that for Elma."

The fans whirred around us, and on the radio, "Will You Love Me Tomorrow" played with the tight harmonies of The Shirelles. Guillermo watched his feet as if they were the most important things in the world. He could move them now, so maybe they were. If I were being charitable.

I slowed my breath and moved Curt's leg through the exercises prescribed. Up. Down. Out. In. Up. Down. Out. In.

Curt touched my hand. "I'm sorry."

I lowered his leg. "Don't be."

But my mind jumped ahead. If the coded messages had come out, people would have found our very easy First Letter messages. Which meant they would know I had been told to look into the explosive stores. They knew I was, in fact, sent to spy on their operative on the Moon.

I'm sure Clemons was looking into who on Earth had leaked copies of our teletype letters, but I still needed to figure out who on the Moon was Icarus. And nice though he was, Curt was our best bet.

I switched to his other leg. "How about you? Anyone special back home worth sending coded messages to?"

I'd been hoping for a flinch or a catch of breath or anything, but Curt just laughed. "Yeah. My mom."

"Really?" I paused before guiding his knee up. "You'd send coded messages to your mom?"

Now he hesitated. "I shouldn't have . . ." Curt let out a sigh and turned his face to the wall. "Yeah. There are some health things at home. She's very private. She doesn't like the fact that someone at the IAC has to read her mail in order to key it into the teletype. A code would . . . you know. I just want to know that she's okay."

Oh, I knew that all too well. I squeezed his foot in solidarity. At the same time, I flagged that he, too, had someone who would never be able to leave the planet. It didn't motivate me to end the space program, but everyone reacted differently to stressors. "They're working on drone mail drops, I hear. I mean, you can send physical mail now, it just takes longer."

Curt plucked at his blanket while I continued to put his leg through the paces. Up. Down. In. Out. Up. Down. In—"Hey . . . they let you go between modules, right?"

"I'm vaccinated, so yes." I omitted that Frisch had confined me to the SciMod, in lieu of my quarters, because I was curious where Curt was going with this question.

He beckoned me closer and waited until I bent down, which was not at all subtle. "Look . . . if you really are a spy, could you check a thing for me?"

"Curt."

He shook his head. "Forget I said it that way. There's just a thing that's been bugging me."

"A thing." I raised an eyebrow. I'd done this before.

Raised a concern that happened to send someone to a place where they could "stumble on" information I needed them to find in order to suspect someone else. "Go on."

"When you found me . . . I was really sick, right? I had been walking all over the place, trying to get my legs to stop . . . you know. I'd tried walking around the track at Midtown. Went to the port. Wandered around there."

This was where he was going to tell me that he'd lost his Swiss Army knife and give me a pretext to look for it or would say that he'd seen Frisch with it. I kept moving his leg at the same, steady pace.

"Anyway, I tripped on this dark block. And the more I think about it, the more I think that it was a CO_2 scrubber filter." He looked at me, line between his brows. "But why would that have been on the floor? And I'm lying here wondering . . . What if there's a problem with the scrubbers?"

"If you think that . . ." I laid his leg back down on the bed. "Why haven't you said something?"

"Because until I heard the news story, I was pretty firmly convinced it was delirium talking." He regarded me with a line above his clear gray eyes. "But there's something else going on. Isn't there? Something they aren't telling us and that makes me think I shouldn't ignore the stuff that's weird."

"I see . . ."

"It's nothing. I know. Some tech just dropped it and that's all. But I can't stop thinking about it and I can't check it because of . . . this." He gestured grimly at his legs in the only display of bitterness I'd seen in him.

"I'll check it out." If he was telling the truth, then it was, indeed, worth looking into. Although I would have to ask the Lindholms or Helen to do it. If he wasn't, then knowing about a false lead would be useful. The trick would be figuring out which it was.

TWENTY-EIGHT

U.N. PLANS DRIVE TO COLLECT DUES

By Thomas J. Hamilton, Special to the National

Times

UNITED NATIONS, Kansas City, May 1, 1963—
Secretary General U Thant has decided to open a
special campaign to collect overdue assessments for
United Nations forces in the United States. The nation
was the hardest hit by the effects of the Meteor and has
used UN forces to supplement its reconstruction efforts.
Unpaid assessments for the peacekeeping force total
about $104,000,000. If the assessments remain unpaid,
the UN may find it necessary to disband their forces by
the end of the year.

N—

Well, we checked the scrubbers. Everything was as it
should be. E. was convinced we were walking into a booby
trap and took a level of precaution that I will embarrass
him about later. Nothing was out of place. There were no
fertilizer bombs. No wires cut. No missing filters.

We did find the filter Curt was talking about, kicked

back into a corner under the stairs. It was used, so our best guess is that a tech dropped it when taking it up to be processed.

H. wants to know if you can see the port from the lounge in the SciMod. If so, would you count the number of BusyBees currently docked?

—M

ON MY NEXT break, I ran up the stairs to the lounge. At a walk, the stairs are the same as they are on Earth, because the anatomy of the leg dictates what is comfortable, but at a run, I leapt them three at a time. I bounded out of the stairwell into the lounge and dawn had come to the Moon.

Long crisp shadows, still black as night, stretched across the landscape. In the light of the early morning sun, the edges of craters blazed white. The surface sparkled with tiny balls of glass from long-ago lava flows and meteorite impacts. And I was not alone.

Frisch sat in a chair by the windows opposite the door, with a blanket drawn up around his shoulders. He looked like he was asleep. There were a lot of confusing things about this and only one simple answer. He was sick. I closed my eyes, hiding from the likeliest illness for a moment longer.

I was furious with him, but I would not wish this on anyone. At least he'd had the sense to come to the SciMod instead of trying to tough it out.

Rising on my toes, I moved as quietly as I could to the window facing the port. Outside, the other modules of the lunar colony looked like a once-grand sandcastle that had been eaten by a sea long-vanished. Buried amid the regolith, the domes and windows sparkled in the morning sun and added their own glow to the dawn. To the northeast the port module lay mostly buried, with just a small viewing area to watch approaches.

I could see four of our eight BusyBees, but the slumped mound of lunar soil that covered the port dome hid everything else. I should have been able to see our rocket, but it was still lying on its side. The other two tall rockets stood on pads around the port, but we couldn't load any of them while the main launch pad was occupied by the crashed rocket.

Which was probably the goal. I sighed, staring out at things I could not touch or fix.

"Are you all right?" Frisch's voice creaked.

"We're concerned about that now?"

His sigh caught and turned into a cough. "Mm." The hiss of pain that followed made me turn. Frisch's eyes were closed and he had a hand pressed to his stomach as he spoke. "I am sorry I yelled. I should not have done that, and yes, I do care. I care about everyone that is up here."

His hand had a reddish-purple rash on the back and he'd lost hair. This did not look like polio. "What's wrong?"

"Dr. Brandão is not certain."

I took a step closer, taking in the hollows under his cheeks and the set of pain in his shoulders. "Did you . . . did you ask her about poison?"

He tilted his head, watching me. "That has not been ruled out."

Could you calibrate a dose to make yourself sick, but not

dead? Sometimes I hate my brain, because I stood there, looking at a man I had known for years, and wondered if he'd poisoned himself to throw us off the scent. I took in a long, deep breath. "Is there anything you want me to do?"

Frisch rubbed his forehead. "I presume you're not offering to do paperwork."

"If that were on the table, yes, I would do it." I chewed the inside of my lip. "Why didn't you retrieve the codebooks?"

"Codebooks? *Mein Gott* . . ." He pulled the blanket about his shoulders, hunching into it like a stork going to nest. "They slipped my mind, I suppose. I have . . . I have had some trouble concentrating."

"I see." I sat on the arm of the chair near him trying to gauge the truth of that. Was he impaired because of poison or was he masking a deliberate effort to obstruct finding Icarus? My best option, either way, was to try to make him an ally. "How can I help?"

Frisch's eyes watered. He blinked rapidly, looking away from me. His Adam's apple bobbed as he swallowed and his voice was hoarser when he spoke again. "I need to do a duty roster." He cleared his throat and straightened a little in his chair. "They're launching the relief ship tomorrow. *Lunetta* is doing an expedited cargo transfer to a lunar shuttle Friday, and we should see them land the morning of Tuesday, the seventh. I've tapped Eugene to act as interim administrator, but he doesn't know the forms and I'm . . . Would you show him the ropes?"

"Of course." Of course he just needed me as a secretary. Never mind that it would be more efficient to let me do the job instead of training a man. But Eugene was a good man and would do a good job covering for Frisch and it would be good for his career and everything was good.

THE NEXT MORNING, I was released from my cage in the SciMod to help Eugene with triplicate. He stood next to Frisch's desk, resting his hand on the back of the chair before he took a breath and sat down. Myrtle gave a nod when Eugene sat, as if to say that this was where he should be. I agreed. Although not under these circumstances.

He drummed his fingers on the desk, looking over the paperwork stacked there. "Silver lining. I have an extra day to get up to speed."

The cargo launch on Earth this morning had been scrubbed. A sensor reading was not what it should be. It was a mundane reason to scrub. I'd been on a dozen launches that delayed or scrubbed because of a sensor.

I sat down in the chair opposite Eugene and crossed my leg over my knee, trying to make this seem normal. "Does anyone else think that scrub was Earth First?"

"Immediately." Eugene's face was grim. "I will not rest easy until Halim lands that thing here."

"Amen." Myrtle looked ceilingward. "I have not had this much anxiety about a launch since your first one."

We always joked about being strapped to a giant bomb and hurled into the vacuum of space to do science. It was less funny now.

"All right . . ." Myrtle turned to face the filing cabinet. "I'm going to start digging while we talk."

Helen was leaning against the doorframe with her arms

crossed, and if someone was playing chess with her, they had already lost. "Nicole? What was the answer to my question about the number of BusyBees?"

"I could only see the southwest side. Four BusyBees were visible in berths one through five."

"Ha!" Helen slapped her thigh. "Berth five was empty, correct?"

"Yes . . ." I stared at the glee on her face. "I look forward to hearing about this breakthrough."

"I wondered how someone could go to The Garden without a ship, which led me to wondering if there was a way to take a BusyBee without it being noticed. The inventory says a ship should be there waiting for maintenance. The hatch indicators show a ship docked there. The porthole is frosted over so you can't tell what's on the other side. But . . . the lighting is wrong. I *thought* it was not a ship but the only way to be certain was to open the hatch and . . ." She spread her hands wide, as if drawing a decompression in the air. "That would be a bad day."

I gave a low whistle. "One more thing there . . . The approach to that berth drops out of visual range of LGC if you don't maintain your altitudes correctly."

At the filing cabinet, Myrtle was nodding, because she flew the same bus routes to the outposts that I did. "A good pilot could stay out of line-of-sight, especially if he were comfortable with night flying."

"Which is great and all." Eugene raised a finger. "But where's the ship?"

The silence sat between us under the whir of fans. That

was a darn good question. If Icarus had taken it to The Garden, then why hadn't he brought it back? We knew exactly where both Curt and Frisch were. But there was a third name on our list. "Does anyone know where Faustino is?"

"No . . . Although we've moved people around so much I don't know where anyone is." Eugene turned to the shelf of notebooks on Frisch's wall, running his finger underneath them. "I'm assuming it's written down, though."

"Let me." I leaned over the desk and pulled the current duty roster from the left side. "If I'm here to be your secretary, let me do this much. Because you don't want me typing for you."

As I flipped through the pages, looking for Faustino's name, Myrtle opened another filing cabinet drawer. "These are a mess . . . I expected better of a British man."

"Swiss German. Just has the accent." I turned another page. "And the pretension."

"Hence the teakettle, I presume?"

At the desk, Eugene said, "Teakettle?" He spun in the chair and spotted the gleaming chrome appliance. "A pressure kettle? Hot damn."

"Language." Myrtle didn't even look up from the filing cabinet.

"It's a room full of pilots! Or are you telling me that ladies can't handle a little salty language?" He picked up the kettle and riffled through the tea things.

"I'm telling you that I want you to watch your mouth. And stop going through the man's tea stash like you're a grave rob—" She gasped, spinning to point at the tea. "We need to take all of that to Ana Teresa and have her test it."

Eugene set down the box of tea bags he was holding. We all stared at it as if it were a bomb waiting to go off. It might be poisoned. Or none of it might be. Or maybe it was the kettle. Or maybe Frisch just got unlucky and randomly developed a liver problem.

"Shit. Goddamn it all to hell." Eugene rubbed his forehead, pinching his eyes closed. "Nicole, will you take it to SciMod when we're through here?"

"Yes." I'd been let out of my cage, but I was still one of the few people vaccinated and Ana Teresa needed me. I reached the last page of this week's roster and flipped back to the beginning. "Faustino isn't assigned to any tasks this week."

That wasn't odd, in and of itself, since the quarantine meant that a lot of tasks were on hold. Except for one little problem. I looked across to Helen, who appeared to be having the exact same thought I was.

"If he had no assignments, why did he have a spacesuit that needed to be serviced?"

THAT NIGHT, I dreamed that it was raining. When I woke, my face was pressed into a damp spot on my hammock's pillow. Truly, the fact that I drool when I sleep is one of my least attractive features and being in 1/6 g should make it happen slower, but alas, does not. My body barely flattened the fabric of my hammock, but fluid dynamics still allowed saliva to escape and saturate my pillow. I was too warm in the small space. Without a fan to circulate the air it felt as warm and muggy as a summer night on Earth. Something plinked in the darkness of my storage locker. From the sliver of light peeking into the room from sickbay, I couldn't tell the time. But I'd been asleep long enough that the phosphorescent labels had faded to nothing.

I yawned and rolled carefully over to check my Omega watch where I'd propped it on a shelf of saline bags.

Two a.m. I had only been asleep for three hours. I set the watch back down, and the shelf underneath it was damp. Groaning, I sat up. If one of the saline bags had sprung a leak, no telling what other supplies were getting wet.

I stood. The floor was damp too. Water dripped in my face.

"What the . . ." I turned the light on.

Condensation hung on every surface. As I stood there, dumbfounded, a heavy droplet fell from the ceiling. Beads of water hung from pipes and ran down the metal shelves. Granted, the closet wasn't intended to have people sleeping in it, but I shouldn't have created that much moisture with my breath. Something was very wrong with the environmental controls.

I couldn't help thinking about the CO_2 filter Curt had pointed me toward, even though those filters had nothing to do with humidity.

Opening the door, I stepped out into rain. Not real rain, I'll grant, but any water falling on the Moon was so off-nominal that the emotional impact felt like rain. The main room of sickbay had only the dim glow of a night-light, but it illuminated enough condensation coating the exposed pipes that water was dripping steadily. Garnet saw me and visibly relaxed on her cot. Her voice was barely a whisper. "Thank heavens. Birgit is on the floor."

One cot was empty.

"Birgit?" Warm water dripped on my arm and ran down my skin, disappearing when it hit my cast. I grimaced. That was going to be a problem.

"Here." Her voice came from a puddle of darkness near the wall.

Hurrying, I slipped on the damp floor and caught myself on Wafiyyah's bed. She was sitting up and wiping water off her face. "What's going on?"

"It looks like the dehumidifiers have failed." Humans exhaled carbon dioxide, yes, but also water vapor. It's why the first generation of space helmets fogged up. "Don't worry. The folks in ops will be right on this."

I found Birgit, on her hands and one knee, dragging the other leg behind her. She dropped back to sit with her weak leg stretched in front of her and smiled up at me. "I nearly was there." She gestured to the wall. "But I have not yet found out how I would to reach the intercom."

"I've got it." I held out my hands. "Let me get you back to bed."

Birgit shook her head. "I'm at the moment well. Call ops so they may first start working the problem."

I nodded, looking around the room for details to tell them. It was much worse out here, with a steady plink, plink of water dripping on metal and plastic. "I'll let them know you spotted the problem."

And that made her last name run through my head. Birgit Furst. Swiss. Worked in comms. It was probably a coincidence, but things turned over in my head. Sure, she hadn't been at the church service, but then neither had Frisch. Perhaps she should have been on my list. Perhaps everyone should have been. Standing, I pressed the intercom button.

A thousand bees stung my hand. Light cracked.

Everything went dark.

TWENTY-NINE

POLAR EXPLORER'S BODY FOUND AS GLACIERS MELT

By John Schwartz, Special to the National Times

NUUK, Greenland, May 3, 1963—The ice cap of this northern nation gave up one of its secrets today, as the body of the scientist and explorer Alfred Wegener was uncovered by the receding snow and ice.

Alfred Lothar Wegener, who came up with the concept of continental drift, died on a Greenland expedition in 1930.

Wegener proposed in 1912 that the Earth's continents were once joined but broke up and drifted away from each other. Wegener was not the first to notice that the east coast of South America seemed to fit together with the west coast of Africa, but he assembled a wealth of geological and fossil evidence to support the theory. While any schoolchild can see that the eastern South America could nestle snugly against western Africa, Wegener did the scientific work of assembling geological and fossil data that substantiated his claims; finding similar fossils of animals and plants across a vast ocean suggested that the separate continents had once been joined in a supercontinent he called Pangea. Mainstream geologists, however, disputed his theory, which languished until the 1960s, when the developing field of plate tectonics showed the underlying mechanism of continental movement.

———————

"Climate change is a global crisis, but it can surprise us with good news," said Peter Harrer, Wegener's grandson. "I am pleased that we will be able to return my grandfather's remains to his ancestral home instead of the bleak Arctic wastes."

"I FOUND HER." Soft hands patted my arms and ran down to grip my right wrist. "There's a pulse."

It was dark. Blinking didn't fix that.

My left arm was a pulsing, stinging, hot-and-cold ache. Water dripped in my face and the air smelled like a thunderstorm. "The picnic will get wet." Even as I said it, I was pretty sure that didn't make sense. I frowned, trying to sort out why it was dark. The clouds were hiding the stars, I guessed.

"I'll find Dr. Brandão." A young woman with a Swiss German accent spoke from across the room.

Another woman, maybe Arabic, said, "Careful you don't get shocked! Everything is wet."

"There's no power."

It felt like dragging my brain through sludge, but I finally got a little traction. Shocked. I'd been shocked. I swallowed and my throat hurt. "I'm all right. Just stunned."

"Stunned?!" The woman who had taken my pulse sounded honestly offended. I knew her name. Arizonan. Imelda. "You were thrown across the room. I can still see the arc burned into my eyes."

"Just give me a brandy and I'll be fine." I pushed myself up on my right elbow. Every muscle in my body ached, but something was very wrong with my left arm.

"A brandy?" Imelda did not sound as if she had gained any more confidence about my wits.

"It's something my mother used to say. Hit by lightning three times." The room was so dark, I was getting phantom flashes of color at the edges. "Just to confirm . . . The lights are out?"

"Yes." Her hand was still on my wrist. "Just rest until we get the doctor."

"*Stärnefoïfi.*" That was Birgit, who said she'd find Ana Teresa. "The door is shut."

"Yes. We lost power." I wanted to curl protectively around my wrist, but sat up, feeling a little more present. There was some reason that I didn't want Birgit to leave, but I was having trouble dragging it out of the morass. "Airlocks automatically close."

"You can still open it, right?" A breathy voice right on the edge of a whisper. Garnet. The computer who had been seeing Kadyn Murphy.

"Yes, but we can't see to check the Delta-v pressure." That might not be reliable even if we could see the gauge. "Did anyone notice what time it started?"

A general murmur of apologies and demurrals went through the sickbay. I rolled onto my knees, right hand resting in a shallow puddle of condensation. The cotton padding inside my cast was damp and cold against my skin. I sighed and let my head drop. It was raining. We didn't have a working intercom, and I was the only person who could walk.

Theoretically walk. I hadn't tried to stand yet, and Mother was always wobbly for a while after a lightning strike. I didn't even have a nine-iron to lean on. At least no one could see me struggle as I sat back on my haunches and decided that standing would need to wait for a minute. A drip splashed on my head and ran through my hair.

"All right, ladies . . . Let's work the problem." I closed my eyes, which bizarrely made it easier to think, even in a dark room. "Roll call and status."

"Birgit Furst. Unharmed . . . Do we talk about the polio?"

Wincing, I turned toward the sound of her voice, which was to my right and presumably near the door. "Only if you are having a status change or need immediate medical assistance." Why flag something when I was the only person in the room who didn't have it?

"Imelda Corona. Unharmed." She was still next to me on my right side.

"Garnet Cunningham. Unharmed." An ironic phrase, since the computer was one of the hardest hit and could barely whisper. Ana Teresa had put her on pure oxygen, but it wasn't that much more than the normal air here. We use an argon/nitrogen mix to reduce fire danger, but oxygen was still a higher percentage than on Earth.

I shuddered, imagining that arc in one of the old pure oxygen capsules.

"Wafiyyah Zinat Abbasi. Unharmed." Also, still in bed and slightly behind me, which made it easier for me to build a mental picture of where I was in the room.

I was perhaps a meter from the wall the intercom shared with the outer door, so I had not been blown clear across the room. I'd probably fallen back and the process of sitting had made me seem to be farther away than I was. That meant the storage closet would be to my left on the other short wall.

"Good." Something else was wrong, besides the water dripping, and my arm, and the blackout. The blackout was . . . there should be emergency lights. It shouldn't be this dark. "Someone else will be working the larger problems, so let's solve just the things in this room. Light. Water. Door. In that order. Any chance someone has a flashlight?"

"The light Dr. Brandão uses to check our eyes is battery powered," Imelda said. "I think it's in one of the cabinets."

"Good call." If the door was to my right and the supply closet was to my left along with most of the beds, then all I had to do was find the door and feel along the cabinets to the left. "Birgit, have you found the door?"

"Yes, but I haven't done anything with it."

"Good. The light should be in one of the drawers to the left of it." I crawled one-handed through patches of water toward her voice, not quite trusting myself yet to stand in the dark. "Just talk randomly so I can follow your voice?"

"I can look for it." She grunted and fabric rustled. "Which drawer is it in?"

Her voice was coming from higher than it had. I stopped. "Did you just stand up?"

"I dragged myself, yes." It sounded as though she were hopping next to the counter. "I also get strength in my left leg back, but it won't support me. Yet. Which drawer?"

I squinted, as if that would make my memory clearer. God, I hurt. "Second set from the door. Top drawer. I think."

Metal rattled and I crawled in that direction. There was something else. Something I should be thinking about. Even if I hadn't just been shocked, the mugginess would make it hard to think. It honestly felt like a summer night on Earth and made me wish for one of Mother's sandalwood hand fans.

I stopped crawling. "The fans are off."

"What?" Then Imelda gasped as she caught up. "How much breathable air is in here?"

From her bed, Garnet whispered, "We have oxygen tanks."

"Good girl." But people in the rest of the colony would not, and it had finally occurred to me that there was no light filtering in from the view port in the door. Power was off in the hall, too. The rooms were big enough that it wouldn't be a problem for a couple of hours, but it would become an issue. "So, we're fine, once we get lights in here we can start addressing the water. Leave solving the power issue to the team in maintenance."

"Found i—*Gopferdammi.*" Metal clattered and bounced. The snap of glass cracking. Something metal rolled across the floor. "Of all the stupid . . . I'm sorry. I dropped it."

It sounded as if the bulb had broken, too. Swell. "Easy to do. Go back to bed and be careful of glass."

"But it's . . . it's so dark." Garnet's voice sounded a little shaky. "What are we going to do?"

There's a thing that happens to people when they are helpless. They become afraid of things that in their normal life wouldn't faze them at all. Garnet probably had not been afraid of the dark since she was a tiny kid, but trapped in a box, unable to move, and with rain dripping on her face? The dark was the one thing that seemed fixable.

"There will be another lightbulb . . . Heck. Probably there's a box of the eye thingies, because the IAC loves redundancy." I reversed course, trying to find my way to the storage closet. Water dripped along my back. "Hey, Garnet, talk to me so I can find the storeroom. Where did you grow up?"

As soon as the words were out of my mouth, I winced. I was so discombobulated that I had asked the question we'd stopped asking after the Meteor and I knew the answer.

"I . . . I grew up in Delaware." The state that didn't exist anymore. In the dark, we were all remembering the day the Meteor slammed into the Chesapeake Bay. Her voice got stronger as she talked, so that was something. "It was a funny little house, white wood. My great-grandfather built it and added on a bit at a time. The thing I remember most is two giant magnolias out on either side of the front walk. These were ancient. The trunks were so big around that I couldn't reach, even with my face pressed against the bark. The branches bent down to the ground and it was hollow inside. We played house in there."

I barked my shoulder against the metal upright of her bed and sent a jolt down my left arm into my wrist. I grunted, tucking my head as if that would keep me silent. Jesus . . . it felt like I'd broken my arm again. But I had a cast on. I sucked in a breath and tried to sound casual. "Found you."

"I grew up in an apartment. We had balconies, but no trees," Wafiyyah said. "Your house sounds magical."

"It was." She gave a little laugh. "No one ever asks about it, so it's like it stopped existing that day. I mean . . . you know."

"Where were you?"

"My cousin was getting married in Texas, so we were all out there." She asked the dark, "What about you? Do you remember where you were when the Meteor hit?"

God. Yes. I had been reading the paper in the breakfast room with my parents when the housekeeper came in and turned on the radio. She hadn't said anything, just turned it on with her face as white and starched stiff as the tablecloth. We'd thought it was another war at first. I set my jaw against the memories of that room getting smaller and smaller as we listened and I felt my way down Garnet's bed to the wall.

"I was at school in Constantine. Teaching," Wafiyyah said. "I heard trucks passing right next to the school. I remember the students, they were standing and running to the window to see what was happening, the way we had when soldiers roamed the city during the war. Except there were no trucks. Later, the principal turned on the school radio and we understood what we heard."

Wall. I patted it until I found the door to the storeroom.

"You could hear it? From Algeria . . . Jesus." Imelda's voice sounded as if she'd made her way back to her bed, which explained why I hadn't bumped into her. "I was out riding with my fiancé. We came back to the house and his mother met us on the front porch. Weeping. I did not think she was human before that moment."

I grabbed the doorframe to steady myself and clawed my way to my feet. I had not been this sore since the survival training they made the astronauts do in the desert. I did not quite keep a groan to myself as my muscles protested every movement.

"Nicole, are you okay?" Birgit asked.

"Just practicing vocal exercises. Oooooo-eeeeee-oooooo . . ." I felt my way into the storeroom, trying to remember how the medical staff had it set up, and a constellation of blue-green stars floated around the walls. I started to laugh with relief. "Oh, bless the IAC and their redundancies."

"What?" Garnet's covers rustled. "What is it?"

"Everything is labeled with glow-in-the-dark paint." I had turned the lights on in here before I went out, so they'd had time to charge before everything shorted. But the sickbay's overhead lights had been off, so any glow was minimal. "So, that's one thing going right."

"Two! You weren't killed." Imelda's voice sounded markedly more cheerful.

"Give me time . . ." Keeping my left arm pressed against my stomach, I scanned the shelves looking for the eye flashlight thingies and the batteries. "While I'm doing this, see if you can work the problem of the water. Prime concerns are your safety and limiting supply damage."

"Roger, wilco." If Wafiyyah had access to a clipboard, I think she would have started making notes right then.

In sickbay, the girls were tossing ideas around, identifying the problems and the goals. I held on to the shelves and let myself have a second to breathe until I spotted the eye thingies, which were labeled "ENT pocket lights."

When I carried them out, the girls clapped. I held one under my chin to illuminate my face. "Welcome to the Lady Astronaut slumber party!" After the complete darkness, the room seemed lit like a dinner party with a thousand tapers. "Do we have a solution for the water?"

Imelda shared a thumbs-up with Wafiyyah. "Yes, we do." She pointed to Ana Teresa's rolling stool in the corner. "And if you get that for me, we can even help."

"You were electrocuted last night and I am only now seeing you?" Ana Teresa glared at me as she snapped her gloves into place. The fact that we were in an improvised sickbay in Le Restaurant in Midtown did not reduce the fury behind her gaze, which felt unjust since I had come to her on my own.

"Technically, I was shocked. Electrocution results in death." The curtains drawn around the examining table did not do much to shield us from the women housed here. "And technically, it was this morning."

If it hadn't been unhygienic, I think she might have spat

on the floor. Instead, she muttered in a long stream of Portuguese.

"Sorry?" I smiled at her as if she were not obviously cursing me out. "Come again?"

From the other side of the curtain, Birgit said, "She's saying that pilots are terrible and that astronauts are the worst. That you could have a propeller through your body and you would insist that you are fine. That she's met donkey's rumps with more intelligence than—"

"I do not need you translating, thank you very much!" Ana Teresa faced the curtain with her hands on her hips. "And it was mule's ass. Not rump. Also, your cast is a mess and will have to be replaced."

I covered a grin. There was something I needed to talk to Birgit about and I could not, for the life of me, remember what it was.

"Sorry. The water was just . . . everywhere." I sat on the examining table and kicked my legs as if I weren't exhausted and in pain.

"The water, I do not blame you for." She took my left hand, turning it over, and I gasped.

Ana Teresa looked up sharply at me, and carefully manipulated my fingers as if I were a manikin. She tapped my index finger, where I'd picked up a small wound, and made a satisfied sound. "Ooh! Jellinek's mark."

"What?"

"The electricity entered you there." She peered at the other fingers. "Haven't seen one outside of literature."

"Oh." I made a note that the way to get Ana Teresa to smile was to present a novel symptom.

"Do you have any idea how lucky you are that you weren't killed?"

"Yes." The short had knocked out power in the entire science module. It had fried things so badly we had needed to move everyone out and into Midtown until the maintenance team finished repairs. Those would have to wait while they got the module dried out, and it had to be completely dry—including inside the walls—or risk another short.

It was nice, I suppose, to have a change of scenery. The men were housed in the library. The women in Le Restaurant. It was not ideal, but the best available option. Watching Eugene organize and run the operation had been a joy. I'd been more than happy to just go where I was pointed.

The pain in my arm ranged from a dull throb to a bullet punch. Any effort to help with recovery made it worse.

She walked behind the examining table. "Remove your shirt, please."

I froze. Funny the moments that will snap something into focus that you know and have shoved to the side. I hadn't been eating. "Oh, but it's just my arm."

Ana Teresa gave a long, aggravated sigh. "Shirt. Off."

Here's the thing. If I fought her too much, she would write that up. So I pulled my shirt over my head and waited with it clutched to my chest as if I had virtue to protect.

She touched a spot next to my left shoulder blade. Ana Teresa pulled her hand away and stood behind me silently for a moment. Then she raised her voice and shouted at the curtain. "I will feel better about eavesdropping if you talk amongst yourselves."

Beyond the curtain, the silence sounded like a rabbit caught in the open and then a conversation sprang into spontaneous life about Garnet's concern for her sourdough starter, which she hadn't been able to feed while in sickbay.

"Put your shirt back on."

As I did, the conversation outside sounded more like people talking about favorite pets than bread-making. Which I suppose it was. What kinds of pets can you have on the Moon? Yeast.

Ana Teresa walked around to her cart and pulled open a drawer. She picked up a foil pouch of bacon cubes, tore it open, and held it out to me. I didn't recoil, but the breath I took was too short and too fast to be casual.

"Oh, I'm not—"

She held up her hand. "Please. Treating a city full of astronauts is already exhausting enough. This is—I went to an all-girls school. Demonstrate to me that this is not a problem."

I swallowed. "Yes, ma'am. I'm sorry." I took the packet. The cube of fat and oil glistened in my hand. I lifted my chin and took a bite. This was its own form of control.

Ana Teresa watched me chew, which only made the thing congeal in my mouth, sticking to every surface. Bacon should not be in a cube. She gestured for my arm. "Let's get that cast off. I should have done it last night."

The plaster was dinged and had crumbled around my thumb and fingers. Underneath, the cotton gauze had turned a nasty gray-brown. The cast had my notes in the form of overlapping signatures and the stars I had decorated it with as reminders. "Oh . . . Oh. But you have a lot to do. This is still functional."

"Besides being an affront, the padding underneath is probably soaked. I don't want to add 'infection' to the list of your other ailments."

"Fair. May I keep it as a souvenir?"

"After being wet for a day, it will reek, but if you wish to, so be it." She dragged her little rolling cart of supplies closer and pulled what looked like a small rotary saw from it. "This vibrates and will not cut the skin."

"Swell, I hadn't been worried about that until now."

"Quite safe. See?" Ana Teresa plugged it in and turned it on, buzzing it against her palm as if I needed to be reassured like a child. She stepped closer to lay it against the cast.

I turned my head to look at the curtain. I couldn't make out any words through the buzzing, although I could hear the rise and fall of voices.

I kept my voice low anyway. "How is LCA Frisch?"

Ana Teresa's lips tightened, but she did not look away from the cutter buzzing through the cast on my arm. "It is not my custom to discuss patients with others."

"You know why I'm asking." I chewed and watched her work. "Would you feel comfortable discussing tea?"

The saw continued to vibrate through the cast, sending soft clouds of dust to drift slowly in the air. Ana Teresa cut through the names of people who had written on the cast to wish me well. She cleared her throat. "The tea was fine. The sugar cubes were not."

"Thallium?" They had used it on Nathaniel.

The saw slowed. Her lids flickered for a moment, but she didn't look up from the cast. "Yes."

The room went very cold. All I could think about was the doctor on Earth who had been grateful for Nathaniel's bleeding ulcer. Without that, he would not have gotten treatment and it would have killed him. "It's treated with Prussian blue, right?"

"Yes."

"Like the paint?"

"The pigment is the same, without the oils, et cetera. Thankfully the launch was scrubbed again, which will allow them to add it. Halim will hand carry it in the command module." Ana Teresa guided the saw across the back of my hand, grimacing. "That is the first time I have ever been grateful for a scrub, although grateful is the wrong word, since it also has the polio vaccines and I would like those sooner rather than later."

I ignored that. "I have Prussian blue."

She straightened, the saw dying in her hands. "Not the paint. Where?"

"Raw pigment." I waved my free hand. "I don't paint. I just keep supplies on hand for the artists. It's in the gallery."

"How much?"

I shrugged, holding my fingers apart as though I were holding a cookie. "A box?"

Ana Teresa took a deep breath, closing her eyes. With a nod, she bent back to my cast. "Good."

"Well, let's go!"

The corner of her mouth twisted in a smirk. "If I let you out without putting a new cast on, I will never get you back. The last thing I need is to reset your arm." She wrinkled her nose at the smell that rose as she pried the crumbling plaster apart. "But you may have saved this man's life."

"I'm glad of— Gah." The plaster snapped, jarring my wrist. I dropped the package of bacon squares. Pain radiated with cold sickness.

"That hurt?" Ana Teresa did not move her hands.

"Yeah." My breath kept hitching. Shaking my head, I blinked back tears. "Caught me by surprise. Keep going."

The muscles in the corner of her jaw worked. Carefully, she let go of the mangled pieces of plaster and turned toward her supply cabinet. Ana Teresa pulled a drawer open and took out a syringe. "I'm going to numb the area before we keep going."

"It's fine." It throbbed in time with my heartbeat. "Really."

"In very rare cases, the tetanic contractions caused by an electrical shock can break bone." Ana Teresa pulled a vial out from another drawer and kept talking, as if she hadn't heard me. Her voice was somehow clinical and angry at the same time. "Typically, with arms, it happens to small children whose bones are fragile. Like someone who has a loss of bone density due to living in space. Or the osteoporosis caused by anorexia."

The bacon squares lay on the floor where I'd dropped them.

Ana Teresa filled the vial. "My X-ray machine is in SciMod. I will set your arm as best I can, but this is going to hurt."

I swallowed. "What about Frisch?"

Ana Teresa snapped the vial down into the drawer and stepped closer. "After. Now? For twenty minutes, you are going to pretend that your health matters."

THIRTY

WIFE OF GOVERNOR WARGIN
ELECTROCUTED ON MOON

ARTEMIS BASE, Moon, May 4, 1963—Late last night, a malfunction of the dehumidification system in the lunar colony resulted in a dramatic rise in levels of moisture in the air to the point that the colony experienced its first rain. Far from being charming, this freak occurrence placed the citizens on the Moon at grave risk as systems designed to operate in dry environments were coated in water. Especially troubling is that the section of the colony most affected by this houses the medical wing where the victims of a polio outbreak are being treated.

Mrs. Wargin, wife of the current Democratic front-runner for president, was in charge of overnight care in the women's polio wing when she noticed the rain. Attempting to call for aid resulted in a short, which, reportedly, threw the governor's wife across the room. The power surge tripped multiple breakers in the module and left them without power for several hours. Despite this, Mrs. Wargin rallied the women and was instrumental in the rescue and recovery efforts.

ANA TERESA TOLD the truth. It hurt.

It . . . it hurt a lot.

I let her give me something for pain and could still feel my arm throbbing inside my new cast. It was muted, but present with every beat of my heart.

What I wanted to do was go back to my bunk, take a Miltown, and lie down. But I had a meeting with Eugene to go over the inventory forms.

If I had hurt like this in training, would it have been enough to stop me? No.

During my endurance desert training, when I had turned up every morning all polished and perky, it had almost destroyed the guys. They had no idea how much I'd been faking. So I dragged my posture up to polished correctness, put on some lipstick, and headed to the AdminMod.

Eugene lifted his head from the stack of forms on his desk. "You're looking better."

Lipstick will do that. Back during the war, I'd once bluffed my way into a German signal office on the strength of a clipboard, my lipstick, and—

I blinked as an idea emerged nearly fully formed in my head. "Eugene . . ." I chased the idea back to Germany and brought it forward to the Moon. "Eugene. I think I have an idea for how to flush out Icarus."

WE RAN THROUGH our plans as carefully as if it were a sim. On Monday morning, when Eugene, Myrtle, Helen, and I walked into comms, the young woman behind the desk looked up and smiled with neutral welcome, but her eyes flicked through the four of us as if comparing us to the schedule in front of her.

I met her gaze with an equally neutral smile. "The acting administrator needs the IAC secure line, stat. Four headsets."

By this point, everyone knew the role that Eugene had played in organizing the relief this weekend. She did not hesitate. "Yes, ma'am." Pulling her roster toward her, she ran a pencil down the list and made a tick mark next to it. "The secure booth is in use. One moment while I clear it."

As she headed to the hall of phone booths to make space for us, a South African man muttered, "A Black administrator . . ."

Eugene pivoted and stepped past me. "Philippus Fourie. Construction. Right? PhD in material sciences from University of Cape Town." His voice was affable, and then he crossed his arms over his chest. Eugene was an easygoing guy. He was funny and charming. It was easy to forget that he wasn't just a pilot. He was a *fighter pilot*. He just stood there, looking at the guy, with this beautifully straight spine and the slightest tuck to his chin.

It was one of the finest uses of posture I have ever seen. Eugene did *nothing*. It was all in his stance. He waited and let the guy build the threat in his own mind. The fellow's breathing got a little bit quicker and he shifted in his seat.

The moment he did, Eugene smiled. "See you around."

He executed a military turn and walked back to us. Poor Fourie wilted in his seat and picked up a copy of *Popular Mechanics* that he almost certainly wasn't reading. Myrtle wet her lips and put her hand on her husband's bicep.

Pretty sure that every woman in the room, and a good percentage of the guys, were envying her right then.

"LCA Lindholm?" The young woman reappeared. "The booth is ready for you now."

"Thank you, Anne." Eugene gave her a nod as we walked down the hall to the booth.

I raised my brows and murmured, "Do you know everyone's name?"

"It was on her desk." He opened the booth door and held it for us. "And I make it a point to read up on the South Africans deployed here. Most of them are fine, but some are . . . 'indoctrinated' is the kindest I can be."

Myrtle took her place at the table. "He means racist assholes."

"Language!" Eugene laughed as he followed Helen inside.

"There's a time and place for cursing. Tell me I'm wrong." Myrtle laid a file folder on the table and sniffed.

"Tell you you're wrong? Oh, no. I'm not walking into that trap." Eugene pulled chairs out for Helen and me, sobering. "All right. Any last questions or second thoughts before I put the call through?"

The levity sucked out of the room. I shook my head and settled into the chair, trying to find a position in which to rest my cast that was comfortable. Myrtle's mouth thinned as she passed out the agendas from her folder. Helen's expression settled into her chess face.

Eugene placed the call. We picked up our headsets and waited as we were patched through *Lunetta* to Earth to Clemons's secretary and finally to him.

"Eugene." Clemons cleared his throat. "Status report and then I'll update you on the supply ship."

During this call, we had to assume that Icarus's counterpart was listening.

We knew they had an operative in comms on *Lunetta* or at an Earth-based station. We were guessing that the "sproing" was the sound of the calls being recorded so they could review them for hidden messages later. In theory, we had a few seconds before they started recording.

And we planned to make them panic.

"Understood. We're activating the Rhode Island protocol. Code four three four echo papa. I repeat. Code four three four echo papa." Eugene looked up from his agenda and pointed at Helen. "Here's the message."

Nodding, Helen lifted her agenda and began to speak in Taiwanese. Her voice was clear and moved each syllable as if it were a chess piece, sliding from square to square. I almost never heard her speak in her native language, except in times of stress when she sometimes defaulted to curses. Listening to her now, you could hear the purpose and power of each character she uttered.

You'd never know that she was reciting lyrics to the popular Taiwanese song "You Can't Raise a Goldfish in a Wineglass" intercut with IAC acronyms and random numbers. There was no Rhode Island protocol.

The Earth Firsters tended to be Americans, so there was a fair chance they might not have a Taiwanese speaker on hand. It had the potential to increase the amount of scrambling they had to do trying to decipher our garbage.

On the handset, I heard the sound of a spring being

struck. I gave a thumbs-up to confirm that we had listeners. Myrtle clicked the timer button on her Omega three and beckoned for Helen to keep going. On Earth, somewhere, her words were being frantically recorded for analysis. Someone would be trying to re-create the text they had missed.

We listened to thirty more seconds of Taiwanese incantations and then Myrtle nodded. We'd hopefully given them enough to stay scrambling and occupied, as well as buying Clemons time to figure out what was going on.

Helen stopped talking.

Eugene crossed his fingers, still looking at the agenda. "Confirm receipt of message. Repeat. Confirm receipt of message."

The lag almost killed me, waiting for all of that to get to Earth and Clemons's response to make it back to us.

He cleared his throat. I could imagine his cigar lowered, smoke drifting forgotten around him as he squinted at the wall. "Confirmed receipt of message."

Eugene punched the air. Myrtle clapped her hands silently together and mouthed, "Thank you, Lord" to the ceiling.

Clemons had just told us that he was going to play along. I closed my eyes, letting out a silent breath of relief, and sagged against my chair.

"Per step twenty-four of the Rhode Island protocol, in the absence of transport, your operative has prepared a verbal report." Eugene looked at me. "Go ahead."

Disinformation and contention within the ranks is a

good way to destabilize an enemy. Confuse them. Make them waste time trying to find a rat within their own ranks.

"Ja." The voice was modeled on a girl I used to be. It could be mistaken for a few different Swiss German IAC employees like Johanna Lehrer or Birgit Furst. Most importantly, it did not sound like me. It made it sound like Icarus had miscalculated.

We hoped. We also hoped that Clemons would understand that everything that followed was a lie.

"The polio outbreak has had a silver lining in that one of the Earth First agents is among the patients. They have agreed to cooperate with us and send false reports to their superiors on Earth. We do not expect them to be completely forthcoming, of course, but the conversation has just begun. However, they did offer the location of the missing vehicle as a measure of good faith. That corresponds to the event on the sixteenth, which led us to the other equipment. Separately, my investigations have uncovered evidence that Herr Frisch was in conversation with the U.S. government about offering refuge in the lunar colony to several highly placed officials, including members of President Denley's family who would not otherwise qualify for spaceflight." Kenneth had said "government," and while it might not be Denley including his name might confuse them. "Given the recent news about coded messages, which implicates Mrs. Wargin, I believe my cover is still in place. Permission to continue. Repeat. Request permission to return to radio silence and continue with the Rhode Island protocol."

Sweat coated the back of my neck for 2.6 seconds. "Good job. Yes, by all means. Carry on with the Rhode Island protocol. Recommend proceeding to section twenty-seven-alpha per the black book."

"Yes, sir." Internally, I applauded his flourish.

"Major Lindholm, do you have everything you need to execute that procedure?"

"I do, sir." Eugene gave us another thumbs-up.

The conversation had basically been "Things here are FUBAR. Request permission to act on our own without checking in," and Clemons had just answered that he trusted us.

"Good. Is there anything else relating to the Rhode Island protocol that we need to discuss?"

"Not at this time. If you have the wherewithal to close that portion of the conversation, I have several operations questions, which are related to my role as Acting LCA."

Up to this point, everything had been a charade. But using "if you have the wherewithal to close" was an actual passphrase from the codebooks that Clemons had sent up. We were hoping the more obvious codes would keep Earth First from looking too closely at this part.

"Confirmed. Please proceed forthwith to the next item."

I breathed out, letting my head drop forward with relief. He'd recognized the passphrase and offered the counter. Helen and Myrtle sagged back into their chairs.

"When the quarantine lifts, I want to do a thorough tour of The Garden to look at early crop plans." None of this was code. That was reserved for an incredibly dry teletype of the inventory that we'd sent down to Earth in a batch of other items. What Eugene had done was to tell Clemons what to look for.

"Mm . . . I'll ask the agriculture department down here to recom—"

The lights went out.

There's a difference between a quiet line and a dead line. This line was dead. In the hall, the emergency lights snapped on, giving us a dim yellow glow through the window of the phone booth. I looked down at my watch to time the blackout. Would we have another sixteen minutes this time? "Well, that was subtle."

"We wanted to make them panic." Helen slid an imaginary chess piece across the table. "Check."

SIXTEEN MINUTES LATER, the power came back on. Eugene looked up at the light when it did and snorted. "At least they're consistent."

"Yes, but that was a tactically poor choice." Helen drummed her fingers on the table. "They just tipped their hand, making it absolutely clear they can hear us."

"Maybe it was a mistake?" I picked at the edge of my startlingly white cast. "Not just stupid, but if the power and the recording are controlled from the same hub someone might have bumped the wrong switch. If they only have a single listening post it would mean fewer operatives."

"A single listening post . . ." Eugene sat forward. "We've been assuming the listener is in comms on Earth . . . Faustino has been up often enough to have set up a post. Convert one of the emergency way stations, say."

In the four days since we started looking for Faustino, no one had seen him. No one had worried because with the quarantine everyone was isolated. People just assumed that he was in another module.

But when Myrtle combed through the rolls that each of the isolation zones had sent in, he wasn't in any of them. How the hell do you go missing on the Moon? I mean, besides stealing a BusyBee. But where do you go?

"He has to come back eventually," Myrtle said.

"Does he?" I leaned forward. "The average lifespan of a 'bird' during the war was six months. We signed up knowing that."

"You lived."

God, she had no idea. "The point is, he might have come here not planning to go home."

The silence between us might as well have been a dead phone line. Eugene whistled and shook his head. "If the explosion was related to his hidey-hole, you saying you'd figured out where it was might be what set him off." He glanced at the door and then at his watch. "I should go make an announcement to reassure people. Would one of you . . ."

Helen nodded. "I'll call Clemons to let him know the status of the lights."

I slid back my chair and hesitated. "Eugene . . . would it be all right if I called Kenneth?"

"What? Sure."

Myrtle paused in the act of standing and stared at me, mouth dropping. "Oh, for Pete's sake. You haven't— Honey, when was the last time you talked to him?"

There are upsides and downsides to having friends who know you well. I swallowed and awkwardly folded my agenda in half. "I haven't been allowed to talk to him since the coded message thing."

"Aw, hell, Nicole. I'm sorry." Eugene put his hand on my shoulder. "Yeah. I'll fix it with comms so it won't be an issue."

I drew a breath, nodding. "Thanks."

Myrtle and I followed him into the hall, leaving Helen the "secure" booth. The silver lining to the power outage was that the people who had been in the booths had abandoned them during the blackout.

I opened the nearest booth and sat down inside. Myrtle knocked on the door. When I slid it open, she handed me a clean handkerchief, and walked away before I could say anything. I have the best friends.

I had to pick up the phone with my right hand.

"Operator." A young woman on *Lunetta* answered. Was she involved with Earth First, reporting on whom I called?

"Earth, Kansas long distance, please."

"Surely." The ritual of talking to the operator gave me time to calm down and shed some of the adrenaline. A different woman said, "Long distance."

"Operator . . ." Or was the terrestrial counterpart the more likely source? Did I have a choice? It was a Monday morning in Kansas City. Kenneth would be in his office in Topeka. My usual call time was Wednesday evening. A daytime call would make him worry. "I'd like to place a call to Topeka: Main one-five-two-five-zero."

"Surely."

The phone rang once, and Kenneth's secretary picked up. "Governor Wargin's office, how may I help you?"

I wrapped the cord around my fingers. "This is Mrs. Wargin. Is the governor in?"

"I'm sorry, Mrs. Wargin. He's just stepping out to a rally— Oh!"

The phone bounced and rattled. And then Kenneth was there. "Nicole? Are you all right?"

"How's the kitten?" Don't ask me why I opened with that. "Knocked over any flowers?"

"The flowers are fine—or wait. Missing. The kitten stole all of the flowers. There are no flowers. Which— Nicole. I . . . I don't know where to start. Electrocuted? Really? I thought your mother had a lock on that."

God damn him for having that squawk box. He couldn't hear me, but he could hear the LGC chatter, and that would have been a very active day. "First of all, I was shocked, because electro—"

"Electrocution leaves you dead. Yes. I've heard your mother say that. So, let's try this . . . You had enough power go through your body to wipe out the entire module."

"Maybe? I mean, I was probably blown clear before that happened." I held the phone closer as if I could snuggle up against him. "I'm sorry if it's giving you problems."

"That's what you're worried about? Sweetheart . . . I almost lost you."

"I'm harder to lose than that." I winced. "How bad are the headlines?"

He snorted. "WIFE OF GOVERNOR WARGIN ELECTROCUTED ON MOON. My PR people would like to know if you could arrange to rescue a small child in addition to a ward of women with polio to complete your heroic picture."

My turn to laugh. "I try to be a supportive wife, by providing you with news sensational enough to distract from other issues."

He laughed, one of the laughs that makes him throw his head back to the ceiling and then melt into a sigh. If I could have sat in that companionable silence forever, I would have. I sighed and rested my brow against the wall. "Speaking of . . . your last letter went missing for a bit. And someone else checked the book out from the library."

Two-point-six seconds later I heard him inhale. Another moment of silence passed and then he said, "I see. The same person had both, I presume?"

"It appears so." I wanted to ask him for details about what sort of investigation the FBI was doing. But even if Icarus wasn't listening to this conversation, it seemed safe to assume the Feds had gotten a warrant for a wiretap of his office.

"Nathaniel had to go back into the hospital."

"Is it . . . ?" Poison? Or did he just stop eating again? "How bad is he?"

"Just stomach pain. They're doing some testing to figure out why." He sighed. "Hershel is flying back out."

"That'll be a help." I wanted to go home. I miss Kenneth when I'm on the Moon, but I have never wanted to go *home* as badly as I did sitting in that phone booth. I just wanted to talk to my husband without having to watch my words. "So does the kitten have a name?"

"Maggie." He switched gears right along with me. "Maggie from *Cat on a Hot Tin Roof*."

"The Elizabeth Taylor character?"

"You should see this kitten's eyes. And she has yet to meet a surface that she won't try to climb. The chair back. The drapes. My leg." Kenneth cleared his throat. "So . . . Marlowe has been drinking a lot of water. A little lethargic."

"Well, he is nineteen." My voice was light, but it was denial.

"His spirits are good, though. I just . . . I just want you to be prepared."

"Thank you."

"For?"

"For not hiding it from me." I swallowed and wiped my eyes. "You were on your way to a rally. You should get moving."

"Hang the rally."

"Kenneth . . . Go. To paraphrase a wise man. I'm fine. There's nothing you can do for me up here, except do your job down there."

He was silent for longer than 2.6 seconds, and when he spoke, his voice was rough. "You're a cruel woman, Nicole Wargin, to use my own words on me like that."

"If you're saying I'm wrong, then I'll catch the next rocket home." Not that we could launch anything right now, but I would find a way. "Now go to the rally and make me proud."

He went. As he should. As I would in his place. As I have.

THIRTY-ONE

HURRICANE TIME STIRS FLORIDIANS

Weather Bureau Preparing with Help of Lunetta
By R. HART PHILLIPS
Special to The National Times

MIAMI, Fla., May 7—A strong weather disturbance last week near the French Antilles, 2,400 kilometers from Miami, brought the attention of the people of Florida once again to the operations of the United States Weather Bureau in watching for hurricanes. In conjunction with the observatory on the space station *Lunetta,* the forecasters are able to accurately predict and monitor the behavior of this unusually early hurricane.

IT WOULD BE nice if I could concentrate on just Icarus, but we still had repairs to do from the "rain day." All of the staff trained to handle that was working to clean up the SciMod, which left mundane maintenance to those of us assigned to help care for the sick. I lay on my side on the floor of Midtown with my head and shoulders inside the wall of the shower facility. My cheek pressed against the plastic wall, I squinted at the clip I was trying to reset on the filter with my right hand.

"Nicole?" Eugene's voice made me jump and drop the clip. Again. I hate doing things with my off hand, but any attempt to use my left was . . . annoying.

"Oh, for . . ." I sighed and fished around for it. "Yes?"

"Can I borrow you for a minute?" He crouched next to the opening, but all I could really see were his feet in their IAC-issue shoes.

"Let me just . . ." My fingers closed on the clip. "Almost finished."

"Okay." He stood and leaned against the wall.

I bit the inside of my lip and closed my eyes while I felt for the socket on the filter. "I can hear you if that'll work?"

He crouched down again. "We have a lead on Faustino."

I fumbled the clip and dropped it. Grabbing the edge of the opening, I pulled myself out so I could see his face. "But . . . ?"

"Danika and Ruben du Preez." He pursed his lips. "Might be more comfortable talking to a white woman."

"Got it. Do you want me to have a '*talk*' with them while I'm at it?"

He shook his head. "They fall into the category of well-meaning and in denial. And the point of having you quiz them is to make them comfortable."

"Copy." I stared up at the translucent ceiling of Midtown. It was noon and the sun hung in the sky, directly overhead. Even with polarized glass, it was too bright to look directly at, just like at home before the Meteor. The engineers who had designed this had given the glass a blue tint, which overlaid the velvet black of space. The shadows moved, if you stayed there long enough, but "noon" lasted for three days.

I grabbed the edge of the access panel and pulled myself back inside to look for the clip. A single task. Simple. Controllable. "Do you have any other details for me about Ruben and Danika?"

"Not much. Rumor has it that they talked to Faustino before he went missing."

The clip bumped along until it snagged on an edge. Carefully, I eased it over and pushed until it clicked into place. I sighed with relief. Almost as good as an orgasm. "I'll see what I can find out."

"Work a little charm and . . ." Eugene straightened slowly. "Come back out. Something's wrong."

I wriggled out of the wall. Myrtle was walking toward us from the airlock, which led from Eugene's office. Her eyes were red and puffy. There's an expression that we wear when someone dies. It's a face anyone in aviation knows, because we all know someone who died.

I clambered to my feet and grabbed the access panel, sliding it back into place. While we waited for her to reach us, I twisted the latches, concentrating on feeling the panel snug into place. Whatever came next, I did not want to leave a task unfinished and cause things to get worse.

"Myrtle?" Eugene caught her hands with his. "Baby? What happened?"

"There's been an accident on the Mars Expedition."

Myrtle squeezed his hands. "Estevan Terrazas is dead."

I sucked in a breath as if I could pull her words out of the air. Terrazas was one of the original *Artemis* astronauts. I'd flown with him. I'd flown *here* with him. The blood leached from Eugene's cheeks. He closed his eyes like he was locking down a heat shield and slid his hands up Myrtle's arms, pulling her in close.

I stood, frozen, next to the shower facility. Around me the activity of the lunar colony carried on as if nothing had happened. Danika was helping Birgit take limping steps on the running track. Ana Teresa was walking from the library to the gallery, talking to one of the nurses. Guillermo and Kadyn were propped on a low bench next to the bunny pen.

None of these people knew Terrazas. Oh, they may have met him in passing, but the Mars Expedition had left Earth last October and some of the new hires probably only overlapped with them by six months. They would know that he looked like a Spanish movie star. They would have heard his resonant voice on the first mission around the Moon.

They wouldn't know about his love for radio theater. They wouldn't know how he laughed with his whole body. They wouldn't know that his little sister was the light of his life. They wouldn't get to hear him tell the story about how he'd punched Stetson Parker on the day they met. They would never taste his paella. They would never hear the giant goofball sit in the CAPCOM seat and announce your mission like you were Flash Gordon. They would never dance with him in microgravity. They would never hang in silence as they orbited the Moon with him, worshiping at the same altar.

Eugene turned his head and held out his arm. He grabbed me and pulled me into a hug with them. I wrapped my arms around them and clung.

Overhead, the relentless noon blazed down, ignoring our grief. I wanted to hang in the shadow that we created from our bodies. But Eugene tightened his hands on us. In the dark, he murmured, "I need to go get briefed and make a statement to the colony."

"Yeah, baby." Myrtle nodded. "Comms brought the news straight to your office. They have instructions not to tell anyone until you do, but . . . it'll get around."

"Helen." I lifted my head. She had been training to go to Mars with Terrazas before they'd rotated Elma on. "I'll find Helen."

SOMEONE, I DON'T remember who, told me Helen was in the library, playing chess with one of the boys. I walked past Central Park and I could feel people looking at me. I tried to school my expression, but there wasn't a damn thing I could do about my eyes. On Earth, I'd throw on sunglasses and no one would blink.

Maybe I could bring the style to the lunar colony for noon-shine days.

From the bench where he was propped with Kadyn, Guillermo reached out a hand as I passed. "Hey. You okay?"

I compressed my lips and shook my head. "Bad day."

He winced and looked toward the gallery. "I'm sorry."

Shit. He thought Frisch had died, which given that he was in seriously bad shape was not surprising. Or maybe Guillermo had poisoned him. "He's—" Not fine. "It's not him. Eugene will be making an announcement soon."

Kadyn pushed himself farther up, looking now to Le Restaurant, where the women were housed. "Who . . . ?"

"No one here." They were doing the same panicked thing we all do, which was to run through the names of people who might have died. The way that every time I heard about something amorphously bad, I worried it was Kenneth. With polio on the Moon, they were running through a list of close friends and colleagues who were right here. "Eugene is going to make an announcement."

I needed to get to Helen, because she should not find out that way. I shoved my hands in my pockets and walked, head down, as fast as I could toward the library.

Inside, the tables had been cleared out. The shelves of books had been covered with plastic sheeting to keep them clean. Ana Teresa had added a bed when Lance Woolen from operations had come down with a fever and weakness in his left arm. He lay on one side, staring at the wall. The men in the other beds were reading or sleeping. In one corner, the radio played "Chattanooga Choo Choo" while one man concentrated on moving his foot in time to the music. One foot. The other lay at an awkward angle on the blanket.

Helen sat at Curt's bed with a packing crate to hold the game and her back to the door. Pillows propped him up so he could reach the board, where it looked like she was trouncing him.

He was laughing as she studied the board, clearly trying to distract her with a funny story. "—so the watch officer looks at me and says, 'But not without the milk,' and I say . . ." His voice trailed away as he saw me and he rested his hand on Helen's arm. Of course, the pilot would know what my face meant. "Helen."

She looked up at him. Her spine straightened as if she were bracing herself. Helen turned and saw me. I watched the recognition go over her face, pulling it into a neutral mask. She reached back and knocked her king over, forfeiting the game.

Curt watched her with worry in the pinch around his eyes, as she stood and walked to me. Helen stopped, looking up at me with steel in her spine. "Outside?"

The men had lowered their books. Even Lance had rolled over to look at us. I nodded and led her out and then . . . where was I going to find a private space for her?

Helen saw me looking around and put her hand on my arm. "Just tell me."

Wetting my lips, I nodded. "There was an accident on the First Mars Expedition. Estevan—"

Her eyes closed, pinching shut so they were nothing but creases of grief. Helen raised her hands to cover her mouth. I stepped forward and wrapped my arms around her slight form. Helen leaned against me, unbreathing. I ran my hand down her back, feeling the tension in every muscle.

Her chest shuddered as she drew in a breath. Against my collarbone, I felt as much as heard, "How?"

I shook my head. "I don't know." Getting words past the broken glass in my throat hurt. "Eugene was finding out."

Helen nodded and slid her arms around me. We waited for the announcement and I could not tell you if she was holding me, or I her. We stood under the unmoving sun and waited to find out how a friend had died on the way to Mars.

And I braced myself for it to have been sabotage.

THIRTY-TWO

ESTEVAN TERRAZAS, 1924–1963

KANSAS CITY, May 7, 1963—The second casualty on the Mars mission comes a little over a month after the crew has passed the midway point. Critics are pointing to the death of Estevan Terrazas as a sign of incompetence on the part of the IAC. An anonymous source, high within the organization, says that Colonel Stetson Parker had objected to sending Terrazas out, saying that he lacked the experience, but was overruled by Director Clemons.

The director of the IAC characterized the death as a freak accident. According to reports, Terrazas became mired in the ammonia cooling system while doing repairs. In an attempt to free him, the crew cut an ammonia line. Tragically, a faulty gauge indicated that the lines were empty, and when cut, the pressure caused the sharp end of the metal line to whip past his suit and breach it. The suit lost integrity, subjecting Terrazas to the vacuum of space.

EVEN IF WE hadn't been observing quarantine procedures, there wasn't anywhere in the colony for all 326 of us to gather. So everyone gathered in the largest common space of the module they were in and listened to Eugene on the address system.

He somehow managed to make space for grief and hope in his remarks. I don't mean that he made us feel good or trotted out a trite aphorism about heroism and sacrifice. He helped us see the connection between our work here and the work Estevan had been doing out there and the work people were doing on Earth. We grieved, yes, but we carried on because that was what made us human.

Late, late that night, long after the shades had been drawn over the Midtown dome, so late that it was no longer the same day, Helen and I sat in Eugene's office. Eugene and Myrtle were making the rounds, doing what politicians do in times of grief. They were comforting. They were listening. I'd done that tour of duty too many times to count.

After the Meteor, there had been too many people who needed comfort and not enough of me.

Helen nudged my foot with hers. "Do you remember when Estevan explained to Bubbles that the title of the film *Casablanca* just meant 'white house'?"

I chuckled. "Bubbles's mouth dropped *so* far. I thought Estevan was going to swallow his tongue laughing."

God, he had a good laugh. The plastic sheeting stirred and Eugene pushed it aside, holding it for Myrtle. She came in, holding a bottle in one hand and four coffee mugs in another. Her eyes looked as if she'd taken too many *g*s.

Eugene followed and dropped into Frisch's chair. He bent forward and buried his face in his arms on the desk.

I rested my hand on his arm. There was nothing to say. I'd seen Kenneth this dragged down and all you could really do was wait it out.

Or, use Myrtle's solution. She twisted the lid off the bottle. "Dandelion wine? I make no promises."

"Does it have alcohol?" I raised my hand. "Then I'm in."

"Same." Helen raised her hand.

Eugene sat back, wiping his face with a sniffle. "God, yes."

She poured us a vivid yellow liquid and handed the mugs around. Sweet floral notes blended with the smell of fresh earth. Myrtle raised her coffee mug. "To Estevan."

The clink of coffee mugs was flat and harsh in the tiny room. I took a sip of the liquid, expecting it to be astringent and funky. It was sweet and tart, with none of the bitter ethanol flavors of her first batches. I lifted my eyebrows. "Myrtle. This is good."

"At least try not to sound surprised." She took another sip. "I've been working on the recipe and used the airlock to force chill it to halt fermentation."

"So, no one believes the busted gauge was an accident, right?" Eugene stared into his mug. He took a healthy swallow. "Just so we're clear. That's bullshit."

Helen shook her head. "If you are suggesting that Leonard or Rafael would be in league with Earth First . . ."

"It's what the FBI thinks about Leonard. That's why they're investigating us." He gestured at Myrtle and himself. "Why the hell not? One of the people I just shook hands with is probably responsible for poisoning Frisch. Why *not* one of those guys?"

"No." Her nostrils flared. "No one on that crew is involved. Not on either ship."

"They wouldn't need to be." I ran my finger around the rim of my coffee cup. "On a three-year mission, it would be a miracle if nothing failed. You want to make sure it happens? Someone installs something wrong. A little bit of extra stress someplace. Install a valve you know is faulty, but certify it."

"But it wasn't an accident." Eugene tipped his coffee mug back and drained it. He sat forward and poured another healthy dose. "Someone killed him. On purpose."

"There wasn't even supposed to be a spacewalk." I shook my head slowly. "It's . . . it's space. Sometimes people die."

"You think they didn't plan for someone on that mission to die? You think they want any of them to come back alive? You think they want anyone on the Moon to live? You think—" He stopped and set his coffee mug down on the desk. "Excuse me."

He got up and walked out of the office with his fists clenched at his sides. Myrtle reached for her husband and drew her hand back without touching him. She stared at the swinging plastic after he walked through. Swallowing, she turned back to us and gave one of the falsest smiles I've ever seen.

Wiping her hands on her trousers, she stood. "More wine?"

"Do you need to go with him?"

She shook her head and poured a little more into her cup. "He just needs a minute." Myrtle sat back down, leaving her mug on the table. "Let's keep working the problem."

"Okay." I gripped my mug in my hands, plaster cast rasping against the cup. "The point I was trying to make was that they would not have needed to place an agent on the Mars Expedition. Any death would serve their purpose. Maybe you weren't the target on your BusyBee and it was set up ahead of time."

She snorted and turned her coffee mug so the handle was aligned with the edge of the desk.

Watching her, I asked, "How . . . how bad was that? You never gave us details."

"Bad." She fished in her pocket and pulled out a handkerchief, which she twisted in her hands. "We weren't supposed to survive that."

The fans hissed, stirring the papers on the desk. Helen shifted in her chair and took a sip of dandelion wine, looking at me over the rim. She lowered the mug. "Do we have two classes of attack? Preplanned and improvised?"

Eugene pushed the curtain open and walked back in as if nothing had happened. "Good thought." As he walked by, Myrtle held out her handkerchief. He glanced down to take it and settled in his chair, wrapping the handkerchief around the bloody knuckles of his right hand. "The BusyBee being improvised and messier."

I nodded and pretended not to notice that he'd apparently walked out to punch something. I understood that feeling. Although I was more likely to throw things. "That would make sense with the dehumidifier. That affected everyone."

"The short." Helen tapped the edge of her mug, considering. "A plan to target Nicole?"

"I don't see how they would have . . ." There was something there, though. I frowned, trying to drag it out of the dark, and stared at the intercom in Eugene's office. How would I have done that? "With the water everywhere, anyone who closed a contact was going to cause a short. So . . . so you'd want to create a situation that would make it likely your target was the one who would be first."

"For instance, a ward full of polio patients?" Helen sat with her feet together now. "If you're the only one who can walk, who else would be the target?"

"Ana Teresa? Any of the nurses? Some of the patients—" There it was . . . on the other side of the lightning. "Birgit."

"What?" Myrtle leaned forward, watching me.

I set the coffee mug down and pressed my fingers against my temples. I should not be drinking on an empty stomach. "Birgit was getting leg function back. She was trying to get to the intercom but fell . . . They could reasonably assume I would be the first one to the intercom, but . . . it was almost her. No—wait. Gah. I was so scrambled. There was something—"

"She's Swiss." Myrtle blinked and stood, turning to the filing cabinets. "Birgit Furst. She's Swiss and works in comms. She could be the mole."

Helen said, "Knowing how to tune a radio is not the same thing as being able to rig a booby trap."

Myrtle set her coffee mug on top of the filing cabinet and yanked it open. She flipped through the files. "No, but. . . ." With a noise of satisfaction, she yanked a file out. "Ha!"

The riffle of pages mimicked the hiss of fans, and then Myrtle slapped the folder down on Eugene's desk. She laid her finger on a line with an air of triumph. Eugene leaned forward to read it and whistled.

"Just so we're clear. If that says she went to Swiss finishing school, I'm going to stab someone." I set my coffee mug down. "Do I need to find a pen?"

She snorted and tapped the page. "Swiss Army. Munitions."

A shudder ran down my spine. I picked my coffee mug up again and took a deeply necessary drink. "So, in theory, she wasn't going to the intercom, she was returning from rigging it to arc." Rubbing my forehead, I tried to press the fatigue back. "That leaves the question of Faustino. Working in league with him? I mean . . . he is unquestionably gone, but neither of them were in a position to do anything to the hand controller in the rocket."

"Curt was. Or it could have happened preflight." Eugene settled back in his chair. "There's no reason to think that Icarus is a single person."

"So all of them?" Helen crossed her ankles. "Earth First managed to get three people on a single ship, all of them with names that contain the letter *F*. The Evil League of *F* Names? This is too complicated. We are focusing on people with *F* names because of the Swiss Army knife, but carrying a monogrammed knife seems like a clumsy mistake."

Eugene's stillness was as alarming as yelling might be in someone else. "It was not a plant. I'm sorry you were not there to see the placement or the damage to the controller, but I will ask that you trust my judgment. It was very clear that the knife was dropped because Icarus was in a hurry and it was not possible to retrieve it without dismantling the controller."

Myrtle laid her hand on his arm. "But they might have stolen it."

"No one reported a missing knife—" I gestured at the wall of filing cabinets. "Look . . . the whole being-Frisch's-secretary was supposed to be cover, but I still had to file a lot of paperwork. People would report losing a box of paper clips, for crying out loud. If a completely innocent person lost that knife, someone would have said something."

Eugene shrugged. "So let's try to reunite it with the owner. Icarus will deny it's theirs, but I'll bet you that someone will remember seeing them pull it out at some point. They know Myrtle and I survived the BusyBee, so the fact that I have the knife is going to be understandable. And frankly, if I encourage them to come for me instead of other people I'll regard that as a net positive."

"There he goes . . ." Myrtle reached forward to pick up her mug.

He rolled his eyes at her and turned back to me. "I've been thinking about Faustino. Looking for him on the sly made sense when we were concerned about Frisch, but . . ." Given how sick he was, even if he had been involved, he was out of the game now. "As acting administrator, I would be irresponsible if I didn't tell all personnel that we had a missing crew member. Let's get all eyes looking for him."

"Smart."

"But—I still want you talking to Danika and Ruben to see if they know anything specific about where Faustino might have gone."

I nodded. "I agree with Helen that we're not looking for a large team of people, but the fact that he and a BusyBee have gone missing at the same time is . . . a problem." I held up a finger and turned to Helen. "Can you talk to Paulo? He was with Faustino when he returned the suit, so might know where he had been."

Helen nodded. "Yes. I can use chess as an excuse for that."

"Good. I'll ask maintenance for the ETA on the report about our rocket crash." Eugene set his mug down and pulled a pad of paper toward him to make a note. "And also find out about the failure of the dehumidifiers, both of which are easily masked as part of my purview as acting administrator."

"Masking . . ." I turned my mug in my hands, thinking. "I wonder if we should stop trying to hide what's going on. The original reason for being quiet was to keep the bad guys from knowing the FBI was on to them, but that went out the airlock when they found my codes."

Helen tipped her head to the side, eyes narrowing as she played through possibilities. Myrtle tapped her finger on the arm of her chair and Eugene said, "Huh."

I had told Clemons, back on Earth, that I was not a fan of the secrecy, even though I accepted it at the time. But now, it seemed as though the fastest way to flush out

Icarus on the Moon was to give them nowhere to hide. It was different on Earth, where there were places you could run. Stealing a BusyBee wouldn't solve the resource problem and sooner or later, if they wanted to live, they would have to come back.

Eugene leaned back in his chair to stare at the ceiling. "The challenge . . . The challenge with that approach is that the clearest example of sabotage relies on my testimony, and I'm Black. We'll need a higher level of proof." He sat up in his chair and studied the sheet of paper again. "Let me see if maintenance has anything useful for us."

God, but I wished he were wrong.

"I can . . . I can ask Kenneth to back you." It wouldn't take much persuading. "If we do multiple calls to split their attention, I should be able to brief him in the morning. Politically, the timing is good, because people will be ready to draw the link to . . . to Estevan. If we wait, the connection will diffuse in people's minds."

Eugene took a long, deep breath, staring at his coffee mug. Shaking his head, he glanced across the table at Myrtle. She gave a small shrug, with an even smaller nod.

"Yeah . . . Probably for the best. So. Tomorrow morning, let's do four calls. I'll call Clemons. Myrtle, you're on Nathaniel. Helen . . ."

"I'll call Reynard. Two husbands will make Nicole's call less obvious."

"Copy. And let's keep eyes on Birgit and Curt for good measure." He grimaced and took a sip of dandelion wine. "At least that should be easy."

Unless, of course, Birgit wasn't as sick as she seemed.

* * *

THE PHONE WAS cool in my hand the next morning. I was apparently the first one to use that booth and I came with a headache from Myrtle's wine. I'd taken an aspirin and then, so I could answer Kenneth honestly, if he asked, I picked up a squeeze tube of applesauce for breakfast. The sticky, sweet pulp still clung to the sides of my teeth, no matter how much I ran my tongue around the inside of my mouth.

In the booths on either side of me, my crewmates were making their own calls. I tried home first, guessing that he, too, would have had a long day yesterday. I hoped he had slept in, even a little, before heading to the office. And if I was wrong, then Chu could tell me Kenneth's schedule for the day.

Chu answered on the second ring. "Governor's Mansion. How may I help you?"

"Good morning, Chu."

"Mrs. Wargin. What a pleasant surprise." He never sounded surprised, even when I was calling from the Moon. "The governor is in the breakfast room, if you'll give me a moment."

"Thank you. Please, please make sure he knows I'm all right." I wrapped the cord around my fingers, the black line a sharp contrast to the unadorned white of my new cast. I pressed the phone against my ear, listening for the faint sounds of home in the background. Was that a bird in the distance, or was my imagination desperate for Earth?

The phone rattled. "Nicole? What's wrong?"

"I told Chu to tell you I was all right."

"That is not the reassuring opener you think it is." But some of the tension bled out of his voice. "It's usually followed by something like, 'I got lucky with the angle of entry' or 'It was only 8 gs.'"

"You make me sound like a daredevil."

"That's because— Maggie, no! Come here. No." He laughed and the phone rustled against fabric as he lowered it. "You little scamp."

"What'd she do?"

"Made off with a piece of bacon." He grunted a little. "She's under the sideboard now . . . Marlowe is being a perfect gentleman and sitting in his chair."

Marlowe had a chair at the dining table and would watch us over the edge. We never gave him food from the table, but he liked to participate. In the background, I heard my old man cat give a meep.

"That's right, Marlowe. She is, indeed, undignified." Kenneth sighed into the phone. "I'm so sorry about Terrazas. He was a good man."

Salt water burned the back of my throat and choked me. "He really was. Helen is pretty broken up, although she's masking it well."

"I can't imagine . . . I'll add her to my prayers."

We all took comfort in the illusions of control where we could. I swallowed. I did not have time for weeping and reminiscing. "That's why I'm calling, actually. I want to brief you on what's happening up here and ask . . . We need your political weight."

The phone rustled for a moment, Kenneth's hand

muffling it. "Chu, clear my calendar for the morning, and give me the room." The air in the line shifted again, and it was just Kenneth's breath crossing the distance to the Moon. "All right. Tell me what you need."

"I'm going to skim through the big-picture details and then you can tell me the things you want a deeper briefing on. We believe Estevan's death was not an accident, but the result of actions by Earth First. Here on the Moon, they've taken a number of similar actions. The faulty thruster coming in, the dehumidifier, the short that hit me. In addition, there have been several more overt—"

On the other end of the line, Kenneth gave a short, shocked breath as my delayed words reached him. "God damn them."

It startled me into silence. I had never heard raw rage in my husband's voice before.

"Sweetheart—"

"I will destroy—If they wanted judgment day, I will oblige." His breathing was harsh. "Keep going. I'm taking notes."

I wet my lips and wished I were home right now. I'd seen him get fired up and he was a force of nature when that happened. His pupils widened and his shoulders seemed to broaden out to fill doorframes. We always had excellent sex when he got like this. I swallowed and cleared my throat. "All right. There was also an overt sabotage attempt—"

The phone made a spring sound.

Naturally. Right when I got to the clearest example. I cursed internally and lightened my voice. "—at The

Garden Club. You know how ruthless the ladies get about their roses. So, apparently, Mrs. Smith went to deadhead—"

"I heard it too." Kenneth's voice was deep and resonant and about as erotic as I could ask for. Yes, I'm attracted to powerful men. "Keep talking. My people will deal with it."

I hesitated. His staff was very good, and if it were just a matter of getting ahead of the news, I would not worry, but the FBI was also investigating Kenneth about the rat poison. At the moment, that was still backstage. It hadn't gone public. If we stirred up the flames with Icarus, they would almost certainly arrange to leak the story to the news, which would damage his run for president.

"Nicole." Kenneth's voice softened a little. "Let me do my job. Please."

Goddamn it. We would have had such good sex if I were home.

And this is why I keep a vibrator on the Moon.

THIRTY-THREE

PICKETING BY CORE STIRS RIOT IN CLEVELAND

CLEVELAND, Ohio, May 8, 1963—Several thousand jeering white persons, primarily teenagers, pelted pickets of the Congress of Racial Equality with rocks, eggs, and tomatoes early this morning outside a White Castle drive-in restaurant in Cleveland. A riot call brought 60 policemen to the scene. At least two of the picketers were injured and taken to the hospital. One was identified as Robert Waldron, a Negro. The other was an unidentified white man. The police said that Mr. Waldron had been knocked down and kicked by white youths.

AFTER TALKING TO Kenneth, I did not go back to my bunk. Alas. Instead I conferred with my crewmates. Eugene and I were the only ones who got spring sounds, although at different points in the conversation. To me, this said they had tried flipping lines, which seemed to indicate a single listening post. There was very little we could do about that, besides trying to let Clemons know.

I was a little frustrated, in more than one way, by the time I found Danika and Ruben walking slowly around the running track in Midtown. Danika had been one of the lucky ones who got a fever, some aches, and then recovered as if it were just the flu. The infirmary had only had two canes, so Ruben leaned on a piece of conduit, bent to have a cane handle and padded with layers of cloth and tape. It had a broad, flat base cut from a packing crate to give it traction in 1/6 g.

His left leg dragged behind him. Ruben had his jaw set and was fighting his way around the track.

I nodded and fell into step beside them. Now all I had to do was wait for Eugene's announcement, which would provide a nice jumping-off point for our conversation. "Good morning."

"Good morning." Danika's hair was in a simple plait around her head, with none of her usual fancy braiding. "I . . . I was so sorry to hear about Captain Terrazas."

I had not forgotten, but I had managed to keep that knowledge to the side. Nodding, I ducked my head. "Thank you." Ahead of us, the relocated rabbit pen from the biology lab in the SciMod was set up by the side of the track. "Have you seen the bunnies?"

She nodded and let me change the subject. "We stop by them on each circuit. So adorable."

Ruben thumped the track with his cane. "Also, by the chickens. By the Gallery. By any available bench."

"It looks like you're doing well, though." Considering that he'd been flat on his back a week ago, being up and around was fantastic. In truth, as bad as the "rain day" had been, moving the patients into Midtown had been good for them. There was no way they could get up to the lounge in the SciMod, and the centrifuge room had been out of the question as a way for them to exercise.

Ruben grimaced. "There is some question of if I will be able to walk on Earth."

Until that moment, it had honestly not occurred to me that he was able to support himself because his body only weighed one-sixth of what it would at home.

"Of course you will." Danika rose on her toes to kiss her husband on the cheek. She dropped back to her heels and pointed. "Look! The bunnies are so silly."

Rabbits on the Moon. They were here to see if they might make a good protein source for the colony's long-term future as well as to look at how gestation happened in lower gravity. Today, though, they had a small group of people gathered to watch them frolic. The rabbits who had been born here moved with a springy economy of motion. One or two soaring hops to cross their enclosure. The ones they'd taken back down to Earth had apparently been miserable and lay on the bottom of their cage, pushing themselves across the woodchips.

Three chimes sounded over the loudspeaker and everyone tensed, orienting to face it as Eugene spoke, "Good morning. This is Major Eugene Lindholm, acting administrator for Artemis Base. Yesterday was hard for our family of lunar-dwellers after two already stressful weeks. I spoke to many of you and I want to say how very proud I am of the spirit and compassion you displayed while grieving the loss of Estevan Terrazas."

While other people watched the speaker, as if they could see him, I studied my targets. Danika put her arm around

Ruben and carefully leaned into him. He tightened his grip on his cane, resting his cheek against her head.

"One of the things I heard time and again was that the quarantine has made you feel frustrated because you want to work. You are here on the Moon because you want to be of service to humanity. Further, because of the separation between modules, you feel isolated. I am instituting morning announcements." You could hear a smile in his voice as he changed tone. "Yes, as though we were in high school again."

People chuckled and the tension began to bleed away.

"Let's begin with Lost and Found. Found: A red Swiss Army knife with an *F* monogrammed on it. If this is yours, you may claim it by notifying my secretary, Mrs. Wargin, in the admin office. Lost . . . Faustino Albino Rios. Please report to your supervisor in Midtown. All personnel, I'd like to take this opportunity to remind you that the quarantine has not been lifted. Please do not go between modules without prior authorization."

I rolled my eyes, pretending that this was news to me, and turned to Danika. "I swear, Faustino is like my annoying kid brother."

Danika crouched to stick her fingers between the mesh of the cage and scratch a soft gray bunny. "I guess."

"What mischief do you think he's up to this time?" I turned to Ruben as Eugene was announcing Halim's incoming flight, which was due to land tomorrow.

Ruben grimaced, pressing his fist into his leg, and looked toward the library. "I don't know where Faustino is."

That was a much firmer denial than my casual question

should have merited. "Any guesses?"

"No." He shook his head, turning away from the bunnies. "No, none at all."

"I hope he's okay." I gestured toward the dome, where the sun still shone at noon. "There's a lot that can go wrong here."

"I told you I don't know where he is. I—" Ruben's hand slipped off his makeshift cane and he tumbled down in slow motion.

In the light gravity, I was able to snare his arm. We danced for a moment as I tried to steady him. Danika jumped up, too fast, and bounded into us.

All three of us went down. I cracked my left elbow against the floor and felt the jolt light up the break in my arm. Closing my eyes for a minute, I waited for the pain to dissipate. It didn't, but I rolled to my side to sit up. Would I have liked to have lain on my back and get my breath back? Yes. But even if I weren't a pilot, as a lady astronaut, I couldn't let the guys have any reason to think I was weak.

Danika knelt next to Ruben. "Are you all right?"

The uncharitable, suspicious part of me was nearly certain he'd fallen on purpose. I got to my knees as other people crowded around us. Someone offered a hand to help me up and I waved him off. "Help Ruben."

I got myself to my feet, dusting off my rump. My arm was still sending distress beacons as a dull throb in time with my pulse.

"Nicole?" Birgit stood next to me, leaning on a pair of lunar crutches engineered with a broad, weighted base. "That Swiss Army knife? I think it's Curt's."

"Oh?" I rubbed the area where my cast brushed my arm and left her a silence to fill.

"I remember him having it in training, because it reminded me of home." She shifted her weight on her crutches. "And he's missing it."

"Is he?" I smiled at her as if everything she said was helpful and not just a frustrating mass of possible lies. "Well, I'll certainly ask him about it."

WHEN I WALKED away from Birgit, I'll admit that my actual impulse was to throw the lot of them into an airlock until we could send them back to Earth. And if a "conversation" happened with some emphasis on the effects of decompression on the human body?

It was not my best moment. Not that I'd had many of them recently. I focused instead on the order of operations rather than things I couldn't fix.

I needed to talk to Curt and to Frisch, but I opted for the easier conversation. Not, mind you, that "Who poisoned you?" is an easy conversation.

I opened the door to the gallery and stepped into the dim shelter of art. They had positioned Frisch's bed so he was facing Bean's landscape of the Taurus mountains. The ground stretched away in burnt ochres and umber, with the occasional vivid spot of hunter green.

Frisch was on his back, propped up a little. Ana Teresa had juggled things so the LCA had an actual hospital bed instead of a makeshift cot.

The light from the gallery lamps shone on the bare

patches of his scalp. "Nicole . . ." I think he thought he was speaking English, but the rest of what he said was in Swiss German. "Have you a status update for me?"

I answered in kind. "Several people are getting leg function back, which is good to see. How are you?"

"I meant about Icarus."

"Ah . . ." I drew a breath, looking at the lesions at the corners of his mouth. If he had poisoned himself, he had misjudged badly. Even if he had been involved, at this point the man was not a threat. "Curtis Frye, Faustino Albino Rios, and Birgit Furst. Any thoughts on them?"

"Faustino is always working an angle." He shook his head. "The other two are new hires . . . I'm not sure I even met Fräulein Furst, although I must have during your arrival."

"Maybe not, given the chaos around the crash."

He nodded, eyes drooping. "Mm . . . perhaps. And you? I heard you were electrocuted? Are you all right?"

I kept the definition of "electrocution" inside my head. "It's the latest exercise fad." I did not mention my trouble sleeping or the fact that I wasn't eating and knew I wasn't. "I have a question about the sugar cubes."

"Where did I get them?" He sighed and it turned into a long, racking cough. Frisch curled into a tight ball, one hand pressed against his mouth, the other outstretched to stop me. I froze, on my toes, watching until he caught his breath and uncurled. "Apologies. Thank you for the Prussian blue."

I opened my mouth and the nonsense words of a politician's wife floated into the room. "Your bravery is a credit to you.

Please let me know if there's anything I can do."

"From Earth. I import them with my tea." Frisch's smile was sad as he shook his head. "These are from the last ship up. I had not felt well, but thought it simple stress. Now . . . I am lying here asking the dark: Have I been slowly poisoned this entire time, or did someone exchange the sugar cubes?"

I had no idea how to answer that.

IN THE LIBRARY, the radio in the corner was tuned to a station playing "Ring of Fire." Guillermo had the table with the radio pulled up to the edge of his bed and was gesturing at Kadyn. "France is your pick for the International Games? I mean, they've been good in the past but are a disaster this year. Are you a masochist?"

"I have to . . ." Kadyn saw me and his voice trailed away. "I'm sorry for your loss."

I inclined my head and took refuge in the old mask of concern and empathy. "Thank you. Estevan is a loss for all of us."

At Curt's bed, the chess game was still set up, king tipped over on the side. Curt was lying on his back, with a fist balled in the covers and his breath a little more jagged than it should be. His smile looked tight with pain. "It sounds like I should talk to you about my pocketknife."

I had been thinking about how I would have played it in his situation. Denial would always be the first, immediate impulse, but . . . if someone had seen him with it, then claiming he'd lost it was the next best step.

"I was wondering who that belonged to." I kept my voice light and breezy as I sat down on the edge of his bed. Mentally, I was noting that Birgit hadn't lied about it being his. "I'm surprised you didn't report it missing."

"Oh, well—" He broke off and closed his eyes for a second. Swallowing, he opened them again and smiled. "Well. It wasn't missing."

"Are you all right?"

"Just stayed out too late dancing."

Here's one of the many cruel things about polio. It takes your ability to move, but not to feel. This does not sound like cruelty until you watch people whose legs are cramping and they cannot stretch them to relieve the pain. We'd skipped physical therapy yesterday. When the news of Terrazas had rolled in, it was all anyone thought about.

Pursing my lips, I stood, and grabbed my rubber glove from the supply cart. "Dancing, huh?"

He blanched. "Oh—I didn't mean . . . Shit. Sorry—I was just joking. I didn't mean to make light about Captain Terrazas's passing."

"I understand. And he loved dancing, so probably would have been delighted if that's what we had done in his honor." I pulled the glove on and threw back the covers. "But for dancers, you should have seen Ruby Donaldson. She was a competitive dancer before she joined the First Mars Expedition."

"Yeah?" He stiffened a little as I took his foot in my right hand. "I'm an off-nominal dancer. I mean . . . even on the best day."

Would he get another one of those? I moved his knee

up toward his chest, using my cast as a guide. The entire time, I kept thinking about what I would have done if I were Icarus in that bed. Try for sympathy? Let my weakness show a little more? Say that I'd loaned the knife to someone else? "So, what did you mean when you said your knife wasn't missing?"

"I knew where it was—I thought I did, at any rate. I'd loaned it to Faustino."

Now that was an interesting choice. "Did he say why he wanted it?"

Curt shook his head. "No idea."

The song on the radio cut off mid-note. "We interrupt this program to bring you a special bulletin from ABC Radio. Here is a special bulletin from Kansas City. Four shots were fired on the steps of the United States Capitol today as Governor Wargin entered the building."

I dropped Curt's leg and turned to the radio. "No."

"This is ABC Radio in Kansas City. To repeat. Four shots were fired on the United States Capitol today at Governor Wargin. We're going to stand by for more details on the incident from Kansas City. Stay tuned for more from your ABC station. We now return you to your regular program."

And Doris Day started to sing.

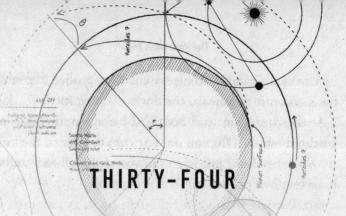

THIRTY-FOUR

U.S. TELLS AIDES IN HAITI
TO SEND FAMILIES HOME

Airlift of 220 Begins Today to Flee Hurricane
Other Americans There Receive Offer of Help

KANSAS CITY, May 8, 1963—The United States ordered today that dependents of its personnel in Haiti leave that country as Hurricane Flora bears down. It also offered to assist in the evacuation of other U.S. citizens from the island. Chartered Pan American World Airways planes will fly to Port-au-Prince, the Haitian capital, tomorrow to begin an airlift of the 220 dependents to the United States. About 1,100 other Americans also may participate. The State Department announced the plans for the evacuation of dependents after receiving advance warning from the *Lunetta* orbital station.

I RAN THROUGH the colony, skidding around corners, and all I could think was *Please, please, please, please, please.* I slammed into the comms module. "I need a phone."

The receptionist looked up with her stupid patient smile, "Mrs. Wargin—"

"My husband was just shot. *I need a phone.*"

Her face changed immediately. She pushed the chair back and moved toward the door. "Follow me."

At the conference call booth, she opened the door and gestured me in. "Do you need . . . anything?"

"No." I pushed inside and grabbed the phone, pulling it across the Formica surface of the table. "Wait— Yes. A radio. Please."

She was still closing the door as I snatched the receiver. On the other end of the line, a young woman in orbit on *Lunetta* answered, "Operator."

Was this the spy who had been listening to us? I was still standing, cast pressed against the surface of the table. My voice did not shake. "Earth, Kansas long distance, please."

"Surely." In my ear, the sound changed subtly, as if my voice were falling down the gravity well of Earth. My throat hurt with the effort of not screaming. A different woman said, "Long distance."

"Operator, I'd like to place a call to Topeka: Main one-five-two-five-zero."

There was a pause, as my voice transmitted across space to her, and I knew the delay was not her fault. "Surely." I waited for the connection to Kenneth's office in Topeka. They would know what was happening. "I'm sorry, ma'am, but the line is busy."

There were four lines going into his office. His staff would be slammed with phone calls going in and out. I bowed my head. "Would you please do an emergency breakthrough?"

"I'm sorry, ma'am . . . This is the office of the governor and it would be best if you tried to—"

"I am the governor's wife. He was just shot. I am calling from the Moon." I was so good. I was not screaming, but every one of my words was frozen in ice. "Please initiate an emergency breakthrough from Nicole Wargin. *Please.*"

That pause. I know why it's there, but the waiting would kill me. "Surely."

It occurred to me, in a strange, calm, rational place in my brain, that I might be about to get bad news and it would be better if I was sitting down. I slid the chair back and sank into it.

"—need to set up a press conference. See if you can get George—" My husband's chief of staff always sounds calm, and hearing Medgar Davis going about his business gave me a gap to breathe in.

"Emergency breakthrough. This is the operator. I have Nicole Wargin on the line from the Moon."

Mr. Davis gasped. "Scott. Get off the line." Whoever he was talking to hung up without hesitating. "Mrs. Wargin. I'm sorry, I didn't think you would have heard yet. I was waiting until I had more details to call."

"It was on the radio. All I know is that shots were fired at the Capitol at the governor." I asked the one question I needed to know. "Is he alive?"

Silence. Waiting. Mr. Davis drew in a long breath that took all of the air out of the room. "I don't know."

"How can you not know?" I hunched over the table. Don't yell at the staff. Don't yell.

"I wasn't there. I'm sorry. This is why I waited to call you, because I'm still trying to find out exactly what happened. What I know at this time is that the governor was shot twice." His voice faltered and in my years of knowing the man, it is the only time I have heard even a gap in demeanor. But he's known me for just as long and he did not coddle me. "Reports say that one of the times was in the head."

I could not draw air and bent tighter, pressing my head against the table. The door to the phone booth snapped open. I couldn't straighten. Eugene crouched beside me, breathing hard, and wrapped his arms around my back.

I fought the constriction in my ribs. "He had bodyguards. How did this happen?"

"I don't know. We're trying to find that out now."

I wanted to scream at him that he had been setting up a press conference and he didn't know how my husband had been shot. He didn't even know if he was alive. I said none of those things, because I knew they had their own set of contingency plans for worst-case scenarios. As did I.

You do not get to be a politician without receiving death threats. You did not watch your husband decide to run for president of the United States without knowing that assassination was a possibility. Medgar Davis was simply following directives that Kenneth would have left him and I resented the hell out of him for it.

There would be people he needed to call. He needed the line clear. "What . . ." My throat clenched and I had to swallow to speak. "What hospital?"

"Washington Memorial." His voice faltered again and that was almost worst. "I am so sorry you found out from the radio."

"Call me the moment you know anything. I don't care

how small." I hung up the phone and sat in the darkness of my arms. Eugene squeezed my shoulders and laid his forehead on my back. I rolled my head to the side. "He's been shot. In the head. Reportedly." I clung to that "reportedly" because that meant it was in doubt.

"Oh God." His hands tightened.

I pushed myself up out of his kindness, and lifted the phone. My hand was shaking so badly I could barely grip the receiver. I wiped my face on my sleeve. "I asked about a radio. Can you check on that for me?"

He hesitated. I'm not sure if he thought the radio or leaving me alone was a bad idea, but he nodded and stood up. "What else do you need?"

"There's—" I had to clear my throat. "There's a folder in my quarters in East Bay. Can you bring it to me?" I could feel his reluctance rolling off of him in waves, but I didn't wait to see Eugene go. I trusted him to trust me about what I needed.

On the phone another young woman on *Lunetta* who might be a spy answered, "Operator."

"Earth, Kansas long distance, please."

"Surely." The sound changed as I stared at the wall opposite, with my feet tucked beneath the chair. A different woman said, "Long distance."

"Operator, I'd like to place a call to Kansas City: Elmwood eight-zero-four-zero-three."

"Surely." Again, the air changed with the hand-off and a different woman answered. "Washington Memorial Hospital. How may I direct your call?"

I wanted to ask her where my husband was, but a

switchboard operator would have no idea. "I'm calling for one of your patients. Nathaniel York, please."

"Surely."

A moment later, the phone rang. And rang. And rang. I'd almost given up hope. "Nathaniel York, speaking."

"It's Nicole." I charged ahead, knowing that my voice was shaking, knowing that he would think the worst about Elma. "Kenneth has been shot. I don't know any details and I hate to ask, but I don't know who else—" Who else would understand what it means to be hundreds of thousands of kilometers away from your love. "He's at Washington Memorial, too. I'm sorry. I know you're— Could you . . . ?"

"Yes. I'm going right now."

"Thank you. I . . . I just don't want him to be alone." And that was when I broke.

LIGHT FOOTSTEPS RAN down the hall and Helen skidded to a stop in front of the phone booth. I became aware that I didn't hear any other voices down the hall as she yanked the door open. Her hair stuck up at angles and her cheeks were flushed from running.

I opened my mouth and words would not come.

"Eugene sent me. I know. You don't have to say anything." She sat next to me and took my hand. "Do you want silence or distraction?"

I wanted to go home. "Distraction."

She compressed her lips, nodding. "My uncle is a classical singer, a tenor. He introduced me to 'You Can't

Raise a Goldfish in a Wineglass,' which is actually a drinking song, but he sang it as if it were opera. When I was very little, he used to sing me to sleep when he visited and I had a favorite song, 'Eighteen Touches,' that I would always ask for. I found out later it was about touching a courtesan, but he had changed the lyrics to be a game about my toys. I found this out by singing it on the school playground."

"No." I pasted a smile on and faced Helen as if I were listening to her. The rest of my body gravitated toward the mascon of the silent telephone.

"My teacher recognized the melody and spoke to my parents, quite upset, to which my father said, 'Why did *you* recognize the song?'"

That seemed to require a laugh. I did. "I asked for a radio. Do you know . . . ?"

"They are working on it, but have to find an extension cord to reach into here, I think." Helen bit her lower lip, then squeezed my hand. "Let someone else listen to the radio."

I shook my head. "I'm not there."

She looked down, and her jaw worked for a moment. "So, my uncle sang with a wonderful orchestra at a dinner club and we would get dressed up to—"

"Did you talk to Paulo?"

"Nicole, you don't have to—"

"If I don't do something useful, I'm going to come apart." My entire body was shaking with the urge to work the problem and it was not a problem I could work. "Did you talk to Paulo?"

She nodded with her whole neck, biting her lips again. She looked so sad for me that I wanted to yank my hand away and scream obscenities at her. "Yes. I did. We were playing chess when Eugene found me, in fact." Helen shifted in her chair to be closer to me. "When Eugene announced that Faustino was missing, Paulo became quite distressed."

I brought my attention around to focus on her and hung on like a lifeline. "Did he know where Faustino had gone?"

"He would not say. But I think he knows."

"I talked to Ruben." I nodded, pulling my hand free as gently as I could, and straightened in my chair. "When Eugene made the announcement, I asked casually if he had any ideas and he did the sort of flat denial that is an admission. What about the spacesuit?"

"According to Paulo, that was a different thing, although I am not convinced. He said Faustino had offered to take someone's shift because his girlfriend had gotten sick and he was afraid he was a carrier and would infect the suit." She shook her head. "I did not get a chance to follow up there."

Because Eugene had found her and told her Kenneth had been shot.

"That would be easy enough to find out." I rubbed my forehead. If I couldn't hear the fans, then I would swear they were off. The air in the booth was so tight and still. "We can also check against the duty rosters in Frisch's office."

Myrtle shouldered the booth door open, carrying a CPK bag in one hand. She dropped it on the table and bent to grab me. "Oh, honey. I'm so sorry."

I buried my face in her neck where she smelled of lilac

talc. "There hasn't been any more news." It was a question as much as a statement.

"Eugene is following with the radio."

Helen said, "I thought one of us could set up in another booth to listen—"

"Let her listen." Myrtle pulled back and gave Helen a fierce look. "When Eugene was overseas during the war, people always wanted to keep the papers and radios from me. Not knowing is worse."

"Thank you." I'm not sure I was audible.

She squeezed my shoulder. "What do you need?"

"Will you . . . will you pray for him?"

"I thought you didn't— Of course, honey. I've been doing that since I heard."

"I don't." I answered the question that she had cut off. I didn't believe in God. "But Kenneth does."

NOT KNOWING IS the worst. Myrtle was right. The radio did nothing to help with that. It sat in the corner with no news, no matter which of our five stations Eugene turned the dial to.

Waiting is the worst. I had to sit on my hands to keep from calling Kenneth's office again. The cast put unyielding pressure against my left thigh. How could they not know something by now? But when I looked at my watch, only forty-five minutes had passed since I'd talked to Nathaniel.

Being powerless is the worst. I stared at the file folder Eugene had brought me. "I need a pen. Please."

Eugene looked around from the radio. What I love best about him is that he didn't tell me things could wait. He straightened and dug in his arm pocket to pull out a pen. My hands were still shaking and I fumbled the pen when he handed it to me. It fell in slow motion, bouncing off the table and spinning to the floor.

Bending, Myrtle scooped the pen off the floor and put it on the folder. She turned to the CPK bag and opened it. "You should eat."

"I'm not hungry."

"I know." She set a tube of something in front of me. "But you need to keep your strength up."

"I'm not hungry."

"Honey . . . I'm not going to fight you on anything else. But you need to eat som—"

I snatched the tube and stood, throwing it across the tiny room. *"I'm not hungry!"* My chair tipped and fell behind me. The tube smacked against the wall, rebounding toward the ceiling.

Myrtle snatched it out of the air.

The shaking had gone from my hands through my entire body. "Goddammit. I don't want anything to eat. He went to the capitol because I asked him to. I will not 'feel better' if I eat something. I will feel better when the goddamned phone rings and they fucking tell me *something*."

My words consumed the remaining oxygen in the room. I wanted to keep screaming. If I ate, then I was going to need to go to the bathroom and then I would be out of the room when they called. I would be out of the room when Kenneth needed me. None of my friends looked shocked or angry or hurt by my outburst. They just looked sad for me. That was the worst.

Myrtle bent down and picked the chair up, setting it back on its feet. She put the tube in the middle of the folder. "I'm not going to play fair and I'm not going to apologize." She rested her hand next to the tube and looked at it. "You're going to eat that because Kenneth would want you to."

"You have no idea—"

"I'm supposed to tell you 'food is fuel.'" She looked at me and her eyes were glittering with tears. "He didn't say why, but I'm a smart woman. So you're going to sit down and you're going to eat that. I'll accept half the tube, but nothing less."

I hated her. I hated him. I sat and ate the goddamned tube. I have no idea what it was.

I did not feel better.

I PUSHED THE half-empty tube across the table. The rest of it sat in a congealed lump in my stomach. "Did you find anything out from maintenance about the thruster?"

Eugene jerked in his seat by the radio, lifting his head. For a moment, I thought he'd fallen asleep, but then I saw his clasped hands and realized he'd been praying. "No . . . No. They're still doing cleanup because the propellant we vented is corrosive enough that they don't want to be out on it in suits when the sun is up."

People think of the Moon as a cold and forbidding place. During the two-week day, the surface can get to 127 degrees Celsius.

He grimaced. "Plus they're down workers because of the quarantine."

"The sun sets . . . on the sixteenth?" Everything would have been exposed to a full day of sun by then and cooked off. "What are they doing about Halim's landing?"

"We're having him set down at the South Pole and then take a Busy—"

The phone rang.

All of us flinched at the clattering bell. I lunged for the receiver and pulled it to my ear. Myrtle moved to stand behind me and put her hand on my shoulder. Eugene turned the radio down, but not off.

"This is Nicole Wargin." My voice was steady and smooth with all the polish of a Swiss finishing school.

In the time it took for my voice to reach the Earth, I could hear the background. I could hear the hubbub of a hospital. A siren outside the building. Voices clamoring for attention.

"Nicole." In Nathaniel York's voice. In the two syllables of my name. I knew. "I'm so sorry."

PART III

THIRTY-FIVE

MRS. WARGIN DISPLAYS A STOIC DIGNITY AND PASSION THROUGHOUT PUBLIC GRIEF

By ANTHONY LEWIS

Special to The National Times

KANSAS CITY, May 11, 1963—Mrs. Kenneth T. Wargin went bravely through her final hour of public grief today. She gave an eloquent and impassioned eulogy via a telelink from the lunar colony. Mrs. Wargin is on the Moon, trapped with some 300 other lunar citizens, unable to attend Gov. Wargin's funeral after he was assassinated three days ago on the steps of the United States Capitol. It had been thought that the cause for the cessation of traffic to and from the Moon was related to a polio outbreak, but Mrs. Wargin spoke of sabotage and a plot by members of Earth First. The governor's office has confirmed that he was en route to the Capitol with information related to this when the shooting occurred.

Nonetheless, it was the first time that many had heard of the alleged reason that her husband's life was taken. She spoke from a tele-conference room on the Moon, projected in the Topeka First United Methodist Church

on a screen six meters high behind the casket holding
the body of her husband.

———————

She wore a simple black sheath, belted at the waist, with
three-quarter sleeves, that made a stark contrast to the
cast upon her left arm. A single strand of jet beads hung
about her neck, barely drooping in the weak lunar gravity.

———————

Mrs. Wargin said, "My husband was a man who loved
the opera and played poker and had a weakness for
kittens. He was a fighter for human rights and dignity.
He believed passionately in establishing a toehold for
humanity in space, even though he had a heart condition
that would prevent him from leaving the planet. He
believed in fighting for the future of the people he
served. And for that last reason, he was murdered."

———————

Her voice faltered here in one of only two times that
her composure broke. It was a vision that few who
watched would ever forget. With the camera trained
on her face, filling the enormous screen, Mrs. Wargin
pressed her hand to her mouth and turned suddenly to
Major Eugene Lindholm, the acting administrator of
Artemis Base, who was a step or two away. Her blue
eyes filled, and for an instant her face looked like that of
a widow burdened with sorrow, instead of a governor's
wife. Major Lindholm pressed his hand to her shoulder.
She drew a breath and stood erect again for the camera,
appearing on the screen over the body of her husband,
tears glittering on her cheeks.

———————

"Kenneth was first and foremost a politician in the purest
sense of the word. He lived to serve the people. He died

to serve the people. I ask you to not let his death be in vain. Find the cowards who killed my husband to stop him from exposing their sabotage on the Moon and on Earth. Find the people who have left me here, trapped on the Moon, and unable to be at his side at the end. Find those who would trap humanity on Earth out of fear.

———————

"My husband sent me to the Moon because there were opportunities for the progress of humanity. He would not say that we should or will abandon the Earth willingly, but that space would give us the tools and the goals and most of all the hope for a future in which we can exercise the best of our potential as individuals."

———————

After speaking, she remained watching the powers of church and state bid him farewell via a camera directed at the church. Few could witness that living portrait of stoic grief and remain unmoved.

I AM FORTUNATE in that I can often delay my reactions to intense events. It is useful when you are in a plane that is going down. It is useful when you have been blindsided in a political conversation. It is useful when your husband has been killed.

The television cameras turned off and I covered my face with my hands. The veneer of resolve that I had pulled around me was cracking and I could not let it yet. Eugene's hand rested against my back again and he tried to pull me into a hug.

I straightened, drawing in a breath, and stepped away. "I'm all right."

Eugene glanced at Myrtle, who had watched from a safe space behind the cameras. Helen stood in the shadows there, arms wrapped around her core. Her lips were tight and the tear tracks on her face nearly undid me again.

I looked down, straightening the sleeves of my hastily dyed dress. There were no mourning clothes on the Moon, but Myrtle used to work for a company that dyed hair. She went to someone in the chemistry department and handed them a formula. Helen used to be a computer and remembered that someone in the pool used to be a seamstress. One of the artists in my gallery had strung the necklace from pieces of lunar breccia, rocks pulverized and melted together by meteors. For this one day on the Moon, I looked like Mrs. Kenneth T. Wargin.

My cheeks were wet and I smeared the moisture away with a hasty swipe of my palm. "Do you have my folder?"

"Maybe you should take a break?" Myrtle pulled it out from under her arm.

I shook my head. Opening the folder, I looked for the next thing to do. I am an astronaut and I am a politician's wife. A politician's widow. We had made contingency plans. All of the business of death written out on the pages inside so I would not have to think. The first page had a list of names and phone numbers. Relatives, funeral parlor, lawyers. All with a check mark next to them. The cats were staying with Nathaniel. The movers had emptied our things from the Governor's Mansion. I turned the pages, moving down the order of operations for grieving.

I put a check next to "funeral."

Interment was next, but they would drive him to

Wichita, where he would be laid to rest in the family plot. The process of letting me see the burial in that remote cemetery could have been done but I had felt selfish about adding a layer of complexity to a day that would already be difficult for his terrestrial family.

And after that . . . there was nothing. I stared at the empty page. If I were home— And home was where, exactly?

I swallowed the rock in my gut. If I were on Earth, there would have been things I could have done, but from here, everything associated with the business of death was finished. There were people on Earth who had handled everything in my absence. I had made phone calls and decisions and delegated, but my *presence* was not required.

And now? I closed the folder.

The fans of the room buzzed around me. Gray snow flurried at the edges of my vision and goddammit, I knew what that was. I did not have time to faint. I stared at the cables of the television camera, trying to breathe the dizziness away. On the floor, the cables curled like snakes; where they weren't taped down, they writhed in the air current without enough weight to overcome the coil of the wire. The snow receded and the fans quieted to a hiss.

I looked up at the young man who had run the cameras. "Thank you." He had a name. I had met him before, but in that moment he was just another young white man from engineering. I walked to him and pressed his hand with the illusion of sincerity. "Thank you so much for your kindness today."

His eyes were damp. "Ma'am, I'm so—"

"Thank you." If he told me he was sorry for my loss,

I might scream at him. You do not scream at the staff. "Would you mind giving me a moment to . . ." I let my voice trail away.

He ducked his head and backed out of the room, leaving me alone with Myrtle, Eugene, and Helen. Looking at the door he had closed behind him, I said, "What has been happening with Icarus?"

Beside me, Myrtle stiffened. She would not approve and I knew all of her reasons for thinking I should stop and rest, so I faced Eugene instead. His face was fixed and impassive. For a moment, his eyes cut to Myrtle, and I could imagine her mouthing instructions behind me.

Eugene twisted his head to the side, "Nicole . . ."

"They killed my husband. Don't you dare finish that sentence with anything else but a plan to brief me on what I've missed." I gripped the folder in both hands, the cast scraping against the paper with a hiss. "What did you learn about the controls of the lunar shuttle we came in on?"

His fists tightened and he looked at the floor. Pursing his lips, Eugene shook his head as if losing some silent conversation. Then he straightened his shoulders and faced me. "Not conclusive. The thruster itself is fine. The hand controller had debris in it, which could have caused the intermittent failure. However, it was not actually impeding anything when they opened the controller. It could have moved on impact, which is why I didn't have problems, or it could have been generated by impact."

"Faustino?"

Behind me, Myrtle said, "Why don't we have this conversation in the cafeteria?"

I frowned. "It's not open."

She and Helen exchanged glances. Helen cleared her throat. "It reopened this morning. Halim landed with the vaccines on Thursday so we were able to lift quarantine."

"Oh. Right." I had been told he had landed. It just hadn't stuck. I had spent the past three days locked in the AdminMod making calls or sleeping under a blanket of Miltown. The cafeteria would be full of well-meaning people who would want to console me. "It's not secure."

"No, but given what you just broadcast, I'm not certain that security is a concern." Myrtle walked to the door. "And lunch would be good for all of us."

"I'm not hungry."

Myrtle stopped at the door, bowing her head. "Kenneth would want you to eat."

"Kenneth doesn't want me to eat. Kenneth is not looking down on me from Heaven and worrying. Kenneth is *dead*." I was away from him for three months at a time. I only got to hear his voice once a week when I was on the Moon. I should not feel his absence with every breath I drew.

And sometimes I didn't. For a moment, while engaged with something else, he still existed in the world. He was still on Earth, in his office, working or playing with his kitten or talking to a constituent or going to the opera. I balled my hands into fists, fighting the grief and rage that filled my throat. "What . . . What is the status of Faustino?"

"You're allowed to take time to grieve."

"This *is* how I grieve!" My voice tore my throat. "The

people who killed him are out there planning who knows what, and you want me to take a nap? Have a little snack? Rend my garments and weep?"

Helen stepped out of the shadows. "Yes. That is what we want. We have been working and I promise you that we will keep working until we find these people and stop them."

I had to remind myself that they were grieving too. Kenneth had been good friends with all of these people. We had lost Terrazas. I bit my lip and looked down at the folder, riffling the useless pages. "I'll tell you that you get two choices with me: you can have me reasonably functional and busy or you can have me stop. Completely."

"You don't know that."

"Oh, I do." The months of numb despair after that final miscarriage rose and tied the grief of losing Evelyn Marie to the loss of my husband. Would it have been easier if she had lived? My eyes burned again and I wiped at them with the back of my hand. "I will eat. Not enough to make any of you happy, but I will eat."

Food is fuel. I had a job to do and I knew the consequences of not eating. I knew the path I was on. But knowing and stepping off the path are two different things.

"Nicole . . ."

"I'm assuming from the way you are refusing to answer the question that Faustino is dead."

Eugene took a step toward me. "Yes." He flexed his hand, which had scabs on the knuckles. I wasn't sure if those were new or from . . . Wednesday?

Had I let four days slip by since we learned about Terrazas? "Are you going to tell me how?"

"According to Ruben, he went skiing."

"Skiing." I was missing something. "We're on the Moon."

"Faustino had been up before. There are places where the regolith is powder. Wood skis, obviously, would be destroyed, but one of Ruben's friends has a PhD in materials science and was able to craft skis out of a packing crate. Several of them snuck out to do this."

The levels of rage and incredulity that boiled beneath the surface of my skin could have cooked veal. "Are you fucking kidding me?"

Eugene's smile was grim. "That was what I said. Ruben defended it by telling me that they were not using any new materials. I explained that this was not the point."

These . . . these *children* had no understanding of how dangerous the Moon was. The colonists flew up here and lived in a dome that had a goddamned rec area and we let them come, undertrained, because that was the only economical way for the IAC to scale increasing the population on the Moon.

"And they knew he'd gone out and said nothing?"

"Ruben did not. Or, at least, not this time. He was down with polio and afterward thought Faustino was just in a different module until we made the announcement and he started to wonder." Eugene ran his hand over his hair. "We found Faustino where they said he'd gone. Walking distance. He'd fallen on his PLSS and had a hiss out."

I shuddered. The Personal Life Support Systems were less bulky than they had been when we'd started coming to the Moon, but still a cumbersome backpack. You had to lean forward to balance the mass. Any time you fall, there's a worry that this will be the time you split a seam on your suit or pop a hose in the PLSS and all your air would hiss out. It's a fast way to die, but not instant. Faustino would have had time to know what was happening.

"Shit . . . Have you told people?"

"While you were asleep." He cleared his throat. "Myrtle . . . ah . . . she had them—"

"There he goes making me the villain." She crossed her arms, giving him a mock glare, and turned back to me. "I had them turn off the loudspeaker in your compartment. You can be mad at me all you want, but it was the first time you'd slept."

Eugene cut back in before I could object. "To get ahead of your questions: there was no BusyBee at the site. We still don't know where it is."

It wasn't possible to walk on the Moon and not leave a trail. There was no wind or weather to obscure your tracks. Things could be hard to see during noon-days when the shadows were straight down or during the two-week night, but even with that, the tracks to an airlock would be clear. "Have you looked for tracks out—"

Eugene nodded. "We've checked all of the airlocks. There are no tracks walking away except for Faustino's. No one else is missing. We think it had to be taken by either Curt or Birgit, with Curt being the most likely."

"What are—"

"To be on the safe side, I've confined both of them and have them under observation at all times." Eugene walked all the way up to me and put his hands on my shoulders.

"I will brief you on all of this. I promise. I'll even give you the choice of your quarters or the cafeteria, but I need you to walk out of this room. Wait— Hold that objection. You need to be busy. You need a purpose. I understand that. Right now, I have a base full of people who are grieving and terrified. I need you to set an example."

That. That was what Kenneth would want me to do. "Goddammit, Eugene Lindholm. You do not play fair."

"No." He smiled even though tears were building in his eyes. "No, I do not."

THIRTY-SIX

EARTH-FIRSTER ACCUSED

Figure in an Anti-Space Group Is Charged

By GLADWIN HILL

Special to The National Times

KANSAS CITY, May 11, 1963—Shane James Cox, a 20-year-old auto mechanic who does charity work through the Catholic church with Meteor refugees, was charged late last night with assassinating Governor Wargin.

Cox was arrested at 7:15 Friday evening, nearly forty-eight hours after the assassination of the governor, in the White Cliff district, five kilometers from where the governor was shot. Chief of Police Alex Charlemagne announced that Cox had been formally arraigned at 1:40 a.m. Central Time yesterday on a charge of murder in the governor's death. The arraignment was made before a justice of the peace in the homicide bureau at Police Headquarters. Captain Dennis Poole, head of the homicide bureau, identified Cox as an adherent of the right-wing "Earth First." This group is the same that Gov. Wargin's widow accused in her eulogy at his funeral, lending credence to her allegations that they have been attempting to sabotage the space program.

BY THE TIME we finished passing through the gauntlet of my peers, I had developed a set of rote responses that rolled easily out of my mouth.

"Thank you, that's very kind."

"Yes, he was the love of my life."

"And how are you holding up?"

This last one saved me, because I could fall back on listening to them talk about polio or Faustino with a concerned expression that I'd honed over decades at Kenneth's side. I had learned the trick of nodding at the right places and tilting my head in response to a change in their tone that worked even when I had stopped being able to understand them. I don't know if the fact that they seemed to feel better was depressing or heartening.

I dropped into a chair in the conference room that Eugene led me to. It was tempting to rest my head on the smooth tan Formica that covered the table, but I would never lift it again if I did. Myrtle set a sip-pack of water in front of me.

I glared at her, but I picked it up and drank because my mouth was so dry that it crackled. My head ached. I rubbed the space over my right eye and looked around the room. "An upgrade from your office?"

"I wanted a map." Eugene pulled out a chair for his wife, nodding to the lunar map on one wall, which was dotted with bright red thumbtacks. "My secretary suggested this."

"Your secretary?" I lowered my hand. "Does that mean I'm fired?"

"No offense, but you're a terrible typist."

I held up my cast as if I wouldn't have been terrible without it. "No argument."

Helen walked over to the map and drew a circle with her finger on Mare Imbrium around Artemis Base. "We have been working with the assumption that the pilot of our missing BusyBee must have walked back from wherever he left the ship. That means we have a two-kilometer radius around the main colony as well as around each of the way stations."

She pointed to each of the red thumbtacks that dotted the lunar landscape in a straight line between Artemis Base and The Garden and the lava tube at Marius Hills. The way stations were essentially BusyBee shells sans engines and placed every two kilometers, which was the formal IAC "walkback" range for an astronaut in a lunar spacesuit.

"But if he's carrying extra air, that range gets bigger." My head felt like I was at the bottom of a gravity well. If I didn't keep moving, I was going to sink through the chair and pass out.

Myrtle opened a packet of crackers and slid it in front of me. "Right. Looking at the logbooks, I think the BusyBee was actually taken on April sixteenth, three days after we landed."

I pushed the crackers out of my way and turned back to Helen. The room seemed to follow a little too slowly. "How do we lose a BusyBee for three weeks?"

Eugene leaned forward in his chair. "That . . . That is one of the things keeping Frisch on my list of people possibly involved. I still think Curt is our man, but can't ignore the fact that Frisch's record-keeping about the BusyBees was incomplete. Inventories come in from each of the outposts and the hangar here. Procedurally, he should have assigned someone to track and oversee those. He did not."

"You think it was deliberate or fuzzy brain from poison?" As I thought about how to figure out which scenario we were facing, I let my eyes lower. The folder was on the table. For a moment, my ribs seemed to fold in and pinch my lungs.

Goddammit. Just one hour. I wanted to get through just an hour without being reminded. Why had I even brought that in here? I pressed my fist against my mouth. They were still talking and all I could do was try to control my breathing.

Clearing my throat, I kept my head bent until the tears passed. "Are we missing other equipment?"

Myrtle nodded. "Some things are natural attrition, like office supplies, tubing, or wire. I'm working with the secretarial department to do a full audit of the books, and the worrying things, so far . . . Oxygen tanks. CO_2 scrubbers. Two missing radio units."

I lifted my head so quickly the room swam with gray spots again. I blinked them away, keeping one hand on the table for stability. "Remote-control bomb."

Eugene's eyebrows went up and his mouth dropped. "That's where your mind goes first? Not listening post? Not that there are two people involved?"

"Tubing. Wire. Fertilizer. Acid." There was something else. Something had tickled at the back of my brain as they were talking, but focusing was slow. "Signal it with a radio."

Eugene wiped his hand down his face and stared at the ceiling. "Swell. And here I thought we were getting things under control."

The door opened, and Halim Malouf bounded in, with the grace of an Algerian film star. Like all the original astronauts, he was a compact man and seemingly chosen for his photogenic properties as much as his prowess as a test pilot. Even now, with his hair matted down and the impressions of a "Snoopy" cap on his forehead, he was handsome. "It worked! I was able to wipe— Oh." He saw me and all the cheer bled out of his face.

He crossed the room and knelt next to me, taking my right hand in both of his. "I am so sorry about Kenneth. We were en route and they didn't tell us until we landed. My dear . . . if there is anything I can do, you must let me."

"Thank you, that's very kind." My eyes were burning again.

"Kenneth was a good man and deadly at poker. He will be sorely missed."

"Yes, he was the love of my life."

"I cannot imagine what you must be going through." Sorrow bent the lines of his face as he gazed at me. I don't mind being the center of attention, but I loathe being the object of pity.

"And how are you holding up?" I pressed the hand with the cast to his shoulder. "It sounded as if you had some good news."

He hesitated, looking to Eugene for advice. Myrtle leaned back in her chair, watching me with all the judgment in the solar system. "She doesn't want to rest. I figure, we let her work until she passes out and then tie her down."

I laughed and stuck my tongue out at her. Pulling my hand free of Halim's, I kept the smile firmly in place. "No, but seriously. What worked? Because I would love some good news."

"Well . . . It is mixed news, really." He got to his feet, resting his hands on his hips. "I tried a couple of different methods to mask my footsteps. A controlled release from an emergency oxygen tank allowed me to obscure my trail. Only for about three meters, but that was just a single tank. It let me get to the rim of a crater, which I was able to use to mask my path."

Helen stared at the map and grimaced. "So really, the BusyBee could be almost anywhere."

"Not if it's the bomb." Staring at the map, I shoved my chair back and stood.

The room tipped sideways, graying. I staggered and reached for the table. My cast thunked against it, slipping off. Halim braced me as I got my balance again. The room narrowed in a tunnel as if I were pulling too many gs and my heart thundered in my ears.

I swallowed, squeezing his hand. "I'm all right."

Other people were standing. When had Myrtle and Eugene moved to be next to me? Halim guided me back down into the chair and his face was tight with concern.

"Sorry." I shook my head. "Sorry. I just caught my foot. I'm all right."

"You are not all right." Myrtle thrust the crackers at me. "Food is fuel."

"Screw you." I pushed them away. She had no right

to parrot words she didn't even understand. "I tripped. That's all."

She planted her hands on her hips, glaring at me. "Everyone out."

Eugene lifted his hands as if he were warding off a bomb blast and backed away from her. Helen, that traitor, turned and walked to the door. Only Halim hesitated. "Is there any—"

"Out. I know you're the chief astronaut, but—out." Myrtle pointed to the door.

I rolled my eyes. "Myrtle, come on. I missed my balance because we're on the Moon. You know this happens."

The door shut behind Halim. She grabbed a chair and turned it so it was facing mine. Sitting down, she leaned forward with the crackers held in both hands. "Do you know how much weight I had to lose to get in the astronaut corps?"

I blinked, memory pulling up Myrtle as I had met her originally, back when Elma was still trying to get any women at all accepted into the astronaut corps. She had been a woman of curves, who had borne three sons and loved to cook and did not regret the extra padding. Now she was trim and athletic without any roundness to her cheeks except when she smiled. Which she was very definitely not doing now.

"Forty pounds. In three months. My body is designed for curves. And I'm sure as hell not shaped like Helen, who could eat an entire French bakery and still be built like a teenage boy. I fast the week before every preflight weigh-in and pray that I haven't screwed up." She held the crackers out to me again. "You are not all right."

"It's not about losing weight."

"I don't care what it's about." The crackers hung in her hand between us. "The last thing Eugene needs is for you to really collapse. Eat the goddamned crackers."

My eyes widened. "Language?"

"Eat the goddamned motherfucking crackers or so help me, I will get Ana Teresa and tell her to sedate you, tie you down, and stick an IV in your arm."

I took the crackers.

OUR COMPROMISE WAS that I ate the crackers and went to bed. I use the word "compromise," because Myrtle Lindholm is married to a fighter pilot and did not find me even a little bit intimidating. She is more stubborn than I am, and my alternative was to . . .

If she had called Ana Teresa, the doctor would have been absolutely correct to hospitalize me. Kenneth . . . Kenneth would have stepped in sooner. I had not eaten anything since the tube of applesauce the morning that—

I went to bed, because she was right. They had everything under control. They were doing all the things I would have done. With the arrival of Halim, they even had an extra pilot—one who could actually fly. Eugene did not need me actually collapsing and I was right on the edge of that. I took a Miltown. I slept.

* * *

I WOKE IN my bunk in East Bay quarters, completely disoriented. My face was wet with tears again. I hadn't slept much for the past several days but I was so tired of waking up crying. I wanted Marlowe to sit on my back and pin me down into the bed. Outside the room, I could hear someone whispering, which might have been what woke me up. Probably Myrtle or Helen. I should get up so they would stop worrying and could get on with their lives.

Rolling onto my back, my body felt like it weighed Earth normal. I stared at the ceiling, illuminated only by the thin strip of light bleeding through from the common room. Everything was dim and gray. I closed my eyes again. Later. I would get up later.

Water dropped on my forehead.

My eyes snapped open. I sat up, room spinning around me. Swinging my legs out of bed, I reached for the light switch and stopped myself. I was out of it, but I was not stupid.

Bracing myself on the wall, I pushed open the thin plastic door. Water beaded on the walls and ceiling of the common room. Helen and Aahana were standing in a whispered conversation. Both women wore their pajamas and the room lighting was set to evening's dim orange glow.

"Don't touch anything." My voice sounded like death, appropriately.

They both jumped. Helen did not waste time, she gestured at the ceiling, which was covered with heavy drops of water, waiting to fall. "We noticed it about half an hour ago. I sent someone to tell Eugene and maintenance."

"The whole habitat module?" I didn't actually think we'd be lucky enough that it was just the women's quarters and Helen nodded to confirm that. "What time is it?"

"Nearly six." Helen was tapping her lower lip, looking at the ceiling condensation. Her eyes widened and she turned to me. "On Monday. You slept through Sunday."

"Well." I sat on the bed and bent down to grab my shoes. Last time, I was barefoot, and having rubber soles seemed like a good idea. "I guess that's what they mean by sleeping like the dead."

"I'm going downstairs." Helen turned to Aahana. "Alert someone in West Bay and get them to help you wake people up, but make sure no one touches the light switches or anything with current. Move them out to Midtown."

"Give me a minute and I'll come with you." What I actually wanted to do was pee. Another drop of water hit the back of my neck as I yanked my shoes on and did not diminish the urge.

"Just go to Midtown with everyone else." Helen started toward the door.

I stood up, too fast, and the entire module spun in a violent circle around me. I grabbed the wall to steady myself. Helen's back was to me and she missed all of that. Aahana saw it. I smiled at her and winked. As I walked past, I gestured to the doors. "Might be best to open them so no one reaches for the switch by instinct."

"All right." She chewed her lower lip. "Are you okay?"

"Just practicing my dance routine for the talent show."

I turned to follow Helen out of the room, but now that I was upright the fact that I'd been asleep for more than a day made me uncomfortably aware of my bladder.

Cursing under my breath, I steered into the bathroom and peed in the dark. If I had been wearing a MAG I'm pretty sure that I would have discovered what the maximum in "Maximum Absorbency Garment" really was.

Five years later, I was out in the hall and feeling significantly less compromised. The condensation in the hall wasn't as bad, with fewer people breathing in it. The door to the West Bay Men's was open and I could hear Aahana talking to someone. I crept down the spiral stairs, carefully not touching the metal banister or support post, just in case.

The equipment room for this module took up the entire bottom floor. This can make it sound huge, but because the domes were more properly bubbles, the lowest floor and the upper floor were the smallest. The stairs came down in the middle, with four aisles that radiated out to a walkway around the perimeter. Batteries, dehumidifier, oxygen, CO_2 scrubbers . . . all in compact packages shipped up and installed in neat quadrants. Each module was designed to be self-contained in case there was ever a decompression event in another. We had central processing for things like power and water reclamation, but basic life support was duplicated. The room was low and brightly lit and far more humid than it should be.

The lighting made it very easy to see the equipment and Helen's body lying at the end of the aisle.

THIRTY-SEVEN

KANSAS LEGISLATURE APPROVES TAX REFORM

Bill Asked for by Wargin

Sent to House by 118–7 Vote

TOPEKA, Kan., May 13, 1963—(AP)—In a special session today, the Senate passed, 118 to 7, a bill urged by the late Governor Wargin to reform taxes by removing exemptions for the very wealthy. The measure, which now goes to the House, would increase state revenue in each of the next three years.

I STEPPED OFF the stairs and my heart was racing. What the hell had happened? Helen had been maybe five minutes in front of me. There hadn't been an arc. No telltale smell of ozone in the air. My eyes burned. Why was she on the floor? I could barely catch my breath and the room was spinning around me. I had to power through, because Helen was . . .

Helen was on the floor. She was facedown on the floor, reaching toward the stairs.

CO_2.

The entire room tilted wildly. There were emergency

masks down here. Where? I couldn't think. The only thing that kept me focused was that we'd done this in training. I knew the drill. I couldn't save my crewmate if I was down too. I backpedaled, turning to the stairs, and staggered. *Come on, Wargin. You can foxtrot while drunk, you've got this.* I held my breath, trying to trap what oxygen was still in my system.

The stairs swam in front of me. Helen was behind me. I should go back for her. I shook that thought out of my head and got to the stairs. Grabbing the banister, which I had been afraid of for some reason . . . Why had that been? *Up. Go up, Wargin. CO_2 sinks.*

By the second floor, I was on my hands and knees or maybe I had been since down below. My left arm yelled every time I put weight on it, which helped me stay focused, so I kept crawling on all fours. The urgency to take a breath made my lungs burn, and on the landing for the second floor, I risked it. The devilish thing about CO_2 is it feels like there's air. It felt like a relief to take in that breath.

The room was still spinning but not any worse than it had been. I was fuzzy-headed, but I could remember where the emergency masks were. Mostly because they were directly across from the stairs and clearly labeled "Emergency Oxygen Mask."

I crawled to the wall and grabbed the handle of the EOM compartment to pull myself up. Just to open it, I had to stand with my legs spread wide and brace on the wall. I pulled out a mask. The familiar, drilled motions to slide it over my head were clumsy with the wrong hand. I fumbled before I found the valve to activate it. Pure oxygen hissed with cold, metallic splendor.

The cobwebs started to peel back from my brain, still clumping and clinging, but I knew what to do. I grabbed another mask. These were small packs, designed to buy you ten minutes to get to safety. Helen had been down there for . . . I wasn't sure how long, but I ran down the stairs.

Everything was still spinning and I nearly tumbled down the last few steps. I grabbed the walls. *Slow is fast.* I walked to Helen because I didn't have enough control to run. Kneeling next to her, I dragged the mask over her face and turned the valve on.

Only then, did I check to make sure she was alive.

Her pulse was frantic and fast as if she'd been running. I sagged over her, catching myself on the floor with relief. The mask pressed against my face. Ten minutes. I had used two already.

I got to my feet and grabbed Helen's arm to hoist her up into a fireman's carry. Even at 1/6 g, when she only weighed nine kilograms, I almost pitched over trying to lift her. My limbs felt like jelly and that wasn't the CO_2 right now. That wasn't the cast. That was my own fault. I wet my lips and rolled her onto her back.

This sucked, but I grabbed her other arm and dragged her toward the stairs. And then, what? I wouldn't be able to get her up them, not in my current state. On any other day, I would try the intercom, but not with this much moisture on the walls. I propped her up against the base of the stairs.

I looked up the spiral. One story up we had offices, the floor above that had crew quarters. Two flights of stairs and I was barely keeping my feet. Could I get up in the . . . six minutes remaining? No. But I could shout from the base of the next floor, which if my brain had been working, I would have done in the first place.

With the order of operations in my head, I scrambled up the stairs. When I came out on the office level, I took a deep breath in my mask and then peeled it off.

"Mayday! Mayday! Mayday!" I stuck my face in the mask and drew another breath, not bothering with the seal. Above me, I heard a reassuring scramble toward the stairs. "CO_2! Get a mask. Repeat. CO_2. Get an oxygen mask."

Above me, Aahana shouted back, "Roger, wilco!"

A breath of metal air. "Helen is down. I can't lift her. Machine room."

"Copy. We're on our way. Hang tight."

I didn't wait to see who the other half of "we" was. I just trusted my colleagues to do their jobs, while the evil part of my brain pointed out that if either of them were connected to Icarus, I could expect to hear the door to the stairs close. If that happened, then I guess I'd find a nonconductive thing and use it on the intercom.

Which, again, if I had been thinking clearly earlier, I could have attempted. It still might have arced, but at least I wouldn't have been fried. I stuck my mask back on and turned to the EOM cabinet, trusting Aahana to take appropriate action. I swapped my mask out for a fresh one and grabbed one for Helen before I stumbled back down the stairs.

As I came out of the stairwell, I saw the EOM cabinet down here, directly across from the stairs. I had been really out of it. Why the hell weren't the alarms sounding?

I knelt next to Helen and leaned over her to check the valve on her mask. Her eyes were open. My heart nearly gave out with relief. She stirred, trying to sit up, but couldn't coordinate enough to get her elbow under her.

She saw me and said something that was garbled enough that I wasn't sure if it was English, Taiwanese, or French. If she had been me, it would have been some version of "What happened?"

"CO_2. Help is coming." I held up the fresh mask. "Hold your breath."

She nodded, drawing in a deep breath, and reached up to fumble with the straps of the mask she had on. I helped her drag it off, dark hair going every which way. We got the new mask on. Above us, feet clattered down the stairs. Moments later, in pajamas and wearing rubber-sole shoes, Aahana and one of the women from computing rounded the last curve of the stairs.

They got us both up and to safety, because, who am I kidding . . . I needed the help too.

HELEN SAT ACROSS from me at the conference table with an ice pack on her head. Her eyes were closed and she leaned her head against the wall. "I keep thinking about Curt and Birgit being confined."

"Yeah . . ." I had a matching ice pack, trying to knock the throbbing in my temples back to a manageable level. "I'll be interested to see what, exactly, went wrong with the CO_2 scrubber."

She cracked her eyes and looked at me. "I don't remember seeing anything off, but this is not surprising."

If Ana Teresa had had her way, we both would have been in sickbay. That was complicated by the fact that the SciMod was still offline from the water damage and even if it hadn't been, she still had polio patients.

"If I hadn't seen you on the floor . . . I would've gone down too." Probably faster, in fact.

In front of me was a tray of food from the cafeteria. Bacon. Buttered toast. And a real hard-boiled egg from an actual space chicken. A glass of Tang and a cup of coffee.

"Do you think Icarus is trying to force us all into one module?"

It was a good question. In Midtown, Eugene and Myrtle were organizing all the people who usually slept in the HabMod, which was a good chunk of the colony. Since the SciMod was still offline, that left us with only three functioning habitation modules. Admin, Midtown, and the OpsMod. There were pilots' quarters at the port, but not enough to accommodate everyone.

Get us all into one place, and then set off a bomb? I grimaced. During the war, I had been Icarus. I had gone places and made friends with the intention of betraying their trust. "It's what I would do if I were—"

I heard the door open and grabbed the hard-boiled egg. Cracking the shell against the table, I concentrated on peeling it.

Ana Teresa came back in, carrying a crate of supplies. Behind her, Halim followed with a couple of hammocks slung over his shoulder. They were speaking in Arabic and switched mid-sentence. "... *almar'at al'akthar eanadaan alty qabalatha ealaa al'iitlaq* but it's close. Let's put the hammocks in the two far corners."

"Hammocks? I take it we're bunking in here." The shell wanted to curl up around the egg without sufficient gravity to help it drop away.

Ana Teresa set the crate on the table. "Welcome to Auxiliary C Sickbay."

The bare egg glistened in the overhead lights. I set it down on my tray and felt the doctor watching me. I picked up the knife and fork. "How are things out there?"

In the corner, Halim pulled out a chair and set it under one of the room's support struts. "Good, actually. Everyone is very much pulling together, which . . ." He climbed onto the chair with one of the hammocks still over his shoulder. "Honestly, I had my doubts about the colonists."

I sliced the egg in half, revealing the sun-yellow orb in the middle. "Good people." Setting down my knife, I reached for the salt and pepper. My heart was speeding up, unaccountably. "Mostly good, at any rate."

"That raises—" He glanced at me, then at Ana Teresa, and grimaced. "That raises my respect for Eugene, that he's doing such a good job motivating them."

What would he have said if we were alone in the room? Helen met my gaze, with the same question on her face. I rotated a bit of egg on my fork, trying to think. If I weren't so wretchedly tired, I would probably have come up with some clever method to send Ana Teresa away, but at the moment, the best I could do was to be quiet and hope she'd finish faster.

Halim seemed to have come to the same conclusion. He hooked the hammock into one of the mechanical receptors built into the support strut and did a pull/twist test on it. Ana Teresa was dragging a chair over to the strut on the other side of the conference table.

The egg was still on the end of my fork.

It is difficult to explain the act of will it took to put it into my mouth. When I was having trouble, sometimes Kenneth would . . . I closed my eyes and fought to keep my breathing even. Behind my eyelids . . . *He stands in his shirtsleeves, whisking a raw egg in a bowl to make a Caesar salad for me. The muscles on his forearms flex and tense. His hair falls forward out of its pomade.*

"Are you all right?" Ana Teresa's voice was soft, elevated as if she had gotten on the chair.

"Fine." I opened my eyes and took a bite of the egg.

The yolk coated my mouth like paste. I gagged. Yanking my napkin up, I covered my mouth and breathed through my nose. The doctor jumped down from her chair and was at my side in an instant. I tried to swallow. Gagged again.

She rested her hand on my back while I spit out the tiny bite of egg, folding my napkin around it. Tears crowded my vision. I kept my gaze down so I didn't have to see Helen and Halim watching this entire little episode.

Ana Teresa crouched next to me and took the napkin away. "Would applesauce be more manageable?"

"It might be. Yes." My voice was hoarse with shame. "I'm sorry."

*   *   *

IN THE EVENING, Eugene peeked through the conference room door. When he saw that we had the lights on, he opened the door and stopped on the threshold. His brows went up as he looked at Helen and me, in our glamorous hammocks, hanging from the ceiling.

Helen waved her fingers. "Surprise."

I lowered the notepad I'd been scribbling on and my IV line coiled through the air with my movement. "Welcome to my parlor . . ."

"Halim warned me, but . . ." He turned to Myrtle. "You ṣeeing what they did to my conference room?"

She smacked his rump. "Are you going to gawk or hold the door for me?"

Grinning, he stepped to the side and held the door for his wife. I had a choice between staring at them with envy, bursting into tears, and counting the mechanical receptors in the ceiling strut. There are five. Two of them were occupied with the hammock and another held my IV bag.

Eugene set a CO_2 filter in the middle of the table. "I'd appreciate it if you'd stop trying to get yourselves killed."

"You'd rather we succeeded?"

He looked stricken, which I think made me regret my joke more than he did his. Wincing, he rounded the end of the table toward my hammock. "I'm so sorry."

"It's the first joke I've made. It's okay." I gestured at the filter on the table, trying to move him past the moment, because even with the joke, my heart was folding itself into a flat square inside. "What did you find out about the scrubbers?"

He looked like he wanted to keep apologizing, but Myrtle said, "That's a fake."

Helen sighed noisily and with much aggravation. "I have just lost a bet, which I do not appreciate." She glared at me. I shrugged and she stared at the ceiling in such a comic portrait of woe that it was hard not to laugh. "Is the fake filter made from in situ resources, including tape?"

Eugene's mouth dropped open and he turned to stare at her. "How the hell do you know that?"

"Language." Myrtle sounded more amused than anything.

Helen pointed an accusing finger at me. "Ask Nicole about her list."

"List." Eugene turned back to me and his gaze dropped to the notepad I'd been scribbling on.

I tried to sit up, which is not easy in a hammock, so I settled for clearing my throat instead. "I started thinking about what I would do to mess things up here. If that had been my assignment during the war."

"Wait until she explains why I'm the likeliest candidate for Icarus."

I grinned at Helen because that was the easiest way to mask the fact that I kept wanting to burst into tears. "You know you like being best at things."

Myrtle pulled out a chair and sat down. "Oh, I need to hear this."

"Helen is Catholic, was in the cockpit of the shuttle on the way here. She trains people on driving the rovers, so could easily have checked one out to deal with the BusyBee."

"I have a grudge against the IAC because they pulled me off the Mars mission." She sobered and then mentioned a thing I had not. Had I thought about this next thing? Yes, but I hadn't said it. She did. "And I had access to the Mars Expedition ships."

Eugene's brow contracted as he put the math together and went into a tailspin of doubt. He pulled out, quickly, and shook his head, turning to me. "Do you suspect everyone?"

"All the time. I suspect you all, too, just to be clear."

Myrtle snorted. "I'd be disappointed if you didn't." She nudged Eugene with her foot. "Wait until she finds out that your first name is really Ferdinand."

I did not have time to stop my double take before realizing that she was pulling my leg. I knew that his full name was Eugene Simmons Lindholm because I'd read his file. I'd read all of their personnel records because I did, in fact, suspect everyone.

I also had absolutely no doubt that I could trust them.

Granted, that sort of thing got people killed back in my war years. On the other hand, Myrtle was now openly laughing at me. "Oh, I got you."

"You did." I pointed to the filter. "So . . . Icarus pulled out a filter, leaving the others in place. That caused the others to expire faster and, with the alarm disabled, we got CO_2 buildup before regular maintenance would catch it. Which gives you a sort of time bomb and allows him to be elsewhere when it happens. Meaning that it could still be Curt or Birgit."

Eugene nodded. "Which raises the question of why Curt pointed us to the CO_2 filter in the port stairs?"

I drummed my pencil on my cast, thinking. It was easier to think, in the way that it is the morning after a fever has broken. Not that I was well, but I was at least clearer. If I had set up a booby trap, why would I give someone the cue to discover it? "Build trust? Avoid CO_2 poisoning since he's trapped in a bed?"

"All right. Here's another piece for you." Eugene tapped the filter. "The frame of this is made from the same packing crate as Faustino's skis."

My jaw literally dropped. I am not sure I have experienced that before. "So . . . so either Curt or Birgit used the same guy to fabricate things as Faustino or . . . or Faustino was Icarus, died stupidly, and has left behind a bunch of time bombs. What about the machinist?"

"Remember the South African guy in comms? Long-timer, so he's had opportunity before this, and wrong type of dumbass." Eugene rubbed his temples and I swear he had more gray there than he had last week. Sometimes that seemed to happen to Kenneth. This whole thing would . . .

I wiped under my eyes with my knuckles. "I'm assuming he did the same thing to the scrubbers in all the modules, but this one expired first?"

"Yeah. Let me see your list." He held out his hand and took the notepad from me.

"I want to see." Myrtle beckoned him to sit beside her. Eugene's face changed as he read my list. It started curious and then went thoughtful and finished with horrified.

He looked up at me. "You are genuinely terrifying, you know that?"

"I'm going to choose to take that as a compliment, and don't disillusion me."

From his side, Myrtle said, "Oh, that's a compliment."

"Hush."

"Do not hush me."

Eugene ignored her and sat forward with his elbows on his knees, staring at the list. "If he's done even a quarter of these, we are screwed."

"Those are fine. We can find and stop them." I plucked at the edge of my cast. "It's the ones I haven't thought of that can kill us."

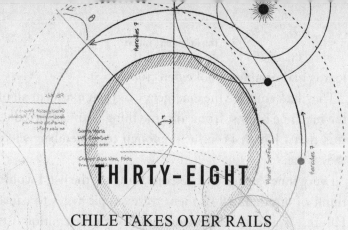

THIRTY-EIGHT

CHILE TAKES OVER RAILS
AS STRIKES AND RIOTS SPREAD

SANTIAGO, Chile, May 20, 1963—A growing wave of demonstrations by thousands of citizens over food shortages prompted the government to place the railroads under army rule today. The government also reinforced guards at strategic points and increased the number of police patrolling the city streets with water-spray cannons.

OVER THE COURSE of the next week, I was, as a Quaker friend of mine says, not my best self. I snapped at people who were trying to help me and— The less said about my behavior, I feel, the better.

While I literally hung around, Eugene worked through my list. He found that Icarus had hidden a steel bowl, filled with perchloric acid, in the guts of the dehumidifiers. It ate through the bowl, and then burned through cables. Icarus had not used my idea to foul the water supply, which is good, because it was really elegant and would have screwed us all.

But Icarus *had* introduced sediment into fuel tanks.

473

Icarus had disabled smoke detectors.

They had emptied the emergency oxygen masks in all of the machine rooms. Ironically, the thing that had saved us was that I hadn't been lucid enough to remember where they were.

Every time Eugene checked one thing off the list, I would think of another. All of them were simple ways to cause failures. It was as if I were going through the caution lists for astronaut training and suggesting everything we were trained not to do. When Eugene found something I'd suggested, it felt like a tiny moment I was being actually useful instead of a drain on resources.

On a personal note, Ana Teresa kindly consented to removing the IV after I kept a meal log for three days running. But she wouldn't clear me to return to work. I still had to keep the food log. I hated her. I hated the log. And I hated myself. It was a party all around.

Aside from that, the week was without remaining incident. Except we still did not know where the BusyBee was, despite sending Halim out looking until the sun set. By the eighteenth, none of the likely spots were still in daylight.

So, the question then was—had we stopped Icarus, or were they biding their time?

AFTER WE TURNED the lights out, with only the sound of the fans, Helen shifted in her hammock. Light from the hall bled under the door and sketched her in charcoal on gray. "May I ask you a question? It is personal."

"Sure."

"With your food difficulties, is there anything you would find helpful?" She asked it, not as if I were broken, but as though this were a problem to be worked.

"'Difficulties' sounds like something my grandmother would say. Just call it anorexia. I know what it is." I don't know why giving it a name made me feel more in control of the conversation, but it did. I readjusted my head on the pillow, staring into the dark. It had been a decade since I'd had a relapse like this. "I would love to tell you it's not an ongoing problem, but I am, at least, usually functional."

"I know, or rather, I know you are functional, because I did not know that you had . . . anorexia."

"Were you about to say 'difficulties' again?"

"Clearly not, it is simply that English is not my first language."

I laughed and, God, that felt good. I did not for a moment believe this was a language challenge. She'd spoken English, Taiwanese, and Mandarin when we met, then added French when she fell in love with Reynard. I have been reliably informed that his Taiwanese is understandable and charmingly hilarious.

We hung in the darkness and I think she would have let me change the subject and not answer her. The problem was that my "difficulties" had endangered her last week. I should have been able to lift her. At minimum, I shouldn't have been struggling to stand.

I rolled toward her, setting my hammock swaying. "Ask me what I had for lunch. Don't police me. Don't bully me . . ." I sighed. "What Myrtle and Ana Teresa have been doing . . . It's necessary. Now. As in, right now, when I'm in what Kenneth calls—what Kenneth called—'a state.' But it's not sustainable. It'll make me dig my heels in more over time. So, just ask me what I had for lunch."

"That won't annoy you?"

"Oh, it will. I'll resent the hell out of it, but it'll remind me to think about if I've eaten. It also just sounds like a social noise to other people." I was weeping again, but at least it was dark and the tears weren't in my voice this time. Kenneth hadn't asked it every day, saving it for times when he knew I was under pressure, when I was most likely to "forget" to eat. When I say I hadn't been this bad in a decade, he is probably why. Was. He was probably why. "I will try not to snap at you."

"Pfff . . . I'm a Taiwanese woman in the astronaut corps. Your drama does not frighten me."

On Monday, my twelfth day as a widow, after I had finally been released from the purgatory of the makeshift sickbay, I sat in a far corner of the cafeteria and had lunch with Helen, who had been cleared to return to work last week. Her hair was still a flattened mess over her forehead from the Snoopy cap because they were letting her fly again.

I was happy for her and intensely jealous. Even jealous of the indentations along her cheeks where the microphone arms had pressed against her skin.

I sat with my back to the room, so I didn't have to make eye contact with anyone. She drew a circle with her finger

on the map of the far side of the Moon in her logbook—
her log was filled with flight time. "It's nearly noon on
the far side, so the shadows are not helping, but there was
nothing at the observatory."

"I've run out of ideas." I sat back in my chair, picking
tiny bits off of a biscuit. We had checked the areas around
all of the outposts and way stations to see if Icarus had
parked the BusyBee at any of them. I say "we," and what
I mean is Halim, Helen, and Myrtle. I'd been relegated to
making lists and keeping notes.

I'd finally suggested checking for the BusyBee in oddball
places like the large-array telescope on the far side of the
Moon, which didn't have a permanent staff. "I'm going to
make a recommendation that, in the future, we paint the
BusyBees bright orange."

"Hot pink. Then none of the men will touch them."
Helen winked. "Job security."

"With a bow on top." I could feel her watching me with
the biscuit, so I put the next bit into my mouth.

"Maybe some lace?" She folded her logbook and tucked
it back into her flight suit.

I laughed, but half of my mind was already moving on
to other ways to find it. "Maybe if we think about where
it could do the most damage and work backwards from
there?"

Helen squinted. "But wouldn't that still involve being
close to one of the places we've already—"

The lights went out.

A collective groan went up from the people in the
cafeteria followed by a weak cheer as the emergency lights

flickered on. In the light, Helen was checking her watch, just like I was.

"It bothers me that we do not know why or how this is happening." Helen pulled out her logbook and made a small dark circle in the calendar in the front. Frowning, she counted and shook her head. "These intervals are very frustrating. Four days. Fifteen days. Eight days. Eight days."

I frowned, because that sounded like one too many. "That's five of them."

She nodded and then looked up, eyes wide and concerned. "Ah. Yes. We had one on Sunday, the twelfth. You were asleep."

The day after Kenneth's funeral. "I see." I looked down and pushed my tray of food away. Across the table, Helen stiffened. Grinding my teeth, I pulled it back and took a forkful of creamed spinach. "I wish someone had told me that."

"Sorry. The issues with the habitat . . . It slipped my mind."

I winced, feeling like a heel. "My fault. Sixteen minutes at random intervals?"

"I want to look at the geometry of the Earth and Moon's relative positions during the power outages. If the Earth is always facing the same way . . ." She drummed her pencil on the table. "The sample size is too small to be certain that my hypothesis is correct, but if a different part of the Earth is facing us each time then we can at least reject that hypothesis."

I stared at her with my fork halfway back to the plate.

It had not occurred to me to try to math the problem, and this was why Helen was a wizard.

On Wednesday, Ana Teresa summoned me to the actual, real sickbay in the SciMod, which was finally dried out and repaired from the water damage. The entire way through the gerbil tubes from Midtown, I composed a detailed explanation of why I did not need to keep a food log and how I would feel much better if I were allowed to work. Had I needed intervention? Yes, even if I hated that I did. However, I was perfectly fine now and continuing to check up on me was a drain on resources that would be best spent on the polio patients.

As I walked through the door into the sparkling room, Ana Teresa wheeled on me with a small saw in her hands. "Come. My X-ray machine is working again. I want to see your arm."

"And hello to you, too." I packed my internal tirade away for later use. It's not that I had forgotten that my arm was broken, but I had become accustomed to it. The ache had muted and become part of the background with my feet. I settled on the stool she had set out for me and propped my arm on the counter.

"I thought X-rays could see through plaster."

Setting the saw to my cast, she raised her voice over the buzzing. "Clearer image without it."

"Ah." I nodded. "Right. For posterity. First broken bone and all that."

Ana Teresa scowled. "The second break confuses

everything. Also, your bone density."

"Well. Sorry to be a disappointment."

She snorted. "You are an astronaut. I expect nothing les—"

The lights went out.

A moment later the emergency lights snapped on. Ana Teresa set down her saw with a huff, as if it were a personal affront. "This is maddening."

"Just wait." I stared at the ceiling, as if I could see whatever was causing the outage. "It'll be back on in sixteen minutes."

She snatched a terrifyingly industrial pair of scissors off a supply cart and pointed them at me. "If I had people on life support . . . Tell the administrator that this is dangerous at my patients."

"Speaking of." Looking around sickbay, with its empty beds, I raised my eyebrows and tried to ignore the jarring crunches of the shears as she cracked through the rest of my cast. "Where is everyone?"

"Mm." She nodded toward Midtown as she worked. "The open space is better for recovery, so I am keeping only the worst cases here."

"But . . ." I looked around the room again. "The beds are empty."

"Yes . . ." She set down the shears and peeled the sides of the cast off my arm. "Eugene rearranged facilities here during the repairs to create a quarters for some of the long-term patients. They're down the hall."

"Who?"

"Currently Major Lindholm has asked me to house Curtis, Birgit, Ruben, Garnet, and the LCA."

Ana Teresa grabbed a smaller pair of scissors to remove the gauze. Without the fans, sickbay was eerily quiet. I could hear the metal blades of the scissors brushing past each other.

The gauze dropped away. My wrist had atrophied in the cast, and had a bulge on the side that I didn't remember.

Ana Teresa huffed looking at it and put her hands on her hips. "Turn your palm up, slowly."

Muscles that had not turned in weeks protested, and I could feel the stretch down the side of my forearm as I began the turn. When my thumb was not quite pointing to the ceiling, my wrist stopped. A low ache throbbed in the center of the bone.

I frowned, straining to turn it. It wasn't that pain stopped it, my wrist just wouldn't rotate farther.

"That's not . . ." I swallowed, letting it relax back down to the table. My palm didn't rest flat. Concentrating, I tried rotating again. Forty-five degrees of rotation. Maybe. "I'm . . . I'm having some trouble."

Ana Teresa slid two of her fingers into the palm of my hand. "Grip."

My fingers moved, but it was almost as if the cast were still there, impeding their range. "It's just . . . This is just atrophy, right?"

"This is a textbo—" The lights came on. In the harsh light, Ana Teresa's frown was deeper than before. She stepped back. "Let's get you on the X-ray and see how bad it is."

"Will physical therapy help?" What had I done? I tried gripping again, as if I were holding a controller. My fingers responded, but with too small a movement. "Will I be able to fly?"

"Let's take the X-ray. Then we'll talk."

I AM VERY good at denial. Some days it is the only thing that keeps me going. Some days, it is the only thing I can control. Some days, I tell myself that my problem is the solution.

I caught Eugene Thursday morning. He was eating breakfast at his desk in Frisch's office and had a report in front of him. He balanced a fork of scrambled eggs in one hand, keeping his place on the page with the other. I stopped in the open doorway to watch him and he had no idea I was there.

He looked really dragged out. Lines I didn't remember on his brow and darkened circles under his eyes. He was slumping into the desk, frowning as he read.

I leaned against the doorway. "What time did you start this morning?"

He jumped, eggs tumbling to the desktop. "Jesus, Wargin." Grabbing his napkin, he wiped the eggs off the report. "Six? I couldn't sleep."

"Hm . . ." I chewed my lower lip, watching him. "May I offer a word of advice?"

"You're going to anyway." He tossed the napkin onto his tray. "Shoo—ure." His voice twisted in a desperate attempt to turn "shoot" into "sure."

It took me a moment to realize that he'd thought saying "shoot" would remind me of Kenneth. It wouldn't have, but the deflection did.

"Kenneth got more done when he stopped doing working breakfasts." Granted, he did that to make sure I ate at least one meal a day, but the results were the same. "Trust me . . . Don't set a pace you can't sustain."

Eugene watched me, drumming his fingers on the desk. He closed the report and turned his chair to face me. "How are you doing?"

There is a sincerity and an earnestness with which people ask that question after a tragedy that is kind and exhausting all at the same time. "In the cast for another two weeks. Weeping less. Eating more. Bored." I crossed my arms over my chest and braced for a fight. "I want to talk to Curt."

He narrowed his eyes. "About?"

"Flying." I braced myself for pity. "I have a permanent loss of rotation in my left arm. From the break. It's not polio, but it gives me a different angle to approach him with. And then see what happens."

Eugene shook his head. "That's not going to work."

I sighed, resenting having to spell this out. "Common ground can usually build a rapport that you can exploit. In this case, we've both lost fl—"

The lights went out.

"Oh, for Pete's sake." I threw my hands out to the side just as the emergency lights flickered on. "Again?"

Eugene turned in his chair to look at the dim bulb. "That was less than twenty-four hours since the last one."

"Yes . . ." Three this week. What would that do to Helen's statistical analysis? "That's concerning."

"Indeed. I don't like that the frequency is increasing."

Nor did I. It felt like we were building to something. "This is part of why I want to talk to Curt."

Eugene turned back to me and folded his hands together. There was a subtle shift in his posture, in the line of his neck and the set of his jaw, that said he was shifting from speaking as my friend to pure business. "I'm going to deny that request. You're not firing on all cylinders yet."

I clenched my hands, knowing that the fresh cast was not what kept my left hand from closing into a fist. "I am not going to collapse in front of him."

He sighed. "No. But you've forgotten that in your eulogy, you talked openly about sabotage. If Curt is Icarus, he will be completely on guard the moment you walk into the room." Eugene leaned forward, holding me with his gaze. "If we talk to him, it has to be a straight-up interrogation."

"All right . . . That's a good point. So let's set that up."

"If you had walked in and proposed that, sure. I'd set it up." Eugene shook his head. "You're not well and it would be a bad choice— Hold that response. Sit on it . . . You know I'm right."

I did. Damn it. I am good at denial, but not that good. I looked at the scuffs on the floor and my eyes were stinging. My cheeks were hot with embarrassment. I nodded, not quite trusting my voice.

"Look . . ." His chair creaked as he spun and papers shuffled on his desk. "It would help me if you'd go through the technical manual for the base. See if there's any vulnerability they're exploiting."

I nodded again and took the binder he held out. If there

was even a chance this would be useful, I'd do it, but I know busywork when I see it.

I SPENT FRIDAY in the gallery. I've made myself familiar with every technical manual since we established the first lunar base. But my eyes ached reading the tiny print and kept drooping. People will talk about the training astronauts go through, but honestly, the hardest thing about our job is staying awake while reading sentences like . . .

Regulation of the array output voltage is required because of the performance characteristics of PV cells; that is, output voltage is a function of the load placed on the cells, and this results in a varying power source, which the SSU accomplishes by receiving power directly from the PV array and maintaining output voltage within a specified range of 130 to 173 V dc (normally 160 V dc that is referred to as "primary power voltage").

Please note, that is a single sentence within a 222-page document, twenty-four pages of which are just a glossary of acronyms. Some of which I used every day and had forgotten what the letters stood for, like PGNCS, which somehow is pronounced "pings." Primary Guidance, Navigation, and Something Something. Others were more opaque. Consider . . .

Secondary power originates in a DDCU and is

then distributed through a network of ORUs called secondary power distribution assemblies (SPDAs) and remote power distribution assemblies (RPDAs), in which modality SPDAs and RPDAs are essentially housings that contain one or more RPCMs.

My personal favorite appeared to contain no actual nouns.

"Once the permanent ETCS becomes operational, the EETCS is deactivated, at which point portions of the EETCS are used as components on PVTCS."

I hoped I would find something useful.
I did not.
But we lost power two more times.

THIRTY-NINE

IAC CHIEF ROCKET SCIENTIST REFUTES CLAIM THAT GOVERNOR WARGIN TRIED TO POISON HIM

KANSAS CITY, May 24, 1963—(AP)—Information leaked from President Denley's office shows that the late Governor Wargin was under investigation for the poisoning of the International Aerospace Coalition's chief rocket scientist, Dr. Nathaniel York. The materials suggest that the governor was jealous of Dr. York, who he suspected of having an affair with his wife.

———

Dr. York, whose wife is a part of the First Mars Expedition, refutes this claim as "insulting," saying that he and Governor Wargin were longtime friends. He went on to say, "It's an attempt by the Administration to sully the reputation of Mrs. Wargin. I'd like to ask anyone to do the calculations on the timing. Why do that to a widow, *now*? Why are they trying to obscure the investigation into Earth First's efforts to disable the space program?"

BY FRIDAY NIGHT, I had a splitting headache from reading print that was too small. I don't remember the font being so tiny when I started at the IAC. Halim caught me rubbing the bridge of my nose over dinner—and yes, I had a companion for every meal now.

He cleared his throat. "Reading glasses."

I stabbed a piece of sweet potato. "I'm not old."

"Calendrically, I am younger than you, but I've used reading glasses for the past two years." He shrugged and sliced his rabbit. "They haven't grounded me, if that's what you're worried about."

Even though I know perfectly well many astronauts wind up using them because of the changes that occur in our eyes in microgravity, most of them were men. For reasons that remained a mystery to the flight surgeons, women's eyes adapted better to space. So the fact that I needed reading glasses was not space related. I just didn't want to remind the IAC that I was "old hat."

Not that it likely mattered. At this point, I was fairly certain I would be permanently grounded the moment I set foot on Earth.

SATURDAY MORNING, I gave up and went to sickbay to ask Ana Teresa for some readers. I'd finished with the current lunar base manual and decided to start on the iteration before, just in case there was a legacy system. It felt like busywork, but I was damned if I was going to dive into self-pity and become more of a burden on my crewmates. I trusted Eugene not to give me something completely useless.

But my eyes still hated me.

When I opened the door to sickbay, Ana Teresa was just visible through a gap in a curtain around the examining table. She said something to her patient about missing her flowers—I don't remember the specifics. I just had to turn around and walk out of the room.

All that trouble and worry about Kenneth's heart and none of it had mattered. I pressed my forehead against the rubber wall, leaning on it as if I were keeping the regolith that buried us from collapsing. My throat was tight and hot with each breath I forced through it. Seventeen days without him in the world. I stared at the rubber wall until my breathing steadied, wiped my face, and went back in.

The curtain had been pulled back and I realized Ana Teresa's patient was Curt. She looked around and their conversation faltered to a halt with my second appearance.

Curt rolled his head toward me, brows turned up in concern. "You okay?"

My eyes were probably red, but I couldn't do anything about that. "Yep. I just didn't want to barge in when she was working with you." I kept my smile calibrated to be approachable but not cheery. Eugene had told me not to question him, and I wouldn't, but I was here now and running away seemed pointless. "Privacy is important."

Curt laid a hand against his forehead in mock anguish. "Oh, the shame if anyone should accidentally learn I have polio." He lowered his hand and gave a small, earnest smile. "Seriously, though, I'm glad you're feeling better."

For a moment, I looked at Ana Teresa with a brief panic that she had told Curt about the anorexia and then realized he only meant that my husband was dead. Eyes stinging, I straightened the curtains as if they needed that. "Has the cramping been as bad?"

"No. It's pretty much stopped." He gestured toward his legs. "Wait until you see my spiffy new braces."

"That's exciting." I turned, with an expression of curiosity, and my breath caught in my throat. In the two weeks since I had seen him, Curt's legs had atrophied visibly. I had entertained the idea he might be faking the severity of the disease, and that idea got crossed off my list. Each leg had a brace, crafted from aluminum and strapped down with equipment tethers. "Wow. Nice work. Who made those?"

"Actual rocket scientists!" His voice sounded upbeat, but he was staring at the ceiling, blinking a little too rapidly. "The right foot was starting to twist, and hopefully this will stop it."

Ana Teresa rested her hand on Curt's shoulder. "It will be better when we can get you home."

"Joy." He rolled his head to look at the doctor. "Here, maybe I can support myself with these if I keep working at it. On Earth? I'll be in a chair and that'll be that."

That surprised me. If I were Icarus, I would not tip my hand about having some mobility. "A chair didn't stop Roosevelt." Having said that, I also knew Franklin went to great lengths to hide his disability from the public. The press had a gentlemen's agreement never to photograph him in it. No one reported on what it cost him to get to a lectern and speak from a standing position. "You can do anything you want to when you get back."

"Not fly."

He wasn't wrong. If Eugene had agreed with my plan, it would have been an opening.

Ana Teresa rolled a wheeled chair over—it was an unholy alliance of a launch couch and an office chair. With it, Curt would be able to sit up and be moved about but completely at the mercy of someone else. With an easy efficiency I envied, Ana Teresa transferred Curt to the wheelchair.

The doctor got behind the chair. "Give me a moment and I'll be right with you."

"Thanks. I'm just in for reading glasses."

"Ah. Certainly. I'll set the eye chart up whe—"

The lights went out.

Blink and the emergency lights popped on. I looked at my watch, even though I knew it would be another sixteen minutes. I did not like how much the frequency of these had increased.

Ana Teresa was scowling at the lights. Curt twisted his head to look at her. "Hey, doc, why don't you let Nicole take me back to the polio ward? That'll give you time to set up."

Adrenaline flooded my body and I stayed in a neutral posture. Why would Curt want to get me alone? He couldn't stand, so I was reasonably confident he didn't want to attack me. "Sure! That'll give us time for the power to come back on."

Ana Teresa shook her head, looking at my cast. "You can't transfer him to the bed."

Curt waved a hand. "I actually want to sit up for a while. The ceiling is getting old."

Before the doctor could object more, I got behind Curt's chair and pushed him to the door. "Back in a minute."

Getting the chair over the threshold of the door took a little effort. My cast dug into the web of my thumb as I tipped the chair back to get the wheels over the lip, but I managed to get Curt into the hall without Ana Teresa chasing us to help.

The moment we were out the door, Curt leaned his head back, trying to see me. "How long do the batteries on the emergency lights last?"

Hot and cold chased along the length of my spine. We were in lunar night right now and the colony got a significant amount of its power from the sun. On my giant list of things, I had not thought about running the emergency batteries down. If something happened to take out the main power plant, it would be another week before we saw the sun. "That's a good question . . ."

"Stop the chair for a second, would you?"

I did, curious about where he was headed but also conscious that Eugene was right. I was not firing on all cylinders. "What's up?"

He reached into the breast pocket on his pajama top and pulled out a folded paper. It was torn from the newspaper our local press office generated from an aggregate of news back on Earth. "Can we talk about this?"

I looked down at the page he handed me. *GOVERNOR'S WIFE CLAIMS TERRORISTS RESPONSIBLE FOR HUSBAND'S DEATH.* I swallowed and wet my lips. "What aspect?"

"That you think I'm responsible for . . ." He waved his hands at the lights. "This."

I handed the paper back to him. "Why would you think that?"

"Let's see . . . One of the incidents you cite in the article was our landing. So the controller was either screwed up ahead of time, or someone did it mid-trip, or it was faked. Two of those scenarios mean me, Mikey, Helen, or Eugene. I was the pilot when we set down."

True. That was the reasoning we had used as well. Was he going to talk about how impossible it was? "Could you have faked it?"

"Sure. I was a test pilot. Half of what we did was getting aircraft to fail on purpose so we could figure out recovery techniques." He twisted his head again. "Could you come around front? It's hard to see you."

True, which was useful. On the other hand, it was also hard to see him. I walked around and watched my shadow from the emergency lights. I kept the shadow of my head just below his chin, which gave me a clear view of his face and left the emergency lights in his eyes. "It will be easier if I understand your goal here."

He sighed and drummed his finger on the arm of his chair. "Trying to help." He pointed at the lights. "The way blackouts are getting more frequent, I'm wondering if your saboteurs are trying to run things down."

"Possible." I let him see me sigh. I pursed my lips in thought and deliberately cocked my head as I considered him. "What would you do if you were me? In this scenario?"

"I wouldn't believe a damn word out of my mouth." He squinted against the light. "How do I change that?"

If he was Icarus, he was very, very good. I might not be firing on all cylinders, but I felt more alive in this moment than I had since Nathaniel had called from the hospital and said my name. I let the moment stretch and unfold, giving him silence to fill.

He waited me out.

I didn't take the bait. I just smiled and got back behind his chair. "I promise, I'll think about what you've said."

Eugene towered over me, hands on his hips, and I felt very, very small, as if I might disappear under the conference room table. "I told you not to talk to him."

The other people in our group studied the architecture, a map, or their nails. Helen made a note in her log. None of them were helping me. I tried to keep my spine straight, but honestly, how had I thought that Myrtle was the scary one? No—it wasn't that he was angry—Eugene was *disappointed* in me.

I lifted my chin. "That is why I disengaged from the conversation as soon as I could."

"No. You did not. The moment he asked you to wheel him out of the room, you could have used that," Eugene pointed a finger at my cast, "as an eeeeeeasy reason to say no. You made a deliberate choice."

I bit my lower lip. I had reported to Eugene the moment I got Curt back into his room. I didn't even pick up the reading glasses. "I was wrong. I'm sorry. I'm aware of the possibility that I'm being manipulated. But now that it's done, what do we do with the information?"

"What information? That he knows you're investigating the sabotage? That's not news."

I sighed. "That he's raised the question of batteries and power supply. Assume he's Icarus. There's something he wants to happen with the power supply that he can't do. If he's not, then he's right that the frequency increase might be an attempt to drain our batteries."

Helen frowned over her notebook. "Then why not have it occur for longer than sixteen minutes?"

"I have no idea."

She kept working, occasionally scribbling a line of numbers.

At the table across from me, Myrtle sat with her ankles crossed, studying the map of the Moon. "Why don't we run both scenarios. Halim and I can take the 'Curt is innocent' scenario." She looked up at her husband. "You and Nicole can work 'Curt is Icarus.'"

"There's another option." I picked at the edge of my cast. "Do you know what a presumptive is?"

"No," Halim said.

"Rather than trying to get him to confess, we presume he is an enemy agent. In this scenario—" The lights cut out again. "Goddammit."

Moments later the emergency lights snapped on and we were all looking at our watches. Halim lifted his gaze to look at me. "So how long *does* it take to drain the emergency batteries?"

"Approximately ninety minutes, depending on draw." So I'd retained something useful during my time reading manuals. "Helen, how many power outages . . ."

She held up a finger to silence me. With the other hand, she scribbled a line of text on one part of the page and then jumped to another to jot a figure down. "I need a map of Earth."

Eugene *moved*. He disappeared out the door at a run that was long and low.

Helen shouted, "And a ruler!"

"Got it," came from the hall.

The rest of us stayed completely still while Helen did her Nav/Comp thing. I gnawed on the inside of my cheek, watching her compute. The four minutes it took Eugene to run two doors down to his office, grab a map, and run back might as well have been spent waiting for a launch. We were that tense and hyper-aware.

I heard his footsteps easily without the fans running. A moment later, he grabbed the doorframe to change his vector state, swinging into the conference room. Eugene arrested his forward momentum with a hand on the table and slapped an atlas and a ruler down next to Helen.

She half-glanced at him and saw us staring at her. "It's a satellite."

"A satellite . . ." Myrtle straightened. "They're bouncing a signal here."

Eugene's eyes widened. "A signal for what? From where?" His gaze dropped to the map. "I'll keep quiet and let you figure that out."

Sixteen minutes later, the lights were back on, and Helen had requested two additional reference books. Without being asked, Myrtle had acquired a yellow legal pad, which she'd offered to Helen by means of sliding it next to the logbook she was working in. Helen switched to it as seamlessly as if it had always been there.

She drew a circle on an enlarged map of the United States. "Kansas. I can't get more detailed with the materials on hand, but deductively it is almost certainly Kansas City. Get me a list of satellites and their orbits and I can tell you exactly which satellite they are hitting."

"But you think it's not *Lunetta*."

She shook her head. "*Lunetta* has a different orbital pattern."

Eugene leaned on the table, looking at the map. "Do you know why?"

Cracking her neck, Helen leaned back in her chair and stretched. "Why sixteen? Yes. That's how long the satellite is in line of sight, which tells us that they have a single base, as we thought. If you want to know what they are sending up on that signal, I cannot tell you."

"You mean, besides 'turn the power off,'" Eugene said.

"There are more efficient ways to do that, if they have a man on the Moon. The power failures started two days after landing, before the polio epidemic struck." She looked back at the notes she scratched and grimaced. "I think we'll get one more outage today and four tomorrow. Regardless of intent, that will be more than enough to drain the emergency batteries."

Eugene steepled his fingers together and bent his head with the tips pressed to his mouth. Not quite praying, because his eyes were open and squinting in concentration, but working the problem in his own head. "All right . . . We can address the lights by pulling backup batteries out of storage and swapping them in key places. We'll hook the emergency generators up to life support for the main dome. I'd give a lot to stop the blackouts from happening."

From deep in the recesses of my mind, an idea scratched. Something related to satellite protocols. I grabbed the manual I'd been reading from a previous iteration of the lunar base and flipped through the pages, trying to jog the idea loose. It didn't feel like something I'd read recently, though. It felt like something I used to know.

"Is there a copy of the first manual for the lunar base?" I stood. "Never mind. It's in the library."

Eugene lifted his head. "Say you have something for me, Wargin."

I hesitated because it was something I only half-remembered from when I'd been one of six people up here. That information had been scraped away and overlaid by new iterations of the base. "I want to look at the original specs for the RPDAs."

"*Remote* Power Distribution Assembly . . ." Myrtle shook her head. "That's just referring to moving power from a central source, though."

"Now, yes. But they also contain one or more RPCMs, which used to mean 'Remote Power Control Modules.'" My heart was beating a little faster as talking dragged that old information kicking and screaming into the forefront of my brain. Of our group—in fact, of the people on the Moon currently—I was the only one who had been stationed in the very first iteration of the lunar base. "Part of the contingency plan was that Kansas Ground Control could assume remote control in case of catastrophic failure. The trigger was a power failure, which caused the system to look for a satellite signal from Earth."

I saw them get it, with the intake of breath and a settling in as they got ready to deal with the ramifications. All of us thinking about that box in Midtown of legacy systems, which were still linked in for redundancy.

I wanted to get to the library to look at that manual. I wanted to be remembering wrong. "I think . . . I think they can assume remote control over every aspect of the base—not just power."

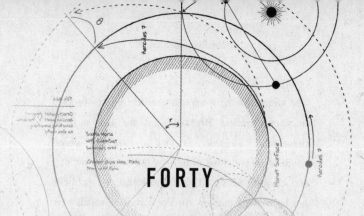

FORTY

AIR FORCE STUDIES SCOPE OF MISSION IN SPACE PROGRAM

By JACK RAYMOND

Special to The National Times

KANSAS CITY, May 26, 1963—The Air Force has undertaken a series of studies of its future that could conceivably lead to dramatic new missions in space or to a sharp reduction in its present roles and missions.

At this stage, it can be reported, the Administration is by no means convinced of the necessity of some ambitious nonmilitary space proposals. The studies were prompted by the changing character of air-weapons technology and Government strategy for nuclear weapons. But an important impulse for the reassessment was the Denley Administration's belief that as resources on the planet dwindle, America must establish dominance in space.

The studies have been named Project Forecast. They have been compared with the famous report "Toward the Stars" that was drafted by a team headed by Dr. Nathaniel York and his wife in the days after the Meteor struck a decade ago.

501

The difference between that earlier report—ordered by then-President Brannan—and the one now in preparation, however, is that a mood of global cooperation prevailed then. Now the mood is that of a service approaching a fight for existence. No publicity has been given the new Air Force studies, which were ordered quietly May 6 by President Denley.

THE AIR IN the conference room, with a gaggle of engineers drinking coffee and arguing across freeze-dried donuts, had grown stale hours ago. My ass was sore from having been in the same chair since that morning. Eugene sat at the head of the table, with his hand on his chin, listening to the chief of every systems department and the lead engineer on the Moon hash out what needed to be disconnected and in what order.

"If you take out water circulation at that stage, we've no way to reject waste heat." Christian Godfrey, lead electrical systems engineer, had the sort of perfect British voice that makes it clear he had gotten the ever-living shit beaten out of him in boarding school.

"What about the EETCS?" I asked. The Early External Thermal Control System had existed just for the first six months of the colony, before we got the permanent external thermal control system assembled. I would have killed for my own copy of the first manual for the lunar base with all of my notes scribbled in the margins, but flipping through the library copy had helped jog my memory. "Parts of that were repurposed for the PVTCS loops, right? Is that something we could use as a patch?"

"Perhaps. See here . . . Our lunar backrooms are quite good, but as I have iterated before, I would feel significantly safer if Kansas ran this as a simulation for us," he protested. Again.

Eugene lowered his hand. "I told you the parameters at the start. We cannot ask Kansas for help without alerting Earth First that we have found their backdoor. If you raise this one more time, I'll ask you to send your assistant in to take your spot."

"I am making a statement about my comfort level, which translates directly to a process you would like me to sign off on. If you simply want people who will say yes, then you're courting disaster." The pasty white man wet his lips and shot a glance at me. "I do not think hysterical panic serves us."

"Hysterical?" I could have killed him with my fountain pen. He only lived because I didn't have one on the Moon. "What a fascinating word choice."

Eugene did that thing where he tipped his chin down just a little and his face hardened, but it was the only movement he made. "Your assistant is Mavis Davis, am I correct?"

"I— Now, see here . . ." He glanced around the room, looking for support, but the other engineers had suddenly found their notebooks very interesting. "I would be irresponsible if I did not voice my concerns."

"Five times in the space of two hours over a parameter I explained at the top of the morning." Eugene checked his watch and held up a finger. "You have thirty seconds."

"To explain everything that's—"

"No. Until we lose power again." Eugene pointed to the door. "You'll want to get to the other side of the airlock to Midtown before that happens. I suggest running. Twenty seconds."

He ran. Twenty seconds after that, we lost power on the schedule Helen had predicted. A little over sixteen minutes after that, Mavis joined us and we had no more troubles with "hysteria."

Also, I was absolutely right about the EETCS. Sometimes, it pays to be old hat.

As much as we wanted to hurry, there is a difference between efficiency and rushing. "Slow is fast" applied to every aspect of the space program. So we spent all of Sunday hashing out exactly how we were going to pull the legacy systems offline.

Monday morning, Mavis Davis—whose parents must have been delightful people—leaned out of the legacy Remote Power Control Module. She was a broad-shouldered woman with a deep Tennessee accent and a wicked understanding of all things electrical. "Nicole? Can you take a look at a label for me? I think it's legacy even for the legacy system."

"Sure." I had been parked by the RPCM just in case something like this turned up. We're supposed to document everything, but there's best practices and actual practices. For instance, I probably would have forgotten to eat breakfast this morning if I hadn't been working with Eugene, even though I know better.

I squeezed past her into the space and followed the beam of her flashlight to a rack of equipment in the bottom of the module. I brought my own flashlight up and squinted at the label in question. Sighing, I slid my brand-new reading glasses down from the top of my head and the handwritten label popped into focus.

VRCS—Do Not Decouple Without Authorization

My brain sent up a flare that this was familiar, except . . . I had no idea what VRCS was. It took staring at it for another second before I stiffened. The upstroke of the *V*, the specific curve of the *S*, the slightly too broad *u*. Those had been on the library card for *The Long Tomorrow* as part of faux Vicky Hsu's name. I could be mistaken, of course, because both were small sample sets, but given the context, I was not taking bets on being wrong. I backed away from the device and kept my face relaxed as I turned to Mavis. "I'm not sure."

"Oh." She knew enough about the situation to understand this might be bad.

It was. On two fronts. With everything going on, we had never followed up with Frisch about the book and how it had gotten into his office. That was bad. But what was worse was that *Icarus had been in the RPCM* and I had no idea what this thing was that he had installed.

I eased out of the RPCM and slid my glasses back onto the top of my head. "I'm calling Eugene. Don't do anything to it, but do look to see what it would take to uninstall it."

*   *   *

EUGENE FOLLOWED ME back to the RPCM, head down as he listened to me brief him on what we'd found. Both of us were moving fast enough that we were having to lean into our momentum. People saw us come out of the tube from admin and got out of the way.

He checked his watch. "Helen says we have another blackout in two hours—assuming they keep to schedule today. You think that's the thing they're using to kill the power?"

I shook my head. "I genuinely don't know. I thought they were exploiting the satellite link."

At the RPCM, Mavis's team clustered around the door. One man had schematics unrolled on the floor next to the module. Another woman leaned in the door with Mavis, nodding earnestly. A third electrician was positioning a large rolling tool chest; he looked around as we came up and tapped Mavis on the shoulder, gesturing to us.

She extricated herself from the RPCM, flashlight in hand, and stood to greet us. "We can take it out. It's a radio."

I wanted to shout "*don't touch it*" even though I knew they would not have. All the same, my heart felt like it was a misaligned engine oscillating in my chest. "Is it wired into comms?"

She shook her head. "Into the EPS."

Electrical power system. There was really only one reason to wire a radio into an electrical system you already had control of. I let my breath out very slowly. "All right . . . Do we have anyone who has defused a bomb before?"

The guy with the schematics on the floor looked up at the RPCM so fast he overbalanced and fell.

Mavis bent to help him up, shaking her head. "The explosives aren't here, dummy." She glanced at me. "Do I have that right? Y'all think this is a remote-control booby trap? We pull it out and someplace else something goes boom?"

I nodded, while beside me, Eugene turned in a circle, looking at all the people who were going about their business in Midtown. He took in a breath and settled his shoulders, getting ready to work.

"Give me a minute to talk to the fellows." She turned back to her team as calmly as if this were a sim, and I could guarantee that "active saboteur" was not a situation she would have hit in training.

Eugene watched them and leaned down to murmur, "Thank God for competent people." He raised his head and looked around again. "You think it's tied to the BusyBee?"

"That is my fear, yes."

He tightened his fists. "I want to evacuate people, but I don't know where to send them because we don't know where that damn thing is."

"Birgit." I pressed my fingernails into the side of my right thumb. "She worked in munitions and has mobility."

"And was nowhere near the cockpit before or during the flight." Eugene rubbed his forehead, grimacing. "But we keep talking about Curt *or* Birgit when it could be Curt *and* Birgit."

"Talk to her and—"

"Okay!" Mavis turned back to us, blue eyes alight with what looked like a plan. Two of the electricians had turned to their large tool chest, while the third crouched on the schematic making notes on the large sheet of paper. "We can put in a dummy load that will mock the radio. The point being, we can pull it out, but doing it during the blackout is best. It's got to have a mechanism to tell that power has been interrupted in such a way that it doesn't go off. If we pull it then and put a line in to span the gap, making allowances for change in resistance, et cetera, and so forth, then it should believe that the radio is still there."

Eugene pursed his lips and you could almost see the silent scales he was weighing his options on. "Sixteen minutes. You sure you can do that?"

Honestly, Mavis looked offended. "Yes. I'm sure as the day is long and the lunar day is two weeks." She jerked her finger over her shoulder. "I have the guys setting up, but we won't go ahead until you give the say-so."

Eugene's jaw worked for a moment and then he nodded. "Do it."

We watched Mavis and her crew work, and my entire body was tight with the urge to do something. The most useful thing I could do was to be on call in case there was something else oddball deep in the belly of the RPCM, so I dropped into the "attentive wife" posture I used so often with . . . I tilted my head back and stared at the dome, hoping that most of the tears would roll back down my sinuses.

The translucent dome was dark with just a glowing orb in the lower quadrant. Earth. With the protective filtering of the dome, it was like seeing the Moon through clouds.

"You okay?" Eugene's voice was low.

I nodded and swiped under my eyes. "You should go." Fishing a handkerchief out of my pocket, I wiped my nose. "In case this doesn't work, we shouldn't both be in the same module."

I could see him want to argue and be too smart to follow through on that. "Agreed. I do *not* like this, though." Eugene set his hands on his hips, shaking his head. "I'm going to do a preliminary evacuation for nonessential personnel. Get them into the BusyBees, so if something does go wrong, they are prepped to move to safety."

Neither of us talked about the scenario in which there was no safe haven. Where Icarus hadn't left bombs in just one location, but in all of the outposts. There are contingencies you can plan for and then there are ones where the people you love have to make plans.

MAVIS'S TEAM HAD used the two hours to come up with a definitive plan and practice it as much as they could without actually touching the radio wired into the RPCM. Midtown was deserted. Downstairs, Lunar Ground Control had closed their airlock and everyone was working in IVP suits, ready to go visors-down as soon as the blackout hit.

The engineering team couldn't. The RPCM had not been built to accommodate a spacesuit. My cast meant I was sitting in my astronaut onesie, with an emergency oxygen mask propped on my head. All I had for tools were a watch and a walkie-talkie. Halim also had a walkie-talkie and was waiting downstairs for us, ready to help with evac if things went meteoric. Eugene had another walkie-talkie in the AdminMod. He'd sent Myrtle and Helen off to pilot BusyBees, which also had the side effect of making sure his wife was in the safest possible spot.

Right decision. And if I were her, I would have murdered him when I got back.

I held the talk button down so Eugene and Halim could hear me, but this was for the engineers. "We're at T-minus thirty seconds on my mark."

"Copy, T-minus thirty." Mavis's voice came from deep in the machine. She and one of her engineers were poised to work the moment the lights went out. One of the other fellows stood ready to hand supplies in, and the third was functioning as an electrician's CAPCOM, reading the procedure they'd written up so that when time was critical, they did not have to stop and think.

The second hand swept around the watch. "Mark."

Every breath was tight. "Twenty."

The lights ringing Midtown buzzed with the fans. "Ten."

They would know when the lights went out. "Nine, eight, seven." But this gave them time to set. "Six, five, four."

Inside, Mavis rose to her knees, hands extended.

"Three, two, one—"

The lights went out.

Around us, the electromagnetic catches on the airlocks released and the doors swung shut. The ripple-bang of the hatches locking echoed in the dark. Inside the RPCM, the battery-powered work lamps they'd positioned seemed to blaze even brighter in the sudden darkness. Giant shadows cut across the walls as Mavis and her team moved.

A moment later, the emergency lights came on. A part of me had honestly expected that we would either not lose power this time or that the emergency lights would fail.

"The settings are eleven papa papa juliet three." In the dim light, it almost sounded like a sim. Everyone was calm and efficient.

"Confirmed. Eleven papa papa juliet three."

I kept my eye on the watch, which was my one actual job here. The second hand seemed to race forward in time with my heart, but if you'd seen me, I was just a woman sitting casually on a plastic chair.

I chewed the inside of my lip, waiting. Across my back, all the muscles were so tight they almost creaked with my breath. The minute hand advanced. "Five minutes elapsed time."

"Copy, five minutes."

Inside they worked in near silence, only responding when they needed something specific.

"You can demate papa fourteen from juliet fourteen."

"Roger, wilco. Demating now."

The engineer at the door took a tangle of cables and set it on the table to the right of the open door. In a smooth motion, she reached to her left and picked up a part, passing it into the compartment. It was like watching a set of wizards dance. Understand that I can do aircraft maintenance. I'm trained in electrical systems on every spacecraft I fly. I had helped install the original unit. My knowledge of electronics compares to theirs like a kite to a T-38 jet.

"Ten minutes, elapsed time."

"Copy, ten minutes."

I was sweating and all I was doing was sitting there, watching a minute hand on a watch.

"J106 alpha in place."

"With that config, you have a Go to decouple the VRCS."

Inside my shoes, my toes curled as if I were going to go on pointe. The VRCS was our mystery radio. It bothered the hell out of me that I didn't know what the letters stood for. Although, for all I knew, it was a random set designed to make anyone who saw it back off because they didn't know what it was.

"Done." Mavis's voice was strong and directed out to me. "We're clear."

I wanted to give her a standing ovation. "Copy. Elapsed time, fourteen minutes." I depressed the walkie-talkie button. "They're clear. We're moving away from the RPCM now."

Eugene's voice crackled in the space. "Good work."

Mavis and the other engineer stepped out of the RPCM. It rankled them to leave their supplies lying around, but they had not argued about the order of operations. I handed them emergency oxygen masks, and we put the EOMs on as we jogged to the stairs. The plan was to get downstairs to the LGC and into their airlock, in case the main dome was breached.

As we came down the stairs, Halim was waiting in his IVP suit, opening the hatch for us. As a group, we crowded into the airlock, which was not designed to have five bodies in it. Halim saluted as he closed the door on us. I wanted him inside. I did not like the plan that left him on the other side of this giant slab of aluminum, even in a suit.

In the tiny space, the luminescent dial on my watch seemed unnaturally bright. We were all silent, except for our breath. I held my watch out where we could all see it, even though we'd know when the lights came on. We'd made it into the airlock with a full minute to spare and it was plenty of time to tense and brace. One of the engineers kept cracking his knuckles. Mavis plucked at the strap of her EOM.

The minute hand hit the sixteen-minute mark.

The lights did not come back on.

FORTY-ONE

EARTH FIRST ISSUES MANIFESTO
Claims Credit for Death of Governor

KANSAS CITY, May 27, 1963—The group Earth First has taken credit for the assassination of Governor Kenneth T. Wargin of Kansas earlier this month. In a manifesto sent to multiple newspapers throughout the country, they claim they had tried a method of diplomacy to try to shift the United States involvement in the space program and have changed tactics because that failed. What follows is their manifesto, printed in full.

"Exodus 32:27—And he said to them: Thus saith the Lord God of Israel: Put every man his sword upon his thigh: go, and return from gate to gate through the midst of the camp, and let every man kill his brother, and friend, and neighbour.

"As the planet Earth recovers from the Meteor strike, the United States atrophies. The needs of our fellow Americans have been ignored in favor of the false idol of the Moon by an elite who strive to enrich themselves at the expense of the poor and forgotten . . ."

FORTY-FIVE MINUTES later, and we were still without power. Mavis had asked Eugene to bring the Hysterical Godfrey back in, because he knew the systems and they had half an hour to solve it before the emergency batteries started dying. The fussy little man strode across Midtown with his chin held high.

He shot a glance at me, and his lip curled a little, but when he got to the engineers, his chin came down. "Mavis. How can I help?"

She looked up from the schematic she and the other electricians were bent over. "Christian, thanks." She stepped over to the table with the parts they'd pulled out of the RPCM. "This is what we swapped out with a VandenHeuvel patch. Figured the blackout would be a time it wasn't going to send a signal and—"

"Good God." His face had completely changed, the color draining out of it as he handled the box. "This is a remote fuse."

She just nodded and none of us said, "I told you so."

He set it down on the table. "Show me."

I am not someone who usually paces, but I found myself wanting to do so as Mavis and her team worked the problem. Eugene did pace. Not a lot, just around in a small circle, with one arm crossed over his body, holding the elbow of the other. His fist clenched and unclenched.

Godfrey backed out of the RPCM, shaking his head. "That's good work in there. Nothing you did should have caused this."

A little tension went out of Mavis's shoulders. "All right." She grimaced. "Although that would have been the simplest solution. Moving on to the mains?"

"Concur."

Eugene stepped out of his pacing. "Status?"

Godfrey opened his mouth and then, in a minor miracle, gestured to Mavis. "I only just arrived. Miss Davis has more current information."

Her brows twitched upward a little, which was understandable since he was still technically her boss. "We don't know what's causing the outage. So we're starting with the simplest solutions and then working out from there." She hesitated and looked at the RPCM. "The thing is . . . we actually have two problems. Because we prioritized pulling the radio out, the existing remote controls are still in place. When we get power back, those will be accessible remotely."

Which meant that Earth First could still control the entire colony. Grimacing, Eugene drummed his fingers on his thigh. "What do you need to field two teams?"

"Some of the folks we sent off in a BusyBee. If I give you a list?"

Eugene shook his head. "The BusyBees are out for another . . ." He checked his watch. "Four hours before they'll send in a team to check on us."

Well, shit. Now I understood why he was pacing and tense. The same shielding that protected the colony from radiation also stopped radio signals. Without power, we didn't have outside comms. Myrtle was in a BusyBee and all she would know was that they couldn't raise anyone in the main lunar colony. The BusyBees would still be able to talk to each other and the outposts, but couldn't reach us.

For that matter, we had no idea if anything had happened elsewhere in the colony.

Mavis chewed her lower lip and looked at the people backing her up. "Split into a three-team and a two-team?" She turned back to Eugene. "Can I keep Nicole?"

I answered for him. "Yes. Absolutely."

"No. I need her." Eugene was looking toward the SciMod. "If it can be done seated, you can have Ruben. If not, we can pull someone from LGC until power is restored."

I took a step toward him, not sure how clearly I could express my discomfort about using Ruben without outright saying he might be involved. Yes, we'd told the department heads that sabotage had happened, but we'd managed to avoid pointing to any particular person. "Are you sure about that?"

"Yeah." Just his head turned as he looked back at Mavis. "That work?"

"Yes, sir."

"Good. I'll send him to you. Split your teams. Draft Halim for anything else you need." He started walking toward the SciMod. "Wargin, with me."

I waited until we were out of earshot, which took a tremendous act of will. "What are we doing?"

"Not being subtle." He jerked a thumb toward the emergency lights. "We need answers, and Curt, Birgit, or Frisch has them."

"And you're *sure* it's not Ruben?"

"Yes. Wrong kind of dumbass." He stopped at the airlock and shone a flashlight on the pressure gauge, then through the window for a visual check. "But I read up on him along with the other South Africans, and he's apparently a damn good electrician."

If Eugene was certain, I was not going to second-guess him. I mean, any more than I already had. At least not out loud. "What do you want me for?"

"You're the spy." He pumped the ratchet handle to release each of the fifteen latches holding the door sealed. "How would you approach questioning them?"

I stopped him with my hand on his arm before he pulled the hatch open. "Question. How much of your urgency is Myrtle?"

His hand tensed on the ratchet handle. "I would be lying if I said she wasn't in my mind."

"She's okay."

His lips compressed for a moment and he broke eye contact. "But she doesn't know that I am."

"All right . . ." I grabbed the hatch. "When the lights come back on, Icarus is going to know we've solved that problem. So that gives a narrow window in which to see if someone will trip up while feeling triumphant."

Eugene could not let me open the airlock by myself and took the handle. "Who are you starting with?"

I'd been thinking about unanswered questions and the handwriting in the RPCM. But I wanted to know how the Lunar Colony Administrator got the book before I talked to either of the other two. "Frisch."

"Not Curt?" He hauled the outer door open and the porthole reflected light from an emergency lamp.

"Eugene . . . Are the BusyBees still in line of sight of the main colony?"

"Yeah. So at least she'll know we aren't venting anything." He shook his head. "I'm okay, really. It's not like . . ."

Not like Kenneth. I shoved that to the side. "The lounge here has 360 degrees of windows. You have a flashlight. Get a mirror from sickbay to use as a reflector to make the light bigger—"

"Morse." He grabbed my forehead and kissed it. Then I've never seen a man finish cycling an airlock so quickly while still following procedure to the letter.

Upstairs, in the lounge, Eugene was signaling APAF to the BusyBees. All Present and Accounted For. I could imagine the sighs of relief going through the tiny flotilla of space buses.

Ana Teresa had taken Ruben off to Midtown, and I had to hope that Eugene was right and we hadn't just delivered Icarus to the equipment he needed.

I helped Frisch walk to my makeshift interrogation room in the geology lab. I would have preferred the biology lab, because it was closer, but a pen full of bunnies did not project the feel I was going for. The geology lab, on the other hand, had tools.

Would I be able to use those on Icarus? Yes. My husband was dead and I am not a kind woman under the best of circumstances. I mask it well, but I am vindictive and selfish. Would I be able to use them to figure out who Icarus was?

No.

"How are you doing?" I guided Frisch to a chair in the middle of the floor and sat down across from him. By my side was a table with hacksaws and hammers.

His skin was dry and sallow. "Distinctly improved, thank you." He gestured toward the emergency lights. "Will you tell me what is happening?"

My gamble was to approach him as if he were not Icarus, nor directly involved. It wasn't an unreasonable position. If he were Icarus and poisoned himself to throw us off track, then he would have made darn sure the medical lab stocked Prussian blue. Also, the class of things happening appeared to have been set up after our arrival. "Icarus has been using a satellite to interface with the lunar colony via an old procedure for the RPCM. We're working on getting the lights back on now."

He frowned, eyes narrowing as he followed what I was saying. That, in itself, was a good sign for his health. "I see. What do you need from me?" He nodded to the door I had shut behind us. "I presume there is some use you have for me or we would not be here."

"There was a book in your office. *The Long Tomorrow.* Do you know it?"

He nodded slowly, watching me. "That was one of the items that caused the IAC's problems with your use of codes. The others were easier to break, but harder to spot if you didn't know. This was blatant. The newspapers had a field day with it *because* it couldn't be cracked and they could suppose it was anything."

I had, truly, expected this line of questioning to be a dead end. I had braced myself for him to not know the book was in his office. Given that it was under the table, I thought Icarus had planted it. "The code, yes. But the book . . . Why did you have it?"

"Oh—Vicky Hsu brought it to me."

The room went cold. "Vicky." At the church services. With my list of suspects. But why the hell would she put her own name in the library when she checked out the book, even if she disguised her handwriting? Or was that a double-bluff of some sort? I rubbed my forehead. "What did she say when she gave it to you?"

"She'd found the letter you'd been decoding in it and thought I should know." He looked down his nose at me like a stork fishing. "You seem confused. Might I know why?"

"I didn't decode it." I chewed the inside of my lip before answering, still trying to figure out how any of this tied together. "When I went to the library, *The Long Tomorrow* had been checked out already. By any chance did she say where she got the book?"

He shook his head. "Just that she'd been reading it when she found the letter. I should have asked, but . . . my mind was a bit fuzzy, which I now realize was because I was being poisoned." Frisch cleared his throat. "I must say . . . when I realized thallium was a rat poison, and it had been used on me, I had a dark period in which I wondered if that was why you never took sugar with your tea. Were you with Icarus, I wondered."

"That seems fair. I wondered the same about you when we found the book in your office." The case against him being Icarus was significantly stronger than the case for it.

There were things he could help with, now that his mind was clearing. I would need to brief him on the Swiss Army knife and Birgit, in case he had any insight from being in a hospital room with her. "What changed your mind?"

His brows came together, turning up in distress. "My dear . . . your husband."

AFTER I FINISHED talking to Frisch, I leaned against the wall of the hallway and stared at the ceiling while I packed my heart back into the little box I needed to keep it in. The moments when the grief hit me were unpredictable. Nineteen days. I would stop counting at some point. Blowing out a breath through pursed lips, I straightened.

Next up. Birgit or Curt. I wasn't quite stupid enough to be alone in a room with either of them. Which meant I needed to pull Eugene away from signaling to the BusyBees.

I bounded up the stairs to the lounge to get him and it was easy to take the steps three at a time. You know those moments when you realize exactly how sick you had been? It felt so good to *move* that I was smiling a little when I soared over the last step into the earthlit lounge.

Outside, the silver-blue light of Earth lay over the ground like a silk blanket. Black shadows etched the rims of craters and deepened the sides of the Apennine mountains. Eugene stood in silhouette, both hands braced against the glass, leaning to rest his forehead against it.

"Eugene?"

He straightened like a marionette being yanked up by its

operator, into beautiful military posture. He took a breath and turned. "Nicole." I do not like it when people say my name in that tone. "Myrtle says they saw an explosion."

I grasped for the one piece of comfort in that sentence. *Myrtle says . . .* So she was okay. But nothing about his body language said anything else was all right. "Where?"

"The Garden. They aren't answering her hails." He wiped his hand over his face. "None of the outposts are."

I braced myself against the back of a chair, my cast scraping the hard plastic. The trouble with a small colony is that you know everyone. This wasn't an explosion in some anonymous far-away place. This was where people I knew worked. Luther Sanchez would have been at The Garden, and Aahana. "Danika. Ruben's wife."

"I know."

It would have been hard to get a full report using Morse with lights. We might be missing details. "They may just have a power outage like we do."

"And the explosion?"

Meteors hit with enough kinetic force to cause a fireball, even on the Moon. I didn't think we were that lucky, and the irony did not escape me. "Are the BusyBees coming in?"

He shook his head. "I sent Helen to check The Garden, but I told the rest of them to stay put until power was restored."

"What do you want to do?"

Eugene bent his neck, staring at the floor, and twisted his head—not quite shaking it, not quite stretching, but more as if he were trying to ground himself. "We'll lose the window for talking to Curt without the lights if we wait." He rubbed his forehead. "Let's kill the power to the SciMod so when they get the main power back on it stays dark here. That'll buy us some—"

The lights came back on.

His head snapped up and he glared at the ceiling. "I know I was praying for this, but Your timing, Lord . . ." Eugene sighed and looked at the stairs and then out at the landscape, obscured behind our reflections in the glass. "How long do you need with Curt?"

"You need to go to LGC. With the power on, people will need guidance on bringing the BusyBees back in." I needed to rethink my game plan with the lights on. "I can ask Halim to be my backup."

"Good call. Thank you." He started toward the stairs. "Walk with me to brief me on Frisch?"

"Sure. He got the book from Vicky, who 'found' the letter insi—"

Behind us, the intercom buzzed. "Eugene Lindholm, please contact LGC. Eugene Lindholm, please contact LGC immediately."

He sprinted across the room, stopping himself with an arm against the wall to control momentum. He slapped the other against the talk button. "LGC, Lindholm. Report?"

"All of the satellites are nonresponsive." Deana Whitney's voice in the CAPCOM chair sounded shaken, which I've never heard. "And we can't reestablish contact with Earth."

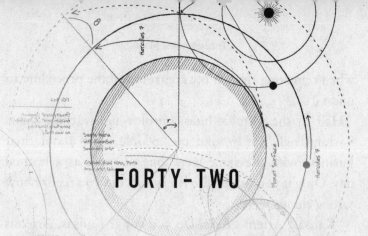

FORTY-TWO

Artemis Base Mission Log, Acting Administrator Eugene Lindholm:

May 27, 1963, 1355—Contact protocols completed. Communication with IAC not reestablished. Satellite Communications and Tracking department is troubleshooting in conjunction with Power.

LUNAR GROUND CONTROL has the same focused concentration as the Mission Control Center in Kansas. On the Moon, it also functioned as air traffic control for the BusyBees and cargo rockets coming from the South Pole mines, but it always makes me feel like I'm coming home.

Today was like coming home to discover your house had been robbed.

I sat at the back of the room, going through every piece of documentation about the early installation to see if I could remember anything that wasn't written down. I wore a headset, so I could be a resource if anyone needed the "historical perspective" that someone had recognized I could provide. In a perfect world, I would find a documented error that we had accidentally triggered when removing the remote controls and the procedure to undo it.

Half of the metallic blue consoles had warning lights flashing red. But around me, people went about their business with the same level tone of voice as a normal day. Only if you listened to the words did you realize how wrong things were.

"Kansas, Artemis Base. Do you copy? Kansas, Artemis Base. Do you copy?"

"BusyBee 6, Ground Control. Have your evacuees report to the cafeteria after landing for duty assignments."

"No response from satellite on low-gain link."

Eugene stood at the Flight Director's desk, resting one hand on the console. He wore a headset, listening to the call-and-response as each station worked the problem, as the BusyBees reported in, as we all kept our cool and went about our jobs.

"Artemis Base, BusyBee 2." Myrtle's voice made Eugene's head come up as if he could see her. "I've done a flyover of where we think we saw the explosion, but it's too dark to see anything."

His hand reached for the comm unit but clenched into a fist, pulling back. He looked to the Ground Controller and bit his lips as if that were the only way to stop himself from stepping into the line of communication.

GC replied, as was appropriate. "Copy, BusyBee 2."

"Request permission to return to base and offload evacuees?"

"Confirmed. You are Go to return to base."

Eugene unclenched his hand and rested it back on the

edge of the console. With a deliberate ease, he lowered his head and kept working.

THERE'S A BIG CLOCK on the wall in LGC. Whenever a rocket is traveling between the Moon and the Earth, the clock counts mission elapsed time. Eugene had them set it to track how long we'd been without contact from Earth. Five hours and fifty-one minutes.

The thing that kept eating at the back of my mind was that Icarus and Earth First had changed strategies. They had been trying to stop the program by making it look bad through subtle sabotage. They had shifted to active attacks.

We had wanted to make them panic. Wondering if our pushing had caused . . . *this* filled a pit of acid in my stomach. Would Kenneth be alive if I had kept my head down? Oh, I know survivor's guilt when I see it—we all saw it often enough after the war. After the Meteor.

But still.

EUGENE STOPPED BEHIND my desk. "Nicole. Take a break."

I looked up over the edge of my reading glasses, blinking. Elapsed time seven hours and twenty-four minutes. Of course, that was not counting the intense day and a half before we lost contact. Eugene's posture was perfect. The only real tell that he was struggling was that his right hand kept clenching into a fist and then opening as if he were forcing it to relax.

Gesturing to the rest of the room, he said, "Second shift is coming on."

That was a sensible time to take a break. They would need to be brought up to speed by the prime team. Some of those staff would stick around, of course, but I probably wouldn't be needed for a few minutes. Neither of us would.

I pulled my glasses off. "When was the last time you ate?"

He squinted at me. "Isn't that supposed to be my line?"

"Myrtle has me well trained. They've got a sandwich station set up in Midtown." I was not even remotely hungry, but I had a log to fill out and knowing that made me realize I had missed lunch. Standing, I stretched and my back let out an artillery barrage. "You can do morale for the Midtown team as we walk through . . ."

He sighed and stepped over to the Flight Director. "Poppy, I'll be back in fifteen. Sandwich?"

"Egg salad, if they've got it." As if this were an ordinary day, these men and women just worked.

Eugene followed me to the airlock, which we were keeping shut, just in case.

I waited until we were inside, with walls of metal between us and the rest of the team. "When do we float the idea that the explosion Myrtle saw was a satellite deorbiting?"

"Deorbit" is the nice way of saying crashing into the lunar surface.

"The frightening thing is I've been praying for that." He grabbed the rachet handle and worked it to open the door. "Because otherwise, that was The Garden."

"Nothing from Helen yet?"

He shook his head as he pulled the door open. "I'm figuring another hour before she's back in range."

Without the satellites, we were limited to line-of-sight communication. On Earth, you could bounce signals off the upper atmosphere, but that wasn't an option on the Moon. Back in the old days, when we had a command module orbiting and a lander on the surface, we used to have to send the signal from the lander all the way back to Mission Control in Kansas and have them bounce it back to the CM. And every time the CM went around the far side of the Moon, the pilot had no signal at all. Elma always said that she found that period incredibly peaceful.

There is a distinct difference between scheduled loss of signal and what we were experiencing.

Upstairs, the engineers had taken over Midtown, setting up conference tables and whiteboards to try to work the laundry list of problems. Eugene started toward the first table and I caught his arm.

"From experience . . . sandwich first. Otherwise, you'll get caught up and forget."

I could have done without the wave of pity that passed across his face, but he didn't actually *say* anything about it, just gave me a simple nod. "Thanks."

It was still a gauntlet to get to the sandwich station at Le Restaurant. He had to shake hands, clap people on the shoulder, and nod seriously when someone asked him if things were going okay. And he managed to keep moving. He was *good*. Things like this were why Kenneth had been pushing Eugene to go into politics since we met. He would have been so proud.

I shoved my hand in my pocket and walked to Le Restaurant. I'd get sandwiches for him and Poppy while Eugene did his thing. The doors stood wide open and all the chairs were still shoved against the walls from when it had doubled as the women's sickbay. Had it only been last week when they were moved back to the SciMod?

Jeanette Arnaud looked up at me and smiled. "Bonjour! How goes it downstairs?"

I switched to French, partly because I like the language, but mostly because I needed to stretch some part of my brain that wasn't involved in remembering acronyms. "Progress. We have removed some possibilities; they are therefore sure to discover a solution."

"Good." She gave a nod and looked down at the sandwiches. "You need nothing special, is that so?"

Special? I froze, panicked. Special as in food that would not trigger my gag reflex? I thought people would have kept the anorexia a secret for me. I use the word, yes. But I also know what it will do to Kenneth's career if people find—I closed my eyes. Goddammit. I was so tired of crying. It didn't matter if everyone knew.

"Nothing halal, or kosher?" She slid a tray toward me. "Ham and cheese all right?"

I swallowed all of that unnecessary fear and the salty snot that filled the back of my throat. "That would be charming, thank you." I looked down to keep my watering eyes from being quite so obvious. "Two and an egg salad, if it does not bother you."

A sheet of paper, covered with numbers, was under the chairs and I knelt to grab it, grateful to have some pretext so I could wipe my eyes without everyone seeing me weep. Again. And frankly, I did not want anyone to lose their calculations if it would help with *anything* related to restoring communications.

"Here you are, madame." She handed over the sandwiches, wrapped in foil. "A pleasure seeing you, as always."

I juggled the things, finally cradling two of the sandwiches between my cast and my body, tucking Poppy Northcutt's egg salad into a thigh pocket in my flight suit. I found Eugene talking to an engineer, head bent over a schematic. He nodded when I came up, taking the foil package when I held it out. He eyed me and then my sandwich, while listening to the engineer. I rolled my eyes at him, and peeled the foil off. Food is fuel . . . Making eye contact with Eugene, I took a healthy bite of the sandwich.

He smirked at me, bending back to look at the schematic on the table. If he'd still been looking, I would have stuck my tongue out at him. But he'd been right that getting out of that room for a few minutes was helpful. I wished I could get Eugene to take an *actual* break, but I knew from experience that politicians could only do that behind closed doors.

Across Midtown, the port airlock hissed open and then closed with the distinctive ripple-bang of fifteen catches activating. We used to always keep the airlocks between modules closed, but I'd adapted to having the doors open and the sound made me turn.

A cluster of engineers walked around the curve of the "street" from the port. At their rear, Myrtle Lindholm strode with her CPK bag over her shoulder. She saw

Eugene, who was still leaning over the schematic, and pushed forward through her passengers.

I opened my mouth to tell him she was here, but Eugene's head lifted as if he felt her presence. He slapped the sandwich into my midriff and sprinted toward her. She dropped her bag and ran. They met in the clear space next to Central Park, Eugene's momentum and mass sweeping Myrtle back a few steps before their bodies in motion came to rest in an embrace.

His head was bent, buried in the side of her neck. Her hands clenched the material of his flight suit. Eugene's shoulders convulsed once, tensed, and the breath shuddered out of him. He stepped back, hands on her shoulders. Myrtle's head tilted up to meet his gaze, and her cheeks were wet as she smiled at him. She said something that I was too far away to hear. Still smiling, she reached up to wipe his cheek.

Turning his head, Eugene kissed her hand and I could just see the curve of a smile on his cheek. He gave a sudden headshake and shrug. The man pulled her in again, one hand behind her neck, and dipped her in one of the most passionate kisses I have ever seen. Myrtle's knee came up and her toes curled down.

Someone said, "Woo!" and I could have killed them.

Eugene immediately set Myrtle on her feet. He stepped back, farther, releasing her completely. I still couldn't see his face, but his posture returned to his military bearing. Myrtle, too, drew her hands away and clasped them behind her as if she were at parade rest and listened as he spoke.

I was so happy for them that it hurt. Swallowing, I turned to the engineer, who was gawking at them. I stepped into his line of sight and gestured with my sandwich to his schematic. "Is there anything I can help you with here?"

"Oh! Um . . ." He swallowed loudly. "I was just explaining that we'd detached and reseated all connectors. Nothing changed."

"Good work." I tried to switch both sandwiches to my left hand and ended up balancing them on my cast. Slightly awkward, but I was able to rest my hand on his shoulder and squeeze. "I'll let Major Lindholm know."

"Hey—" He wet his lips and looked toward Eugene, who was listening to Myrtle. "Do they know who did it?"

I took a slow breath. This type of suspicion could destroy the colony in ways that blowing it up couldn't touch. "Leave that to Major Lindholm."

"Oh . . . sure." He tugged on his ear. "Should we be doing anything about that?"

I glanced over at Eugene. He was walking back to us, wiping the sleeve of his flight suit across his eyes. I squeezed the young man's shoulder again. "Just keep doing good work."

Before he could ask another question, I walked over to meet Eugene. He cleared his throat, fooling no one. "Just finished debriefing Myrtle—"

"You could have gotten a room for that."

Let me tell you, making Eugene Lindholm blush is a thing of beauty and a joy forever. "Is that my sandwich?"

I held it out and yanked it away before letting him have it. "Sandwich for details on the debrief—the actual debrief. I don't need to know about the state of her tonsils."

The color of his skin deepened with a beautiful rosy undertone. He snatched the sandwich and started walking back to the stairs to LGC. "No sign of any explosion or impact, but as you heard the night makes it too dark to see much detail out there. Coming in, she used a flight path that let her circle the base. From the outside, everything looks nominal."

"That's good . . . although something definitive would be useful." I sighed. "For future problems, we have a morale iss—"

"Nicole, what is this?" Eugene had stopped in his tracks. In his hand, there was a grease-stained piece of paper, covered with numbers.

Or rather, covered with a cipher in a very specific handwriting. "It was under the chairs. I just . . ." I sucked in a breath, turning back to look at Le Restaurant. "Oh shit."

"There's something worse?"

"When it was the women's sickbay . . . that's where Birgit's bed was."

I SEQUESTERED MYSELF in the conference room with the cipher and a notepad. To brute-force a cipher, it helps to know what language it is written in. I knew of a fellow who used a simple Caesar cipher, but wrote his notes in Middle English. They were indecipherable.

This could be anything from English to French. Since Birgit was Swiss, it could also be German. I spoke all three of those, fortunately. Or it could be some random language, in which case all bets were off.

Once you get a crack, the entire thing can unfold in minutes. It's finding the crack that's the tricky part.

Someone tapped lightly on the door.

"Come in." I straightened, sliding my reading glasses off my nose.

Eugene poked his head in. "Helen's back. Are you . . . interruptible?"

"Yeah." I tossed my glasses on the table, massaging the bridge of my nose. It wasn't quite an ice pick between the eyes, more like someone trying to enter my head using their knuckle.

He pulled the door the rest of the way open, holding it for Helen, Myrtle, and Halim. Myrtle was carrying a CPK bag and set it down at the end of the table. Methodically, she pulled out food and set it in a rigid grid. Her jaw was tight.

I grabbed my papers, to make more room for her. Myrtle shook her head. "Don't lose track of what you're doing. I've got plenty of space."

Helen's hair was disheveled and matted against her head from her Snoopy cap. The indentation of her microphone arm was still pressed deep into the curve of her cheek as she dropped into the closest chair to the door.

Sitting down opposite me, Halim rubbed his nose and picked up one of the pages. I held still, hoping he would magically say, "Ah-ha! But it is Arabic!"

No such luck.

Eugene pulled the door shut. "First things: I talked to

Vicky and asked her about *The Long Tomorrow*. She says Birgit gave it to her."

"Troubling." Which was a fairly significant understatement.

"There's more. Go ahead, Helen."

"The big picture. The Garden is fine. They have not lost power, but did lose comms for anything outside the facility. Because they did not lose power, they were able to tell us when the satellites went offline. It was at the top of our initial blackout window."

I twitched. "That was before our team had removed the radio fuse. So . . . so the loss of satellites is not related?"

"I do not believe so." Her voice was almost Katherine Hepburn crisp. "At the same time, their telemetry picked up a series of five impacts or explosions. The timing coincides with the flash Myrtle saw."

There had been five satellites in orbit around the Moon. I'm guessing there were none now. For a man whose prayer had been answered, Eugene did not look happy.

"While we were docked, it occurred to me that the logs we have here regarding the BusyBees were incomplete, because Administrator Frisch was struggling with poison." Helen folded her hands in her lap. "I took the opportunity to look at the logs at The Garden to see if anyone from our list of suspects had arrived there."

Myrtle nodded and slid a sip-pack of soup to Helen. "Good thought. When we did the inventory of potential explosives, we didn't look at the log."

"Birgit Furst is recorded as arriving to do some work in their comms department. She was the only passenger. The name in the pilot's slot was empty." She turned to look at me. "Birgit was at the 99s the day your plane was sabotaged."

The blood drained out of me and iced over the floor. "Flying a BusyBee is not the same as an airplane."

Leaning forward, Halim groaned and rested his face in his hands. "I gave her simulator time."

Hell . . . The first time I flew a BusyBee, all I'd had was simulator time too. In theory, Birgit actually could have flown herself out to The Garden.

I looked at my watch: "22:36 . . . So do we haul her out of bed and question her now, or wait until tomorrow?"

Eugene stood. "Fourteen hours without contact with Earth. We question her now."

FORTY-THREE

Artemis Base Mission Log, Acting Administrator Eugene Lindholm:

May 27, 1963, 2306—Contact with The Garden and Marius Hills has been reestablished via BusyBee. Dispatched a reconnaissance flight to the South Pole outpost at 23:00. Pilot: Armstrong. Copilot: Aldrin. Nav/Comp: El-Mohtar.

EUGENE *REALLY* WANTED to be in the room when we questioned Birgit, but they needed him in the LGC more. I'd unscrewed a couple of bulbs in the geology lab, so when Halim escorted Birgit in, my interrogation room was dim in the right ways.

Balancing on a pair of crutches, she was walking fairly well, with a makeshift brace on her left leg. When she saw me waiting she stopped and looked over her shoulder at Halim and beyond him to the astronaut standing guard outside the door. "What is going on?"

"Have a seat." I patted the back of the chair we had set up for her in one of the bright spots of the geology lab. "We have some questions."

Her eyes widened a fraction. "All right . . ." Birgit

made her way to the chair and sat down with her left leg stretched out in front of her.

As soon as she was seated, I walked to the table opposite her and picked up a clipboard. I do love a clipboard. Halim shut the door and stood beside me, which put him in the shadows. He crossed his arms over his chest and spread his legs into a wide, comfortable stance. I picked up a pencil from the table and flashed a smile. "We'll try to be quick."

"Quick about what?" She played with the wrapping on the handle of her crutch. Nervous, yes, but because the situation was odd or because she knew she was caught?

Always start with something known and verifiable. Get them used to answering questions, and then move on to harder ones.

"Your personnel file says you worked in munitions for the Swiss Army during the war." I touched the eraser of the pencil to my lower lip, to make my curiosity clear. "Tell me about that."

"Um . . ." She tucked a strand of hair behind her ear. "Well, they were mobilizing and . . . You know Switzerland has mandatory military service for able-bodied males, correct? So then, my brothers were conscripted and I wanted to with them go, so I volunteered."

I nodded encouragingly, as if she were not telling me things that I already knew.

"As it happens, I was not stationed near them. In hindsight, it was foolish to hope so, but I was very young. Only fourteen, although, of course, I lied on my application. I was assigned to a munitions plant." She shrugged. "It was hot and dusty and not very glamorous."

On the clipboard, I made a note to confirm the math. It had not occurred to me to check her age for those wartime activities. According to her files she was thirty-eight, so . . . Fourteen. Fourteen when she started, but the war went on for years. So verifiably true and misleading because there is a vast difference between a fourteen-year-old in a munitions plant and a twenty-year-old.

"What did you do at the munitions plant?"

She looked at the piece of cloth she was worrying on her crutches. "I swept the floor."

"Pardon?"

"I think they knew I was underage . . ." Her head came up suddenly and she leaned forward, trying to see past the shadows to my face. "Is this about the fuse they found? I can't— If you need someone to disarm it, I can't. I'm not qualified."

She had jumped to the subject of the bomb very quickly. My challenge was to withhold judgment until I had a big picture. Any single piece wasn't enough, so I waited to see if she would fill the silence with more information.

Birgit fidgeted in her chair for a moment. "I'm so sorry. I know I should not have let anyone believe I did work more complicated than that. It is only that I wanted so much to go into space. All I did was sweep the floor at the munitions factory."

"I understand that." I tapped my pencil on the clipboard, watching her. "Did you enjoy *The Long Tomorrow*?"

She blinked at the sudden change of topic and then the color drained out of her face. "The letter. This is about the letter." Birgit's head dropped forward. "I am so, so sorry."

"Could you be more specific?"

"I just found it—the book, I mean. Outside the door to my sleeping compartment. There was a note 'for Vicky' and I thought that whoever left it had just put it in the wrong place, so I took it to Vicky. She didn't know anything about it and then there was the letter and . . ." She glanced up at Halim, almost as if she were looking for reassurance, and then faced the floor again. "I'm so sorry, Nicole. When I realized the letter was yours, I should have brought it to you immediately."

I tilted my head. "And why didn't you?"

"It was—There was a code. I'm in communications and it is hard for me to see a cipher and not want to crack it." She drew a breath and sat up straight, facing me directly. "We invaded your privacy and I am very sorry about that. It was unforgivable and I am ready to face whatever disciplinary action is mandated."

"Mm." I shrugged as if that were not important, and honestly, in this context it was not. What was interesting was that she had said *we*. "*We invaded your privacy.*" Again, true. They had, but "privacy" was a conversational tangent I did not need to explore. The "we," though . . . "Then what happened?"

"Given the content, we thought it best to let Administrator Frisch know. So Vicky took the book to him."

The fact that she had taken it to Vicky was consistent with Vicky's story. The timing felt off, though. "There are a couple of things I don't understand. If you don't mind helping me with them I would appreciate it."

"Of course." She knit her hands together in her lap and

leaned forward, in a picture of bright-eyed eagerness.

"Approach these in any order." I ticked the inconsistencies off on my fingers. "One: the book was checked out of the library in Vicky's name, but in your handwriting. Two: I only got the letter that morning and the airlock doors closed that afternoon. Let's say, about four hours later. So I'm curious about how the letter got into the book, then to your door, and then you were able to find Vicky and translate it in enough time for her to get to the administrator before the airlock doors closed."

Birgit's eyes blinked rapidly. "The first is easy. It was a library book and we'd hoped looking at the records would tell us who left it for her. There wasn't anything and it was filed as still being on the shelf. So I checked it out for her while she went to the administrator." She aligned her crutches with the side of her chair. "But . . . But I got the book the night before the airlock closed. At first, I thought it was someone who knew I was sick, and then there was Vicky's name."

"Sick?"

"I thought it was the flu." Her mouth twisted and she rested a hand on her left leg. Even through the trousers, it was visibly thinner than her right. "I was sick for a couple of days, and then better for about a week, and then . . . this."

"Hm . . . You got a copy of this mysterious letter before I did. What are your thoughts on how that happened?"

"That's easy. Or . . . I mean, mechanically, it is easy. Mail comes in via teletype to comms and then we have to sort it. If it came in after you checked your box, then you wouldn't see it until the next day." She shook her head. "I don't know who would have taken it, though."

"So you're saying a random person took a letter from my box, checked out the one book that could decode it, and just *happened* to leave it for you?"

"I told you! It said it was for Vicky. I got it by mistake."

Beside me, Halim shifted his weight. "Do you still have the note that said 'for Vicky'?"

"I gave it to her with the book."

I fed Birgit more silence to see what she would fill it with. The geology lab fans whirred with an almost static hiss. Outside the room, wheels squeaked as something was rolled down the hall.

Birgit swallowed. "I really am very, very sorry about reading the letter. I just . . . Can I blame it on having a fever?" She laughed nervously and then shook her head, sagging into her chair. "I'm sorry. I know better."

I could not count the number of times I had played the contrite Mädchen. Her rendition looked sincere, but so had mine. The tricky thing about reading body language is that it's only one piece of a larger whole. I mean, she certainly reeked of guilt. But one of the easiest ways to mitigate being caught is to pin your guilt to a different action than the Big Thing that you don't want to be accused of. She had jumped straight to "I'm bad" the moment I had brought up the book.

"On Tuesday, the sixteenth of April, you went to The Garden. Why?" According to the more detailed briefing Helen gave us after her big-picture synopsis, Birgit did some unscheduled work in comms for about two hours and then excused herself, not feeling well. Her BusyBee's departure time was not logged until nearly six hours after that, again with no pilot.

"To work in comms."

I waited. Birgit tucked her hair behind her ear, but stayed silent.

"The Garden has you arriving after the start of the morning shift, why so late? And then only staying two hours."

"I didn't get the notification on time. By the time I got out there, they were covered. I'd started feeling sick, so, since they didn't really need me, I left." She picked at the wrapping on her crutch again, grimacing, and shuddered. "In hindsight, I was already sick with polio. I'm just so grateful no one there caught it because of me. I keep thinking about that—I'm so, so glad I was out of the room before I started . . . you know. Vomiting."

"According to the schedule, you weren't supposed to be on duty at all."

She looked up, frowning. "No. I was."

I flipped to a page on my clipboard where I had the staff sheet from the week of April fifteenth. "I have the schedule right here."

When I held it out so she could look at it, Birgit shook her head. "That's the original one, which is why I thought I wasn't scheduled. They revised it after our rocket crashed, but I didn't see it immediat—"

The lights went out.

I straightened. This wasn't supposed to still be happening—the engineers had removed remote access to the RPCM, I thought. The emergency lights gave a brief flicker and died. We'd replaced the batteries in critical areas, but the geology lab was not one of them.

Reaching into my pocket, I pulled out a flashlight. Beside me, I heard a rustle of cloth from Halim. His flashlight clicked on a moment before mine did. In the halation of the light, I could just make out his face. He nodded toward Birgit and trained his light on her.

Whatever was happening was not something that would be solved by us running out, no matter how much I wanted to know why we'd lost power. Instead, I pointed my flashlight at my clipboard and collected my thoughts. "Do you have a copy of the version that says you were scheduled?"

"No. Why would I keep that?" She shifted in her chair, squinting against the light. "They didn't need me, anyway."

"Mm." I tapped my pencil on the clipboard, giving her just a moment longer to be uncomfortable. "Here's my other question. You missed the morning BusyBee route . . . How did you get out there?"

Birgit froze. Her eyes darted around the room, but with the flashlight in her face, she had to be nearly blind. She took a rapid breath and swallowed. "A friend flew me out."

"A friend . . . Funny thing. There's no pilot listed."

"I feel like you are accusing me of something specific, but I don't understand what." Birgit lifted her chin. "No offense, but why am I talking to you instead of Administrator Frisch?"

Defensive and, oh, so interesting that she wanted to involve Frisch instead of Eugene.

Halim leaned forward on his toes just a little. "As a

reminder, I am the chief astronaut."

"And head of your department, but I'm—"

The lights came on.

Birgit looked up and, thankfully, missed the moment of complete confusion I'm sure showed openly on my face. That had not been anywhere near sixteen minutes. What the hell was going on? I powered off my flashlight and lowered it.

Frowning, Birgit looked back to us. "I'm . . . I'm a colonist. I'm in a different department."

Halim shook his head, doing an excellent job of staying in the game. "On the Moon, everyone ranks below astronauts because we're the ones trained to keep you alive." He turned the flashlight off and stowed it. "Also, this question involves a spaceship and a pilot, which is very definitely in my department. Who flew that BusyBee?"

She clenched her hands together, staring at the floor again. "I don't want to get anyone in trouble."

"So you're saying you didn't fly it there?"

She shook her head, still looking at the ground. "I'm not certified to fly a BusyBee."

"You're a pilot." Halim shrugged. "I let you have simulator time."

"That's— Come on. I'm not stupid enough to think a simulator is the same as flying in actual vacuum."

I crouched, trying to make eye contact with her, in a posture expressing concern. My voice was couched to be low and sympathetic. "Just tell us who flew you. Don't make this worse than it already is."

She tensed before leaning forward to rest her elbows on

her knees, head hanging. "I guess we're both grounded, regardless. Only . . . He was being kind. Please. Do not let this reflect on him." Birgit took a slow breath. "Curtis Frye flew me out. We did not list it in the logbook, because he was grounded."

Curt. Curt went out to The Garden? Birgit was at least accounted for during a two-hour period, but there was no record of him being out there at all. Or did he go? There was a scenario in which she flew herself out and framed someone who would have ample reason to deny being in a BusyBee.

Bringing my chin down, I asked, "Where is the BusyBee?"

"The one we flew to The Garden?"

"The one you stole."

Birgit gaped at me. "Stole? What are you . . . ? I don't—" Her eyes widened. She gave a breathless laugh. "You think I'm with Earth First? No! *Mein Gott,* I was stupid and inconsiderate but I'm not—No. *NO!*"

"Darling." I smiled at her and it was as cold as I could make it. "Do you understand why you might not be believed when you say that?"

"I don't care what you believe. I had nothing to do with the power outages or losing contact with Earth or the Lindholms—"

"What do you mean, the Lindholms?"

Birgit cut herself short. "They were—Someone sabotaged their BusyBee."

That was a detail we had not told anyone outside our little group. Save for Frisch. "I don't recall mentioning that."

"Someone else told me."

"Who?"

"I don't know!" She ran her fingers through her hair, flattening it against her skull. "I can't believe you'd think I had anything to do with any of this. I have polio. What am I supposed to have done, dragged myself around doing all sorts of wicked things?"

"You can walk."

"Now! Barely." She hit the crutches with the flat of her hand. "This is better than Curt or Ruben, but it is not easy. I am not subtle and built for sneaking around doing any of the things you are accusing me of."

"So far, those are all from before you got sick." Folding back the papers on my clipboard, I exposed the page of ciphers, which I still hadn't been able to crack, and turned it to face her. "Would you like to explain this?"

She sighed, looking up to the ceiling. "*Mein Gott, ist ein Albtraum* . . ." She gestured at the paper. "It is a game that Curt and I play. People would run the papers between us when we were confined to bed. We were having an affair. There. Are you happy now? All of my laundry you have. What next? Firing squad? Airlock?"

"Who else are you working with?"

"I'm not working with anyone!" She flung her hands out as if she could push the question away. "Curt and I are— Do you know what it's like to be confined to the same room with him and I cannot touch him even? And you think now we are collaborating on . . . what? What exactly?"

I smiled sadly at her. "I'm sure this is hard for you. If everything is the way you say it is, then the simplest way to demonstrate that is to tell me what this cipher says."

Birgit's cheeks flamed. She crossed her arms over her chest. "I can't."

I raised my eyebrows. "Can't. That's awkward, if you really want to help us."

"I didn't crack it."

"The thing is . . . it's in your handwriting."

Her nostrils flared. "Yes. I know. I couldn't get it, so I copied a clean version to start again." She blew her breath out and stared into a corner with spots of red still flaring like alarms in both cheeks. "If you want to know what it says, you'll have to figure it out on your own."

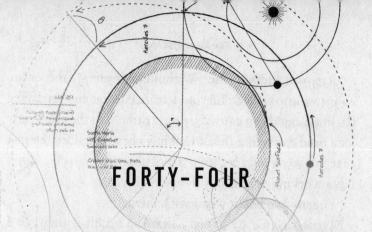

FORTY-FOUR

Artemis Base Mission Log, Acting Administrator Eugene Lindholm:

May 28, 1963, 0103—Still no contact with Earth. Tasked comms department with confirming that main radio dishes are capable of receiving by scanning for signals from anywhere on or around Earth. Have been told they will not be able to isolate any channels due to low SNR of non-IAC sources. Backup LGS is non-operational due to Aerozine corrosion from the lunar shuttle crash.

WHEN WE FINISHED asking Birgit questions, we stowed her in one of the offices that Eugene had converted to crew quarters. He'd made the door lockable. Halim still asked one of the astronauts who was a long-timer to guard it, figuring that if he was involved with Earth First, we would already be dead. It was not an entirely reassuring thought.

The moment Birgit was out of the geology lab, I turned to the intercom. "Could you hear all of that?"

Helen's voice crackled out of the small speaker. "Aside from when we lost power, loud and clear."

"What happened with the lights?" Halim asked.

"The engineering team turned the whole system off—"

"Are you kidding me? Without warning." The entire room went hot with fury as I realized that the terrifying darkness had been caused by our team. "Do they have any idea how damaging that could have been? Besides the fact that we were interrogating a possible terrorist, we don't have working emergency lights in here."

"Eugene has had a word with them."

Myrtle cut in. "By 'word' what she means is they got a 'Come to Jesus' moment of Biblical proportions."

That made me chuckle, but only slightly less likely to stab the person who had decided to just cut the power. "Why in this or any other world did they decide to turn things off?"

Helen's voice slowed down and became more precise. "They cannot find anything mechanically wrong with the communication channels to Earth and were hoping that when they powered the system back up it would reconnect to the Earth downlink automatically. It did not."

"It did not as in, it did not power up, or it did not connect automatically?"

"It powered up and went through the correct connection procedure. However, we can neither send nor receive a signal."

At my side, Halim's face was as tight as mine felt. He checked his watch. "To confirm . . . Fifteen hours and eleven minutes without contact?"

"Confirmed."

Mission Control in Kansas must be in a panic. Engineers would have flooded into the facility as everyone buckled down to work the problem and—I grabbed a chair to steady myself as a thought went through my head. Even though it was nearly one in the morning, the IAC in Kansas City would be fully staffed right now. Astronauts, engineers, technicians, computers . . . everyone would have come in.

Earth First had issued a manifesto calling for blood.

Halim touched my elbow. "You all right?"

Clearing my throat, I wanted to be in two places at once. I wanted to be in LGC to help them and I wanted to be here, talking to Curt. "Could you ask them to see if we can pick up signals from anywhere other than Mission Control or *Lunetta*?"

"They've done that . . ." Myrtle's voice was hesitant. "What are you thinking?"

Earth rotates, so there are three large radio dishes placed around the planet every 120 degrees. That used to be all we had, but they added satellites as a layer of redundancy for the radio dishes. When everything is working, the comms run through satellites around Earth to *Lunetta* and then down to Earth. Mission Control was based in Kansas City and could be relocated to Brazil or Europe, but it still took the massive radio dishes or the satellites to cross the distance to the Moon without signal loss. Losing one would still leave the others. So why couldn't we contact them?

"If we can detect other signals from Earth—even if we can't reply to them—then it's not our system."

"Nicole, honey . . . You don't have to solve all the problems."

I clenched my jaw as rage flooded through my veins in

disproportionate amounts. I had just enough presence of mind to be aware of that and to ride it out, but I wanted to snap at her that she did not need to solve all the problems either and I was certainly not a problem to be solved.

Swallowing, I let out a breath. "My point was that if everything is fine here, then something is wrong on Earth. Everyone will be at the IAC trying to reach us. *Everyone.*" I took another breath to steady myself and charged on. "And we already know they are willing to kill."

The intercom was silent for a moment and then Helen said, "I'll ask about receiving other signals."

Her voice was so even it hurt. Her husband, Reynard, was an engineer and would be there. If Earth First had decided to bomb the IAC, there was nothing we could do, but not knowing is the worst.

So what could we do? I bounced on my toes, thinking. Curt would have seen us take Birgit out of the room and note that she didn't come back. "Let's get Curt. Tell them not to turn the lights off."

"Confirm."

Halim hesitated. "Should we pause for a snack?"

I almost threw my clipboard at him. It's hard enough having Helen and Myrtle know about the anorexia. Having Halim know and nursemaid me? We work well together. I like the man. I'd even call him a friend, but he's not a close friend. More importantly, he's my boss. I do not like being reminded that he knows about this weakness.

I shook my head. "Afterward. I don't want to give Curt any longer to think about why we pulled Birgit out of the room in the middle of the night than we already have."

"It won't take that much longer." He shrugged, smiling with a real effort at innocence.

Over the intercom, Helen said, "What did you have for lunch today?"

"I forgot. But I had a sandwich for dinner. With Eugene, so I have a witness." The lie rolled off my tongue with disturbing ease. I did have a sandwich. Eugene would remember that I had a sandwich. He would remember seeing me take a bite. I had two bites of that sandwich and then we got busy. The rest of it was wrapped in foil in my pocket.

The smart thing to do would be to pull it out and finish eating it. The smart thing to do would be to not resent the friends who were trying to help.

I clapped my hands together. "Shall we get Curt?"

It was the same setup as before. Curt sat in his wheeled chair under the good light. Halim and I leaned against a table opposite him in the shadow.

Curt looked up at the light and then down to me. "So . . . I guess this is the interrogation portion of my night?"

I winked at him. "Let's get right to it, then, shall we?" Start with the known answers. "Your file says you were Air Force. What did you do with them?"

"How do you know if a fighter pilot is in the room?" He gave a wry smile. "They tell you."

Hell, if I'd been allowed to fly combat, I would have told everyone I was a fighter pilot too. I gave him a courtesy chuckle to build rapport, which was also probably what he was trying to do.

"Although since you've read my file you know I was a fighter pilot. So in the interests of complete honesty, I only flew one combat mission in Korea before we were recalled to the States after the Meteor. From there I was on reconnaissance to help spot refugees. Later, I went to test pilot school at Edwards AFB."

"Why join the IAC?"

"That was where the interesting flying was." Curt shrugged. "I mean, the answer I gave in my interview was, 'To serve my nation' and something about 'the survival of mankind' but really it was about the rockets."

"What did you do at The Garden?"

"Tricky . . ." He tilted his head to the side, eyes narrowing as he watched me in the shadows. "I haven't been to The Garden."

Interesting. He might have delayed to protect Birgit. He might have straight-up admitted it. Or . . . denial. "And yet, we have a witness who saw you there."

"I don't know what to tell you. I haven't been there." He chewed his lower lip. "You won't tell me who . . . Will you tell me when I was supposed to be there?"

"April sixteenth. Tuesday. All day."

"Huh." He rubbed his chin and frowned. "I'm trying to think if there's anyone in the new hires who looks enough like me to be confusing . . . Anyway, Tuesdays are my scheduled phone call home. I can't account for the whole span, but I was talking with my mom during part of that time."

"That's easy to check." I made a note on my clipboard. "How's your mom?"

"Fine. Although apparently, Mike is back from Venezuela

and having a hard time because Bert has uterine cancer."
His voice was relaxed and breezy as he said this, then his
eyes widened. "Oh! Wait. It's a soap opera. Sorry. Should
have been clear about that up front. Mom loves *Guiding
Light,* so a lot of our phone calls are updates on what's
happened. You should have heard her last season when
Anne got shot. Whew! Nothing but that for days. I think
she went into actual mourning— Oh, shit. Ma'am. I am
so, so sorry. I didn't mean . . . Shit."

The funny thing is that I had been so focused on trying
to read Curt that I hadn't drawn the connection until that
moment. I'd been living in the reality where I was just
doing my job and Kenneth was still alive. My heart beat
sideways, touching parts of my chest it had no right to.

I swallowed to clear my throat and turned the clipboard
around to show him the coded letter I'd found. My voice
would be goddamned level. "Tell me about this?"

Curt hesitated, still trying to look past the clipboard to
me. Damn him. As derailing tactics go, bringing up my
grief was an easy target, but that had been *so* well done.
His gaze dropped to the clipboard and he leaned forward.
"Well . . . it's a cipher."

I waited, giving him silence to fill and my eyes a chance
to clear.

He beckoned. "Can I see it? It's kinda in the shadows."

Nice try at getting me closer. I passed the board to
Halim. "See but not handle."

"Fair." Curt nodded as Halim walked it to him and held
it just out of reach.

The fans whirred as we waited for him to read through

the page of text. Curt frowned, mouth moving slightly as if he were reading to himself. "Do we know what language it's in?"

"How would you determine that?"

"Looking at common letter pairs? But cryptography wasn't really my area of interest. I just took one class in it and . . ." He shrugged. "I passed, so that was good."

I gave him some more time to look at it and also to get my own brain back on track. What had we been talking about when he derailed me? His mom. That seemed like an innocuous topic, so what had been before that? His schedule. He'd given me one thing that could be a partial alibi and then used my question about his mom to change the subject.

"May I assume you think this is linked to me in some way?" Curt was resting his elbows on his knees and squinting at the page.

"Birgit says you gave it to her."

Curt raised his eyes, brows going up. "Excuse me?" He pointed at the page. "But that's not my handwriting."

"She says she copied it over from text you gave her."

"From . . . ?" He looked back down at the page again, tilting his head to the side as if that would change his focus. "I'm trying to think of how to convince you that I've never seen it before in my life and I can't think of a single thing I would find compelling if I were in your place."

"She says you're having an affair."

"What? No!" Curt stared at me. "No. She's *married*, for crying out loud."

"That is why it's called an affair, I believe, instead of dating or going steady."

"Look—" He held his hands up as if he could stop the conversation. "Look, she's ten years older than me. I mean, she's pretty and all and yes, I definitely flirted with her when we met, but we never . . . I mean, as soon as I realized she was married I stopped, because there are things you just don't do."

I kept going as if he weren't protesting. "Is she the one that helped you with covert communications to Earth?"

He tensed and looked like he was going to yell. Instead, he balled his fists and slowly relaxed back into the chair. "Every protest makes me sound guiltier. I don't know why she said we were having an affair or that I gave her— Wait. Back up. Is she the one who said she saw me at The Garden?"

I could tell him yes. I could tell him she said he'd flown her there. But I was very interested in what he did when he had nothing to play off, so I simply tapped my pencil against my clipboard. "Why do you ask?"

"Because I *did* see her that morning." He compressed his lips and shot a glance at Halim. "She said you'd given her simulator time, and wanted her to apply to be an astronaut. She asked me to show her a BusyBee. My pilot credentials get me in, even when I'm grounded. It seemed harmless, so I did it. But I was . . . I was already starting to feel sick, so I left her in there, unescorted."

That could even be true. It was four days before we found him on the floor. The timing on polio meant he could have been having flu symptoms that seemed to clear up before paralysis. Or . . . admit to something small to distract from the larger thing you've done. The question was, which rendition of events was correct?

"Where is the BusyBee?"

Curt wiped his hand down his face. "What BusyBee?"

"The one you stole."

His shoulders slumped and he looked exhausted. "Listen . . . I want to help, but honest to God, I have no idea what you're talking about. None of this. I can make guesses, but every guess I get right makes me look guilty—like, I was right about the emergency lights, wasn't I?"

I pursed my lips. "All right . . . I'll play. What guess would you make now?"

Curt scrubbed his face, and ground the heels of his hands into his eyes. "Okay . . . Okay, since you think I'm involved, it has to be stuff that happened in April, right after we arrived and before I got sick. There have been problems with environmental controls and power outages. This last one wasn't sixteen minutes long—and please, please tell me I'm not the only one timing them."

In truth, I would be surprised if multiple people in the colony hadn't been timing them. I timed blackouts on Earth, too, just from idle curiosity.

"So we're talking about things that could have been set up in advance." He lowered his hands, and scowled at the floor. "Something is happening at The Garden. With Birgit, I guess. There's a missing BusyBee . . . Oh, and coded messages, presumably to Earth First. Heck, it could be anything from fouling the water supply to blowing up the base to scuttling the rocke— Oh. Oh . . . that's good."

I raised an eyebrow. "Good? Interesting word choice."

Curt winced. "A good guess; an appalling thing.

BusyBees fit in the cargo bays of the translunar shuttles. Load one up with fertilizer from The Garden, turn it into a bomb, and park it inside a rocket. Now you've got the bomb, plus the propellent and oxidizer to ignite. Pick the right rocket, and you could flatten everything."

"You're right. That is appalling." Also, it would involve a BusyBee being parked there for over a month and it seemed unlikely that no ground crew would have noticed. "You'd guess the BusyBee would be booby trapped, I assume?"

"Undoubtedly." Curt drummed his fingers on the arm of his chair. "Or a lava tube. Like, if there was one running near the base or something. Or . . . a parking orbit, timed to decay and crash into the main base—although I don't know how I would have gotten back from that one. Or any of them, really."

That problem, at least, we thought we understood. Icarus walked back and obscured his footprints with compressed air. For the rest, I wasn't actually closer to knowing where the BusyBee was than I had been.

At least the lights hadn't gone out.

FORTY-FIVE

Artemis Base Mission Log, Acting Administrator Eugene Lindholm:

May 28, 1963, 0300—Seventeen hours and thirty-six minutes without contact. Have requested that engineering develop a solution to allow us to flash a Morse message to Earth using the colony exterior lights. They have promised a solution in 24 hours, but cautioned that it would likely not be visible to the naked eye. That is acceptable. I have to believe that at least one Earth-based telescope is trained on the Moon.

"HERE'S A THOUGHT . . ." Eugene was lying on the floor of the gallery with his feet up on the bench. "What if Birgit or Curt set up something with the BusyBee and then couldn't follow through on it after the polio hit?"

Myrtle, who was sitting on the bench, tapped his ankle. "Are you saying we should stop looking for it the same way I should give up about feet on the furniture?"

"Both of them are wishful thinking?" Eugene lifted his hands and covered his eyes. "It's three in the morning, Myrtle. Let me put my damn feet up."

Myrtle pursed her lips and inhaled to speak.

I cleared my throat, which was as close to jumping in the line of fire as I was willing to do. "So, Halim. *Did* you ask Birgit to apply for astronaut training?"

"Yes?" He swept a hand over his hair. "Understand, please, my preference would be for everyone to go through astronaut training because it is more rigorous. Did I ask her specifically . . . Maybe? Birgit is very good with comms and we'll need that for future Mars Expeditions."

Which was consistent with both versions of reality that Curt and Birgit gave us. And being good at comms meant she'd be good at resolving a weak signal or patching into a line she shouldn't.

Turning that over in my mind, I stared at the moonscape across the gallery from me, with bright orange oxidized regolith at the foot of an astronaut taking a core sample. I was on CAPCOM when Terrazas and Halim had spotted that first patch of orange. Their shock and excitement had been infectious in the main Mission Control room and apparently left the back room of geologists nearly wetting themselves with glee.

I blinked and shook my head, trying to keep from drifting off. "What are the things we need to follow up on?"

In her seat by the door, Helen stretched. "Smartest strategy would be to take a rest period. We are at the point of diminishing returns."

"Past it, I think." Halim stood, reaching toward the ceiling with a groan. "All right, people. I am exercising my prerogative as chief astronaut and sending you all to bed."

I was so tired I could have curled up on the gallery floor and slept while simultaneously sure that my brain would not shut off. "I'm going to spend a little more time with Birgit's code."

Helen paused as she was standing, before straightening with something like an *ah-ha* on her face. "Is there a reason we aren't using the computer department to decode that?"

I opened my mouth, raised a forefinger, and blinked. "No." There was no good reason, except I kept forgetting what computers were capable of. "If I say that I think it's probably a homophonic substitution cipher, would they know what to do with that?"

She shook her head. "But if you give them the steps you would go through to break it, they can do those, but distributed between multiple desks."

"I'll write that up and—"

"Excuse me. What part of 'sending you all to bed' was unclear?" Halim glowered at us, and the man can smolder. "Out. Sleep. Reconvene at eight hundred, which is less sleep than you need. We'll meet in the cafeteria because we need to eat."

That last involved a glance toward me and then studious attention to Helen, as if I wouldn't notice.

"Could we not—" I bit it off and just started to haul myself to my feet.

"You need to—"

"Stop." I did not raise my voice. My voice was very level. My voice was dead calm. "Nagging me makes it worse. Could we not add a layer of extra importance every time we talk about food? I had my condition under control for a decade and the circumstances in which I slipped are, I think, entirely reasonable. I know how to manage it. Your concern is appreciated, but you are making me worse."

Everyone was quiet and I could feel them looking at each other, as if holding a silent conference about who would speak first. Into the midst of this, Eugene snored.

Not a small snore. A snore as if the ground had torn open and swallowed the entire lunar colony.

His arms had relaxed away from his face, and he was lying slack-jawed on the floor. "Sawing logs" is not the correct phrase, unless it is with a diesel-powered saw that has never been tuned.

Helen stared at him with the same horrified amazement that I felt. "You *sleep* with that?"

"Wax earplugs and love." Myrtle gazed at him fondly. "I'm going to let him sleep, because if I wake him up to move him, he'll try to go back to work and I'm too tired to fight."

Helen said, "I'll get you pillows and blankets."

I could not stop staring. "Why don't I remember this from when we did missions together? The capsules were tiny."

She shook her head. "It's only when he has dairy. Which we figured out because the early missions had such a limited menu."

I winced. "I gave him a ham and cheese sandwich."

"Oh, don't worry. This is all on him. The man knows better, but he loves cheese, so . . . Most days, I figure he's worth it."

When we left the gallery, a couple of the engineers were staring toward it with some concern. Halim wandered over to let them know the sound it was man-made and not an equipment malfunction. Helen went to get blankets and a pillow.

I went to the cafeteria. Because I also know better, and if I had problems—if I became a problem this week—it would be entirely on me.

FIVE HOURS LATER, I was back in the cafeteria, listening to Eugene and Halim work at deconflicting the duty roster, which acknowledged that we still did not have contact with Earth but the regular business of the colony needed to continue.

As I needed to continue. Rehydrated cottage cheese, canned peaches, toast, and scrambled rehydrated eggs with saline, pepper in oil, and hot sauce. Carefully logged.

Beside me, Helen chewed absentmindedly on a piece of toast while she read through my list of instructions for the computers.

"Compare quadgram statistics from the plaintext to quadgram statistics of English text . . . All right. We'll have to have them working at the same table so they can compare fitness levels of the text as they work." She nodded, laying the paper back down. "This is very clear. I'll pass the algorithms to the computer department with the text. I'm not sure what else they have on the docket so don't know how long this will take."

Without looking up from the duty roster, Eugene said, "Tell them I said it was priority."

"Roger, wilco." She looked at the sheet of instructions again. "Nicole . . . One question."

I swallowed a bit of peach and raised my eyebrows.

"Why were you not a computer?"

"Codebreaking is fun." I shrugged, stirring the cottage cheese with my fork. "Numbers are just . . . numbers. I can do them, but they don't come alive the way they do for you and Elm—"

Across the cafeteria, someone shouted, "Get your goddamned hands off of me!"

Near the line for coffee, a scuffle had broken out. It was hard to see details, as the knot of people surged back and forth, but it clearly wasn't about a lack of caffeine. Colonists and astronauts scrambled up from their seats around it. Eugene and Halim ran toward the mess, with Myrtle not far behind them.

"*HEY!* Knock it off!" Eugene's bellow cut through the noise.

People let him through. The initial pair was on the ground now, kicking and hitting each other in a morass of testosterone. Eugene and another astronaut grabbed one of the guys while Halim subdued the other, who was lying on his back, panting.

"What the hell is going on?" Eugene forced his guy down onto a bench.

It was Kadyn. The tall botanist had a bloody nose and the skin over his eyebrow was split. "He said this was our fault. Not being able to contact Earth. The lights. Everything. That we didn't belong here."

My hackles raised. Kadyn was a Black Caribbean British man and the other man was white. Eugene's jaw clenched, the muscle by his temple pulsing.

Halim knelt by the other man, holding him down with one hand on his chest. I recognized him from the fifth class of astronauts, one of the long-timers on the Moon. His white skin was streaked with blood, but none of it seemed to be from his own wounds.

Keeping a hand on Kadyn's shoulder, Eugene turned toward the astronaut on the ground, and his voice was frighteningly level. "Care to explain what you meant?"

He glared up at Eugene. "Come on, man. Anyone can do the math. None of this stuff started happening until that ship came in. Every time we get a new bunch of colonists, shit goes wrong. Undertrained, ill-considered—"

"Hold your tongue." Halim's voice was a well-placed scalpel. "You are grounded, pending review. And with the state of affairs, a review board is not my top priority."

I WENT TO the astronaut-pilot staff meeting, even though I couldn't fly, because Eugene asked me to. Given my choice, I would rather be in the conference room, trying to work out another strategy for finding the BusyBee. Halim stood at the front of the room next to a whiteboard that was covered with a duty roster. I held my cup of coffee, feeling bloated and gross from breakfast, and sat at the back of the room with Helen and Myrtle. The twelve astronauts around me sat in clumps, men and women, pilots and Nav/Comps alike, shoulders stiff as if they were under attack.

Which, technically, we were.

At 9 a.m. on the dot, the public address system gave

three chimes and Eugene's voice joined us in the room. "This is Eugene Lindholm, acting administrator for Artemis Base. Yesterday, you exhibited the best qualities of the IAC as you worked the multiple problems we faced. Most of those were resolved through your hard work. I'm going to briefly give you the big picture and then your section heads will take over from there on individual assignments." He paused for a moment as if waiting for everyone's full attention. "It's been a full day since we've had contact with Earth."

Everyone in the room knew that, but it's one thing to guess and another thing to hear it from a voice of authority. The pilots reacted in various ways, heads coming up to look at the speaker, or bowing as if in prayer, or staying rigid in their seats.

"I won't beat around the bush, we're in a rough spot right now. The longest communication blackout in the IAC's history was just over three hours. The engineering team has been working around the clock and can't find anything wrong on this end, so at this point, we're considering our options if the problem is on Kansas's end."

I noted he said "Kansas" rather than "Earth," which made the problem seem smaller. Slightly. Until you thought about how many people in the IAC had family who lived and worked in Kansas City.

"What I'd like to address specifically is how I want you to approach this. It is very easy to fall into the trap of blaming someone else for the problem. Blame does not lead to solutions. The IAC sent us here to build a home for the future. We have done that. There are people who want to destroy our work—but I want to be clear. The physical presence of mankind on the Moon is not the accomplishment of which we should be proudest. It is not what frightens them. What we have created here is a community. That is what they want to destroy by making us suspicious and fearful of each other. We have seen this path on Earth. We have seen the wars and injustices that fear leads to. My challenge to you—the problem I want you to work—is how to keep our community whole. I believe that we have the best of humanity here on the Moon and I believe—I *know*—you are collectively capable of solving the problems ahead of us."

He would have been a brilliant preacher. I caught one of the male astronauts wiping his eyes furtively as he sat up straighter in his chair.

"Division heads, the floor is yours. Lindholm out."

Halim stepped to the center of the room and gathered our attention with his gaze. "Our department, in particular, is going to bear the brunt of the work over the coming period. Without the satellites, navigation will be more complex between the main colony and the outposts. As a first step, while we wait for new satellites from Earth—"

"Hang on." Aldrin sat forward in his chair. "Lindholm said the engineers 'can't find anything wrong.' Can you explain how that factors in the downed satellites?"

"And the remote fuse." Mikey was frowning at the board.

"Neither of those affect communications with Earth. The satellites are strictly navigation, and the remote fuse, although concerning, has been removed and deactivated."

"That's great, but I'm more than a little concerned about the cause of both." Liz Hara gestured at the intercom speaker. "Stirring speech aside, there's a person who did both of those things. This isn't about blame, but what else is pending?"

Halim nodded, accepting the question as the legitimate concern that it was. "I'm not going to downplay this. We don't know. What I will tell you is that we have a task force that is specifically addressing it. I am aware you would like to help, but I have also read your files and none of you have worked in intelligence."

"You can say that again . . ." Myrtle's stage-whisper was unsubtle.

"Hey! I represent that remark," Lovell said, tossing a wad of paper at her.

She snatched it out of the air as it began its slow fall to the floor and mimed throwing it back at him. The levity broke the tension that had been building in the room. But the undercurrent was still there.

I leaned forward. "Seriously, though. I've worked with all of you long enough to know that you're good, intelligent people with an unrivaled strength of character. You've also worked with Eugene and Halim long enough that you should know they will not waste your skills." I hesitated for a moment before saying the next piece, because I was fairly confident I was going to cry and did not want to. But it needed to be said. I studied the edge of the table in front of me with great care. "I think you all know I have a personal investment in finding the people responsible for . . . all of this. If I am of best use as CAPCOM, I'll do that. If it's reading manuals, that's where I'll go. I am trusting the people who can see the big picture to make the decisions for the best reasons. And believe me . . . I do not trust easy. But I trust Eugene. I trust Halim."

Helen rested a hand on my back. It was as if the weight of her hand pushed the tears over the rims of my eyes. I closed my eyes, trying to tell myself that seeing me weep would drive home my words. Tears were a useful manipulative tool. I clenched my jaw and breathed through my nose and tried not to let myself descend into anything uncomfortably maudlin.

At the front of the room, Halim tapped the whiteboard. "All right. The Satellite Communications and Tracking department has come up with a plan to link the way stations' comm systems together so they can be used as a relay network for the two closest outposts, The Garden and Marius Hills. This is the flight schedule and assignments for getting those teams out there." His marker squeaked on the board. "You'll note that all flights, even on BusyBees, must now have a Nav/Comp in addition to a pilot. Any flights to the South Pole also need a copilot, since that route does not have way stations as navigation beacons and you'll be flying by dead reckoning. I want two eyes on the instrumentation and landmarks at all times. Questions so far?"

"Circling back to the communications with Earth." That sounded like Mary Marguerite Harding. Darn good pilot. Glass artist who I'd been trying to get work from for the gallery. Levelheaded as only a mom can be. "Just as a point of information. Are we sitting tight or sending a ship to *Lunetta*?"

"Both. Sitting tight initially. If the problem is on their end, we won't be able to do anything to help them fix that. It's a three-day transit from *Lunetta*, so if there's information they need us to have, it makes more sense for them to send a ship to us." Halim capped his marker. "But we're also going to prep a flight for a free-return transit to Earth if we don't hear from them within the week."

Free-return transit. It was a wonderful thing about orbital mechanics. We could aim a flight with enough precision that it would reach a planet, loop around it, and the gravity assist would fling it back to its origin. That had been the plan with the first lunar mission, in case the engines malfunctioned; the crew could have looped around the Moon and returned safely to Earth.

I saw the men and women in the room get it. I saw the tension come back. They were pilots and Nav/Comps and understood exactly what a free-return meant. The only reason to plan that for a trip to Earth was if you thought there might not be a place to dock.

FORTY-SIX

Artemis Base Mission Log, Acting Administrator Eugene Lindholm:

May 30, 1963, 0941—Three days without IAC contact. South Pole outpost reports being in good condition. We are maintaining regular shuttle flights to the Pole as well as The Garden and Marius Hills.

When dawn hits tomorrow, the engineering and astronaut departments will begin setting up a visual flight path to the South Pole to make that route safer without the navigational satellites.

Two days after I gave Helen the coded letter, I left the centrifuge room, sweaty and still breathing hard from my required 1 g exercise time. I was damned if I was letting Ana Teresa keep this cast on me one day longer because I wasn't putting a gravity load on it. If I'd been disciplined about it in the first place, it might not have rebroken when I got shocked.

As I pushed the door open, Eugene was reaching for it and we had one of those moments where we both startled at the sight of the other.

I was still calibrated to Earth gravity and jumped too high, catching my crown against the doorframe. "Gah!"

As I landed, he steadied me. "Sorry. You okay?"

I nodded, keeping my hands down instead of rubbing the spot the way I wanted to. I didn't want him to worry and it didn't hurt that much. "What's up?"

"We decoded it." Helen stood behind Eugene, with a folder in one hand, picking at the skin of her thumb with her other.

"Let's go upstairs." Eugene had a fresh bandage on the knuckles of his right hand and the "flesh" tone stood in garish contrast against his medium brown skin.

I followed them up to the lounge. "No Myrtle and Halim?"

"I've got them on flight duty this shift." He didn't even check his watch. "She'll be back at 17:30. Helen says this shouldn't wait."

Helen said, "I've only given Eugene big picture. I wanted you here for the details."

I did not like the sound of any of this or the bandage on Eugene's hand, which had not been there last night.

As we came out into the lounge, the nighttime lunar landscape lay around us in a silver-blue vista with the Apennine mountains forming a lighter black against the ink of the sky. A moment later, the lights from the landing field and a wide bank of external work lights threw dozens of stark shadows across the colony.

They blinked on and off in a rhythmic sequence spelling "APAF" in Morse. Three days, and we still couldn't reach Earth, but we could at least try to let them know that we were All Present and Accounted For. Assuming someone had turned the orbital telescope on us, or really any telescope that could see through the clouds. Sometimes the ones in Hawaii and Australia had a clear view of the night sky. Clear enough to see this message flashing in the dark of the Moon.

All Present and Accounted For.

Please, please tell us that the same is true back home. Because my mind is cruel, it reminded me that Kenneth was not present. He was accounted for, though. I blinked the sting back in my eyes and followed Helen to one of the card tables set up in the lounge. She sat down and laid the folder on the table.

Eugene pulled a chair out for me. I was still sweaty and too keyed up to sit. When I shook my head, he shrugged and sat next to Helen.

I leaned over their shoulders to peer at the folder.

Helen pulled out a map of the Moon, with two areas circled on it. One near The Garden, the other near Marius Hills. She set a neatly printed translation beside the original grease-stained copy. "The document is in three parts. The first and second parts caused the most trouble, because it was impossible to get a fitness check on it in any of our three target languages. We eventually realized we should be including numbers in our trials and it resolved into a flight plan."

Resting a hand on Helen's shoulder, I leaned forward studying it. Thrust, burn times . . . "For a BusyBee, it looks like."

"That was my assessment as well." She tapped the page. "Given this and the launch position listed, a pilot would be able to set a BusyBee into a decaying orbit that would crash into the main dome. If it was launched at the time listed, that crash will occur in two days."

Eugene flexed his right hand, the bandage wrinkling as he moved.

"However, the launch time was after both Curt and Birgit contracted polio, so it is possible the flight did not occur. If so, it is within the realm of possibilities that the starting coordinates tell us where the BusyBee is parked."

"I would very much like some good news." Eugene wiped his mouth and looked from the translation to the map of the Moon. "This is near Marius Hills, isn't it?"

She nodded. "I have a flight plan ready to go."

"And if it's not there?" I was still frowning at the pages. "Can we do an intercept course if it launched?"

"Possible."

Eugene nodded. "Work that as a contingency when we're through here. Anything further on this section?"

"Not at this time." She flipped the page to reveal three short lines. "Here we have a different set of coordinates. These are west of The Garden within an easy drive by a rover. I've compared this location with our big map and it is in the region we searched for the BusyBee; however, none of us documented anything of note."

"Huh." Eugene rubbed his chin, still looking at the page.

"The impact." I stepped around them to lean on the table so I could face Helen. "You mentioned an impact during the second blackout."

"Ah . . . Interesting thought."

Eugene's brows came together in confusion. "What impact?"

"When you and Myrtle were doing the inventory on . . ."

Helen flipped some pages in the folder and consulted her notes. "On Saturday, April twentieth, Luther Sanchez told me that the ground telemetry station at The Garden recorded an impact, but couldn't triangulate specifically where because Artemis Base was offline."

I nodded. "That was a week after landing and only a day after Curt came down with polio. If—and I realize I'm making suppositions here—but if someone launched a supply dumb drop, they would have done it before they knew he was sick. That could be the impact."

Eugene squinted one eye as he studied me. "So, you think this might be something that could survive a hard landing, sent out but not retrieved?"

"Or perhaps retrieved. Birgit didn't hit the paralytic phase until Monday, the twenty-second." I gnawed on my lower lip, looking at the map of the Moon and desperately wishing that I didn't have a cast on my arm. "Or it's a trap."

Eugene leaned back in his chair. "So . . . let me get this straight. You're suggesting that they set up a trap in the middle of nowhere on the Moon, which we would only learn about by finding a secret letter by accident in the sandwich line, in order to get . . . which two of us out of the way? 'Cause only two people fit on a rover, so it can't be all of us."

I held up my hands. "Hey. My role here is to be the paranoid one and I like to think I acquit myself admirably."

He snorted and turned back to the pages on the table. "Last section?"

"Gossip." Helen turned the page. "The target language turned out to be English and the page contains socially damaging information on a number of different people within the IAC."

I reached past Eugene to tap a name. "Not gossip. Blackmail."

Florina Morales—spacesuit technician—Husband recently promoted to project lead. Gambling debts.

I cocked my head, staring at the page. Turning over reasons that I might have given this sort of incriminating text to someone if I had been Icarus. To frame her? To get help with translation? And why would you need that if your own people had sent it to you? "Assuming Birgit is lying about not being able to decode it, then she would have a lever to use on Florina, which would get her access to a suit."

If Icarus had contacted Florina, she could tell us who she prepared an off-schedule suit for, when she did, and how long they were out on the surface. It was really the first time that I felt like we'd gotten out in front of Icarus.

Eugene nodded. "All right. Order of operations. Wargin, take the list of people and check to see if Icarus contacted them. I'll send Myrtle to Marius Hills to check the BusyBee launch site. Helen, you're on the potential drop site. Pick the copilot you want to go with you and we'll arrange to clear their schedule."

"I am comfortable flying solo to there."

Eugene made a flat negation with his hand. "No one flies solo. Not until I'm confident that we've cleared every trap Icarus has left for us."

* * *

THE DONNING ROOM hummed with the first shift coming back from Marius Hills or The Garden. Sweaty astronauts and colonists shucked out of their IVP suits chattering about the nothing sorts of things you discuss at the end of the day.

Florina Morales stood at her station by donning stand 6 conducting a post-EVA inspection on one of the colonists' suits. Her hands were graceful and sure as she assessed the seams and closures for tears or degraded material. She looked up as I approached and her gaze dropped to my cast. Florina narrowed her eyes as she straightened. "Do not for a moment think you will convince me to let you into a suit."

I laughed. "No, thanks. But I'm supposed to get the cast off next week, so we can discuss then."

"Hmph." She removed a glove. One of her dark curls escaped its ponytail and bobbed by her cheek. "And you are here . . . just to visit?"

I bent down to pick up a wrist mirror and hung it on the wall. "I have a question, but it's a bit sensitive. Have a more private place to talk?"

She paused with the thermal garment folded back away from the glove. "I do not like this class of questions."

"Fair. I don't like asking them."

Florina glanced around the room and then jerked her head toward the back. "Come on. The fans in the shop are loud enough that someone would have to be on top of us to hear."

The workshop behind the donning room was a clean industrial space dominated by a large table surrounded by women doing suit repair and maintenance. Sure, parts of the suit were sewn on a machine, but the gloves required such precision work that it could only be done by hand. Any spare bit of fabric or wrinkle felt like it turned into a rigid piece of wire when the suits were pressurized.

Florina set the helmet and Hard Upper Torso down on a workstation with her back to the table of stitchers. "So?"

There were many ways to approach this. I could ease into it. I could try to shock her by making an accusation about off-schedule suit use. Or I could simply ask. We wanted her as an ally, so I chose the closest to honest route that I could. "Has anyone tried to blackmail you to let them use suits off-schedule?"

Her brows came together in surprised confusion. "No . . . Blackmail me how?"

I lowered my voice and leaned in. "Information about your husband's gambling debts?"

Florina's face paled. "No." She grabbed my arm. "He just got the promotion. Please. He'll get it sorted out."

I rested my hand on hers. "I'm sure he will. It's okay. The debt isn't what I'm interested in." Her pupils were dilated with fear. In that moment, I realized Birgit might have told the truth about at least one thing. She hadn't been able to decode the letter. Or, she just hadn't approached Florina. I asked anyway. "No one has tried to put pressure on you?"

She shook her head. "He's a good man. He's just . . . For an engineer, you'd think he would be better with balancing a checkbook."

I recognized the terror she felt for her husband. She would do anything for him, but I didn't think that she had done anything. The desperation was the wrong shape. It was the fear of a potential future, not of something she had done.

I squeezed her hand again. "I won't tell, but you can use me as the bad guy if it'll help you get him into shape."

She laughed and then sobered. I saw the sympathy coming before I could stop her. "I'm so sorry for your loss."

"Thank you, that's very kind." I looked at the floor and did not cry. "He was the love of my life."

FOUR DAYS WITHOUT contact from Earth. I rounded the corner to Eugene's office and nodded to his secretary. She was an efficient Black woman who attacked the keys of the typewriter as if it had personally offended her.

She looked up and gave me a brief nod. "He's in."

I pushed the plastic sheeting of his office door aside. Eugene had a cup of coffee steaming on the desk and was scowling at a report, massaging his forehead.

"Careful, or your face is going to stick that way."

He snorted, and marked his place on the page. "That will be the least of my problems." Eugene turned to a thermos sitting next to the pressure kettle. "Coffee?"

"Depends. Is it poisoned?" I settled in the chair opposite his desk.

"Depends." He grabbed a coffee mug and poured. "Am I going to like whatever you're about to tell me?"

"Depends." I leaned back in my chair. "I've talked to everyone on the Icarus list. None of them have been contacted. Not by Birgit. Not by Curt. Not by anonymous note."

"Huh." Eugene frowned and handed me the cup, correctly

remembering that I took it black. "You believe that?"

I nodded. "All of them panicked when I brought up their potential blackmail lever. But when I asked if anyone had pressured them, none of them gave any sign of having been contacted."

"You sure? I could see scenarios where they were lying."

"There was no overt extra confusion about why I was asking. No regressive motion. No feigned disinterest. No self-soothing by, say, plucking at their collar."

Eugene shook his head. "Regressive motion? Self-soothing? Why did I even raise the question?"

"A question I ask every time I try to demonstrate competence." I winked over my coffee mug.

Sighing, he picked up his own mug and turned it in his hands, staring into the milky depths. "So Birgit was telling the truth when she said she couldn't translate it. Presumably Curt couldn't either. Any thoughts on why they would have a coded message but no key?"

"Some. Nothing I'm happy with." I took a sip of the gloriously bitter brew, with all the tannins and complex chocolate and nut layers that you could ask for. I'm not much for food, but can be a real snob about beverage. "One. The key was in their quarters, and if we search, we'll find it. Two. Curt translated it and gave it to Birgit to frame her. Three. One of them translated it, but didn't need to blackmail anyone. Four. They translated it but polio hit before blackmail opportunity. Five. Neither of them is Icarus."

"Come on . . . one of them has to be. How else did they get the letter?"

I raised my forefinger from the handle of the coffee mug. "Birgit said Curt passed her notes. He says he didn't. What if there's a third party that is pretending to send her notes from Curt who also left the message 'to Vicky'?"

"Occam's razor."

"So you're saying the simplest thing is that Birgit is Icarus with Curt?" I shook my head. "If they were, they would have coordinated a story that wouldn't incriminate the other. That's not the case."

Eugene drummed his fingers on the desk, gaze dropping back to the report. "Kansas is dark."

The sudden topic shift tilted the floor under me. "Excuse me?"

He rubbed his mouth and chin, looking again at the report on his desk. I waited, giving him space as if he were a mark I needed to draw out. Or just a friend, who needed to get his thoughts into alignment. In my seat, I was a picture of calm attention, but my heart raced.

"I asked the astronomy department to look at Earth." Eugene's gaze lifted for a moment, his mouth quirked sideways. "I wanted to know if another meteorite had hit."

Once upon a time, we worried about A-bombs. Those, at least, diplomacy could keep in check. One had hoped. The Meteor . . . I swallowed. "I take it there are no signs of another strike?"

He nodded. "But Kansas is dark. They used the infrared observatory, and even through the clouds, they should pick up lights. Electricity. Something . . . They can see Chicago. All of Illinois. Michigan. L.A. is a glowing mass. But all of Kansas. Most of Missouri. It's dark."

FORTY-SEVEN

Artemis Base Mission Log, Acting Administrator Eugene Lindholm:

May 31, 1963, 1834—Four days without IAC contact. Met with the agriculture department today to discuss plans for accelerating work at The Garden as part of a long-term contingency plan. We have food stores set for six months. It is unlikely that we will need to be growing all of our own food at the end of that time, but much like the situation post-Meteor, if we wait until it is necessary, it will be too late. I would rather plan ahead for making the lunar colony self-sufficient and discover that we do not need it.

THERE'S INFORMATION YOU can act on and information you can't. Knowing that Kansas was dark . . . What could we do with that? Nothing for Kansas. Nothing for Nathaniel. Nothing for Helen's husband. Nothing for my ancient cat. Or my husband's kitten. Nothing for the thousands of men and women who worked at the IAC.

But for the Moon, we could try to prepare the lunar colony, as best as we were able, for an extended period on our own. We could try to keep Icarus from destroying more things. I say this as calmly as I can, but my insides were a sodden mass of despair and fear. I wasn't afraid for us on the Moon. I had trust in the people I worked with. It would be hard, but we would work the problems as they arose.

My fear was about the news we did not have. Kansas was dark.

Not knowing is the worst.

In the evening on the thirty-first, Eugene and I sat at a desk in comms, headphones over our ears with a staticky connection to Marius Hills. Eugene had his eyes closed, listening to Myrtle and Halim . . . who am I kidding—he was listening to Myrtle.

"There's no indication the BusyBee was here." She sounded beat. "There are footprints, but we followed them all over and there are no blast-off patterns in the regolith at all. It's dark, but . . . I dunno, baby. I don't think it was here."

"Could they have wiped the pattern with oxygen tanks the way Halim wiped his footprints away?" Eugene rested his head in his hands.

Halim answered. "No. Blowing the dust around wouldn't have hidden the color change from the landing blast."

I wasn't sure if this was a good thing or a bad thing. On the one hand, it probably meant we didn't have to worry about the BusyBee crashing into the domes. On the other, we still had no idea where it was. If we were lucky, Icarus had parked it someplace and never been able to go back to it.

If we were unlucky, this was a wild goose chase to distract us from finding the real thing.

With his head still in his hands, Eugene said, "Tell me about the footprints."

"They crisscross the area, mostly running northwest by southeast, with some excursions to the side. We think there are two sets."

I asked, "Two as in two people or two visits?"

"Two people. Maybe."

Eugene opened his eyes and looked at me. "Two."

Curt and Birgit. Possibly. Or possibly one of them and an unknown other. The possibility remained open that one of them was innocent of all of this and yet another party was the coconspirator.

"Can you tell me what makes you uncertain there were two people?" I twisted the cord of the headset in my fingers.

Halim filled in the gap. "They're both wearing medium boots. The stride length is different, though. One of them is doing the skip-hop. The other is shuffling. It's either two people, or one hauling things."

"That's a good observation." It was. The suits were modular to make them as customizable as possible, but there were still a limited range of sizes. Extra-small, small, medium, large, and extra-large. "I'll ask the suit techs what size Curt and Birgit wear."

"I'm not going to hold my breath on that," Myrtle commented dryly. "We're not going to get lucky enough that one of them wears an extra-small."

"Alas. You are probably correct." Most of the people tended to use mediums or larges, so a medium boot didn't narrow it down as much as if they'd seen an extra-small. "What about stride length? Did you measure the distance between steps?"

"N-no . . . Sorry. Damn." Halim sounded annoyed with himself and sighed. "You could use that to tell height, couldn't you? I've read my Sherlock Holmes, I just didn't think."

"It's all right. It's not like there's been a study of forensics in lunar gravity." I gripped the cord so tightly my fingers turned white. I wanted to be there. I wanted to be able to look at the things they were looking at and assess it on my own. "Too much to hope that you could you tell anything about the depth of the footprints?"

Silence at the other end for a moment and I could imagine Myrtle and Halim looking at each other, negotiating who would answer me. Myrtle said, "We also didn't check that. How would we go about it?"

"Slide a ruler vertically into the impression. See how many millimeters deep it is from bottom to the rim." I shook my head, even though they couldn't see me. "It's all right. I was just curious."

Eugene had let me have my tangent and brought us back on target. "Where did they go? The footprints."

"We didn't find an origin point." Halim cleared his throat. "The problem is . . . it's quite dark. The Earth is only at a quarter and waning. We'd like to go back out there with more work lamps tomorrow. It would mean staying overnight, but—I asked the geologists here about other lava tubes in the area. We were apparently within a couple of dozen meters of a skylight for a large one, which connects to the main Marius Hills site."

Myrtle joined in and I could almost see her leaning forward as if she could touch Eugene's arm with her earnestness. "They have to go somewhere. I suppose there's a possibility we're seeing tracks from a geologist on legitimate business." She laughed, but there was no humor in her voice.

Eugene rubbed his temples. "I want a specific plan before I'll even think about authorizing you to go into a lava tube."

"Roger, wilco. We'll have that for you in the morning."

If I were Myrtle, I would have so much more to say my husband, but the radio just buzzed with the static awareness of present witnesses. Halim and I were occupying the space between them.

I cleared my throat. "Hey . . . I'm pretty beat, so I'm going to play it smart and get some shut-eye. Halim, you've been doing double duty, so let me nursemaid you for a change. Go to bed."

"I'm all right." He did sound unfairly alert. "Myrtle has had the longer day. I can finish the debrief if—"

"Halim." I cut in and gave up on subtlety. "They're a married couple. Let's you and me get scarce and let them have some time."

"Oh." I could hear his blush over the airwaves.

Eugene looked up and mouthed, "Thank you."

I winked and nearly fled the room. I was fine. I was tired. But that was all. The hollow running down my middle was just fatigue. The jittering under my skin was nothing that I was going to cater to. Twenty-three days since Kenneth had been murdered. I just needed to wait this out.

Stopping in the corridor, I pressed my hand against the wall. The jittery feeling did not dwindle.

And then the tiny part of my brain that has a sense of self-preservation asked: *What did you have for lunch?*

When had I eaten last? I closed my eyes and breathed through my teeth. When had I last filled out my log? For that matter, where was my log? What kills me is that I know I forget to eat when I'm stressed. Nothing about this was surprising. And yet. Here I was again.

I drew in a breath and straightened. Fine. I would go to the cafeteria. I would get something to eat. I would find my logbook. Then I would make decisions about what to tackle next. I would do things in that order.

I walked out of the AdminMod, pausing to perform the ritual of passing through an airlock with all the minutia of Delta-v checks and the ripple-bangs of ratchets catching. The Midtown side hissed open and I stepped through into shouting.

I raised my head, trying to pinpoint where the sound was coming from under the parabola of the Midtown dome. The far side moving toward the gallery. I leaned forward, digging in to build momentum into a lunar lope. If they did anything to my gallery, I would flay them.

Coming down the street, I burst into the clear area in the middle of the dome. Central Park. Someone had pulled up plants from Central Park. I know they are dandelions and prickly pear and at home I would think they were weeds, but here? Here it was like seeing someone set fire to Yosemite.

Across the park, moving in a knot, people were herding a hunched figure down the street. I ran forward to the edge of the group, desperately wishing Eugene were here.

"Hey! *HEY!*" Drawing in a deep breath, I bellowed, "Laaaaaadies and geeeeentlemeeeen!" as if it were the start of a masquerade party.

The incongruity broke the crowd's fixation on the figure in the middle, and I grabbed that moment of silence and ran with it.

"Senior astronaut in the house! Who has a status report for me? Stat." They turned, blinking, faces flushed from shouting, and looked at each other as if passing the hot potato with their gazes. I spotted Jennifer Weaver in the mix. A former flight attendant turned astronaut, her blonde hair was pulled back into a loose bun and she looked dangerously pissed. "Jennifer. Report."

She drew herself up and pointed behind her. "I came in after the shouting had started, but Emmett said Imanol was trying to steal plants." A young white man stood hunched against the wall of the gallery, with a dandelion clutched in his hands, white taproot like a contrail of guilt. A Basque botanist from Spain, if I recalled correctly, from the rotation before ours. So one of the group of short-timers who should have gone home when our ship arrived. I didn't know him well.

"I told him I wasn't!" He shook his head.

Emmett Baldwin was being held back by a knot of other people. A colonist, but a long-timer. One of the astronomers. A Black man, with small dark scars on his forehead and arms. He'd been in Harlem when the Meteor hit and somehow survived for months before getting out. "You have a plant! In your hands!"

"I'm doing my job!" Imanol started to step toward me,

but Jennifer blocked him with a hand to his chest. "I'm supposed to rotate plants with The Garden so we can optimize the rootstock for the conditions here. We got off-schedule with . . . during the quarantine. So there's overgrowth and stress and—"

"You were just ripping them out of—"

"I'm supposed to, you big—"

"That's enough." I stepped in between the two of them, desperately wishing Eugene were here. A Black man and white man going at each other and I was about to have to side with the white man. I did not like that dynamic. "Imanol, you go back to work."

"You're going to let him just throw them away?" Emmett's face went red and he clenched his fists. "We can't afford to be wasting food—"

"Hold it. Stop. You're getting written up and you need to think about how you want me to frame that when I speak to Major Lindholm." I walked toward him as I spoke, getting closer than I really needed to, trusting that he was reasonable. "I'll give you a moment to decide what you'd prefer. Do you want a chance to explain this to me, before I make my report?"

He sputtered, looking around the group for help. I kept my gaze fixed on him, not giving him even a hint of uncertainty in my stance. Finally, he sagged, just a little, in the arms of the people holding him back. Some of the tension leaked away and he nodded. "But I want to be on record that this is a shitty policy."

"We have not begun our chat yet, but I'll make a note." Now, I looked around the group. "Thank you for your attention in this matter. I've got it from here. If there's anything you think should go into my report . . . Jennifer, can you collect statements for me?"

She nodded with the calm competence I expected from her. Really, I expected it from all of them, which made Emmett's outburst all the more troubling.

I walked to the door of the gallery and pulled it open. "In here."

The people holding him let him go reluctantly. One of them had a red welt on her chin where she'd taken a blow, but she turned calmly to Jennifer as if nothing had happened. Emmett went into the gallery and stopped, just inside the door.

I stepped in, shutting the door behind us. He was staring at a small bust of a Black woman in a space helmet that stood on a makeshift plinth in one corner.

Walking to his side, I joined him in looking at the sculpture. Ed Dwight had done it on his last rotation as an experiment. She looked up, as if gazing into space, and had a yearning expression that seemed to beg to go beyond. He'd fiddled with a composition of regolith and water and filler and come up with something he called luna cotta. It sculpted differently than terra cotta did, with a higher grog content, but the tiny grains of glass made the clay sparkle in the light. I loved her.

She wouldn't survive a trip down to Earth.

"What happened out there?" I kept my voice soft.

Emmett sighed and dropped his gaze to the floor. "I genuinely thought he was stealing food."

"I gathered. Why?"

He rubbed the back of his neck. "It's been five days . . . Kansas is dark. No one is coming, right?"

I'd meant "what action made you think he was stealing," but he'd answered "why would someone steal." The trouble with being surrounded by smart people is that they can paint a picture as well as we can, but Emmett had a perspective I did not. I'd been safely in the middle of the country when the Meteor hit. He'd been living in a part of New York the powers that be had just "forgotten" to evacuate. He had survived, not only the initial blast, but the acid rains and the cold and the months of scarcity.

And as an astronomer, he had access to the telescopes. He could see and understand the dark patch with visceral clarity.

"All we know is that they've had a massive blackout. That would affect launches."

"Not from Brazil. Not from the Euro spaceport."

"Right. There you go, see?" I said with a lightness I did not feel. We could move the people of Ground Control, but the main relays for the Outer Space Tracking Network had been built in Kansas. With the state dark, any ship that came our way would be navigating without ground communication to back them up. It would all be up to the pilot and Nav/Comp on board. "We've been sending them an APAF signal via Morse, so Earth knows we're fine. That's going to reduce urgency to get to us. We have stores laid in for six months, and that's not counting The Garden."

"It's not producing yet." He lowered his hand and kept looking at the sculpture.

"Here, I will gently point out that keeping people from doing their jobs is not going to speed that up."

He bent his head, jaw clenching for a moment. "He didn't say any of that stuff about optimizing rootstock. Just that he was pulling plants. Didn't tell me he worked in agriculture."

"All right . . ." I thought through my options. Emmett and I did not overlap much other than when I flew him out to one of the observatories. He was a long-timer on the Moon and generally pretty easygoing. The past months had been . . . brutal. "I'm going to talk to Eugene, informally. I'll tell him it was a misunderstanding and that my judgment is it won't repeat. Is that correct?"

He swallowed. "Yes, ma'am."

"Is there anything I need to address with Imanol?" I turned to face Emmett directly. "It is not my experience that you would jump immediately to trading blows with someone."

His mouth worked for a moment as if he were swallowing several responses. Squinting, he looked back up, but still not at me, at the sculpture. "There was some language. Not the first thing he said. But . . . Why didn't he just tell me what he was doing?"

"I see." I wasn't going to make him tell me exactly what Imanol had said. That was clear enough. "I'll address that with him. I'll use some . . . language of my own."

He gave a little laugh but didn't look like he really believed me. Fair enough. Trust was earned by actions. Kenneth always said that our collective actions meant there were centuries of work to be done to prove ourselves trustworthy.

I stepped back, toward the door. "Thank you for talking

with me." I paused, watching him still looking at the sculpture. "Do you like art?"

Emmett looked around, scars pocking his forehead and making a bare spot in one eyebrow. "Mom was a sculptor. She would've liked that piece."

I looked at the luna cotta, with her gaze of hope and longing. Wasn't that why we were all up here? Trying to build a place for the future. "I'll handle things with Imanol and Eugene." I gestured toward my makeshift bench. "Stay here as long as you like."

As I left, he was settling on the bench, hands clasped in his lap like he was praying. Meanwhile, I was about to . . . educate a young man who would not understand why he was in trouble when what I wanted to do was rain down righteous indignation on him. Eugene had been right that keeping the community together would be the hard part.

I found Imanol next to Central Park, with Jennifer standing in front of him. She was projecting full Valkyrie aura, backed by Guillermo, who I hadn't even seen earlier, and Christine, one of the young Black women from the computer department. Imanol was standing with his head down, chewing his thumbnail. The dandelion rested in a packing crate on the floor with a couple of other plants. It, honestly, was easy to see why it looked like he was taking things at random.

". . . are we clear about why this is a problem?"

"I didn't mean anything." He shifted his weight. "The word is just so close to Spanish."

Guillermo sighed and stamped his cane against the floor. "No. No, this is covered in the English-language training for any Spanish astronaut heading to the United States. Even if it were not, why would you refer to him by his race in this context?"

"Well, someone had been littering!"

"Oh, for— You did not just say that." Christine threw her hands out. She saw me coming, and I had, in fact, started to move faster. She took a step back. "You know the acting administrator is Black, right?"

"That's not—" He turned to Guillermo and said something in Spanish.

Guillermo shook his cane at the young man. "No. I will not back you on this. You were wrong and you will say so. In English."

I stopped next to them. "You can practice the apology on me, and then I'll have someone escort you to Emmett, where you can issue it."

"He pushed me!" The young man's face went red and hot.

"Before or after?"

He opened his mouth. Closing it again was an answer, but he didn't apologize. He knelt and grabbed something out of the bin. "Look. See! Litter in the dandelion beds."

In his hand, he held a candy Easter egg, wrapped in dirt-stained cellophane.

I looked at him and laughed in his face. "You know who left that there? A white man. Last month, as part—"

My brain clicked, losing everything else I was going to say. I'm fairly certain I stood there with my mouth open for a moment. Why had Curt hidden Easter eggs?

To be a nice guy?

Or as an excuse for poking around in Central Park? I turned and walked to the edge of the beds, looking at them as if I were Icarus. We'd gone through his and Birgit's quarters with a fine-toothed comb and found nothing incriminating. If either of them had a key for the encoded letter, they hadn't kept it with their things. I wouldn't have either.

"How often do you change plants? Without the quarantine. What's the schedule?"

"Um . . . It depends. We try to come through weekly, though, to make sure moisture levels are okay and the irrigation system is working." The cellophane rattled in his hand. "That's why putting things in the park is a problem."

If it were me . . . The beds were filled with carefully ameliorated lunar soil, contained in a rubber liner. We'd quarried lunar granite and put retaining walls around the liner, both to reinforce it and for beauty. We were trying so hard to make this place into a home. The irrigation system meant I would have had to worry about water, but the space between the liner and the wall would be dry. A corner. There'd be a little more space there. I walked around the edges, leaning over to look at the gaps at the corners.

The second bed, in the third corner, there was a little piece of cellophane just visible. I wedged my stiff fingers into the gap to push the rubber and soil back, wrist twinging, and grabbed the little corner with my right hand.

It wasn't cellophane. It was a plastic envelope, filled with six or seven sheets of paper. My pulse was firing as if I were trying to put a plane down on an aircraft carrier. I opened the envelope, sliding the papers out.

The top page was a list of characters from *Guiding*

Light followed by a string of digits. "Holy shit . . ." I barely remembered to look back at the group. "Jennifer, I'll get your report later." Head down, still reading, I left the baffled group of people and walked straight for the AdminMod.

Curt was Icarus.

Curt's "mom" had been telling him which cipher to use based on which characters she talked about with him on the phone. I had no idea how they were getting messages up to him without someone in comms flagging strings of coded text coming up— Oh.

Oh . . . He had recruited Birgit for that. We knew they had someone on the ground. That person must have been sending the messages up when they knew Birgit was on duty. Suddenly the affair snapped into focus. He'd created a lever to use on her, which is why she admitted it and he denied it.

I turned to the next page.

It was a letter from Kenneth.

FORTY-EIGHT

Dear Nicole,

I hope you are enjoying reading the book I recommended. The two characters at the heart of it remind me so much of some of the refugees we saw after the Meteor, eleven years ago. I know that the author is writing about life after a nuclear war scenario, but I can't help feeling the parallels—though I'll grant that this is only the third of these "post-apocalyptic" books that I've read.

It's occurred to me that, in many ways, the Ring cycle could also be considered post-apocalypse, especially the third opera. The seven Valkyries (or is it nine) are faced with many of the same loyalty questions that people face today. Government or family? Duty or love?

You will forgive me for being a little contemplative today. At a rally with a whopping 115 people, two constituents asked me if space is really the way to recover from the Meteor. Recovery is not the point of the space program; it is about survival. If I had a nickel for every time they respond, "But how does that help *me*?"

I offer words such as "jobs" and "economic growth," but the truth is that I know we are going to be abandoning people. It pains me. True, we have a score of programs that are attempting to recover and salvage life here on Earth, but even if we can use lunar technology to build terrestrial underground cities, they won't hold everyone. Every third person I see is likely to die. Good lord, I am a melancholic man without you around to balance me. I'll just get a cat-o'-nine-tails and do some self-flagellation while I'm at it, shall I?

Marlowe is doing well. He is curling on the pillow by my head at night, but I think he misses you. Out of thirty days this month, I'm gone nearly thirteen nights. Perhaps if we had two cats? One of my assistants reportedly has a cat with kittens.

Be well, my love,

Kenneth

PS I forgot, again, to buy flowers for the house.

I was kneeling on the floor, halfway to the AdminMod. I didn't have any memory of kneeling. In my hands was a letter from Kenneth that I had never seen. It was filled with numbers, a coded message hidden in the conversation, and I needed *The Long Tomorrow*. The paper rattled in my grip. It was hard to see.

I HAD A letter from Kenneth.

Curt had stolen a letter from my husband and I was going to kill the bastard.

Around me, people were saying things. Someone was running.

There were more pages. There was another letter.

Dear Nicole,

The house is still without flowers for at least the hundred and fifteenth day in a row. Seven days in a week, and yet somehow, I forget on every single one. I miss you so much that I think it will take yesterday's letter and tomorrow's to say everything I want. Even then, I expect I will wake at some forgotten hour of the night with another unspoken thought.

The interview you did yesterday is playing very well, which is unsurprising. Medgar tells me it's been replayed on 217 different stations. Three different people have told me that they listened to you and that's just since nine this morning. I know it is hard on you, but, darling, you are so good at this. Sometimes I think that you should be running for office instead of me.

And then I remember that you are essentially a cat and really only tolerate people. There are, perhaps, twenty-seven people in all the worlds that you find genuinely appealing. This is one of your charms, I think, but I am somewhat biased. I might be counting high. Maybe you only like ten.

Speaking of kittens. I've been told that my staffer's cat has had six kittens. They are nearing ten weeks of age, which is the perfect time for adoption. I am sorely tempted. Not for myself, of course, but for Marlowe so that he has company. If I wanted to horrify you, I would adopt three of them and name them after famous presidents.

In all seriousness, Nicole, I miss you more on this trip than any in recent memory. Please come home to me safely.

All my love,

Kenneth

"Nicole." Eugene was in front of me, walking backwards. "Nicole. Talk to me."

Pins prickled along my airways with every inhalation. The dome of Midtown had narrowed to a tunnel of red edged with black. Two letters. Kenneth had sent me two letters I had never seen. Kenneth had sent two letters that Curt had stolen. Curt had made arrangements to have my husband killed.

I was walking toward the AdminMod. Curt was being held in SciMod. I turned. There were other people around us. One of the men held a garden trowel. I transferred the letters to my left, pinching them in an awkward grip, and took the trowel. He flinched but I was already moving again.

"Nicole!" Eugene grabbed my arm. "Hey . . . Hey. Nicole? Nicole. I need you to stop and tell me what's going on."

I twisted away from him, breaking the grip just the way I'd been taught. Curt had answers I needed and Eugene was in my way.

Wait.

This was Eugene. I was frightening him, which was a bad strategy. If I worried Eugene, he would try to restrain me. He was bigger than I was and he would succeed, unless I hurt him, which I did not want to do.

He got in front of me again, blocking my path. "Come on, Wargin. I need your report. What's the sitrep?"

Situation report.

I blinked and my lids scraped over dry eyes. He was still in front of me, waiting for my status update. Wetting my lips, I handed him the first page, the one with the keys to the codes.

Eugene glanced at it, as if he were afraid to look away from me, then did a double take. "Holy . . ." Looking to the side, he found a person in the crowd. "You said she found these in the dandelion bed?"

Why wasn't he asking me? Probably because I wasn't talking. Which raised the question of how long Eugene had been here? I was . . . I was not right.

"Okay . . . Wargin. Show me the other papers?" He reached for them.

They were for me.

I stepped back. It hurt to breathe. Eugene's eyes were wide and he looked alarmed. Not the way he was when he worried about Myrtle but as if he were assessing a threat.

Oh.

I had lifted the trowel. That had been a poor choice.

I lowered it. Eugene needed to not see me as a threat. I needed to not be a threat. I relaxed my posture, but my face was a hard mass. Lowering my gaze was the best I could do. I lifted Kenneth's letters and held them up so Eugene could see but not touch.

"Jesus . . ." Eyes wide, he looked up from the page to me, and then at the people who were still around us. "All right . . . Okay. Nicole? I want you to come with me to the AdminMod. We'll talk this through and come up with a plan. All right?"

Curt was in the SciMod. A trowel was not a perfect tool, but it was what I had. I didn't like working with my right hand, but it was what I had. I turned the handle of the trowel over in my grip, weighing it.

Eugene's gaze flicked to the trowel and back up to me. "Wargin, I need a confirmation. Do you copy?"

"Copy." The word emerged on its own from the call and response of pilot litany.

"Thank God." He closed his eyes for a brief moment and I could have gotten past him in that flash of inattention.

But that, too, would have been a bad strategy. I stayed still. No, wait. I needed to do more than that. I needed help, because the problem with packing all your emotions away so you don't become a weeping mass on the floor is that it leaves you cold and dead and ready to drive a trowel into someone's guts and watch them choke on their own blood and that would cause problems.

It would upset Eugene. It would upset Myrtle. I thought Helen would understand, but I was not certain my judgment was entirely sound. I reversed the trowel in my hand and held it out to Eugene, handle first.

He took a slow breath and reached out just as slowly, as if I were offering him a gun. "Thank you."

I dragged language out of the crypt. "I'm sorry I am worrying you." My voice sounded flat and wrong.

"I'll admit that you are." Eugene handed the trowel off to someone. "Formation flying to the conference room. Take point. I'm wingman. Copy?"

"I'm upset, Eugene. Likely in shock. I have not gone stupid."

"Great. Glad to hear it." His smile was off-nominal. "I still need verbal confirmation. Just reassure me. We're going to the conference room. Not a request. Do you copy?"

"Roger, wilco." My smile hurt, but his shoulders relaxed a fraction, so that was good. "Is *The Long Tomorrow* in your office?"

"Yes. We'll get it for you." He nodded, looking again at the letters clenched in my hand. "What else do you need?"

I needed my husband. I needed to not screw up. "A tube of applesauce. I forgot to eat lunch."

"All right." He shot a glance to the side and nodded. I heard someone moving off at a run toward the cafeteria.

"Thank you." I turned around and headed back to the AdminMod with Eugene trailing off my port side. I needed to work the problem before this dome of calm fractured.

EACH LETTER HAD five sets of numbers. Ten words my husband had tried to make sure that I knew.

GOVERNMENT HEAD BACKING EARTH FIRST
TRYING TO PROVOKE SPACE WITHDRAWAL

"He thought I knew." I slid the translated page across the conference room table to Eugene and followed the motion through to rest my head on the table next to the empty tube of applesauce. "I told Kenneth I hadn't translated his most recent letter, but he thought I'd gotten these two."

The paper rattled and a moment later, Eugene whistled.

"I wouldn't have asked him to—" My throat seized and

I braced, tensing on the table, until the wave of grief and anger rolled over me.

"He knew what he was walking into." Eugene's voice was low.

"But I didn't!" I slammed my cast on the tabletop. "There were other solutions. Other—"

Clamping down, I held on until I could breathe again. Eugene waited. I heard him shift once as if he were going to reach for me, but he only set his hand on the table close enough to mine that I could feel the warmth.

"It's okay to cry."

Three horrifying sobs tore past my guard. Sounds that should not come from the human throat. Holding my breath, I tried to stop the noise. My back shuddered with the effort of managing my airflow.

"I don't—" I swallowed. "I don't want to."

"What can I do?"

Wiping my eyes, I sat up, leaving my hands pressed against the sides of my face, the plaster a chalky cool. "Show me how you punch the wall?"

His brows went up, gaze dipping for a moment to the bandage on his knuckles. Surely he hadn't thought that was subtle.

"I can't figure out how you do it without rebounding across the room." I swiped the skin under my eyes again and lowered my hands to my lap. Everything ached with the tension knotted in my joints. "I'm trying really hard to not murder Curt."

"I'm not going to lie . . . I thought you were going to."

"Probably was."

The fans whirred, pushing air across the tears drying on my cheeks.

"It's a filing cabinet." Eugene pushed his chair back from the conference table. "Grip a drawer handle and brace with a foot against the wall opposite. But if you break your other hand, I didn't show you how to do this and wasn't anywhere near."

"I'm sure Ana Teresa will be delighted that you're afraid of her."

"The doctor?" Eugene shook his head as he opened the door for me. "Myrtle will kill me dead."

My laugh felt as if someone had stabbed me. "Leave the murdering to me." I caught his arm before I stepped through the door. "I really am sorry I frightened you earlier."

Eugene lowered his head and gently closed the door again. "Wargin. The problem isn't that you want to murder Curt. It's that you were nonresponsive. By rights, I should pack you off to medical and I'm not because . . . I understand blind rage." His gaze was level and serious. "I need you to tell me that you're okay. That I can trust you to not act without authorization."

Things inside my chest broke and tore as I drew in a breath. I pulled myself up into perfect posture, leveling out my shoulders, and nodded. "Yes, sir." I wished I had lipstick as a shield. "I'm compromised, but clear."

"Okay."

His trust nearly fractured me again. I bit my lips and looked to the wall beside the door, waiting for the burning in my sinuses to pass. I cleared my throat. "I have a suggestion you won't like."

"Then make one that I will?"

Snorting, I turned to him because I needed eye contact for this. "I think you should let me question Curt alone."

Eugene laughed once, and it was breathless as if he'd tried to stop it. "No."

"I'd want you outside the door, in case there were any problems."

Still staring at me as if I'd lost my mind, which was fair, he shook his head. "With him or with you?"

"Either is a reasonable question. That's why sending me in is an interesting choice. Once he knows we found the letters, I will be terrifying in ways that you could not be." I kept my arms nice and relaxed by my sides. "It is a ploy that stands a high statistical likelihood of making him break faster, which we need."

Honestly, I had no idea if there were statistics on things like this, but I'm good at manipulating human emotion and I knew I was right about the effect I could have on Curt. There was a twinge of guilt about trying to work Eugene, but not as much as there should be. I was retreating into that safe, calm vacuum where I could move without friction. Reentry was going to be hell later. But that was a tomorrow problem.

"So you're proposing that you rage in and—"

"No." I shook my head. "I'm proposing that I go in cold, saving the rage until the right point. He'll know it's there. The potential danger of setting me off, that's the motivator." I tilted my head and kept my voice level and reasonable. "I'll give you a list of questions before I go in.

I'll include a passphrase for the rage moment. If it's not there, then you know I've gone off script and you pull me out."

Eugene stared at me, but I could see the idea starting to kick around in his head. He hadn't said yes, but I'd opened the door to the possibility.

I smiled, aiming for the right degree of self-aware dry humor. "Heck. If you have to pull me out kicking and screaming, Curt will see you as a savior and that bond will increase the likelihood he'll talk to you. So, even if I lose it, it's still a win-win."

"Unless you kill him before I get in there."

"Flatterer." I shrugged. "You can frisk me for weapons before I go in."

"I'm not sure you need weapons. Don't— I see you. Don't try to push this right now." He put his hand on the door. "Let's go punch a filing cabinet."

EUGENE LET ME join him when he called Helen to get her update on checking the coordinates near The Garden. He hadn't said anything else about my suggestion and I knew better than to push. My right hand ached from slamming against the filing cabinet and that small finite pain made quantifiable sense. I knew why it hurt. I knew how long it would last.

The control was seductive. It was probably not a safety valve I should reach for often.

Speaking of control, I had picked up a packet of crackers on the way to talk to Helen. It wasn't a lot, but I was disproportionately proud of myself for doing it. And equally ashamed that I was just breaking a cracker into smaller and smaller bits as Eugene caught her up.

When he was finished, her voice crackled on the line with awful static as she began her report. "The coordinates were not an impact site. They pointed to the landing site of *Artemis 17*, which I feel that I should have caught, but looking at old missions did not occur to me."

I had been on that mission. It had been me and Terrazas with Elma orbiting above us as Nav/Comp. What had we done that would make someone go out to visit the site? I started running through the list of experiments and mission goals, trying to drag something—

"Oh, shit." I put the bits of cracker down and pushed the packet away. "I was on that. We were testing a jet pack."

"I remember that." Eugene sat forward. "I was jealous because I wasn't out of training before they decided not to build more of them."

"The design was questionable, and the rovers worked better for most things. We left it on the surface. Is it there? Six legs spreading out for stability around a middle backpack. Looked like a spider?"

Helen was quiet and I could imagine her replaying her visit. "No. I did not see that. What I did note were parallel lines leading away . . . I think they are ski tracks. They intersect with and are obscured by the rover path between The Garden and the cargo ship landing pad."

Eugene massaged his forehead. "Just one set of ski tracks?"

"Multiples. Too overlaid to count."

Even without getting the coordinates from the coded message, if Curt had known they were sending him to retrieve the jet pack, he could have figured out where from publicly available information.

Eugene looked at the ceiling. "I am ready to have some answers instead of endless questions." Sighing, he closed his eyes. "All right. We know Curt has a coconspirator. There were two sets of footprints at the Marius Hills site. Helen . . . you're at The Garden. Can you look at the logs to see if any of the skiers were out there?"

"I already came to the same conclusion when I saw the ski tracks and have looked." Naturally she had, because Helen was the kind of casually brilliant person who thought playing two chess games simultaneously was fun. "The day the quarantine lifted, Philippus Fourie is logged as arriving at The Garden on the morning shuttle and returning on the afternoon one. He was not scheduled for work that day."

Eugene ran a hand down his face and sighed heavily. "Naturally."

I almost knew the name but could not quite pull it to the front of my brain. "Who?"

"Remember the South African guy in comms that day? The one who didn't like me being administrator?"

I dragged the moment forward out of my memory and saw the guy sitting hunched behind his copy of *Popular Mechanics* trying not to wilt under the force of Eugene's gaze. "Blond guy? Wide-set blue eyes?"

Nodding, Eugene looked like his teeth hurt. "Construction. PhD in material sciences from University of Cape Town. He's the guy who made Faustino's skis."

"Well, shit." Admit an easy, known guilt to draw attention away from the larger one.

"So there's a jet pack, a missing BusyBee, explosives, and a fully mobile bad actor loose in the colony."

"Curt practically told me . . ." I groaned and leaned back to stare at the ceiling. "When he was talking about a decaying orbit for the BusyBee he said, 'But how would I get down?' The jet pack would do that."

Eugene shook his head. "Why would he tell you?"

"I don't know." Taunting me? Bragging? Trying to warn us because he was having second thoughts?

Helen's voice slowed, becoming more precise. "I have just done some back-of-envelope calculations. There is nothing to prevent the BusyBee from being launched at a later time with the same parameters. It would only delay the crash date."

Eugene clenched his fist on the table, light bandage stretching across the knuckles. "We'll pick up Fourie. Get him locked down. And Wargin . . ." He looked across the table and my pulse sped up in anticipation. "You get to talk to Curt."

FORTY-NINE

Artemis Base Mission Log, Acting Administrator Eugene Lindholm:

June 1, 1963, 0112—Entering the fifth day without contact. We've apprehended Philippus Fourie and have him confined in an office under guard. I am authorizing Nicole Wargin to question Curtis Frye and I take full responsibility for this choice.

"I was joking about frisking me." I faced the wall down the hallway from the converted office where Curt was being held. My arms were outstretched, with a clipboard in my right hand and a partial tube of applesauce in my left.

"I wasn't." Eugene was methodical and impersonal as he ran his hands down the sides of my legs. "I know your sense of self-preservation is null and void right now, so let me be very clear. Your actions will reflect on me because I am making the judgment call that you are stable enough for this."

"I am."

"You are not stable." Eugene stood and came around to my front, checking my pockets, bosom, and rib cage area as if I were a mannequin. "I am trusting that you are stable *enough* because I have damn few options. I'm not going to make threats, because I don't think you care right now. Am I wrong?"

It took me a moment to swallow. "No, sir."

"So what I want you to hold in your head is that I am a Black man and if you hurt Curt, or let him hurt you, it will *all* come down on me. People won't know that you were a spy in the war. What they'll know is that a Black man ordered a white woman—a grieving widow—into a dangerous situation. They'll wonder what sort of 'savage' would do that. Do you copy?"

"Copy." A different form of grief and rage pulled my shoulders down. He was right and I knew exactly how that would play. "Yes, sir."

Eugene stepped back and held out his hand. "Clipboard."

I lowered my arms, frowning. The clipboard was an important prop.

"If you hesitate to follow *any* order, I will take it as a signal that you are unreliable." He did not move his hand or issue the command again, just looked at me with an unflinching gaze.

I handed him the clipboard.

"Good job not asking why." He tapped the edge of the aluminum board. "You can't take weapons in."

I knew better than to protest. Partly because he was not going to tolerate any pushback from me, and partly because I had thought about what the edge of a clipboard could do to a windpipe.

He removed the notes from the clipboard and held them in one hand. "Confirm the passphrase for the 'rage' moment?"

My voice was so level it hurt. "You bastards murdered my husband."

Eugene nodded. "And the next parameter?"

I was allowed to improvise, but he didn't trust me to not get carried away, which was fair. "I am not allowed to use profanity except that phrase, in order to demonstrate to you that I remain in control."

He held on to the clipboard, but handed my scripted list of questions back to me. "If you don't get him to talk, that is not a failure. Physical harm to either of you is. Am I clear?"

"Yes, sir."

"Finish the applesauce."

I wanted to make a crack about how Eugene had become my Space Dad, but I was pretty sure he had no sense of humor at the moment. I unscrewed the lid and transferred the tube to my right hand to squirt some of the grainy sweetness into my mouth. It had gotten warm in my hand and was more like unflavored pie filling than anything else. It had enough liquid in it that it didn't cling to the roof of my mouth and was easy to swallow.

Mostly. I could feel each mouthful drop into my stomach and lodge there. Eugene waited, looking just over my shoulder so he wasn't staring at me while I ate. He was still watching me out of his peripheral vision, and I resented that even as I knew he had to.

I managed a half-dozen swallows before my body sent a warning wave of queasiness.

Yanking the tube away from my mouth, I stared at the wall, breathing through my nose. When I swallowed, the back of my throat was burning and sour. Eugene's gaze shifted to me. He waited.

I closed my eyes and tried to wait for the queasiness to pass. Shit. "If I finish this, I'm going to throw up." I managed to sound as if I were reporting on engine trouble. "I'm sorry."

"All right." He sighed and fabric rustled as he shifted his weight. "Nicole . . ."

"Please don't be kind." Opening my eyes, I tried to cap the tube and fumbled the lid, dropping it. I didn't curse, to demonstrate that I had control of my brain, if not my fingers. "We want me to go in cold, so I don't want to start crying yet."

"Noted." He snatched the lid off the floor and held out his hand for the tube. "I'll be right outside the door."

I'm not sure if that was to reassure me or him. Or to warn me. Probably the latter. He led me down the hall to the room where we were holding Curt. Eugene stepped to the side of the door. I held up my hand to get his attention. It had occurred to me that he needed to see me put on the mask so he would believe I was at least starting off in control.

I gestured at my face and mouthed. "Watch."

He cocked his head, brows coming together in a question.

Looking away from him, I took a slow breath and deliberately thought about finding Kenneth's letters buried like part of his corpse. I used the memory of pain and rage to shift my posture forward. My fingers curled toward my palm, not quite into fists. My head tilted down, pushing forward with just a touch of aggression. The animation in my face bled out on the floor, leaving an expressionless facade.

I said I was letting Eugene see me put on the mask, but it was probably more accurate to say I was taking it off. I'd been pretending to be human for him and that was not, at all, what lay under my skin.

Pivoting, I opened the door to Curt's room. The lights were off inside. The hall light sent a shaft of amber slicing across his bed. He opened his eyes, blinking at my silhouette in the doorway.

I stepped in and reached to the side, flicking on the overhead light.

"Nicole?" Curt rubbed his eyes and pushed up in the bed with his arms. "What time is it?"

In a room without a watch or clock, there was no way to judge the passage of time. He could have been held for a day or a week and the only thing to let him know the difference would be the weakness of his own body. The urge to piss or shit. The urge to eat.

I pulled the door shut. Leaning against it, I watched Curt and very deliberately put my hand on the lock. "I found the letters."

He frowned as if he had no idea what I was talking about. "Letters?"

"It took some doing, but I convinced Eugene I was calm enough to be the one to question you." Very gently, I twisted the lock, easing it home without a click. "He's standing right outside. For your safety."

Curt's gaze dropped to my hand on the lock. Just for a

moment, I saw his pupils flare as he understood that he was locked in with me. "Okay . . . I see a problem with that."

I pulled the room's one chair away from the wall and set it down facing him. Leaning forward, I rested my hands on the back of it. "He even frisked me to make sure I didn't have a weapon." I rocked the chair forward on its front legs, getting a sense of the balance. It was plastic with aluminum legs, like most of the other chairs in the colony. "You know how I found my husband's letters? The Easter eggs."

He watched me testing the heft of the chair. It didn't have a lot of mass, but it had plenty of hard edges.

"I wondered, why would you go to the trouble and expense of bringing up candy eggs to hide in the dandelions."

Curt was very good at looking confused and a little frightened. The latter was probably a real emotion that he was trying to use to mask other reactions. "Because it was Easter? Also, I was the new guy and figured I could bribe people into liking me."

As if he had not spoken, I lifted the chair again, flipping it over. It was an elegantly simple design with a single six millimeter bolt going down into the main shaft of each leg. Just twist to the left to unscrew it and voila, a club. "How's your mom, Curt?"

"Well, there's no way for me to know, is there. Even if you didn't have me locked up in here, last I heard, we didn't have contact with Earth." His posture was fairly relaxed, but the vein in his neck was beating visibly now. "Or has that changed?"

"Does she still like soap operas?" I unscrewed the chair leg, watching him.

"Lives for them." He pulled a pillow around into his lap as if he were fluffing it. If it were me, that pillow would either be a shield or hiding a weapon. "She's going to be pretty worried because I missed our weekly call."

"You know the soap operas are what gave you away, right? Should never have told me that you and your mom talked about *Guiding Light*. But it was such a good opportunity to get in a dig about my husband. Derail me a little." I got the leg off and laid the rest of the chair on its side on the floor. "Drop the pillow off the side of the bed."

"Oh, come on—"

"*You bastards murdered my husband!*" My throat hurt. I slammed the chair leg on the mattress, right next to his foot.

Curt couldn't flinch away from the club. He stared at the chair leg resting on the mattress a centimeter from his leg. He'd have felt the impact on the covers. He'd have heard the hard slap of it, even if it hadn't made a sound that would travel outside the room.

He was breathing fast now. I set the chair leg down gently on his right leg. "Drop. The. Pillow."

The fans whirred as he hesitated.

I raised my right hand, with its makeshift club, not taking my gaze off his face. I snapped a smile on, full grin with a painfully cheerful voice. "Funny thing. I was a spy in the war, basically doing your job. Get in. Make people like me. Cause chaos. Did that come up in your briefing for this mission?"

If I brought it down now, it would slam into his ankle.

"Curt. Darling. I have nothing to lose. Are we clear?

You took everything I actually cared about. You took my one reason for going through life as if I were a good and decent person. The way I figure it, you weren't planning on still being here when the sh—stuff hit the fan. If you were on an actual suicide mission, you wouldn't have tried to warn us about the things that might be fatal to you. You still have a sense of self-preservation. I don't. So you're going to drop the pillow and then you're going to answer my questions."

The vein in his neck pulsed like he'd been running. A bead of sweat made its slow way down his temple. With an almost audible snap, the resistance drained out of his body. He shook his head, shrugging. "What the hell . . . This will be easier." Curt dumped the pillow off the side of the bed.

It hit the floor with a hard metallic thump.

"Easier than what?"

"Than trying to warn you about pending problems without getting caught as the person who caused them." His smile was bleak. "Tricky. And you've been slow on the uptake."

"Curious. You set up a series of disasters and then . . . I'm to understand you had a change of heart?"

"Polio changed things. Yeah."

I pulled the chair leg away from him and walked back to the chair itself. "I'm going to ask a series of questions. You're going to answer them fully and completely."

"I didn't have anything to do with your husband's death."

The entire room went red and hot. I clenched the chair leg so hard that my fingers cramped. Only by stopping completely. By holding my breath. By planting. Only by freezing myself was I able to keep from driving the chair leg into his temple.

Eugene had been so right to tell me I wasn't allowed to have a weapon. My hands were shaking with the flood of adrenaline as I knelt to screw the chair leg back into place. This was why I had a script. I laid the folded paper on the floor and wished I had my clipboard.

"Where is the BusyBee?" The leg slid off the bolt and I had to pause.

"If you found the letters, then you have the codes, so I'm going to assume you already found the BusyBee and are testing me." He sighed and leaned back to rest his head against the wall as if he were exhausted. "You've got the coordinates. There's a lava tube close to that, which connects to The Garden. If you give me a map, I can draw the route to the entrance."

"How do you have it booby trapped?" I managed to get the leg seated on the bolt and started to twist it back into place.

Curt scowled and shook his head. "I don't."

I raised my eyebrows. "Fully and completely."

"Honest to God." He crossed himself. "I didn't have time. In the original plan, I was supposed to go back to it, but I also wasn't supposed to get sick. Heck, I was supposed to be gone by now. The whole colony was supposed to evacuate. Look—I've been trying my best to warn you about the things I set up. That has to count for something."

I lifted the chair and put it back on its feet. Leaning on the back, I studied him. "It's not exactly a sign of virtue when it's self-preservation."

Curt's jaw clenched, and he ran his hand over the blanket covering his legs. "I'm not the only one this affects. Like, Garnet won't survive reentry."

It took me a moment to find a connection. Garnet was one of the polio patients who had been in the women's ward with a reedy thin voice because the polio messed with her lungs. Not enough to need an iron lung, but bad enough that she was on oxygen.

"Ah. Right. Altruism." Though in truth, I had not known Garnet's condition was that bad.

"Yes. Altruism. This entire space program is basically a eugenics project." He sat up, leaning toward me as if he could convince me of his righteousness. "You haven't thought about the people who won't get to come up here? The people who don't have the right education because they're the wrong color? Or the ones whose health is just a little off-nominal?"

I did not scream at him. I did not shout that I thought about that every day, because I had a husband with a heart condition. I *had* a husband. I did not take Curt's bait any more than I already had. I waited out the heat, pushing air through my clenched chest, and then I sat in the chair. I bent down to pick up my list of questions from the floor.

"Let's start with your plan. I want you to step me through what you did." Eugene had wanted me to start by asking about sabotage that was still pending, but I needed things I could verify before we moved into unknown territory.

He spread his hands. "I want to be up front, before we start, that I'm not giving up anyone else. You get me. That's it."

"We decide what's appropriate."

He shook his head. "No. This is the deal. I'll talk about myself and my actions, but you absolutely do not get anything about anyone else. No names. No genders. No personal details at all."

I shrugged. "You can try. We'll see how long it lasts. The original plan?"

He sighed, with his lips compressed. "The idea was to make the IAC withdraw from the Moon with a minimal loss of life."

"Minimal loss." I raised my eyebrows. "You hit the CO_2 scrubbers."

"Yes. I know. I also tried to warn you about that. I could have ruptured the dome. We were hoping if we did enough small system failures the IAC would order an evacuation." He gestured at his legs. "Polio wasn't in the plan."

"Why did you give Eugene food poisoning?" That was a bluff, because I only guessed it was deliberate.

He didn't bluster. "I needed him out of the pilot's chair. I was supposed to make the landing look bad. Make it look like another unsafe rocket."

I crossed my legs, watching him. "But you snapped it down too hard, didn't you. Breaking the landing strut was an accident."

That made him blush, oddly. As if messing up as a pilot was the worst thing he could do. "I'd never landed in lunar gravity and misjudged. It's not like I could practice it in the simulator. I didn't plan on getting grounded. That . . . complicated things." Curt smiled and it was grim. "But I didn't lie to you when I said I could fake a misfiring thruster."

"I need a complete list of the sabotage you set up after landing." Taking notes with my right hand, on paper on my knee, was going to be a mess. I wanted my clipboard. "Take a minute to think about it while I bring Major Lindholm in."

Curt watched me as I went to the door and unlocked it. The lock snapped open with an audible click. Shit. I'd been so good about securing it quietly.

Eugene was standing right by the door. He looked from me to the lock and gave me the kind of glare that suggested, strongly, I was going to get a very serious "come to Jesus" talk later. That was fine. It had worked and he hadn't told me *not* to lock the door.

"May I have my clipboard, or would you like to take notes?" I smiled at Eugene.

Based on the look he returned, I imagine his sons did not get out of line very often. Eugene held the clipboard out and followed me into the room. I sat in the chair facing Curt again, with Eugene looming behind me.

Once my papers were clipped back into place, I nodded to Curt. "Start talking. List of sabotage."

"The plan was to set up as many delayed reaction problems as possible for two reasons. It gave me a chance of having alibis when things went wrong and we also figured I had maybe two weeks before getting caught. The more things I could set up at the beginning, the better."

I leaned forward in my chair, just a little. "That's not a list. That's a rationale."

His jaw clenched. "All right. I swapped out filters in the CO_2 scrubbers in all the modules with a fake. I used perchloric acid to make a time delay to disable the dehumidifiers. I added moon dust into the fuel tanks of the BusyBees and rovers. I disabled smoke detectors. I stripped wires to increase the likelihood of shorts." He looked at me and winced. "I was going for small shorts and I'm genuinely sorry you got hit."

Doubtful. More likely, he was trying to pull suspicion away from Birgit now that he'd decided to talk. "You'll need to tell us where you stripped them."

Curt shrugged and shook his head. "At random, everywhere. Any time I was alone in a room, I'd open the nearest panel and fray things."

"Continue."

"I emptied emergency oxygen masks. I've punctured the oil drums on the fans, which is taking longer to fail than I expected. There's a slow leak in the seal of BusyBee berth six. Hoping for a rupture, but it's being more resilient than I'd like." He frowned and looked at the ceiling. "I think that's everything I got to before the nineteenth."

"The nineteenth?"

"Friday, April 19th. It's the last day I walked. Kinda remember the date, just a little."

Here is where I was supposed to feel sympathy for him. I did not. "The list seems incomplete. For instance, you haven't mentioned the fertilizer you took from The Garden." Or sabotaging the Lindholms' BusyBee, or the remote-control fuse, or the jet pack.

"Yeah . . ." Curt sat forward. "Here's the thing. We're still cut off from Earth, right?"

From behind me, Eugene said, "What do you know about that?"

"I know what the plan was when I left. There were two schools of thought in our group. I favored the first plan, which was to try to get the IAC to lose enough credibility that people would stop throwing money at you and start taking care of things on Earth. That didn't work." He glanced at me and wet his lips. "So, we're getting more . . . direct, in our action."

I gripped the clipboard, pressing it into my lap. He was trying to piss me off to distract me. This was not how someone with a change of heart behaved or cooperated. This was how someone who had been caught attempted to still cause problems.

Lifting my pencil, I tested the point, watching Curt. "Less commentary. More details."

"They've blown the radio dishes, deorbited the communication satellites, including the two for the Mars Expedition, bombed the IAC, and taken out the power grid for the area surrounding Kansas City." Curt's voice was level and matter-of-fact like someone discussing a flight plan. "There's no one to come to your rescue."

"Slight miscalculation there. This is the *International* Aerospace Coalition. The spaceports in Brazil and Europe are still fine." The Garden was designed to feed thousands, and while it was still young, we had six months of stores and only 326 people to feed. It would be difficult, I had no doubt about that. I also believed this group of people could do it. "Even if they weren't, surviving without the Earth is exactly what this colony is designed for."

"Sure." Curt shrugged. "And as long as you're up here, people on Earth are going to want to come to your rescue.

I told my group this would just make 'saving the Moon' a project. So what we want is for you to voluntarily abandon the Moon. Minimal loss of life."

Behind me, Eugene said, "Why the heck would we do that?"

"Because it's the right thing to do. Jeremiah 22:3: 'Thus saith the Lord: Execute judgement and justice, and deliver him that is oppressed out of the hand of the oppressor.'"

"There's more to that verse than that." Eugene shot a glance at me. "'. . . and do no wrong, do no violence to the stranger, the fatherless, nor the widow, neither shed innocent blood in this place.' You have shed innocent blood."

"Verse 13. 'Woe to him that buildeth up his house by injustice, and his chambers not in judgement: that will oppress his friend without cause, and will not pay him his wages.' People on Earth are dying and the resources being pumped into this are criminal. For what? The Meteor was eleven years ago. There are still people in North Carolina without running water and—"

"I don't need your monologue." I jumped in before they could continue arguing theology. "I just need to know what you did."

"All right. Then moving to plan two is on your heads. You want a reason to abandon the Moon? Here it is. I wired Marius Hills and the main colony to blow. It's remote controlled." He folded his hands in his lap and leaned back against his pillow. "When you regain contact with Earth, if the United States government has not agreed to withdraw from the Moon and funnel money into helping our own people, then Earth First will set off a remote detonation. That's why I didn't damage any of the main ships, just FYI. Let me know if you need help planning the evacuation. I already did the preliminary work. You're welcome."

In my head, a film played in which I stood up and backhanded him with my hard plaster cast, sending blood in a slow spray across the walls. Curt's head would snap to the side and I would feel the contact in a jarring sting up through my elbow and to the base of my teeth. Eugene might or might not try to stop me.

Instead, I moved my pencil to the next item on the list. My breath was hot in my lungs but I kept my posture relaxed. "Next question. What instructions did you give Philippus Fourie? Just a reminder, we have him in custody so we'll be cross-checking your answers. You're welcome."

I would be damned if I let this man control me.

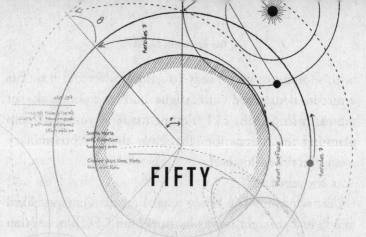

FIFTY

Artemis Base Mission Log, Acting Administrator Eugene Lindholm:

June 1, 1963, 0337—Maintenance order: Overhaul all fans, checking for damage to oil drums.

THE PAGES ON my clipboard were covered with notes I had taken as Curt talked. At some point during the hours we questioned the man, Eugene brought in another chair. He sat next to me, occasionally interjecting a question, but mostly just looking intimidating.

As Curt yawned wide enough that his jaw actually popped, I flipped through the pages. "What was Faustino doing for you when he died?"

He was fatigued enough that for a moment his constant slightly cocky mask cracked and I saw what looked like a real emotion. Regret. Curt sighed and lowered his hand. "Nothing. And I wish to God I hadn't introduced him to the skis." He looked down at the covers, tugging on them. "Funny, that that's the thing I feel guilty about."

"But you did use the skis?"

He nodded. His hair was tousled out of its crisp part,

with mouse-brown strands sticking up like old hay. His entire body drooped with fatigue, and I did not think that was an act. "Yeah . . . Philippus made them, which you already knew, but he thought it was all aboveboard."

Eugene raised his eyebrows. "Nothing about those skis was aboveboard."

Curt winced. "You know what I mean. They just liked skiing and thought it was harmless fun." Stifling another yawn, he said, "Philippus probably told you he helped me move some gear. He legitimately thought it was a work assignment but that we were cheating by using the skis to make it easier."

That did, actually, match what Philippus had said, although with a great deal more crying. "What gear?"

"Fertilizer. We transferred it out of the lava tube to the jet pack and then I moved it to . . . a surprise location." He spread his hands and shrugged. "Sorry. I'm not giving up where the bombs are."

"Mm . . . you did already, actually." Flipping through my notes again, I ran the pencil down the page. I made a random tick mark. "Just circling back, Birgit's involvement was also 'innocent,' you said. Seduced her, et cetera. I didn't catch how you were going to explain the contents of the coded letter you asked her to translate for you. Just curious, really."

"She . . . she liked codes." Curt looked like he was trying to figure out if I was bluffing about knowing where the bombs were. That was fine. He could enjoy wondering. "Part of the seduction was pretending we were both secret agents. It was like a game of dress-up. She liked handcuffs, if you know what I mean."

"Yes, those can be fun with the right person." If he thought he was going to shock me, he had been paying no attention. On the other hand, Eugene coughed and lifted his glass of water, so that could have been aimed at our clean-cut leader. "You might remember, in the letter you stole from me, that my late husband mentioned a cat-o'-nine-tails. It's mink."

Eugene sprayed water out of his nose. Curt's mouth dropped open and he went flaming red. I will honestly never understand why men, who seem to spend so much of their lives thinking about sex, get so flustered when a woman discusses it.

I ignored the fact that Eugene was wiping his chin and nose on his sleeve and carried on, watching Curt. "The problem I'm running into is that Birgit already told us about the affair, so 'I thought it was a game' would have been a natural thing for her to bring up as a defense."

Curt shook his head, shrugging. "I don't know what to tell you."

"All right." I turned to Eugene, who did not look much less tired. "I'm finished. Did you have any follow-ups or circle-backs?"

He pursed his lips, studying the bastard. "No."

"Let's go." I stood and the room spun around me. It's not a good thing that I have enough experience at almost fainting that I know how to wait it out. The edges of the room snowed dark ash for a moment and then things steadied. I tucked my clipboard under my arm and turned very carefully to walk out of the room.

When we got into the hall, Eugene locked the door behind us and gave instructions to the astronaut on guard. I waited, with one hand against the tunnel, until Eugene joined me.

"What do you thi— Are you okay?"

"Dizzy." I am very proud of myself for not lying to him. "I need to eat something."

He inhaled, nodding, and looked down the hall. "Lounge? I'll get a tray for you?"

"Thanks." I straightened, steady enough to go upstairs and grateful not to have to face even the tiny late-night crowd in the cafeteria.

"Anything you . . . find appetizing?"

"Caesar salad and a rare steak?" I'd meant for that to be a joke since neither was available on the Moon, but the image of Kenneth whisking egg yolk in a bowl came to haunt me. I bit the inside of my cheek and then cleared my throat. "Sorry. Kenneth always . . . Here, the peaches usually work. Cottage cheese, sometimes."

Eugene nodded as if we were out together at any normal restaurant and I was placing a completely normal order. "Copy. I'll run— Or. Or I could use technology and ask someone via the intercom to bring us both some food."

"Glad we're both brilliant." I smiled at him as we walked to the stairs to the lounge. "And in answer to your question, Curt spent most of the time sowing disinformation mixed with just enough truth to make us check every statement he made."

Eugene paused to let me precede him up the stairs. "And . . . *do* you know where the bomb is?"

"Oh yeah." I hauled myself up the steps. "It's still in the BusyBee. The jet packs can't carry a load. That's why we didn't use them after the test. They're unstable. The footprints Myrtle and Halim saw are him loading the jet pack, realizing the problem, and then unloading it. Stride length is different because he was tired or having the first signs of leg weakness from the polio."

"Um . . . And Fourie going out after the quarantine lifted?"

"Retrieving his skis. Curt wants us to think that he's got the main colony rigged to blow, which is why he wants us to think that Fourie helped with unloading the BusyBee. Three problems there. One. We found the main colony detonator. Two. The aforementioned difficulty with the jet pack. Three. Despite Curt's efforts to confuse us, the logs give us independent verification that Fourie went to The Garden outpost, not Marius Hills." I did not remember the staircase being this long. "Also . . . Curt is not pushing to get moved elsewhere. He's not worrying about anything happening to the main colony."

"Just to be clear. The BusyBee is rigged as a bomb in the lava tube that Myrtle and Halim want to explore in . . . four hours?"

"Yes. Tell them not to go in." I finally walked into the lounge, squinting against the long shadows of lunar dawn. The brilliant sunlight, even with the polarized glass, was a jarring contrast to the wee hours of the morning. "We'll need to get . . . I dunno. Mavis and her team out there to defuse it."

"That's not in your skill set?"

I snorted and dropped into a chair. "I was a spy, not a bomber." Exhaustion threatened to pull me down a gravity well of fatigue. "Oh, and Kenneth doesn't have a mink cat-o'-nine-tails."

The present tense sat there.

Eugene opened his mouth and inhaled, shaking his head as it turned into a yawn. "I didn't think so."

"It was suede."

He choked on nothing. It was impressive. Pounding himself on his chest, he watched me slowly smile. Eugene shook his head. "I am, suddenly, very glad you never played poker with us."

"Actually, it was zebra."

He rolled his eyes and went to the intercom. "I'm calling in for food. Hush."

I settled in the chair, and could feel myself starting to fall asleep, so I sat up and dragged the clipboard onto my lap. As Eugene talked, I went through my notes looking for other discrepancies and information in the gaps of what Curt had told us. The thing I had realized as he talked was that Curt had been improvising wildly since he got sick. If Birgit had decoded that letter for him, I had no doubt he would have used blackmail to get people to do his dirty work for him.

He did do that with Birgit and Fourie, but in both cases, those were blackmail items he'd created on his own. Birgit and the affair . . . I was sure that was real, even if not the way either of them described it. I'd used seduction in the war. He'd lured her into being a coconspirator, even if she didn't believe in Earth First's goals. He'd trapped Philippus

Fourie by getting him to make the skis and use them. Both things broke so many rules Fourie would have been sent home immediately if he'd been found out. Unlike Curt, he wanted to be here. Fourie was not innocent, but he was not a danger.

My eyes were crossing, trying to focus on the page. Where the hell had I left my reading glasses? Probably with my logbook. My head dropped forward, eyes drooping. I snapped them open and straightened.

Eugene was sitting in the chair across from mine, with his chin propped on his hand, watching me. I did not remember him sitting down. The corner of my mouth was damp and I wiped it furtively, checking to see if I'd drooled on my clipboard.

I had not. Funny the things we're grateful for.

He lowered his hand. "You locked the door."

"I did." I sat straighter in my chair and tried to come back up to alertness. "I needed to frighten him and had a limited range of threats available."

"You should have discussed it with me."

"I know. But please acknowledge that I didn't disobey anything in the parameters you'd set." He'd also said I couldn't take a weapon in, but he hadn't told me not to improvise one. "At no point was I—"

"You know better than that."

"Come on, Eugene. It's a plastic door. If you'd needed to get through, you could have."

"Are you telling me it wouldn't have bought you enough time to kill him?"

"I'm telling you I wouldn't have needed that time." That

was probably not true. When I'd been in the field, in my early twenties, and fast? Sure. In my fifties and exhausted? With a broken arm? With anorexia? I would have needed the time.

"That does not reassure me."

"You made the consequences clear." I held up my hand as he drew breath. "Hang on. I resent how right you are about my motivations. My career with the IAC is toast. My reasons for wanting to go back to Earth right now consist of a twenty-year-old cat and a kitten I've never met. But you? I wasn't going to risk you. I skirted the line, but I wasn't going to cross it. Besides, Myrtle would have killed me dead."

He laughed. "Yeah, well, she's going to do that to me when she finds out I sent you in."

Which she would know because he would tell her. The same way I would tell Kenneth. Delayed and off-handed and underplayed as if it were no big deal. I sighed and shifted the clipboard in my lap. "We need to send someone out to check all the old landing sites."

Eugene frowned. There was a two-year gap between when I started launching and when he did. He'd never come to the Moon without satellites. Of the people up here currently, only Halim and I had used the old-style landers.

"Before we got the navigation satellites, we had high-gain antennas on the landers." Later missions had them only on the orbiter because the satellites provided the coverage.

He sat up, eyes widening. "Can we use that to contact Earth?"

"Yes? Maybe. It depends on someone having a way to listen, but—" I shook my head, before I let myself get distracted. "If any of them are missing, then Curt's threat about a remote signal from Earth might not be a bluff. And they might not need to wait for the IAC to reestablish contact."

Eugene stared at me as shock slackened his face, followed by widening, horrified eyes, and then his jaw tightened with rage. "I should have let you kill him."

"He may have uses later." I rotated my cast as much as I could, picking at the plaster. "But I have another suggestion you aren't going to like."

He shook his head. "This isn't time to play."

"After we eat." I said it out loud to remind myself that I could *not* skip another meal. "Tell Ana Teresa to take my cast off. Halim and I are the only two people on this whole tiny world who are trained on those landers."

THE PROBLEM WITH my brilliant proposal was it required waiting for Myrtle and Halim to return. More specifically, waiting for Halim to come back wasn't a problem. It gave me a chance to rest and to eat something. Eugene dispatched Mavis and her team to the lava tube at The Garden. Ana Teresa, with much grumbling, removed my cast. That was all fine.

The problem was that Myrtle came back with Halim and was . . . displeased.

Halim and I sat in the conference room and tried to pretend as if Myrtle and Eugene had not just left to have an argument.

They were in the office next door, and occasionally one of their voices would vibrate down the hall.

"... you did *not* let her."

I cleared my throat and pushed my fork around in the boiled dandelion greens on my tray. My left arm was shockingly thin, and gripping the fork made the base of my thumb ache with strain.

The tray contained my second meal today and I had wanted to make certain Myrtle saw me eating. Two problems. She was yelling at Eugene and nothing on the tray looked good.

I abandoned the fork and picked up a cube of bright orange cheddar with my right hand, rolling it between my fingers like a die. They'd been out of cottage cheese and this was the closest option. "I thought we'd start with the landing sites near The Garden and Marius Hills before moving to the ones near the main colony."

"... think I *wanted* to ..."

Halim paused with a piece of chocolate cake partway to his mouth. The lines from his Snoopy cap and mic had mostly faded, but his hair was still a tangled mess. "More efficient to split us up. Send us each out with a BusyBee loaded with engineers who can safely dismantle whatever we find."

"Good thought." The cheese left greasy residue on the ends of my fingers. "Although I'm not sure how many people we have who actually know how to defuse things. We might have to wait for Mavis's team to come ba—"

The door to the conference room opened. Myrtle stalked in and glared at me, shaking her head. "Pilots."

Halim looked at the empty door. "Where's Eugene?"

She straightened the stack of maps on the table, aligning them with the edge in rigid geometry. "If you get him fired, I will . . . Well, I'll just have to hope God will forgive me."

"It's only a moonwalk." I set the cheese on the tray and wiped my fingers on my napkin. "It's not doing anything we haven't trained for."

"You know how it will look in the news if you die out there?"

"Yes." I picked up the cheese again because the last thing I needed was for her to see me not eating. "I've spent most of my adult life being evaluated for how I appear in the news. Thank heavens we don't have to worry about Halim's appearance in the news."

Myrtle winced a little. "You know it's different."

I was the widow of a beloved politician. I was white. I was a woman. If Halim died trying to defuse a bomb, he would be heroic. I would just be a tragedy. A senseless tragedy and the blame for it would rest on Eugene. I tore the cube of cheese in half. "Believe me, I considered going out unauthorized so it wouldn't blow back on him."

Halim looked aghast at the suggestion of doing a solo moonwalk. Myrtle just looked sad.

"I'm trying very hard not to be stupid." I put the piece of cheese in my mouth. It had enough lactic acid that my mouth watered a little. "But I do know my judgment is . . . off. That's why I *suggested* it so we can work the problem together."

Myrtle rested her face in her hands, with her elbows on the table. "He's calling the department heads. God help us all, but we're doing this."

Halim and I exchanged glances. All I'd had time to do was tell them about the idea before Myrtle had hauled Eugene out of the room. Halim's idea of splitting us up hadn't been posed to the group yet. "We?"

She lowered her arms and looked at me. "Don't think for a second I'm letting you go out there without someone who knows you very well."

I wish that I could unsee the specific fear she carried in her heart. Myrtle was not afraid I would perform badly or that I would make a mistake on the surface of the Moon.

She was afraid because she saw my attempts to gain a modicum of control over my life as attempts to self-destruct. She was afraid that I wouldn't care enough to be careful. She was afraid of the risks that I would take.

She was afraid that I wouldn't care if my suit ruptured and hissed out.

FIFTY-ONE

BusyBee 2 Mission Log, EV1 Myrtle Lindholm:

June 2, 1963, 06:00—Completed suit checks. All EMUs are nominal. The suits are rated at eight hours of consumables, so for each site, I've allotted a maximum of four hours with a refresh between sites. The overall walkback limit is set at fourteen hours.

MY BREATH WAS loud in my helmet as I stood in the airlock of the BusyBee waiting for the air to finish cycling out. Myrtle was by my left shoulder, giving a thumbs-up to the three engineers waiting in the main cabin of the BusyBee for us to assess the site. Mavis, Eunice, and Yung-Chiu, who was also rated as a pilot. Just in case.

We were pretty sure that if Curt wasn't bluffing, the antennas he was using would be at one of the landing sites near the Marius Hills outpost. That's where Eugene sent Halim. But if we were wrong and something happened to Myrtle or me, the engineers had a way home.

Myrtle checked the indicator on the outer hatch. She wore the red stripes of EV1 and was in command of the mission, which was fine with me. My role was solely to examine the lander, make sure nothing was off-nominal, and then we would move to the next landing site.

Under my Snoopy cap, the comms gear pressed against my ears and cheek. Myrtle's voice crackled over the tiny speaker. "Airlock pressure going toward zero. Verify suit circuit 36 to 43."

I used my wrist mirror to check the settings on my suit. "That's verified."

"FIPGA pressure above 4.5. Okay. 4.7, coming down. Ready to open the hatch when we get to zero." Waiting for that needle to move the last fraction always seemed impossibly long. "There we go. 0.1. I'm opening the hatch now."

The tiny remainder of atmosphere evacuated the airlock, appearing as a brief mist, and was gone before the hatch fully opened. Myrtle climbed down the three steps from the BusyBee to the surface of the Moon. Her shadow stretched long and dark across the ridges of the tiny craters pocking the floor of Mare Crisium.

I clambered down after her, working against the stiff pressurized legs of my spacesuit. Dust puffed around my feet, falling back in perfect trajectory arcs undisturbed by air. The lander module was only ten meters away, all shiny gold and silver, except for the scorch marks where we'd separated the ascent module and launched back into orbit.

Myrtle had set us down so the sun was to our right; that way we didn't have to walk directly into it on the way there or back. Above us, the sky was velvet black.

"See anything out of place?"

"Negative." Footsteps ringed the module, marking places where we'd walked to set up experiments or collect samples.

Were there new prints? It was impossible to tell. Without wind or weather, the prints I had left years ago were as fresh as the ones I made today. "Let's take a closer look."

"Roger." Myrtle turned to the module and skip-walked toward it.

I leaned forward a little in my suit to counterbalance the Personal Life Support System I wore on my back. The PLSS had thirty-eight kilograms of mass and even if it only weighed six kilos on the Moon, it was still a significant percentage of my mass. For all of that, it felt good to be outside.

Granted, I was in my own person-shaped spacecraft, but there were no walls. Just the black arc of the sky backing the tans and grays and whites of the lunar landscape. I caught a flash of green to my left and my brain automatically went "olivine basalt" the way I had drilled for the early missions.

Up close, the ship was pocked with micrometeorite strikes. Each had raised a tiny ridge of knifelike blades around the impact points.

Myrtle stood in front of the ladder. "I don't like the idea of climbing that."

The suits had twenty-one layers, each designed to keep us safe in a different way. In theory, they could stop an 8mm round. But the gloves . . . those were more vulnerable because they had to be flexible. They were puncture resistant, yes, but this was just our first stop. Spending a day pressing my gloves against tiny knives was not appealing.

"Yeah . . ." I looked around us at the landing site. "Hang on."

"What are you thinking?"

"We left a bunch of garbage behind." My feet sent up their first mild complaints as I walked over to the stack of white bags next to the leg of the lander. I had to bounce up a little to be able to come down with enough force to bend the knees of my suit. I opened the first bag and lifted out one of the plastic packets inside.

"Are you serious?" Myrtle came up behind me.

"I think the correct question is 'Am I shitting you' and yes, yes I am." I held a half-frozen fecal containment bag in my right hand, filled with mashed brown space turds. I rested it on the ground so it could thaw in the sunlight. "The bags are sturdy, and we need something we can shape around the rungs."

Myrtle's sigh was loud over the VOX. "I thought I was done with this when the boys were out of diapers."

"Hey. It's in plastic. And be happy you joined the program after they built the zero-g toilets." I laid another bag on the ground. "Taping a bag to your rump is exactly as delightful as it sounds."

She laughed. "I've heard horror stories."

I grinned through my helmet. "So . . . funny story. During training, a certain astronaut of our acquaintance did not take the suggestion to shave his nethers seriously. When it came time to remove the tape . . . I wasn't in the room, but could hear the screaming. It is one of my fondest memories."

Myrtle nearly bent double laughing and had to stagger to get her balance back. "You have to tell me who."

I pressed my left hand to my chest and lifted the right in

a Girl Scout salute. "I promised I would not."

"The temptation to look at who you trained with is very strong . . ."

I poked the first of the bags to see if the sun's rays had softened it up enough for use. "He's lucky it wasn't en route, or that would be in the transcripts."

"Don't make me laugh anymore. I can't wipe my eyes."

"All right . . . but then I can't tell you about Terrazas and the floating 'Milk Dud.'"

"No."

"Yep. That one is in a transcript." I sighed and looked up, trying to spot Mars amid the millions of stars overhead. "How do you think they're doing out there?"

She turned so her back was to the sun and stared into the vast space between us and the First Mars Expedition. "Last we heard, they were fine. It's been a week without contact . . . so they may still be trying to troubleshoot the ships."

I compressed my mouth. Without the Outer Space Tracking Network, the First Mars Expedition would be too far out to pick up anything from home. They didn't even have the option we had of sending a ship to Earth.

"Nathaniel must be losing his mind." Assuming the people at the IAC were all right. I poked the plastic bag and my glove depressed it a little. "Poop's warm."

Myrtle crouched down to pick up a couple. "Let's do this shit."

"Language!" I laughed, even as I was aware that she was trying to keep me from getting melancholy. Unfortunately, I know from experience that telling someone you aren't in danger of offing yourself has very little impact in the context of behavior like mine.

So I carried warm bags of space poop to the lander and formed them around the rungs. It was like clay. Warm, very brown clay. The tiny abrasions in the surface of the rungs gave traction to the bags and I carefully did not think about the fact that they would start to leak through those little punctures.

I grabbed a rung wrapped in poop. The bag gave a little more than I would have liked. "Brace me?"

"Got you." Myrtle's hands balanced the mass of my PLSS as I hoisted myself up. My left hand could barely close on the crosspieces, but it was enough to get me up the nine ladder rungs to the "porch" of the descent stage.

The lander looked solid, but it was really just a bunch of engine parts and tubes wrapped in tinfoil. Excuse me. Wrapped in Kaplon. Still. You had to know exactly where to step or you'd punch through the gold foil and hit one of the "no-go" zones. The danger wasn't that you would damage the engine, but that you would rip your suit.

And knowing where to step was why I was out here.

I tethered myself to the handrail of the "porch" and balanced very carefully on the support truss as I bent over the Quadrant 1 compartment. When we'd been here, the ascent stage's command module had been affixed to the lander, providing hand grips. Without it, this was an awkward, painstaking process. There was no scenario in which a human needed to interface with this part of the ship without the lunar module in place.

If that had happened on a mission, it would have meant

someone had been abandoned on the surface of the Moon. Cheery thought and a little too close to home.

When I finagled the compartment open, the high-gain antenna was still nestled inside with the IAC seals in place. "It's here." I bent down to begin deploying it, so it was in a position for our engineers to decouple it from the lander. "BusyBee, EV2."

Mavis's voice joined me on the surface of the Moon. "Go ahead, EV2."

"The antenna is here. I'll be ready for your team to uninstall it in about forty-five minutes."

"Copy, EV2. We'll complete suit-up and head out to you."

Of the two problems we were working, this was the more straightforward. We'd haul all of the S-Band antennae back to the main colony and let the engineers work their magic.

For the second problem, all we knew was that Curt hadn't been to this particular lander. One cleared, five to go.

After the third landing site, we tramped back through the BusyBee hatch and let the airlock cycle up to partial pressure. Fans turned on and sucked the air and moon dust out to vacuum. Then it cycled up for real. My feet were throbbing and my left hand ached from fighting the suit for hours.

Myrtle looked at me. "Stop for a meal break after this?"

It wasn't on the schedule until after the fourth lander. "Sure. That sounds great."

She toggled off her microphone and leaned over to me, pressing her helmet against mine. I sighed and turned my mic off too.

Myrtle's face was lit along one side by the reflection of the sun off the lunar surface. "How are you doing?"

"I'm fine." I smiled at her with exhausted good humor. "Tired of this shit, though."

"I'm serious."

I let my expression go flat and dead, because I figured she would believe that. "There's a piece of paper that says 'Government Head Backing Earth First.' I keep thinking about it. So, for our purposes here, I'm fine. I have reasons to stay focused and a problem to work." I brought back enough of the smile to soften my face. "And I will not balk at an early meal break. Because I really am tired of this shit."

THE FIFTH SITE had a rover. It had a high-gain antenna deployed on a pole like an inverted gold parasol that they'd used to beam pictures of the worksite back to Earth, so we had two to check. The rover's and the one in the descent stage. This hadn't been one of my missions, but it was easy to see that the rover hadn't been moved, because the bags of poo had been stacked next to one of the wheels.

We'd worked our way far enough east that the land we were walking over had been in sunlight for a couple of days. I could feel the heat radiating from the surface when I knelt. "At least we won't have to wait for the bags to thaw."

"I try to thank God for small blessings, but this one just doesn't quite . . . I'm not even sure how to form that prayer."

I handed her a couple of bags, which drooped over her hand. "Holy Father, thank You for this sh—"

"Don't you dare."

"You're the one who started talking about praying and poo." I gathered my bags of excrement and stood, overbalancing slightly. I did the lunar jog, to get my feet back under me. It's fun. You fall slowly enough that if you start running, you can usually get your feet under you again. Usually.

Momentum carried me up against the rover and I dropped a bag onto the driver's seat.

"You all right?"

"Yep." I picked up the bag and paused. On the seat under the bag, there was a small piece of paper with Stetson Parker's distinctive handwriting on it. It wasn't anything significant, just a checklist which he'd left behind when they'd finished at this site. "You know . . . if I were Curt, I would have used the rover's antenna."

Myrtle nodded. "Sure. Safer to get to."

I held up the paper. "I don't think he was here."

If he had been, the paper wouldn't have still been in the driver's seat. This was not surprising. With each stop, we were venturing farther from the colony or any of the outposts. Halim was working the ones close to The Garden and Marius Hills because they were all still in the dark. Doing a night moonwalk was riskier, and I'd known better than to fight Eugene.

Chances were that Halim had already found the lander that Curt had visited. Without the communications satellites, we wouldn't hear anything from the colony until we were back in line of sight.

I really wanted to rub the ache between my eyes but a helmet stood between me and that goal.

Myrtle said, "So tempting to skip checking the lander and go to the next site. But . . ."

"Yeah." We would check anyway because skipping steps was how people died in space.

Myrtle frowned and rotated one of the bags. "Why is Parker's excrement blue?"

"Too much disinfectant." I shifted the bags, still looking at the note on the seat. I turned to look up at where the Earth spun slowly above us. It was in the last quarter, so just a slice of brilliant blue and white floated in the heavens. I talk about the colors that you can see on the surface of the Moon, but it fades to monochrome when you face the Earth. Stretches of white clouds masked most landmasses, so I wasn't sure who was facing us right now.

I looked down at my watch. It was nearly 7 p.m. Central Time, so Kansas would just be slipping into that curved shadow of night. "I'm going to—I'd like to try the radio."

Myrtle looked at me and at the rover. Her mouth pursed and I waited it out. The deal I had made with her and Eugene was that I would follow instructions and wouldn't push. I wanted to, but if I misjudged something, I wasn't the one who would have to deal with the consequences.

"Tell me why?"

I gestured to the solar array and the sun. "It's probably got a full charge. Right now, Brazil and Kansas are both facing the Moon. While it is unlikely that I'll get through, the possibility exists that someone got an old tracking station up and running. The worst that can happen is I'll get an earful of static."

Technically, the worst that could happen was that a micrometeorite had hit something vital at exactly the wrong angle and the vehicle shorted. But my mom survived three lightning strikes and my suit was insulated.

"How long will it take?"

I couldn't shrug in the suit, so I waggled my right hand. "Five minutes to power it up. Give me ten to check a couple of bands?"

"All right." Myrtle raised her wrist mirror to check the gauges on the chest of her suit. "All right, we've got six hours of consumables and that's more than enough to finish here. We can refresh them from stores in the BusyBee for the next site and still stay within our walkback limits. Let's do it."

I grinned and climbed into the rover. "You just want to avoid handling more feces."

"That was true when I told Eugene we were done having children." She rested a hand on the rover. "Is there anything I can do to help?"

I shook my head, before realizing that my suit was at the wrong angle for her to see. "No. But maybe don't touch the vehicle in case I'm wrong and it shorts." I waited for her to remove her hand and flipped the power toggle.

The instrument panel lit up as if it had been turned off yesterday. It was still tuned to suit broadcast settings and we got an earful of hum over our comms as the tubes warmed up.

Myrtle whistled. "The IAC really knows how to build—"

". . . Brazil. Over. Arte." Static buzzed but the human voice was still there ". . . ase, Brazil. Over."

I choked. Days of fear and grief clogged my throat. I swallowed, eyes stinging. "Brazil, Artemis Base. We read you. Broken but loud. Over."

"Thank . . . od. This is Cristian . . ." In the static, I could barely recognize Cristiano Zambrano's voice at the CAPCOM desk. ". . . re's room full of enginee . . . all just fainted behind me. Boy ar . . . glad to hear from you."

"This is Nicole Wargin. I have Myrtle Lindholm with me." I held out my hand and she grabbed it. I could feel her prayers radiating out of her suit. "We're out at the rover from *Artemis 14*. Repeat. The *Artemis 14* rover. Over."

"Copy . . . *rtemis 14* rover. What is the . . . of the colony? Over."

"Good. We're all fine up here. All systems working well." That wasn't completely accurate. Prioritizing information given the spottiness of the connection was hard. "Tell Clemons we caught the saboteur and are cleaning up the last of his messes. What's the situation down there? Over."

The static was bad enough that I was afraid we'd lost them. ". . . fires. Director Clemons . . . relocated operations to Brazil while . . . ppens. The UN has sent in additional tr . . . offer aid. We lost many good peo . . . Over."

I wanted more details. I wanted a list of who had been lost. Lost. That's the wrong word. I wanted to know who had been taken from us.

But that was a question for later. For now, we had contact with home and a problem to work. We were the IAC and that was what we did.

FIFTY-TWO

LUNAR COLONY SAFE

CHICAGO, Ill. June 2, 1963—The world thrilled today to receive word from Artemis Base on the Moon that all is well in that far outpost of humanity. An earlier use of Morse code had been spotted from telescopes in Hawaii, but the International Aerospace Coalition lacked the means to respond following terrorist acts by Earth First two weeks ago. Contact was restored by Mrs. Kenneth T. Wargin, widow of the late governor, who managed to revive an ancient radio system left from the first days that mankind walked on the Moon. Mrs. Wargin reports that the citizens of the Moon "are all safe up here and will keep working until the IAC is ready for us to come home."

MYRTLE SET A trajectory that was high and fast to get us above the curve of the horizon and into radio contact with Artemis Base as soon as possible. It was hell on fuel consumption, but that was low priority. We'd been out hours past our scheduled return time. Sending a report back with Yung-Chiu via the BusyBee would have left us without a life raft if anything went wrong, so it never even came up. We just flew, fast and high.

"Artemis Base, BusyBee Two. Over." I held the microphone in my right hand. My left was so fatigued from the gloves that I couldn't close it. "Artemis Base, BusyBee Two. Over."

I stared out the windows of the BusyBee as the lunar landscape rolled below us. Crisp shadows and undulating craters. Almost, even with my left hand in this state, I almost asked if I could fly while the ship only needed the right-hand controller, because I could not see a future in which I got to return to the Moon as a pilot. I didn't ask.

"Artemis Base, BusyBee Two. Over."

"BusyBee Two, Artemis Base. We read you loud and clear." Helen answered from the CAPCOM chair for our flight. "Permit me to say that you have had us a little worried."

"Sorry about that. The sites were all clear of signs of Frye's presence." I imagined Eugene had been standing right by her desk as our scheduled return time ticked past. "Please let the acting administrator know that we are all well."

She cleared her throat. "The acting administrator would like you to know that Halim found a bomb, defused it, and still beat you back by four hours. Although the administrator used different words."

Myrtle glanced at me. Eugene might be staying off the comm, but he was hearing every word we said. She had the helm, so I continued to talk to CAPCOM. "We stayed out to our walkback limit because we got one of the rovers powered up. We made contact with Earth."

"That is . . . that is good news." A roaring static backed

her words and it took me a moment to realize it was the sound of all the people in Lunar Ground Control. Helen's voice returned, level and calm. "We look forward to hearing the details when you're back in. Dock at berth one."

"Roger, wilco." Just another day at the office.

WHEN WE OPENED the hatch at Artemis Base, Eugene gave Myrtle time to step out of the airlock. He took the helmet and gloves out of her hands and passed them off to a suit tech. He looked at me. "Wargin. Good work. Get some food and then report to the conference room at twenty-hundred hours for a full debrief."

"Yes, si—"

As far as Eugene was concerned, the rest of the lunar colony had ceased to exist. He pulled Myrtle to the side and dipped her into a deep kiss, spacesuit and all. You had to admire the man's strength, even at 1/6 g.

I gave them as much privacy as I could by looking away as I stepped out of the BusyBee. As Mavis and the other engineers clambered out, I turned to them to draw their attention away from Myrtle and Eugene. "Good work out there."

Mavis shrugged. "All we did was uncouple a few connections." She glanced over her shoulder and frowned. "Is there . . . Do they need help with gear?"

Eugene and Myrtle were stepping back into the BusyBee. He had his hand on the hatch and was pulling it shut.

I caught Mavis's arm and steered her toward the donning room. "No." Smiling around a jealous ache, I walked away from them. "They need to do a private debrief."

A moment of confusion crossed her face, then a grin appeared like the sun popping over the horizon of the Moon. Mavis winked. "Got it."

The BusyBees had many wonderful qualities. One of which was that they were soundproof.

I spotted Helen waiting by the door to the donning room. The cuticles on her thumbs were picked raw. I abandoned Mavis and went straight to Helen.

She gestured to the donning room. "Forgive me for this, but when you're done, I'm supposed to go to the cafeteria with you."

"Copy." I was sweaty and ached and wanted a shower more than I wanted food, but none of that was important right now. I held my helmet and gloves in my right hand and rested my left hand on Helen's shoulder. "Reynard is in Brazil. He's fine."

At the sound of her husband's name, Helen's face crumpled. Her hands came up to cover her mouth. I pulled her into a one-armed embrace with care so that I didn't bruise her with the controls and couplers of my suit.

She sniffled and shook her head, stepping back. "Later, please?"

I understood all too well. Besides which, we didn't know the status of everyone at the IAC in Kansas City. Mavis and her crew had managed to boost the signal through some electrical magic, but getting a full list of those hurt or killed had not been the top priority.

But some I did know about.

I walked into the donning room and went to Florina.

She turned as I came across the floor and she knew. There is a face that we wear when someone dies.

She knew her husband was dead.

HELEN WALKED ME to the cafeteria and on the way there, I started pulling on the armor of my public face. Word had spread that we'd reestablished contact with Earth and people were moving with an extra lunar bound in their step. They kept veering out of their way to thank me and I developed a set of rote responses that rolled easily out of my mouth.

"It was a group effort."

"Yes, it's such a relief."

"I'm afraid I don't know. How are you holding up?"

Not knowing was the worst. Helen tried to keep me moving through the groups of our colleagues but didn't have the practice at extricating me that my husband's handlers did. Besides. I knew my job here.

I listened to every inquiry. I patted shoulders or shared a laugh or fears.

I was genuinely not going to have time to eat, and I'd have Helen to back me that I really had tried to go to the cafeteria. But Eugene had given me instructions. I had promised him I would not balk at any of them. Beneath my armor of public hopeful concern, I seethed with resentment because this was work that needed doing.

The Moon was full of people with ties to Kansas City. I'd simultaneously given them hope and confirmed their fears. They were smart. The ones with families who worked at the

IAC needed . . . not reassurance, but the strength to wait.

So I worked the problem. Between one cluster of people and the next, I turned to Helen. "I'm sorry—can you get a tray for me? I'll eat in the conference room."

A champion chess player on two worlds, Helen assessed the situation and was nodding before I had finished speaking. "Cottage cheese, peaches, and toast?"

"They're out of cottage cheese and the cheddar is appalling. So . . . something? And coffee." I could feel another group approaching on my right. "All the coffee."

THE CONFERENCE ROOM was crowded with department heads when I arrived. I had not anticipated that when I'd suggested to Helen that I eat during the debrief. I'd assumed it would only be our little group, but in hindsight, Eugene had said "full debrief." We'd just reestablished contact with the IAC. Of course, Eugene would want all hands on deck.

Helen looked up from the near end of the conference table and waved me over to the empty seat next to her. It had a tray in front of it. Joy.

But if I could eat at a table with the Honorable Ambassador from France *sans difficultés*, then I wasn't going to let a little thing like a roomful of engineers stop me.

"Mrs. Wargin—" The Hysterical Godfrey appeared in front of me. "I want to apologize. It's been weighing on me that I was dismissive of your concerns. I was very wrong. Thank you for your work today."

"It was a group effort." I wanted to gawk at him for actually apologizing, but instead smiled, because that was what was required.

"Miss Davis and her team are definitely getting commendations in their personnel files." He grinned. "I'm just glad the old hardware powered up."

"Yes, it's such a relief."

He cleared his throat and looked down. "I don't suppose you know the status of Building 7A?"

"I'm afraid I don't know." That was the engineering department in Kansas City. Most of his colleagues would have been there. "How are you holding up?"

"Fine. Thanks." He gave a watery smile. "Well . . . I just wanted to apologize."

"Accepted."

The door opened, as a slightly breathless Eugene held it for Myrtle. His flight suit was not zipped quite all the way to the top.

I used their arrival to make my escape and joined Helen at the table. My tray had canned peaches, dry toast, and a covered bowl.

"I don't know if you'll like this, but it is soft and mild." Helen reached across and lifted the lid. Inside was a bowl of rice, which looked like runny risotto, and smelled of chicken broth and . . . something savory. "It's called *mwei,* or sometimes congee."

A moment later, Myrtle sat with us. She had a sheen of sweat at her temples and her cheeks were a little rosy.

"How was the debriefing?" I said innocently.

She wet her lips and stifled a smile. "Thorough."

"Glad to hear it." The tray sat on the table and I pulled it toward me. The back of my throat was closing and some of it was from knowing that Helen and Myrtle were watching. Both of them were trying not to, but . . . they cared. I lifted the bowl. "Spoon or fork?"

"Spoon." Helen slid a wrapped foil packet to Myrtle. "I got a sandwich for you."

"You are blessed." Myrtle opened the packet and bit into the ham and cheese sandwich with a relish that I envied. "Eugene wants us to be first on the agenda."

"Noted." I dipped the spoon in the *mwei* and gave it a try. It was . . . palatable. The texture was creamy without being sticky. I nodded. I could eat this.

"Would you be willing to do it solo?"

I raised my brows. "You were EV1."

She nodded. "I'm also his wife. I think it will look better if I fade back."

I knew this dance and I hated it. The charges of nepotism. The belief that you advanced only because of who you were married to. For me, getting into the IAC, that had been true. They never would have let me in if I hadn't been married to Kenneth.

But I had carried my own weight, hadn't I.

"I think you should do it." I scowled at the room. "The more you hang back, the less able people will think you are."

Myrtle pursed her lips. "We talked about it and this was what we decided."

"This was my entire life." I reached for her arm. "Please don't bury your own ambit—"

The door opened again and Halim entered, walking with

an obvious limp. I don't know who it was, but someone started applauding. A moment later the entire room was. Considering that he had defused an actual bomb, while all I did was turn on a radio, that seemed fair. Halim tried to wave the applause away, which only helped a little.

He had been hurt? Why didn't anyone tell me he had been hurt? I turned to Myrtle to see if she had known and she was glaring at Eugene. Someone stood up and offered the chair across from me, which Halim took gratefully. It was clear that more than just his knee was injured.

I set my bowl down and leaned over to him. "What happened?"

Halim shrugged. "I was mauled by bears."

"Jet pack?"

"Jet pack. One of the charges was accessible only with the jet pack." He shrugged, blushing. "I never trained on it and should have waited for you to come back. But I figured if Curt had used it . . ."

Myrtle shook her head. "Pilots."

"It was fine on the way up."

"Everything is . . ." I grimaced. "You had a load on the way down, didn't you."

"The charge." He nodded. "Who designed that?"

"Not a pilot." I leaned back in my chair and picked up the bowl of *mwei* again. "Glad you aren't dead."

Eugene gathered the room's attention again. "All right. We've dodged some potentially meteoric disasters and that's all due to the men and women in this room and the support teams that you all work with. There's still some ejecta we have to deal with. So we're going to start with a debrief of the Earth contact team and move on to readjusting our plans for the next six months. Wargin?"

I looked at Myrtle. If she didn't move, I would stand up and do the job, but it wasn't right. She shrugged and tossed her sandwich on the table.

Standing, Myrtle said, "I was EV1 on this, so let me walk you through what we learned. Earth First had several people within the IAC. Specifically, they had someone in the computer department who sent up bad code that deorbited the satellites both around Earth and here. They took down the power grid in the area surrounding Kansas City and also ignited several fuel storage facilities on the IAC campus. Evacuation procedures meant that most people got out; however, not everyone did." She swallowed and there was the face we wear when someone dies. "The death toll at the IAC is currently at fourteen with sixty-three unaccounted for."

Someone in the room moaned and I was honestly surprised it was only one person.

"The spaceports in Brazil and Europe are unharmed and most of the operations are moving there to—"

"Who?" The voice came from the back, interrupting her in a way they would never have interrupted Eugene.

Myrtle shook her head. "We don't have a list yet. The connection was spotty. I'm sorry."

"I meant who did this? You said it was people within the IAC. We know about Frye. Who else?"

"What would you do with that information?" Myrtle stepped away from the board. "Is that the problem you want to solve tonight? Because we have only three ships that can do the Earth-Moon transfer and even with the spaceports open in Brazil and Europe, it's not clear when the IAC will be able to launch more. So I ask you . . . do you want to spend time talking about a vengeance we cannot enact, or working for the future of our home here?"

There are times when I hear a song or read a poem or listen to a politician speak and find a resonance. Myrtle was not speaking to me directly, but words sprang into my head in response to her.

"*Forgive us our trespasses, as we forgive those who trespass against us . . .*" For a moment, Kenneth was sitting beside me so clearly I felt as if I could reach to my left and take his hand.

Forgive Curt? Hell, no. But myself, yes. I could work toward the future the way my husband had. The way I had before I . . . before I got lost. It wasn't much, those words, but it felt like a guide star that I could use to navigate home.

ONE MONTH, ONE week, and three days after Kenneth died, Eugene knocked on the door to the gallery. We had been back in touch with Earth for two weeks and the lunar colony had settled into something that looked normal.

"Busy?" He was carrying a clipboard in one hand and I was happy to see that neither hand had Band-Aids on the knuckles.

"Just looking at memorial designs." I straightened the drawings I'd been going over and gestured to the bench opposite. "What's up?"

He sat down facing me and the gallery light above his head burnished his hair with gold. "Ana Teresa tells me you're doing better."

"Regular meals, yes." I sighed and looked at the ceiling, where the skylight let in the artificial light that filled the dome. "If you need to see it, Helen has the logbook, and I've been given to understand that I've gained weight."

He shook his head. "And the arm is doing well?"

"Physical therapy is a miraculous pain." I lifted my left hand and closed it into a fist. I felt the pull in the tendons at the base of my arm as I showed him that I could do nearly a hundred degrees of rotation. Ana Teresa said it was likely all I'd get without corrective surgery. I lowered my hand and regarded him with some suspicion. "What are you about to ask me to do?"

"We're going to send the first ship back to Earth in approximately three weeks. I want you to be on it, but—" He held up his hand. "But. Curt and Birgit are going to be on it. How would you feel about being on the same ship?"

I'd known it was coming, the return to Earth. Home. I loved the Moon, but if I were Eugene, I would have put me on the first ship back to Earth too. I shrugged. "Not thrilled, but okay." I rubbed the slight bulge in my left wrist. Even to a layman, it was visible. The oddity delighted the medical community. "Thank you for giving me the option to say no."

He sighed. "All right . . . Next question. Halim has requested you as copilot. Helen will be Nav/Comp. Clemons approved the request. Is three weeks enough time for you to be ready?"

My brain filled with a flat buzzing. All of my joints felt as if they were filled with liquid oxygen. "Did you just ask me to copilot?"

"Yes." He held up his hands. "If you're not up for it, there are other options."

"That's not—" I sat up, waving my hands as if I could pull the right words out of the air. I only needed to be able to turn my hand to ninety degrees to grip a controller. I could compensate by using my shoulder if I needed extra rotation. Most spaceflight was done with the right-hand controller. None of that was the question. "After all of . . . After my breakdown, why the hell would the IAC let me fly?"

"They don't know." He looked down, running his thumb along the edge of his clipboard. "I kept your personal difficulties out of the logs."

"Halim knows. Ana Teresa knows." I stared at him. "You know."

"I also know that the crew making this flight will not have radio contact for the majority of the trip." His brow creased as he spoke. The IAC had cobbled one radio dish together and we had communication with them only when Brazil pointed toward the Moon. Eugene lifted his head and met my gaze across the tiny gallery. "I know I need a crew that is experienced and damn good pilots. I know that the head astronaut requested you. And I know that if you aren't up for this, you will tell me."

It wasn't one of the big rockets that launched from Earth. Under normal circumstances, it was a nursemaid transit from the Moon to *Lunetta* and one I'd done countless times. Was I up for this? Not my arm. Not my feet. But was *I* up for this? I looked at the small luna cotta in the corner and the yearning on her face. "I'm still crying randomly. Eating is sometimes a challenge, but I haven't missed a meal since we made contact." I turned my hand over as far as it would go, forcing the fingers apart. "I'd want to do a couple of check rides and some sims."

"Already planning on it."

"Three weeks?"

"Yes."

I nodded. "Then yes. I'm stable enough."

How many places do you call home? For me, it could mean my parents' home in Detroit. Or an empty pied-à-terre in Kansas City. Or my bunk in Artemis Base.

Or the middle seat in the cockpit of a rocket ship.

I settled into the copilot seat with Helen in the Nav/Comp chair to my right and Halim in the commander chair to my left. The cockpit was cramped and gray with a view of a velvet black sky overhead. The sunlight that caught on the edges of the ports was the odd ruddy color of a blood moon. I'd been on the surface during a lunar eclipse with its hours of coronal display, but I'd never launched during one. I kept feeling as if there were a fire outside the window.

The window explodes in a shower of glass and flame. I grab Kenneth and spin him away . . .

I swallowed the memory and focused. In my lap was a clipboard with the checklists for launch. I'd done this so many times over the years I could probably have set the switches in my sleep, but we live and die by checklists, so I worked my way through as if this were the first time.

"Okay. Ascent feeds are open and shutoffs are closed."

Over the comm, Myrtle's voice was a soothing presence in the CAPCOM seat. "Roger."

Halim flipped a switch at his position. "And I've got the cross feed on."

"Trans-Earth Shuttle, Artemis, little less than ten minutes here. Everything looks good and we assume the steerable's in track mode AUTO."

I nodded, even though she couldn't see me. "Roger. It is in track mode AUTO. And both ED batteries are Go."

"Indeed." Halim's voice was on comm. "All nominal."

Much of what I was doing, in fact, was reading the checklist for Halim to set the switches. We knew he could fly this solo, but I read the items aloud anyway. "ATT translation, four jets. Balance couple ON."

He joined me in the litany. "Balance couple, ON."

"TTCA jets, prop pushbutton reset, deadband, minimum. ATT Control to mode control; mode control auto, both."

He nodded. "Reset. Auto, auto."

"Trans-Earth Shuttle, Artemis. You are Go for launch. Repeat. You are Go for launch."

Helen watched the clock, with her pencil poised. "Two minutes to launch, on my mark."

"Roger." Halim lifted his hands away from the controls. He toggled the mic for the people riding in the passenger compartment below us. "Two minutes downstairs. Please confirm you are secure and in launch position."

Below us were some of the polio patients, but not all. Garnet would not survive the crushing g-forces of reentry to Earth. Someday, she might be well enough to go home, but for now, she was alive on the Moon and working as a computer with a pencil held in her mouth and a workboard positioned above her. Guillermo stayed behind, with a limp that did not interfere with his work, but he was afraid that if he went back to Earth they wouldn't let him launch again. Eugene had talked Clemons into transferring Guillermo to the roster of long-timers.

"Mark."

Halim replied, "Roger. Guidance steering in the AGS."

I double-checked the indicators. Every call and response calmed me and brought me closer to peace. Eugene and Myrtle have their church. I have mine. "Master Arm on."

"One minute downstairs."

Downstairs, Curtis Frye was restrained in a launch couch. I had not spoken with him since Eugene and I questioned him. I was fine with that. I did not want to see his face again until he was in court and I was on the witness stand. And he was not my problem.

I turned to another page in the checklist. "DSKY blanks."

Halim's hands settled on the controllers. His touch was delicate, as if he were a violinist and the trans-Earth shuttle were a Stradivarius.

On my left, Helen watched the clock and counted us down. "Nine, eight, seven, six, five . . ."

The main engine ignited, utterly silent in the lunar vacuum, with only an indicator to tell us the ship was alive.

"Three, two, one . . ."

And we had liftoff. Gravity grabbed us, trying to keep us on the Moon. As we rose on a column of fire, g-forces dragged us back into the couches. I worked my panel. "Eight, eleven meters per second up. Be advised of the pitchover."

The rocket rolled in silence as we adjusted our angle to slot into lunar orbit before our trans-Earth injection burn.

"Balance couple, OFF." The light in the cabin shifted, and the cold gray metal went warm with the amber of a sunset. As we rolled, a corona of long red and gold streamers rose in the window. It formed a ring that glowed brightest where it brushed the paper-thin skin of atmosphere wrapped around our hidden planet. In the center of that shifting, ethereal halo lay a black velvet orb eclipsing the sun. Earth.

Home.

EPILOGUE

FIRST MAYOR OF LUNAR COLONY ADDRESSES UNITED NATIONS

ARTEMIS BASE, Moon, May 28, 1965—Today, Major Eugene Lindholm addressed the United Nations via telelink from the Moon after his historic win as the first mayor of Artemis Base. Major Lindholm, a handsome Negro man, has been serving for the past year as the International Aerospace Coalition's administrator of the lunar colony but will step down to take on this new role. In his address, he thanked the United Nations for their vision in allowing the Moon to be a self-governing and independent world. He invited all nations and all peoples to think of the Moon as a new cradle for humanity. He was joined by his wife, Mrs. Lindholm, who wore a navy belted pantsuit, with a matching feathered cloche.

THE BALLROOM WAS stifling as 250 guests circulated in a swirl of Kansas City's social hierarchy. At the front of the room, on the stage where we held press conferences, a fantastic big band backed Ella Fitzgerald. I smiled at my guests as I moved among them with the cool stem of a martini glass in my right hand. Having learned from mistakes with Kenneth, this party was cocktails and hors d'oeuvres, but honestly, I think I could have thrown a twelve-course banquet and no one would have objected.

We were welcoming the First Mars Expedition home.

Even if you didn't approve of the space program, these men and women were worldwide heroes. Each of the crewmembers who had made it home from Mars stood with a knot of people around them. On the far wall, I'd had them hang the official astronaut portraits of those we'd lost.

I spotted Nathaniel York trapped by Senator Mason from North Carolina, who had backed the man into a bouquet of gardenias. Nathaniel had one hand in the pocket of his tuxedo trousers, and nursed a martini while he looked past the senator to the press of people around Elma. He would be stuck there for hours.

I worked my way through the crowd in a swirl of robin's egg taffeta. "Well, good evening, Senator. Dr. York."

The senator turned, chest puffing over the cummerbund of his tuxedo. "Madame President. Such a pleasure to see you and such excellent timing. Dr. York and I were just discussing the budget constraints that the space program faces."

Nathaniel, standing slightly behind the senator's line of sight, mouthed, "Save me."

"Now, Senator . . ." I put my left hand, clad in white kid glove, on the sleeve of his tuxedo to build rapport. "You know I will have those conversations with you at any time. In fact—you're on my to-do list for next week. I want to sit down and look at a job creation program for North Carolina."

His greedy little eyes gleamed. "That is mighty considerate of you, I must say. I am glad to hear you thinking about the interests of the states of this great nation."

"Of course! Maybe I can take you up in my plane?"

"Oh." He blinked, because flying with me had become a coveted distinction in the Kansas City circles. Oh, the Secret Service hated it every time I went up, but I changed more minds by getting them above the cloud layer and into sunshine than with all of my rhetorical power. It had been worth every penny I'd spent on the modified controls. And for this climber . . . Private time with the president? How could he turn that down? But I also knew for a fact he was afraid of heights and I had a reputation for doing stunt flying. Senator Mason cleared his throat. "That's very . . . very kind."

"Wonderful. I look forward to having that conversation with you. Now, you're a family man so you'll understand as few others can." I gestured to Nathaniel without slopping gin over the edge of my martini glass thanks to years at an actual Swiss finishing school. "This man has not seen his wife for three years and she only got home days ago. So, I'm going to use my presidential powers and escort him to her."

"But of course."

My private secretary trailed my left shoulder at these events and would set something up with his people. I'd used the code phrase "having that conversation" so she would *not* set up a flight with him and would limit it to a fifteen-minute meeting. He'd be grateful to get out of flying and wouldn't push for more.

If I looked over my right shoulder, I would see one of the bodyguards who followed me everywhere public, even when we were, technically, in my own home. The ballroom was part of the public areas of the New White House and I was a new president with people who demonstrably did not like my policies of expanding the space program.

Nathaniel sighed with relief as we walked away. "Thank you." The pinch of worry that had gripped his features for the past three years was not quite gone. "I would thank you for inviting us, but I can't get to my wife."

"Sorry. I worried about that." I tried to peer through the crowd, but could really only make out her hair. Why the IAC didn't give her a handler, I would never understand. We would have to talk. "Watch this."

I approached the crowd and formed my flight plan as I went, marking out the terrain and where the hot air was likely to be gustiest. "Ambassador Ferdowsi. Such a pleasure. Have you met Dr. York? I'm just taking him through to his wife. Oh, hello, General Tanii. Have you met Dr. York? I'm just taking him through to his wife. And Mrs. Henson. Tell your husband I loved the show! Have you met Dr. York? I'm just taking him through to his wife." The floor cleared. "Elma! Darling."

"Nico—Madame President." Elma turned with such palpable relief I could almost see the numbers of the Fibonacci sequence forming over her head.

"Lady Astronaut! I've barely seen you tonight." I embraced her and whispered, "My staff have instructions to show you to the Washington bedroom if you need to make an escape."

"Thank you."

Pulling back, I drew Nathaniel forward. "I've brought you your husband."

"Nathaniel! I was wondering where you'd gotten to."

Stetson Parker, the commander of the First Mars Expedition, stood near her with that ferociously charming smile of his. He'd lost most of his hair while away. Stress, solar radiation, or male pattern balding. Hard to tell. He was still a handsome son of a bitch. "Madame President! Sure we can't tempt you back into space?"

"My place is here, doing the work my husband started." I turned to the assembled group who were still vying for time with the famous Lady Astronaut and the First Man in Space. None of them were paying attention to the fact that I'd booked Ella Fitzgerald for this event. "Friends . . . There's a wonderful band, and these lovebirds haven't seen each other for three years. Shall we let them sneak off to the dance floor?"

"Oh yes!" Elma's anxiety looked like bubbling enthusiasm if you didn't know her. "I haven't danced in years—so don't watch too closely."

Nathaniel led her away without a backward glance.

Parker winked at the crowd. "We're used to one-third of your gravity so . . . tripping the light fantastic will not happen tonight. Except maybe the tripping part." He held out his hand to me. "May I have this dance, Madame President?"

"Of course." I tucked my arm in his and handed the martini off to my secretary. Parker had a line of tension in his shoulders I wasn't used to seeing. I lowered my voice and murmured, "Gravity giving you trouble?"

His gaze shot my way and he shook his head. "My world mostly consisted of a handful of people in a tin can until three days ago." He nodded to Elma and Nathaniel, who were gliding through a slow foxtrot to "Blue Skies." "She's weathering it better than I am."

"She's got years of practice." We moved into dance position, my left hand not quite settling into the correct frame on his shoulder, and I was aware of the crowd taking note that the First Man in Space was dancing with the President of the United States. This would be in all the papers tomorrow. I'd have to make sure I danced with at least two of the other male astronauts or the papers would romantically link me with Parker, which was a headache I did not need. "But do let me know what I can do for you and your team now that you're back."

"Actually . . ." He swung us in a three-point pivot. "I did want to pick your brain. I'm . . . I'm going to retire from the IAC and was thinking about politics as a next step."

I raised my eyebrows. "I didn't think anything could pry you out of space."

"I've got two teenage boys." He promenaded us slow-slow-quick-quick across the dance floor. "So . . . any tips?"

"Well . . . what's your platform?"

"Er . . ."

I threw my head back and laughed. "Sorry. It's just so delightful to actually stump you." I squeezed his shoulder. "You need a platform that helps people understand why they should vote for you."

"What was yours?" He smiled wryly as he turned us in another pivot step. "Our news was . . ."

"Censored. I know. I told them I thought that was wrong." I sighed, thinking about the world the Mars Expedition had left versus the one they'd come back to. "Okay. Platforms. For instance, I linked job creation and economic growth to the space industry, coupled with increasing accessibility to reduce people's fears about being abandoned on Earth. The fact that I was nearly killed—"

"What?!" He did not actually stop dancing, because Parker is still a pilot, but it was close.

"Oh. Right." I shrugged. "Terrorist on the Moon. Lost environmental controls. Got shocked."

"You were electrocuted?"

"No. I was shocked. If I'd been electrocuted, I'd be dead." Which brought us to the other part of my platform. "The point is, your platform has two prongs. The policy and the person. My policy focused on space, but I sold it based on how it would benefit people on the ground. For the person . . . I rode the coattails of a martyred husband. It sold well."

Parker guided me to the edge of the dance floor and stopped. "I was sorry to hear about Kenneth."

Two years, two weeks, and three days and it still hurt. "Thank you, that's very kind."

"They didn't tell us . . . Damn it. He was a good man."

"Yes, he was the love of my life." I put my hand on his upper arm, belatedly realizing why the fact that he had teenage boys was different now than when he'd left. His wife had died during the Earth First blackout. "And how are you holding up?"

Parker covered his mouth and turned abruptly so his back was to the dance floor. A moment later, he cleared his throat. "I . . . I was doing okay until we got back. The house is . . ."

"I know." I squeezed his arm, knowing exactly how empty his home felt. "I'm going to stand here and babble about nothing while you pull yourself together."

He nodded. I caught my secretary's eye and flashed two fingers. In a moment, we would each have a martini, and in the meantime, I launched into a highly embellished version of being shocked. He laughed at the right moments, but I think it was a while before Parker actually heard me.

Outside the velvet drapes that framed the tall windows, the clouds broke for a moment and the ballroom filled with long shafts of blue light. Conversation stumbled to a halt as people turned like moths to the flame at the rare sight of a waxing three-quarters moon. My gaze went automatically to the right "eye" of the Man in the Moon. Dawn would just be breaking over Artemis Base. Wisps slid across her face, and the Moon drew her veil back around her, leaving only a glow in the sky to mark her location.

How many places do you call home?

The party went on longer than any of the astronauts would have liked. At some point, Elma and Nathaniel disappeared. The moment the other members of the First Mars Expedition were safely out of the ballroom and escorted to their guest rooms in the New White House, I made my own escape.

The door to the ballroom shut behind me. The hangers-on would continue to schmooze for a while before realizing the influential guests had left. The reporters would be the last to go, leaving only when the last canapé had been consumed.

I let the first piece of my public armor fall away and tugged off my long kid gloves, exposing the bulge in my left arm. One hallway, a set of stairs, and a door were between me and the private areas of the New White House. I exercised my presidential powers and kicked off my heels—would that my power extended to the fashion industry. Sighing, I let my aching feet sink into the thick pile carpet for a moment. Bending, I scooped the shoes up and headed for the stairs.

At the bottom, I paused outside the door to my private suite. Glancing over my right shoulder, I nodded to the Secret Service agent. "Thank you for your work tonight."

"Good night, Madame President."

I stepped through the door and let the second layer of public face drop away. Tu Guanyu Chu, now my New White House chief of staff, waited in the hall to take my gloves and shoes. "Good evening, Madame President. Your dinner is waiting in your sitting room."

"Very good, thank you, Chu." He was the only person on my staff who knew. He kept a log, and on nights like this where an hors d'oeuvres reception gave me an easy excuse to not eat, he had a carefully calibrated plate waiting for me. Food is fuel and I had a job to do.

From the inner recesses, a small gray streak bounded across the room, fluffy tail held high. Maggie the Cat billowed as she hurried to me and rubbed against my legs. Her fur was like a thundercloud and, as Kenneth had promised, her eyes were iridescent. She was the most beautiful cat and had a voice like a dying sheep. "Miaaaaaah."

I crouched to greet my cat. "Well hello, beautiful."

She bleated again and twined around me.

"Yes, I know. The state of the world is worrisome." I scooped her up. "What should we do?"

"Mah. Mrah. Ma-a-a-aaah." She twisted on her back in my arms and let me rub the soft fluff of her belly. Unlike every cat I have ever known, she will stretch out to give better access and go limp in my arms.

"That's a very sound plan." I rubbed the lighter gray fluff of her belly as her green-blue eyes squinted shut and then I looked up at Chu. "Sorry. Is there anything I should attend to before dinner?"

"No, Madame President." He would say that regardless, except under very specific parameters. "The correspondence that requires your personal attention is on your desk. Per your instructions, I've confirmed breakfast with the Yorks in the morning before they depart on the European tour."

"Thank you. Good night and good work." I sighed and carried Maggie partway across the room. She squirmed in my arms and I let her down to scamper away still full of kitten energy in an adult cat body.

The light in my little sitting room was on and the curtains were drawn to shield me from the outside world. I closed the door, leaning on it for a moment. Kenneth's portrait hung over the mantle and I waved at him. "It was a good soirée. Parker wants to go into politics."

On the table in the middle of the room, a covered dish sat on a starched white tablecloth. I walked over and pulled the lid off. Caesar salad and a bowl of *mwei,* rice still steaming from the kitchens below.

From my chair, a dark fuzzy head poked out from under the tablecloth and meeped at me.

"Well hello, sir." I bent down and scooped up my old man cat. He shoved his head into my chin. Marlowe was ancient and rickety, but scratching under his chin still made him purr like a Sirius IV rocket escaping Earth's gravity. "Hey, sweet boy. I'm home."

ACKNOWLEDGMENTS

WE SAY THAT writing is a solitary act, but I have found that it is much more like staging on a one-person show. There's one person in the spotlight, but there's a lighting designer that allows them to be seen, there's a stage manager, a costumer, a director . . . A book is similar. I get the credit, but I am supported by a wealth of people. This book, in particular, would not be in your hands without a vast crew of people. While I was writing it, my life was disrupted by a series of family illnesses and a move from Chicago to Nashville. It's the first time I've blown a novel deadline, turning it in two months late. I limped through writing this, supported by people that are only visible to those of you who have stayed to read the program notes.

My agent, Seth Fishman, helped me find the core of the story before I even started writing. He's my advocate, yes, but some days the person who he is advocating to is me, reminding me why I write. Eileen Cook, C. J. Hunt, and Jared Hunt let me ignore them to write. Kathy Chung listened to me ramble at length. The Whiskey Chicks,

Elizabeth, Suzanna, Nephele, Eileen, and Crystal, keep me steady.

Thank you to the entire board of the Science Fiction and Fantasy Writers of America, who were graciously understanding when I was a largely absentee president for the first month of my term as I wrestled the ending to the ground.

Alyshondra Meacham, my first reader and my assistant, is fantastic at "bespoke enthusiasm" and is so good at unpacking how a story hits her, that—in my extended theatrical metaphor—she's invited to all of my rehearsals, as rough and ragged as some of them are. If I make her laugh or weep or cringe, then I know I have something. Beth Meacham, no relation to Alyshondra, is my editor. When I emailed her and said, "I need help" she started reading and commenting on chapters as I wrote them, brainstorming with me when I had lost my way amid the chaos of my external life. Also, she rolled with it when I turned in a 180,000 word novel. The last one in this series was 99,000. I cut it down, with her guidance, but still.

I blame the length on Brandon Sanderson.

He, Dan Wells, and Howard Taylor make up the core cast of the *Writing Excuses* podcast. I remember sitting around after a recording session and talking about how I couldn't find the ending. They have a knack for asking the right questions.

There's some specific help as well. Bobak Ferdowsi figured out the frequency of translunar shuttles departing from the *Lunetta* space station in low Earth orbit. Interestingly, the launch windows are tiny, but more frequent. You're still restricted by when you want to arrive on the moon. (I'll talk about that more in About the History.)

The airplane sequences were greatly helped by Derek Benkoski, who is an air force pilot with an interest in historical planes, and my father-in-law, Glenn Kowal, who was a fighter pilot in Vietnam, a test pilot, and a commercial pilot. When he was forced to retire from carrying passengers, he went back to being a test pilot for as long as he legally could. A lot of Nicole's refusal to give up flying comes from him.

4thewords.com and Habitica.com are companies filled with good people who keep me writing. Seriously, it is embarrassing how much more likely I am to write to earn a pair of virtual wings than I am for an actual paycheck.

Volumes Book Cafe in Chicago was my happy writing place. If you visit, try the Shades of Oats and Honey latte. Parnassus Books in Nashville is my local indie store and filled with lovely people.

I have very smart beta readers. In particular, my Patreon supporters and the members of the Lady Astronaut Club: Rachel Gutin caught a major, major plot hole and helped me brainstorm to plug it. Maggie Watson told me about Cameroon Dwarf Goats, which we know today as pygmy goats. Someday, I really want to write a story about someone spinning yarn in low gravity. Marzie Keifer helped me with the chemistry of how Icarus was setting up delayed reaction meltdowns of the dehumidifiers. M. Warshaw helped me with some of the mathy language that Helen uses when figuring out what Icarus is doing with the blackouts. Rebecca Kuang, Yung Chiu Wang, and

Vicky Hsu helped me with Taiwanese music, language, and food questions.

Mark Zeman very graciously helped me with the Swiss German when I pounced on him at WorldCon in Dublin. I explained the scenes and he gave me the phonetic spelling of what he would say.

Brendan Minish sent me a note about radio communication in *Fated Sky* and got roped into helping with the communications in this book. Without him, Bill Barry, Stephen Granade, and Max Fagin, I'd have some technical holes.

Fábio M. Barreto, who is a talented Brazilian author and audiobook narrator, translated all of the Portuguese dialogue for me so that it isn't glaringly wrong. We met when he tutored me on pronunciation for the *Fated Sky* audiobook.

Dr. Sheyna Gifford, Dr. Stacey Berg, and Dr. Jennifer Chu helped me with the polio outbreak, figuring out how people would respond to that and how it would spread. Dr. Chu, in particular, is my "unofficial official orthopedic surgeon" and helped me figure out how to break Nicole's arm the right way.

I need to thank a couple of real people who lent their names, but nothing else, to the novel. Nicole Wargin gets her name from a real person. Nicole was originally a tuckerization in *Calculating Stars*, which is when you insert a real person's name. I offer that as part of fundraisers sometimes. I liked the character that grew out of the name and when I asked the real Nicole if it was okay if I used her name for an entire novel, she happily said yes.

Curtis Frye is also a tuckerization. It was supposed to be a throwaway in *Fated Sky*, before I knew I'd be writing *Relentless Moon*. In the real world, he's one of my oldest friends. I've known him since college when we met at a debate tournament. The real Curt is a great guy and, thankfully, laughed when I told him what I'd done to his good name.

Astronauts Kjell Lindgren, Cady Coleman, and Jeanette Epps answered various and sundry questions. Cady flagged a ton of things that were specific to the experience of women astronauts as well as helping me with the escape sequence. As a shuttle astronaut, she trained to rappel out the side of the shuttle in a Mode V evacuation.

Kjell . . . Okay. Chapter 14 and 15? I rewrote that *multiple* times with his input. Not only is he an astronaut, but he has an innate sense of narrative. We were trying to balance the mechanics of the crash with the needs of the plot. I'd hand it to him and he'd shake his head. "Everyone is dead." I'd try again, incorporating notes. "Still dead." Again. "The rocket is in one piece, but how are they breathing?" Again. "They're alive, but now it's . . . boring." Rockets are easy to crash, and hard to do without killing everyone.

I sometimes feel like that is also true of books in general.

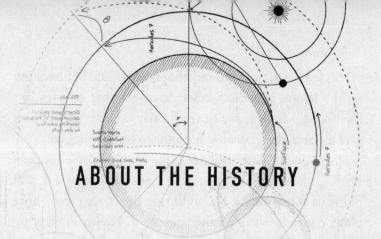

ABOUT THE HISTORY

No matter how far we get from the Lady Astronaut Universe's cusp point of the Meteor, there are things in the real world that continue to serve as models for the alternate LAU time line. I think they are rather fun to look at.

The actual Moon landings were scheduled to take place at dawn. Without an atmosphere, it was incredibly difficult to judge scale, so the long shadows of dawn helped with depth perception. The longer the shadow, the taller the object. It also meant that the surface had not had time to heat all the way up to 250 degrees Fahrenheit. That didn't affect the ability to land on the moon, but it did affect the length of time the astronauts could be on the surface. When we go back, those will still be considerations.

In the LAU, the preference is still to land at dawn, but they have ground control, visual markers, and satellites that help with the issues of knowing how far above the surface you are. As such, they can land or launch at any time. I'll note that I took great pains to make sure that the time of day on the Moon was correct throughout the entire book.

This led me to the discovery that there would be an eclipse on the Moon and the further discovery that eclipses last for hours. I look forward to the day when a real person gets to view that, because it ought to be spectacular.

The plans for Artemis Base come from multiple sources. NASA, the Air Force, and the Soviet Union all had plans to settle on the Moon during the space race. Those plans continue through the present day with interesting iterations. The Lunex base that the Air Force proposed would have resulted in a shuttle-like vehicle and aimed to place a base on the Moon by 1967. My favorite of them was from NASA in 1989, which proposed inflatable domes with multiple floors. Until that point, I'd been thinking about the base as being a single buried level. Finding those plans gave me partially buried structures with the machine room on the bottom floor.

When writing these novels, I want the science to be as correct as possible, but there are times when I need to handwave past something. For instance, I know that they've solved radiation shielding in the LAU but, aside from the regolith, I don't know the specifics. Generally speaking, if a character interacts directly with something, it is as right as I can make it. If it is a plot point, very much so. The radiation shielding is never, ever going to break down because I have no idea what it is. Currently.

The other fun thing about the lunar colony plans is that we know more about the Moon than people did in the 1960s in our world. NASA scientists knew about the Marius Hills. Those are volcanic domes in Oceanus Procellarum on the west of the near side of the Moon.

They considered it as a landing site during the Apollo missions and it was a backup for *Apollo 15*.

But we know about the "Hole." The hole was spotted in 2011 by the Japanese SELenological and ENgineering Explorer (SELENE) as a thirty-six-meter, well, hole. The Lunar Reconnaissance Orbiter got good images of it, confirming that it was an underground cave that's somewhere between eighty and ninety meters deep. Researchers think that it might be the skylight to a lava tube. There are other confirmed lava tubes on the Moon, including a massive one in that region spotted by the *Chandrayaan-1* orbiter. And yes, in the real world people are considering them as a possible location for extended human habitation on the Moon.

The Moon is covered with a ton of interesting things. Including ninety-six bags of human waste. Yes. Poop. When the astronauts needed to launch from the surface, every pound counted, so they did not follow the cardinal rule of hiking to pack it in and pack it out. Ninety-six bags of poop on the Moon, ninety-six bags of pooop. Take one down, pass it around . . . In all seriousness, modern scientists would like future lunar visitors to return the "fecal containment units" so that they can see if anything is still alive after fifty years on the surface. Science is glorious.

Radiochef Speedy Weeny was a real thing. I'd just wanted to find out what would be in a vending machine and found this . . . thing. Go ahead. Look it up. It's very odd.

With the polio outbreak, the LAU has a significant change from the real world. In our world, Jonas Salk developed an inactivated virus vaccine and through the March of Dimes, a massive vaccination campaign took place across the United States. It was delivered by injection and required boosters to be effective. A decade later, Albert Sabin brought out his attenuated virus vaccine, which was administered via a sugar cube.

Both methods were controversial at the time. The headline about Chicago refusing to vaccinate children? That is real. The vaccination program did work though and brought the polio epidemic to a standstill. The last case of wild polio in the United States was in 1979 in an unvaccinated Amish population.

In the LAU, when the Meteor hit in 1952, Jonas Salk was working on his vaccine, as he did in our world, in Pittsburgh. The March of Dimes was headquartered in Washington, D.C. His vaccine was never completed. This means that polio would have continued to be a problem so I extrapolated based on historic trends.

When I wrote this book, COVID-19 didn't exist. As we go to press, we're in the middle of what my husband calls being "ensconced in situ," and I have to tell you that the choices that I've made to be religious in my social distancing and mask-wearing are directly influenced by the research I did about polio. My father says that he remembers movie theaters being shut down, how no one would get into a public swimming pool, and that "everyone was afraid of getting it." Everyone knew someone who had gotten polio.

Polio was originally a childhood illness that hit in infancy. Most children got a little cold and then got better. Very rarely, one would lose some limb function. Then in the late nineteenth century, outbreaks began to occur. These grew steadily worse. It stopped being a childhood disease, striking adults. Influenza was a deadlier disease, but polio survivors remained part of their communities. They were also, largely, white and affluent. This, more than the deadliness of the disease, made polio dominate the headlines.

Houses were scrubbed. Children were kept isolated from each other. Towns were quarantined with checkpoints in and out. And massive temporary hospitals were set up in places that were experiencing outbreaks.

It is very easy to think of polio as a historic disease. While it is true that we have gone from 350,000 reported cases worldwide in 1988 to 22 in 2017, there are still polio survivors in every country. More disturbingly, people who had the disease as a child and appeared to recover symptom-free can experience post-polio syndrome decades later. Since it was possible to get polio and have no more than a fever, some people never realized that they had it as a child, which makes diagnosing post-polio syndrome challenging.

Anorexia is, similarly, an illness that can be difficult to diagnose. The common depiction of it in the media is of a teenage girl obsessed with her appearance. There's a reason for that. Cultures that value thinness have a higher incidence of anorexia and women are often taught that our value is linked to our appearance. But anorexia affects men. It affects older women. It affects people who are not concerned with being thin.

We think of it as a modern condition. Medical literature

documents religious fasting as early as the Hellenistic era. In medieval Europe, self-starvation with a goal of religious piety was called anorexia mirabilis. 1n 1873, Queen Victoria's personal physician, William Gull, named the disorder "anorexia nervosa."

The Mayo Clinic says this and I think it's worth quoting in full. "Anorexia isn't really about food. It's an extremely unhealthy and sometimes life-threatening way to try to cope with emotional problems. When you have anorexia, you often equate thinness with self-worth."

We have so normalized an obsession with weight that it can be very easy to miss early warning signs until the condition becomes life-threatening. Here are a few: Preoccupation with food, which sometimes includes cooking elaborate meals for others but not eating them; frequently skipping meals or refusing to eat; denial of hunger or making excuses for not eating; eating only a few certain "safe" foods, usually those low in fat and calories; fear of gaining weight that may include repeated weighing or measuring the body; frequent checking in the mirror for perceived flaws; complaining about being fat or having parts of the body that are fat. . . .

I tried to be very careful when I was writing this to not include triggering behavior. There's a thing called "thinspiration," in which people with anorexia will read about a character who has the disorder and rather than taking it as a warning will mimic the behavior. I remember doing this when *The Karen Carpenter Story* came out and I often think that the film may have been the only thing that saved me. The only time in my life that I haven't felt like I was overweight was after I had dysentery.

If you recognize yourself or a family member, I encourage you to talk to a doctor or to at least learn more about the disease. As a starting point: www.nationaleatingdisorders.org. The National Eating Disorders Hotline number is 1-800-931-2237.

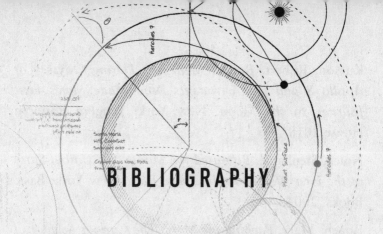

BIBLIOGRAPHY

Chaikin, Andrew. *A Man on the Moon: The Voyages of the Apollo Astronauts*. New York: Penguin Books, 2007.

Collins, Michael. *Carrying the Fire: An Astronaut's Journeys*. New York: Farrar, Straus and Giroux, 2009.

Etzioni, Amitai. *The Moon-Doggle: Domestic and International Implications of the Space Race*. New York: Doubleday and Company, Inc., 1964.

Hadfield, Chris. *An Astronaut's Guide to Life on Earth: What Going to Space Taught Me About Ingenuity, Determination, and Being Prepared for Anything*. New York: Back Bay Books, 2015.

Hardesty, Von. *Black Wings: Courageous Stories of African Americans in Aviation and Space History*. New York: Smithsonian, 2008.

Holt, Nathalia. *Rise of the Rocket Girls: The Women Who Propelled Us, from Missiles to the Moon to Mars*. New York: Back Bay Books, 2017.

Jessen, Gene Nora. *Sky Girls: The True Story of the First Women's Cross-Country Air Race*. Naperville, Illinois: Sourcebooks, 2018.

Kurson, Robert. *Rocket Men: The Daring Odyssey of Apollo 8 and the Astronauts Who Made Man's First Journey to the Moon.* New York: Penguin Random House 2018.

Nolen, Stephanie. *Promised the Moon: The Untold Story of the First Women in the Space Race.* New York: Basic Books, 2004.

Roach, Mary. *Packing for Mars: The Curious Science of Life in the Void.* New York: W. W. Norton & Company, 2010.

Scott, David Meerman and Richard Jurek. *Marketing the Moon: The Selling of the Apollo Lunar Program.* Cambridge: The MIT Press, 2014.

Shetterly, Margot Lee. *Hidden Figures: The American Dream and the Untold Story of the Black Women Mathematicians Who Helped Win the Space Race.* New York: William Morrow Paperbacks, 2016.

Sobel, Dava. *The Glass Universe: How the Ladies of the Harvard Observatory Took the Measure of the Stars.* New York: Penguin Books, 2017.

Teitel, Amy Shira. *Breaking the Chains of Gravity: The Story of Spaceflight before NASA.* New York: Bloomsbury Sigma, 2016.

von Braun, Dr. Wernher. *Project MARS: A Technical Tale.* Burlington, Ontario: Collector's Guide Publishing, Inc., 2006.